THE Heirloom

MaryAnn Minatra

HARVEST HOUSE PUBLISHERS
Eugene, Oregon 97402

Scripture references are taken from the King James Version of the Bible.

Except where well-known historical figures are
clearly identified, any similarity to persons living or dead is unintentional.

THE HEIRLOOM

Copyright © 1995 by Harvest House Publishers
Eugene, Oregon 97402

Library of Congress Cataloging-in-Publication Data

Minatra, MaryAnn, 1959–
    The heirloom / MaryAnn Minatra.
       p. cm. — (The Alcott legacy)
    ISBN 1-56507-235-9
    1. World War, 1914–1918—Fiction. 2. Family—United States—
    Fiction. 3. Americans—Europe—Fiction. I. Title. II. Series.
    Minatra, MaryAnn, 1959– Alcott legacy.
    PS3563.I4634H45   1994
    813'.54—dc20

94-30954
CIP

Printed in the United States of America.

This little story is dedicated to those fathers and their daughters who are unreconciled and separated....
There is Hope. There is Jesus.

Kinsale, Ireland
1972

❖ ❖ ❖ ❖ ❖

*W*hen he stepped from his rental car, he paused a moment to listen for the pounding of the North Atlantic. He knew instinctively it was just beyond the line of low stone cottages, just beyond the stretch of green. He knew from the spiraling sea birds, from the moist, salt-smelling wind that blew in his face, from the pale horizon to the east that seemed like an unruffled ocean in itself.

It was cold and wet, just as he expected. He walked past the courthouse to the edge of the cliffs that stood like an ancient wall against the sea; the fog had shrouded the beach like a dripping blanket and muffled the surf.

He glanced around at the little square of Kinsale—so simple and unassuming, so plain, so Irish. He could count three pubs in one block alone. There was no advertisement, no proclamation other than the museum, that anything dramatic, newsworthy or historical had ever happened at this somnolent fishing village. Nothing more than the passage of Irish sons and daughters. Nothing outward—but he knew.

Storytelling is in the Irish blood like verdant green is the carpet of the Irish earth. History, from ancient conquerors and their bloody battles, to family narratives of birth and death is an oral record—a gift entrusted from generation to generation, a precious thing. Any of the town's old timers could give him the facts with great relish. Yes, the facts...and surely they would add their own flavor to the telling. That was the story-teller's prerogative.

His family chronicle had a beginning here in this village called Kinsale, of the Emerald Isle. But perhaps the real beginning was thousands of miles away, on another continent entirely, in a place as unpretentious as this, called Peppercreek, Illinois. So he had taken this out-of-the way side trip to the coastal village. He patted one coat pocket for the book there, the other pocket for the camera; perhaps after the tour the light would be better for pictures. He pulled up the collar of his coat and climbed the courthouse steps.

It was Thursday afternoon, and the caretakers of the obscure little museum in the courthouse felt especially energetic. It was time to dust the displays. Irene and Isabel Shaw, twin sisters, spinsters by design and temperament, were the careful and conscientious custodians of this one room museum situated in Kinsale square. They kept their charge tidy—the windows that offered a stunning view of the Irish sea were always spotless, the tile floor clean and shiny. The displays, the map, the books, the photographs were all inoculated against dust and decay. The only real menace to the musuem was that it could easily become a yellowed page in history in a volume of more spectacular pages. The subject of this little room had claimed international attention 57 years ago. The sisters hadn't forgotten any detail, but they wondered if most had.

The sisters wished the room was visited more often, but Dublin and Cobh and Kilkinney drew the tourist crowds. They didn't want crowds exactly, but more interest would be nice. They went about their dusting now in silence—until the etched glass door opened—and a young man's face popped in.

The sisters exchanged a glance. It was appalling to be caught cleaning, so undignified.

"Excuse me, are you open?" he asked cheerfully.

The two women exchanged another look. They could not lie.

"The museum is open," the eldest said stiffly.

She felt stiffness in tone and posture were the unspoken demeanor of a museum curator—even in a little out-of-the-way place like this.

The man's smile broadened. "Great!" He came in, a hopeful look on his face.

"I left Dublin this morning. Just wasn't sure...I could follow the directions just right. Your lingo is hard to follow sometimes."

The sisters passed a look.

"Oh, well, I mean...I meant no offense. I'm sure you could have trouble with my accent, you know..." He shrugged and smiled widely again. "I'm an American, you see."

Yes, they could see that.

The younger sister felt an immediate liking to the young man with the red hair and deep blue eyes. She gave him a timid smile.

"Irene, you finish the dusting. I will give our guest the tour."

"Oh, you don't need to interrupt your work for me. I can show myself around." He glanced over the room. "There isn't much."

Again that look between the two women.

"What I meant was, what there is, is nicely cared for."

The two sisters allowed themselves slight smiles.

"We've been curators here for 30 years," the elder sister said proudly.

"Wow! That's great! Then you know all about it." He flung his arm around the room.

"We do," they said in unison.

So he was given the tour—the scrapbook with the yellowed clippings, the model replica of a ship, the details of the event and the local reaction, the surviving remnants under the glass of a long table that commanded the room.

Isabel spoke confidently, and thoroughly. She stood at his shoulder and described with amazing detail a day now 57 years ago. She told him about the Kinsale folk and how they had taken the drama so suddenly cast upon their shore. She was surprised the young visitor asked so few questions.

"Were you living then?" he asked without taking his eye from the glass.

"Yes, but we were Queenstown girls then," Isabel replied. "I remember the crowds in Queenstown, now called Cobh, the day after. And then the procession to the cemetery. Very sad, very sad."

Forty minutes later and he had seen everything. They expected a cheery, American goodbye. But he walked back to the display case, his forehead creased in thought.

Isabel shrugged at her sister.

"Well…" he murmured to himself.

"Have you any other questions?" they asked together.

"Well, yes, I do. Just one, a request actually."

He paused by the table. He glanced at the beaded purse, the tea cup with the famous logo etched in gold, an evening slipper, and a red leather volume.

"How do you explain this book here?" he said pointing. He leaned forward over the case. "It's remarkably undamaged by water. How do you suppose that happened?"

He had posed a challenging question, but they were undaunted. They exchanged their customary look.

Irene spoke confidently. "We believe this is a journal, a diary as you Americans call it. Of course, it was in the display before we became curators. But we understand it belonged to a passenger and was found in one of the rescue ships. Any identification mark had been smeared by water."

"The *Bluebell,* if I remember correctly," he said mildly, "was one of the boats in the channel that day. The book could have been in that boat. Belonged to a Padraic Falconer, I think," he continued casually.

He did not look up to see their shocked look.

Then he turned to them. "Do you suppose…I could…hold it?"

Their eyebrows rose in perfect concert.

"Hold it?" Irene sputtered. "Open the case?"

He nodded eagerly.

"Oh, no sir, that is never permitted."

"It was once, sister," Isabel said. "Remember that magazine that did a story? We opened the case so they could photograph."

"That was at least twenty years ago," the older woman objected.

"This is very important to me. You see, I've come a long way," he pressed. "And I'm not sure when I'll be back."

"I'm afraid we simply couldn't." Irene gave her sister a stern look.

"I'd be very careful. It would just take a moment."

"I—"

"Oh, sister, I think we should." The younger woman looked imploringly at her sister—as if she could cry! "What could it hurt? He seems very sincere."

"Oh, I am!"

The case was opened. They watched him closely as he looked over the case again. It amazed him, so little remaining...from such opulence and abundance. He gently lifted the leather book and slowly opened it. They were impressed with his reverence. Why had he chosen this book?

Some of the pages were blurred as if the book had fallen open and been splashed. He turned to the last page with writing on it.

"Here, here it is," he said in a low voice.

They were completely intrigued now, all professionalism gone. They stretched forward to look over his arm.

May 7, 1915

Last night the orchestra played Strauss until midnight. It was so wonderful. There is no one like Strauss, no one! I could have danced until dawn. But Clark is far more practical than I. He took me to my cabin door and wanted very much to kiss me again. Oh, I wish I could feel about him the way he feels about me. But he doesn't stir me. Maybe no one can. Maybe I should be a nun! But when I look out at the moonlight that spills over the water like a shimmering bridge of gold, I wonder if there isn't someone, somewhere who sees the same moon and is hoping and waiting just for me. Captain Turner says we will be joined by an escort late this afternoon and be in Liverpool by evening...

He closed the book with undisguised tenderness.

"It was written on May 7th, the very day," Isabel whispered in awe. "Her journal survived, but I wonder if she did."

He handed the volume to her then pulled a book from his pocket.

"She liked red," he said simply.

He placed the two books beside each other. Both red bound books, both with identical, flowing script.

The two sisters were shocked again. Who was this young man?

"What is this book?" Irene pointed to the young man's book.

"It's called Emerald Portrait," he said.

They did not miss the pride in his voice as he began to read out loud.

" 'I saw it first, just after sunrise, when the Atlantic looked so cold. It was a thin gray line, only slightly darker than the gray line of ocean. Then the mist began to thin, blown away it seemed by some gentle breath. The line became darker, not gray at all, gradually muting to a filament of green, such green! I was getting my first real look at the Emerald Isle. I had stood at the rail all morning, absorbed completely in the land some twelve miles in the distance. It seemed so remote. I saw no evidence of life besides the circling sea birds. It was like an ancient rock, pushed up from the sea, a desolate but determined promontory. And though we had no plans to disembark there, I wished we could. I wanted to walk along the shore and climb into that verdant green. I didn't know in that first glance, in that first hour, I would come to know that rock. I didn't know it would become a beginning for me, a place where my past and future seemed to merge together, and now I set to paper—Emerald Portrait.' "

"Emerald Portrait," the sisters murmured together.

"They are written by the same woman," Isabel continued. Here in this narrative she knew so well was a part she knew nothing of.

"Yes." The young man grinned. "My grandmother wrote them both. That is her journal she kept as a girl. And this book is our family journal she put together years ago." He ran his fingers over the cover of the oldest journal. "I had no idea I'd find this here."

He placed it carefully in the case, then opened his book to the cover page, to the name penned under the title.

"Have you ever heard of her? She's written other—"

"We have every book of hers!" they gasped in unison as they read the signature.

He laughed at their surprise and enthusiasm.

"Her murder mystery, that's my favorite!" Isabel said gaily.

"Yes, well, she did have…true life to draw from you know," he said.

" 'Tis a grand thing," Isabel bubbled, "her being American and becoming so, so Irish! And she your own grandmother!"

The two sisters would have no end of new information for visitors now! This would add a sparkle to their sedate tea time for quite awhile!

"Is this your first time to Ireland?" Irene asked shyly.

"Yes, ma'am. I'd like to come back for a longer stretch. This is just a jog I took. I'm off to London. Got a job with the *Times*."

He glanced out the spotless window at the Irish channel. He turned back to them after a moment.

"So you see," he said with a wide smile, his fingers tapping the book, "she did survive!"

Part I

Summer
1914

*The human heart is the starting point
of all matters pertaining to war.*
—MARECHAL DE SAXE, 1732

*N*ewspaper dispatches crossed the Atlantic. They carried dark tidings from distant and unfamiliar places. Propped up on the breakfast table or read by the evening fire, the events in central Europe were insignificant to most Americans. It was troubling to be sure, unfortunate for certain, but how could it affect a people an ocean away? After all, President Wilson was in the oval office, firm and quietly resolute that America would remain neutral in the regrettable conflict. He could be trusted to keep an eye on things.

Yes, things were tidy at home—while the people of Europe thrashed things out. Looking youthful, President Wilson announced his engagement. Henry Ford's millionth Model T rolled off the line in Detroit. Ty Cobb set a major league record for bases stolen in one season. Americans found diversity in their reading—the poetry of Robert Frost, the novels of Edna Thurber, and *Tarzan the Ape Man,* Edgar Rice Borrough's bestseller. George Cohan, John Barrymore, Marie Dreisler and Al Jolson were the toasts of Broadway while *The Birth of a Nation* played in scattered movie houses.

But such quiet, or indifference, or isolation, was destined to fade. The promise of summer could not last forever...

Chicago

The Model T clipped along at 40 miles per hour—a heady, exhilarating speed to the four occupants of the vehicle. The two young men decided the country roads around the big lakefront city were perfect for pushing the car to its limit. The two girls alternately screamed or laughed as the new invention took corners, hills and smooth straightaways. When the driver made the car careen around a corner nearly on two wheels, the girls shrieked and clung to the young men. The driver winked at his friend in the back seat—this driving had a fine assortment of thrills.

It was a gloriously clear, cool May afternoon. All four should have been in their dorm rooms studying. But who could resist a day like this? It was perfect for racing around in a vehicle, perfect for protecting terrified young women. On a straight stretch the driver spied a farm cart headed toward them. It wasn't a surprising sight—farms were scattered thick around Chicago, bringing their labor to the markets. As yet, the car and truck had not completely taken over American roads; buggies, farm carts, horse and rider were still seen on the roads and country lanes. Their day was not yet over, but their glory was definitely gone.

The driver had gassed the Model T to its maximum speed for the unrutted road, and he could see that the approaching horse and driver were nervous. Loud, brash technology was hurling toward the farmer.

"Don't slow down, Ben!" the young man in the back seat shouted. "He'll pull over!"

The driver didn't apply a brake, but he did steer the car over as far to the shoulder of the road as he dared.

"Make him take the ditch, Ben," the young man in the back seat commanded again. "We don't want to put a dent in my dad's wheels."

The girls clapped and squealed as the old and the new came closer and closer. Now Ben saw the farmer's face clearly—a classic mixture of anger and fear. The Model T sped by. The girls waved their hats, the farmer shook his fist and cursed. The frightened horse skittered into the narrow ditch while the passengers in the car laughed.

Ben turned to look over his shoulder. The wagon was stuck and the farmer was slowly climbing down. The Model T began to slow.

"Ben! Hey, what are you doing?"

The car came to a stop on the edge of the road.

"Ben, what's the matter?" his girl added. "Why are we stopping?"

The boy in the back pulled his hat over his eyes and drew his girl close. "Don't you know how conscientious Ben is? Might as well settle in. He has to go do his Good Samaritan act."

"I'll be right back." The driver smiled as he climbed out.

It was amazing how genetics were prone to hurdle generations and appear suddenly in a nose, a chin, a mannerism. At 21 years old, Ben Alcott looked far more like his paternal grandfather Ethan, than he did his own father. Similar in looks, similar in temperament, Ben Alcott was known as fun loving, loyal, generous.

The farmer was trying to move one of the rear wheels when he heard the steps on the dirt road. He looked up, an angry expression on his face. This was not the first time this new invention had rudely bumped him off the road to Chicago. He cursed Henry Ford every time he took to the ditch. What was wrong with the horse and wagon? Hadn't it proven itself for centuries? Who needed to go faster? Who wanted to ride in something that sped you along so fast you hadn't time to appreciate the scenery? But his temper cooled just a bit when he saw the young driver coming back—this was a first.

Ben Alcott was the picture of athletic health—just over six feet, well built, dark, wavy hair. The farmer noted the school sweater. Ah, one of those spoiled and wild college boys! It figured—sons of the wealthy had nothing better to do than run poor farmers off the road with their expensive toys!

"Good morning!" The boy smiled cheerfully.

"Feelin' guilty, huh?" the farmer snapped.

Ben shrugged and continued smiling. The farmer looked away. The boy looked too much like one of his own boys—mischievous and loving.

Ben examined the wagon wheel then laid his shoulder to it. "You steady the mare, all right, sir?"

The farmer went, grumbling, to the horse.

"All right, give her a go!" Ben called.

The wagon lurched forward, and the farmer led the horse back to the middle of the road. He moved around to the back of the wagon, his tobacco wad working vigorously in his mouth. He eyed Ben, then the car down the road. They could both hear girlish laughter. He pulled out a clean handkerchief and tossed it to the boy to clean his hands.

"Thanks," Ben replied with a grin.

"Schoolboy?" the farmer asked.

"Yes, sir, University of Chicago."

"Studies include runnin' old men off the road?"

Ben shrugged. "No, sir. What's your load here? Oh, cabbages. Heh, those look nice."

"'Course they do. It's a wonder, though, that I don't have a ditch full of slaw."

Ben smothered a smile. "My father is a corn farmer. An orchard man too. Grows apples."

The farmer began to settle down. "So, why ain't ya at home helpin' him like a good son?"

"Well, I...well, he wants me to do what I'm interested in."

"If ya ain't interested in apples, what are you interested in?"

Ben looked down at the muddy wheel a moment then back to the guileless eyes of the farmer. He shrugged. "I haven't figured that out yet exactly."

"Humph..."

They leaned on the wagon comfortably as if they were close neighbors. Ben had forgotten entirely his friends waiting in the car. A bird spiraled up from the prairie grass, his shadow purple over the land he soared above. Ben watched it until it was out of sight.

"There...that's what I want to do..." he murmured.

The farmer followed his gaze. "Fly? You want to fly? One of those aeroplane things? Ain't a car thing deadly enough for ya?"

Ben smiled and said nothing. He couldn't explain it to the old fella. But something had happened on a remote stretch of beach at Kitty Hawk, North Carolina, 11 years earlier, and had forever altered the course of young Ben Alcott's life.

"Ben! Hey, Ben! Come on!"

The voices from the car pulled him from his daydream.

"Better stick to apples and things on the ground, boy," the farmer said with the first touch of real softness in his tone. "Birds and clouds are the only thing that's meant to be above God's green earth."

Ben smiled. "Good luck with your cabbages, sir!" He jogged back to the car.

His friend was now in the driver's seat.

"You lost your spot, Ben. We can't have you stopping for every farmer on the road!"

Ben shrugged and climbed in beside his girl in the backseat. "How 'bout a kiss for my gallantry?" he said as she snuggled up to him.

Peppercreek, Illinois

In the fragrant shade of an apple tree, the young girl sat listening intently, pen flying over the page.

"I always thought President Lincoln was a...beautiful man, in his own way," the old woman said thoughtfully.

The young girl frowned. "He looks terribly homely in all the photographs I've ever seen. Big ears, big nose."

"That's because you just see a black and white picture on paper. How can a paper capture his heart, his kindness? That's what made him beautiful. He would stoop over the men's beds and you could see in his eyes he would gladly have traded places with them if he could have. He cared very much."

"Didn't you...I mean, weren't you afraid of catching something from all those men you came in contact with?" the young girl pressed.

"Certainly not!" the old woman returned tartly. "It never occurred to me to be afraid."

"Well, I would have been afraid. I could never have been a nurse like you, Grandma. It would have made me positively ill!"

The old woman smiled and fastened her eyes on the girl. She did love this high spirited, temperamental granddaughter. So different from her own youth...

"Your...passion is writing," she said simply.

A blush rose up the girl's neck. She was insecure enough to feel uncomfortable with the reference.

"Well, yes…I do like to write. I'm good at it," she added with a touch of unneeded defiance.

"That's one reason we spend so much time together, isn't it? You want to record my stories. Why?"

The girl fidgeted. "I…enjoy hearing them. I'm not sure why…I don't want them forgotten, I guess."

"You want your children to read the stories of their great grand-mother who was a Civil War nurse."

"Oh, Grandma! Heaven forbid! Children! Never!"

Sara Alcott chuckled. "Too modern, Katie?"

"Too smart!"

"Ah…so you're to be a career woman, a journalist."

The girl's chin came up. "Precisely."

"Well, if you ever put my memoirs together, you must remember two important facts."

Kate was silent. She knew them already. Perversely, she did not want to give the old woman the pleasure of telling her she knew.

"Emphasize how generous the Lord has been to me. For 73 years, Katie girl. And…" Her voice lowered and her rheumy eyes gazed across the yard to a hill, crowned with an iron-fenced plot. "And, my love for your grandfather."

Her eyes lingered there.

Kate was philosophical. Oh, well, that's all I'll get out of the old lady now. Kate was never close to her grandfather Ethan. She resented his in-trusion even now. She knew he still held the old woman's heart though he'd been dead ten years.

"You met Grandfather there at…at Carver Hospital, didn't you?" she prompted.

Sara did not look away from the plot.

"Goodness, no! I loved him since I was a girl of eight. Loved him…"

Kate sighed and closed the notebook, capped the pen. Minutes passed. Kate closed her eyes and leaned back in the wicker rocker. Sometimes quiet could be so satisfying. Sometimes, not often.

"You know, you were very vocal about this family plot here, some years ago," her grandmother interrupted. "Do you remember?"

Kate's eyes snapped open. "Who, me?"

"You. Quote, 'I think a place that has a cemetery near the house is positively creepy! Think of it, you could go to plant a garden and dig up a relative!' "

Kate laughed. "Oh, Grandma, surely I didn't say that!"

"My eyesight and hearing aren't what they used to be, I will admit, but there is nothing wrong with my memory, Miss Kate. You did say just those words. It was one of the first times your father brought you here to Peppercreek. We were sitting down to Sunday dinner. The room got very quiet. Melanie looked horrified—"

"I can imagine," Kate interrupted sourly.

"Ben held back a laugh. Your father and grandfather looked quite shocked—"

"As usual."

"But I laughed. I thought, this young Alcott has spirit and imagination!"

Kate's frown deepened for a moment. "And a troublesome tongue." She stood up and stretched. "That wasn't the first blunder I made to embarrass Daddy, nor the last, I'm afraid."

Her tone was light, but it did not conceal the bitterness.

Sara pressed her fingertips together. "Your father loves you, Katie girl, no matter what you think."

Kate gave her grandmother a patronizing smile and patted the wrinkled hand. Better Grandma should stick to her stories of the past...

New York City

It was an Italian restaurant on the lower east side of New York City—one of many. It was called Valentino's and it was classic with its red-checked tablecloths, candles dripping down empty wine bottles, Italian operas playing on a scratchy Victrola. But you hardly noticed the poor quality of the phonograph. You hardly noticed the music itself, for there was always laughter at Valentino's—lots of laughter. Valentino's was not the place to come for contemplating life, transacting a shady business deal, perusing a book or pursuing a romance. Valentino's was laughter and cheap wine and lots of hot, heavy, delicious pasta.

Lilly O'Hara could easily afford one of the many Italian restaurants on the upper east side, near Broadway, where she made her living. Those places had spotless white linen, expensive wine, mustachioed waiters in short white jackets, and expertly placed miniature palm trees in the dining room. They also had reputations—boasting New York celebrities and social architects as varied as their elegant menus.

Lilly didn't go to those places much and never on Sunday nights. She far preferred Valentino's where she had eaten his special Sunday night pasta dinners for over 20 years. In many ways she had grown up or at least matured at Valentino's. She was a part of the place as much as the robust Valentino himself or his timid, brown-haired little wife.

Lilly often dined alone, though sometimes she brought a troupe of her theatrical friends with her. The Italian owner made enough from Lilly's generous crowd to last for weeks without another customer.

When giving an interview, she always insisted on the obscure, little Italian diner. Sometimes Valentino or one of her friends or another customer would coax her to sing while they waited for the spicy viands. Lilly always obliged them, singing a cappella.

She went to other places occasionally, New York's finest like Dominique's and 51 Club, but Valentino's was her favorite. Lilly often reflected that anything of importance that had happened to her in the last 23 years had begun or been celebrated at the diner. Here she made her first New York friends, Valentino and his wife. Here she read her first script for an off Broadway play. Here she brought a crowd of friends a short five years later to celebrate her huge success in *The Little Millionaire*. Here she brought the director who, over a steaming plate of linguine, asked her to marry him. And ten months later, here, she silently stared into her coffee cup just hours after his funeral. The big city of New York was her home, her work, her family. And there was Valentino's.

Valentino and his wife Tess sat with Lilly O'Hara one day as a formidable spring wind chased trash and leaves down the stone corridors of the great city. Lilly had a two o'clock rehearsal and it was noon. She wouldn't think of leaving the couple until they were calmer—if that was possible. Their youngest daughter had eloped the night before with an Italian sailor. Valentino was not in the least consoled by his new son-in-law's nationality—the young man had stolen their daughter and that was all that mattered. Valentino wanted to contact the coast guard in the New York harbor. Perhaps the steamer was not well out to sea and could be stopped. All he could do at this moment was shake his fist in the air and mutter Italian curses at all naval men. Lilly was trying her best to steady the couple. She laid a hand on Valentino's big, beefy arm.

"Now, Valentino, I think we must try to be rational about this. I'm sure...What was his name?"

"George!" he spat out.

"George loves your daughter and is going to take good care of Victoria. He—"

"He's a cad to steal my daughter! To not come and properly ask for her hand. It is...it defies everything...proper!"

"And no engagement party, no wedding..." Tess moaned.

"Well, weddings are expensive these days," Lilly offered lamely.

Valentino's chest swelled, a thing hard to distinguish for the casual observer, for Valentino's...considerable midsection.

"I would have spared nothing for Victoria!" he said fiercely.

"I know, I know you would have," Lilly soothed. "And I'm sure Victoria knows that, too. She is just a headstrong girl who wanted...a little excitement perhaps."

"Let her go to the theater for excitement," the big man gruffed. "That isn't something you want in marriage! Tess and I were chosen for each other by our parents. We were engaged two years!"

"Ten months," Tess Valentino corrected sorrowfully.

"Just so, the old ways are best. Children! Where is their heart?" Valentino waved his hand in the air. "Do you know, Miss O'Hara, last night I ruined the marinade for the chicken cacciatore? It was the first time in 20 years! I was so ashamed!"

He looked like he was going to cry over the memory.

"He added a cup of salt instead of a cup of sugar," Tess explained.

Lilly shook her head. This was serious—Valentino spoiling his famous marinade!

Valentino looked across the table. Miss O'Hara had not changed much since that first time he'd seen her—some cad was bullying her in the alley behind his restaurant. They had become instant friends. Why was it he, Valentino, could count the years by added pounds, migrating hairline and wrinkles, and Miss O'Hara looked— He stopped to consider. No, she didn't look just as she had when they first met. No indeed, she was far too thin in those early days. He had fed her plenty of pasta dinners that had put some meat on her bones. But now, there was a finer quality to her face, a maturity. He could not help but compare her to the elements he traded in daily. Lilly O'Hara had aged beautifully like a fine wine. Her skin was fair and unblemished, and her trademark hair was just as vivid. Her sparkling green eyes were Valentino's favorite feature. Other men had found them equally attractive over the years, equally captivating. Ah yes, Miss O'Hara, a dear friend, a daughter to him—a lovely bouquet like the finest wine.

"And a sailor!" Valentino muttered.

"Now really, Valentino, that isn't fair and isn't like you at all. What you are implying is like...like saying all Italians are hot-tempered," Lilly said with gentle reproof.

"Most are," Tess whispered.

Lilly ignored her. "Or...or all German Americans are in favor of Germany in the war or worse that they are all spies. In all the years that I've known you, you have been as fair as your big, loving heart."

"I thank you, Miss O'Hara. Such kind words are soothing to my greatly troubled breast. But sailors are still so, so—"

"You're being silly," Lilly said with a smile.

"Vulgar and unstable, that is what they are. Now I ask you, what kind of a husband will that make my poor Victoria?"

Now Victoria was back to being 'poor'. Lilly smiled again.

"Valentino, come on, not all sailors are like that."

"I do not wish to contradict you, Miss O'Hara. Goodness knows I think you are a brilliant woman but—"

"Oh, Valentino..."

He held up his hand. "Can you name me even one sailor that you have ever known who is...decent? That you'd pick for your own beloved child, hmm?"

Lilly smiled down at her coffee cup. A sailor...decent, and more than decent. His face came to her instantly, a memory held in the sweet shadows of her mind. Tall and slim, vivid blue eyes, a golden-brown beard. Like a chivalrous gent of old, he had rescued her. Twenty-three years had passed since she'd seen him, since she'd laid her hand on his cheek and said goodbye. Nineteen years since she'd received that last letter. He was happy, the lines had said—he was getting married. So much had happened, so much had changed, and yet, she was still the same big-eyed girl as she was years ago in New Orleans when this sailor had come so suddenly into her life. A meeting in a park, a divine appointment. No years, no distance, no changes in her own life could ever steal those precious memories.

"Yes, I did know a sailor...once. It was years ago, before I came to New York." She fingered the rim of her cup for she did not want to meet their eyes. "He was the best man I've ever known."

The Valentinos exchanged a look. Miss O'Hara did look sorrowful. She must feel their pain.

Valentino stood up with a deep sigh.

"He took our little girl off on a, a common steamer!" He gave Lilly's hand a pat and went back to his kitchen muttering and wringing his apron.

Lilly smiled and shook her head. Chances were good that Valentino's famous sauce would be spoiled again tonight.

New Orleans

He stood at a large drawing table, one hand tapping blueprints in front of him with a pencil, the other absently rubbing the small of his back. His shirt sleeves were rolled up, and he wore a gray vest, with a tie loosened at his throat. A half eaten sandwich and an orange were at his elbow. He had taken a few obligatory bites, then forgotten the food entirely. Occasionally he glanced up at the huge window behind his desk. Sometimes he would walk to it and stare at the impressive sight below him. The harbor of New Orleans was a cauldron of animation and energy, throbbing with life, never silent, never still. Ships of every nation found a berth in the port city, a convergence of every tribe and tongue.

His face was creased in a frown—a habit that indicated he was deep in thought. He sketched a line, erased another, measured a third, then stood back for a critical look. He consulted a sheaf of papers, chewed his lip, then bent over the table again.

The door opened and a man in his mid thirties entered the room. He tossed the sandwich in the trash but saved the orange. He placed a stack of mail on the desk. Then he stood beside his employer taking the same posture of critique. The designer glanced at the desk, then tossed the pencil aside. "Anything worth looking at?" he asked.

The secretary hesitated. He knew this man he had worked for, knew him well. He's worked for him for nearly 15 years, and he knew his talents and weaknesses. He knew his eating habits—and he knew just what frustrated the man more than anything.

"Uh...well, actually, there is—"

The older man smiled. "You're hesitating. I know when you hesitate, Collins, you have something unpleasant to tell me."

"Just a few, items, concerning...Miss Katherine, sir."

"A few items, huh?" he replied tiredly. He picked up the orange and strolled to the window, his back to the secretary.

"What are these few items? Is it Mrs. Morton, saying Katherine isn't welcome for another term? Or is it something else?"

"It's a bill from Saxons, a rather substantial one. You said last time to let—"

"Yes, yes, I know. Inform me when she's gone and spent a small fortune and not bothered for my consent. What else?"

"A Mr. Daniels from Boston keeps calling."

"I don't know any Daniels in Boston."

"I know, sir, it's about a school there, a journalism school. It seems Miss Katherine has applied for admission—"

"So now she wants to go to school in Boston!"

After 15 years, the secretary knew when to be prudently silent.

Andy Alcott slumped into the deep leather chair and swiveled it to the window. A multitude of ships floated in the harbor this morning. Freighters and tankers and liners with their belching smoke, yachts and pleasure craft with their trim sails a little farther on, fishing boats and tugs. No clippers or stern-wheelers, those boats of his youth. No, you never saw those anymore. He rubbed his chin. He was getting old. He thought of his own clipper, *Magnolia Remembrance,* that he had captained years ago. Seemed like a century ago now. Wasn't life simpler then?

He began to peel his orange. How was it his daughter could still stir up trouble from over a thousand miles away? He smiled grimly. Packed off for two weeks to his mother's home in Illinois—what mischief was she making there? When would the phone call come from her uncle or grandmother demanding he come and get his wayward child? He shook his head. That wasn't likely to happen. Sara Alcott was a tolerant and loving woman. She knew how to handle her temperamental grand-daughter. And maybe the only one who did.

Eighteen years old! Old enough to quit giving him such aggravation. He flipped the peel angrily onto his desk. Being her father wasn't ever simple. No, not simple, easy, or peaceful. Any moments of peace and tenderness between them were brief. Now that he thought about it—it was always that way, from the beginning, from her first lusty baby cry. She had come into the world absurdly small to be making so much noise and fuss. She pushed, demanded, rebelled. She wouldn't cuddle, compromise, or conform. She was always a stranger. A stranger, his own flesh and blood, his own daughter!

Her first cry. He closed his eyes, remembering that picture without any difficulty. She was so small. A tuft of reddish hair on a silken head, a waving fist that grabbed his finger, a piercing cry. He had stroked her head awkwardly, hoping the nurse wouldn't see how nervous he was. She had stopped crying.

He had looked up from her, to her mother. Amy lay so still and white in the hospital bed. She had given him a weak smile, a sort of congratulations that he had calmed the baby. He would do fine. He had looked back down at the infant who was suddenly relaxed and sleeping in his arms. A daughter born of their love. Another smile from Amy, one of the last she had given him.

He would use that head rubbing technique on Katherine over the next few years, for colic, or earaches or scratched knees. It always worked. Then one day, undefinable in his memory, it didn't work. She had screamed and shoved his hand away. He didn't try it after that.

Andy tossed the orange into the trash. The memory was too painful, like a brilliant gift ripped savagely from his hands. He had worked hard, and he had been successful. But it was always a bit tarnished, a bit cold without Amy to share it with. But then, he mused, he would never have worked so hard if Amy were there. Only two years. Two years with her, and now 18 years alone. Alone...

"Ahem, sir?"

"Oh...pay that bill. Call Saxons and tell them to refuse service to Miss Katherine Alcott the next time she comes breezing in. I should have done that long ago."

"Yes, sir. And—"

"And while you're on the phone, call the other shops she always goes to. Stop the credit there too."

A facial muscle did not twitch on the secretary's face. He didn't say a word. But the two men knew each other well.

"What's the problem, Collins?"

"Well, sir, I don't mean to presume."

"Of course you do. It's your job. You think I'm being too harsh, is that it?"

"I..."

"Go ahead, say it."

"I would allow Miss Katherine is...is a highstrung girl. Very energetic and, and fun loving."

"Headstrong and spoiled," the father returned flatly. "I've no one to blame but myself. I've made a mess of raising her."

"She's a good girl, really, sir. That is from what I've observed."

"Yes, from an observation point she is very sweet. You don't live with her, though. You don't have a daughter of your own."

"Yes that's true, sir," the secretary said calmly.

Andy ran his fingers through his hair and closed his eyes. "I know she's a good girl...I know..."

"Like Miss Melanie is. Both good girls in their...in their own way, sir."

Andy opened his eyes and gave his secretary a tired smile. "Years ago, when I was paddling Kate for something, she turned on me, and I'll never forget what she said. 'Melanie is an angel. And I'm the opposite of an angel!'"

"An interesting and, and enlightening comment, sir."

Andy stood up and shrugged. He walked back to his drawing table. "Maybe Mel should have been a little less of an angel, and Katherine a bit more. A balance would have made my little kingdom a bit more peaceful, don't you think?"

"Yes, sir."

He picked up his pencil. "Daughters..." he mumbled. "Designing ships is far easier, Collins."

Chapter 2

Vienna, Austria
July, 1914

◆ ◆ ◆ ◆ ◆◆

The little girl held tightly onto her mother's hand while column after column of marching men passed in front of her. She knew in her own childish way she should be impressed. But she wasn't. Their shiny black boots were so loud, so cruel looking—like they could smash anything underneath them. This parade confused her; everyone seemed so happy, yet she felt frightened. Everywhere people were talking about something called mobilization. It was too big a word. She didn't understand.

Later they went to Demel's for pastries. The outdoor cafe was crowded, and everyone was still in a holiday mood. She was just hungry. Soldiers were everywhere—laughing, boasting. Even her older brother Kurt was there in uniform. He did look nice and smart in the gray—but so strange. Not like the Kurt who took her to the Burggarten, or the Schonbrunn Zoo, or boating on the Danube on Sunday afternoons. He seemed so busy, so occupied with that strange, undefinable thing called politics. She couldn't remember the last time he had pumped her on his bicycle to their cousin's house outside Vienna.

His friend was with him, too. They were together a lot these days, she noticed. She didn't like her brother's friend; he was so angry looking. He wasn't the kind of friend she would have picked for Kurt. But then, she was only six and no one asked her opinion.

"Yes, Adolf can be...moody," Kurt had agreed. "But he sees things, you know."

"Sees things? What kind of things?"

Kurt had shifted, rubbed his chin, then pulled her silky braid affectionately.

"He just has visions, ideas...and just...things. You're too young to understand, little one."

Still, she didn't like him. Didn't like him leaning down and asking her to hurry and grow up so she could be his girl. Didn't like his intense dark eyes and the droopy mustache that seemed too large for his thin face.

Later when her mama tucked her into bed she sleepily asked, "Why is Austria...I mean, why is Austria angry and so many soldiers about?"

Her mother lost that holiday look, and she only shook her head sadly. Maybe she was too young to understand too...

And so, from a single shot, it began—and on such a beautiful summer day...

Queenstown, Ireland

The young woman opened the door and stopped on the threshold. Immediately she recognized the odor—violets. Only one person she knew wore the cheap perfume. She closed the door reluctantly. She was tired and hoped the smell was merely her imagination.

But sitting in the small parlor was an older woman. She was smoking and studying her nails. And she had not heard the door. In the sunlight that streamed through the windows, she looked almost like a mannequin, stiff and painted. And aging. Over the years, every attempt was made to hold the youth. But the youth was too tarnished to bequeath any beauty. And so, still she aged. She sat there, a picture of the young woman in 20 or so years.

She finally looked up, and they assessed each other in hostile silence.

"Well...you didn't answer any of my letters, so I had to come," the older woman said in a heavy German accent.

"I didn't even open any of your letters," the young woman returned bluntly. "I felt no need."

The older woman smiled, a slow, crooked smile. It reminded the younger woman of how a cat must look just before he devoured a mouse.

"But I found you anyway," she teased.

"So it seems."

The young woman tossed her coat and purse into an overstuffed chair.

"No more welcome than that, pet? Such a way for a daughter to greet her mother who she has not seen in so long. Ah well...I made myself some tea." She glanced around the room. "Nice little place you have."

"Why are you here?"

Again, the teasing smile. "Aren't you curious to know how I found you?"

"Not really. I'm sure you coaxed my letters from cousin Walther."

The woman nodded. "At least you care for some member of your family, if not your own mother." She pouted.

"I'm tired and very busy," the girl snapped irritably. "Get to the reason you've come all the way from Berlin. Not to see the lovely Irish countryside, I'm sure."

"No, this place is hideously provincial. Bicycles everywhere, not a decent tram. I don't see how you stand it! But I don't like your bluntness at all."

"Like it, or leave."

The mother shook her head sadly. "Pet, such a bitter tongue you have." She snuffed out her cigarette with exaggerated daintiness.

"The constable's office is at the end of the block. I'll go there in one more minute if you don't get on with what you came for."

The older woman drew herself up haughtily. She could be just as hard as her daughter—after all, she had taught her everything she knew.

"And tell him you are German while you're there, hmm? Your tuition is late. Your rent is late. You have very little money, and therefore small reason to be so harsh to your dear mother."

The young woman cursed inwardly. "That is none of your business!"

"Ah but it is, pet, it really is. There is a war coming on. Did you know that?"

"I'm surprised you do."

The ample shoulders shrugged. "I keep...company with an officer very close to the kaiser. And I do know. I also know England will be compelled to join in. It is only a matter of hours." Bitterness filled her voice. "Dear England, always ready for a fight—sends the least, and claims the most in the end."

"Did you come here to give me a civics lesson?" The young woman rose from her chair. "You are pointing out that your country will be fighting against my adopted one. Imagine that..."

The older woman rose also. "Imagine yourself kicked out of school and out of this cozy little flat because you have no money. Imagine yourself on a cold street corner or perched on a stool in the pub, making up to a fat Irishman with garlic on his breath!" She went off into a fit of laughter.

"As you have," the young woman said without pity.

The laughter ended abruptly. The coldness from her eyes was almost tangible. "We understand each other, pet. My officer is being transferred to Emden where he will be the head of intelligence. Very important position, you can imagine." She looked puffed up as if the promotion were her own. "He wants information about British liners, merchant and otherwise, that pass through the St. George channel. He was intrigued when he learned I had a daughter close to the channel."

"There is a Cunard office a few blocks over. You can get a timetable for free. You don't have to sell anything..."

"Of course, but he wants more details than that. Details that a pretty girl could get easily enough if she tried. Passengers may be the only thing on the manifest. Munitions, of course, would not be."

"And what would that matter?"

"Don't be a dummkopf!" the mother snapped irritably. "Germany will go to war and Germany will win! And we will sink anything in St. George's channel we desire. You see now, pet?"

"A spy is what he wants."

"A brilliant daughter, I have, yes. A spy on this ugly little rock! And a fortune to be made for a girl with a smart head on her shoulders. Simple."

The young woman sat down wearily. She no longer felt like jousting. She wanted her mother to go. That she did not protest any further was her first great mistake.

"You are perfect for this…assignment. You have friends—"

"You've been very busy snooping," the young woman said with less acid in her voice now.

The mother drew a map from her purse. A thick finger with a blood-red nail traced along the Irish coast. She had come prepared. She had done her homework.

"You should find a friend, a school chum perhaps, a boyfriend, someone who lives on the coast. Perfect. The fishing fleet would know the particulars of what is going on in the channel."

"Ignorant, illiterate fishermen?" the girl asked with exasperation.

"They will watch for the liner, see any naval operations that Britain would prefer to conceal," the mother continued nonplused.

"This does not concern me," the girl said firmly. "Why would I turn against Ireland? I care nothing, absolutely nothing for Germany!"

Still that steady calmness, that assurance, from the older woman.

"Of course, this concerns you, pet. You like to eat, don't you? And being your mother's daughter…" Her smile widened with the taunt. "…you like nice things and you're willing to do almost anything to get them. How did you earn your passage from Berlin to here, may I ask?"

The girl crimsoned. Then her eyes grew hard. "So the mighty German government must resort to a college coed to help it out, is that it?"

"The mighty German government will have a hook wherever it cares to have one, pet. And you'd do well to not forget how sharp a hook can be…" She smiled again.

"Is that a threat?"

The older woman pulled on her expensive wool sweater and checked her reflection in a small mirror. "It would be a…pity to lose this little flat…"

"Get out!"

"Does anyone know you are German, pet?"

"I am not German!"

A pitying smile. "Ah, but if you aren't then…what are you?"

The younger woman could not answer. She felt nothing but seething hatred and self-contempt now.

"It could become very uncomfortable for you if your identity was known. I've heard landlords kick out tenants for less. And with Walther rising in the navy and your affection for him, how can you not help?"

The young woman said nothing. They both knew who had won this struggle. Her mother opened a leather bag and pulled out a small stack of bills. It was more than the young woman had seen in her whole life. She tried hard not to gawk.

"Each month this amount will be deposited in your account—if there is a transmission each month of vital information. Very simple...and very painless...and you don't have to be pawed by anybody!" She went off into another spasm of laughter. But it was an ugly laugh, entirely void of joy.

"Auf Weidersehen, pet, it really has been lovely."

Then the flat was quiet and the young woman sank into a shabby chair and cried.

London
July, 1914

"So...there I...was," the speaker said, caring little that her mouth was full of food. "So fresh, he was absolutely all...hands. Then...my mum comes in the room...and my mum likes him. But me? I just can't decide. Are you going to eat all that custard, Alice? Thanks. So anyway, I shove this cream bun in his mouth...to slow him down!"

The three other girls joined in the laughter.

"What would you have done, Molly, if you had been on the front porch and your father came to the door with...with octopus arms beside you?" Alice asked.

The fourth girl finished her bite completely before she answered. She was like that, deliberate and unhurried in her speech—which caused her peers to think her just a bit odd.

"Well, since Janet says she doesn't care for Fred and only went out with him to please her mother, I would probably have slapped him."

"Ouch!"

"Molly, you have no romantic illusions!"

"No, I just prefer not to wrestle with someone I care nothing for," Molly said easily.

"Which implies she would wrestle with someone she did like! There is hope for Molly, after all!"

"Yet she won't go out with anyone I try to set her up with!" Janet laughed.

Molly smiled and took another bite of her sandwich.

"It's because she's a vicar's daughter," a young woman named Judith said snippishly.

"Well, the wildest girl I ever knew was a vicar's daughter!" Janet protested.

"Molly prefers her Bible," Judith continued cuttingly.

"You do like men, don't you, Molly?" Janet asked with concern.

Molly Fleming sighed. Lunch hour was always like this—it was the hardest part of her day. She would prefer to take her lunch at her desk or even nicer, up on the roof for a bit of fresh air. But to do that would further ostracize her from her coworkers and cause more jaded remarks. So she endured lunch hour at Whitehall Shipping with patience, and tried not to think about the future yawning out at her, year after year of listening to the romantic trials and triumphs of her fellow secretaries. But then, there was Martin. Martin was a part of her future...wasn't he?

Molly Fleming did not like London. Yet another difference between her and 'the girls'. London was nightlife, opportunities, shopping, fun at Picadilly Circus—and lots of men. Molly didn't like London not only because of her stuffy job, but because of the crowded streets, the noise, the smelly air, the fog, the fussing at the market, the flat she shared with her father that gave a grand view of the alley bisected by laundry lines, and the billboard advertising a remedy for gout.

And now in the heat of July, the stifling London summer was almost unbearable. Not at all like the home she had left where the scented breezes and brooks and fresh-mown fields didn't radiate heat. When the crickets and the mockingbirds came out at dusk, there was a coolness that the city could not duplicate. The country was all she had known for most of her 21 years. Life in the country village north of London was a simple pleasure in a thatched cottage. Bicycling to work, teaching music at the local school. Yes, life was different since they had come to London. But she would not begrudge her father the teaching fellowship at King's College. It meant so much to him. Like a prize, it had restored his self-worth.

"I'm sure Molly has never even kissed a man," Judith said with a contemptuous laugh. From the beginning, she was against Molly, unexplainably cold and hostile.

"Oh leave off, Judith!" Janet snapped with sudden loyalty. "Molly has her own ideas."

Judith pointed her nose higher and tossed her yellow-blond curls. Molly wanted to laugh.

"Then tell us what you do in the evenings," Judith pressed.

Molly wanted to tell Judith to mind her own business, to toss the remains of her lunch in the trash and go back to her desk. And the truth?

What she would tell them would only bring down more sarcastic remarks. She took a deep breath.

"Well, some evenings my father and I read together, or play chess."

The three fun loving girls looked shocked. Judith looked triumphant.

"On Tuesday evenings, I work with the children's choir at Halley Street Church. Wednesday nights I volunteer at the library."

"And Friday nights and Saturday nights?" Janet asked in a near paralyzed voice.

"Friday nights we go to lectures or stay home or—"

"Or knit baby booties for the Red Cross! Lovely..." Judith's voice dripped sarcasm as she stood and gathered up her things. "You belong in a convent, Miss Fleming. Tooda-loo!" She waved.

Molly quietly folded her bag and brushed away the crumbs from her skirt.

"Don't mind Judith." Janet pressed Molly's hand. "She's a cross one... Has it out for you for some reason."

Molly shrugged. One more lunch hour over.

"Molly, you're very pretty," Janet continued, trying in her simple way to be diplomatic. "Much prettier than Judith."

"Thank you, Janet."

As Molly Fleming walked the six blocks home in the coming London evening, she hardly noticed the cabs that passed her on the street, or the press of people that passed her on the sidewalk.

"Get your paper!" newsboys croaked from every corner. "Russia mobilizes! Get your paper!"

But Molly was thinking of Judith. Judith and her acid tongue. "You belong in a convent, Miss Fleming!"

For some reason, she couldn't seem to shake Judith's jabs like she usually could. She stopped suddenly in the tide of people and stepped up to a clean plate-glass window. It was a watch shop with a variety of timepieces for any purse or preference, but she barely saw them. She took a good look at her reflection in the window. Average height, average weight and figure. A slender face, olive complexion, a decent nose, brown eyes, respectable lashes. Dark hair, straight, just below the line of her shoulders. A working girl, in no way remarkable. Decent. Like a nun. She smiled to herself and resumed her steady walk home.

It was like clockwork, her day—meriting the scorn of the girls at work. Her hand on the doorknob to the flat at 4:23. Her purse on the bench by the door, next to her father's rumpled jacket which she would always smooth and hang up. The sound of water on the fire that her father set for tea. She knew it gave him pleasure and a feeling of usefulness to have the water on and the tea things laid. She would pull off her pumps and toss them by her chair in the little living room. She'd bend over his chair, kiss the top of his head and pat his shoulder. He'd take her hand and give it a squeeze. Like clockwork, every day the same.

"Hard day?" he'd ask, his face bent over the *Times* crossword puzzle in his lap.

"So so. And you?"

"Fighting against the encroachment and enslavement of ignorance is always hard, Molly dear."

Always the same answer, and always she would laugh. She knew he was happy in his work. She would slip to her room then to pull off the stockings that were so vicious in the heat all day, run a comb through her hair, and washed her face which she felt always accumulated London grime. Then she finished the tea preparation and carried it in to her father.

Thomas Fleming was approaching 60, and it held no fear for him. He counted his life blessed, rich indeed. A quiet, steady man, he had accepted all the varied experiences of his life with calm equanimity. When he looked over his shoulder at the march of years, the heartaches and disappointments, the failures and pain, they carried no bitter point to prod him. Even when Molly's mother was killed, even when a stroke enfeebled him and left him temporarily unable to provide, even then Thomas Fleming remained steadfast in his trust that what remained was a treasure, and he was a fortunate man.

He was the picture of an Englishman—tall and spare, lean-faced with thinning gray hair, glasses perched on the end of a slender nose. He wore a thin sweater even in the July heat and rumpled tweed trousers. A pipe and a cup of tea waited at his hand. He wore a slightly absentminded, benevolent look in his eyes. Yes, English to the marrow. Now as he sat in the old overstuffed, floral chair with the paper in his lap, he felt rich. And he always felt richer when he heard Molly's step on the threshold.

He glanced up when his daughter entered with the tea tray. He frowned—she looked tired to him. He didn't like to see London taking the country blush from her cheeks, shading her eyes with care. He knew she didn't like London, though she had never voiced a word of complaint. He didn't like it either. He hated leaving the village that Molly had known all her life for the congestion of the city. It seemed an unfair trade, but it had provided a living for them beyond the meager vicar's pension. And too, he reflected, perhaps Molly needed the opportunities, the stimulus of a more cosmopolitan environment. Maybe she really needed London. He worried over her in his own tender way—a nameless concern that life was slipping by Molly. She was as calm, assured and content as he—a true daughter taught well by a loving father. Weren't his nagging concerns just so much silliness?

"So who was truant today, Dad?" she asked as she poured their tea and glanced over the mail. "Maxwell the third or David Davies the second?"

Fleming removed his glasses carefully. Molly knew the gesture. The students of Greek studies at King's College knew it, as well. It was preparatory to the scholar saying something serious. He was not in a teasing mood. He was troubled about something.

"No, Max and David were present. Jonathan was absent however."

"Jonathan? Hasn't he had perfect attendance? Your star pupil."

"Apparently Jonathan has had other things on his mind besides Greek. His sister came by after class. Jonathan left for Paris yesterday. Left a note saying he was joining the French foreign legion."

"What?"

Fleming nodded and sighed. "Just like that."

"Well, that seems rather, rather rash of him."

"I suppose..."

They settled in for their tea.

"What else, Dad?" she asked gently. "What's upset you?"

"Molly, did you hear about Russia?"

"Just vaguely. The girls don't talk about things like that much on breaks, you know."

"I had lunch with a fellow who works in the admiralty offices. Some sort of undersecretary to Churchill."

"Who's he?"

"Only first Lord of the Admiralty. Anyway, inside government workers are saying within the week Germany will declare war on Russia, then France, then..."

"Us," Molly finished quietly.

"It seems inevitable. The Grand Fleet's been on maneuvers and Churchill's directed them to war stations." He took a long drink of tea. "I don't like the look of this, Molly. It looks like a mad race to fire the first shot. Like a bunch of adolescent boys eager to try out the pop guns they received for Christmas!" He shook his head. "No, no, that's a silly illustration. This is far more serious. I get in these rare, prophetic moods from time to time, daughter. I'm in one now."

"And what does your mood tell you?"

"That this may be far more than a little scrap between Austria and Serbia. I can see the whole of Europe caught up in it. Young men sacrificed for old men's follies."

Molly shivered. "I hope you're a poor prophet, Dad."

He nodded and studied the rim of his cup, instantly regretting the worry he may have given his daughter. For 21 years he had loved her, and for 15 of those years they had lived a peaceful, quiet life together—

just the two of them. He was always pleased to look at her and see that she did not bear an English stamp in her looks. Her dark hair testified to her French mother.

"So, what's the news from Martin?" he asked to change the somber mood.

"May be down next weekend, or the one after."

"Hmm. Medical school keeps him very busy."

She nodded.

"Rather inconvenient having to go all the way to Glasgow to study," he continued.

She shrugged. "Well, when you have a rich bachelor uncle who'll pay for your entire schooling, I suppose you don't fuss."

"Like you here in London, hmm?" He smiled above his cup.

She returned the smile, and they enjoyed their tea in silence a few moments.

"What's the challenge today?" she asked finally, pointing to the *Times* puzzle.

"No real challenge at all. Painfully easy. I must write the editors about it."

She laughed.

"And your challenge today, Molly?"

She hesitated, then, "Oh, nothing much. Mr. Whitehall was a bit crosser than usual. Fussed at Janet for taking too long a break."

"Martin being there in Glasgow and you here makes courtship a bit...awkward, it seems."

Carefully, slowly, he wanted to talk about young Martin.

"Well, I think the mail service appreciates us, Dad."

He began to polish his glasses. "Hmm...suppose he studies most of the time. And when he's not studying he..." A gray eyebrow lifted to punctuate the sentence.

Molly seemed genuinely surprised at the comment. "Are you thinking I should worry over Martin?"

"No, no, not worry," he hedged. "Not exactly."

"After all, we're not married or anything!" Molly laughed easily.

"No, a marriage conducted at such a distance would be rather difficult. Only..."

"Only?"

"Only you and Martin have been engaged for a rather lengthy time."

Molly looked shocked. "Dad, your comments are a bit odd."

He peered over the rim of his glasses and smiled.

"And actually, Martin and I aren't officially engaged like the girls at the office would call it."

"An understanding then?"

"An understanding, exactly."

"Hmm…could I have another cup, my dear?"

She leaned forward. "Dad, you do like Martin, don't you?"

"Of course, I do. He's a fine, steady lad." And as Thomas Fleming spoke, he could not help but pose the question to himself. If he was so fine, so steady, so apparently right for his daughter, what was he nagged about? Of course, Fleming had the romantic opinion one shouldn't marry even the most sterling man if it was simply for convenience or comfort. "We've known Martin for years. There's always been Martin."

Molly's eyes narrowed in suspicion. "You make him sound like, like a favorite pair of carpet slippers!"

Fleming smiled indulgently. "When I think of Martin, I…" He glanced down at the paper a moment. "I think of the word ambiguous."

Molly could not help but laugh. "Oh, you've done too many puzzles! How in the world is Martin vague?"

The father leaned forward with sudden intensity. "Does he excite you, Molly?"

"Excite?" she echoed cautiously.

"Do you thrill to see him when he walks through the door? Is he the best-looking man you think you've ever seen?"

Molly Fleming attempted a weak laugh.

"Molly, have you and Martin ever had a decent row?"

"You want us to fight? We have never raised our voices in all the years we have known each other."

"There's nothing wrong with little sparks now and then. Where there's sparks, there's flame. And where there's flame, there's warmth. You don't get lonely, you don't get disappointed, you don't get bored…and you don't get cold when there's a fire in your love, Molly."

Molly crimsoned a healthy country pink.

"Of course, when there's flame you feel its absence so much more.…"

"Dad, why are you…saying this now? Have you heard from Martin?"

Thomas Fleming respected his daughter. He could not bluntly ask her if she loved this man with whom she had an 'understanding.' She did have her dignity and privacy.

"No, I haven't heard from Martin. I just want the best for you. You're such a precious girl, and I want the man you choose to be worthy."

"And you don't think Martin is…worthy?" she asked slowly.

"Martin is a good fellow. But is he the fellow for you?"

He looked past her, drawn into memories that kept only a tender claim.

"Your mother and I had that warmth," he said softly. "Not for long. No, not for long, but a lovely flame while it burned. And loving you, Molly, has kept me from being a broken, frigid shell."

Darkness had settled on the crown city with little relief from the cloistering heat. Molly climbed to the roof of the adjoining apartment building. She had followed their cat to this place once and found a private little sanctuary. Sitting in a shadowy corner now, hugging her knees, she was in her own little world. The chimney pots, the noise, the imprint of a place still new and foreign to her were far away. She could think anything—and not worry that her father would see her frowns or tears. She was basically a happy, contented girl, but coming to London made her feel small and exposed. She would give herself a proper talking to, 'You're too provincial, Molly girl, been too sheltered. You really must toughen up.' So she would adjust to this new place. She looked up into the purply black sky—as many thoughts competing in her mind as twinkling stars in the heavens. Was she like a nun? Was excitement a much needed part to life? Was she unfufilled without it? And what could her father's unexpected, untypical comments about Martin mean?

Martin. Steady, fine, constant. She carefully reviewed the questions. Did he excite her? Did she think him wonderfully handsome? Was their relationship so boring that a fight was unthinkable? She forgot for a time the threat of war that loomed in the distance. Right now, on this warm July evening, only one question was uppermost in her mind. Was Martin the right one?

Kinsale, Ireland

He stood in the muddy field watching the last smudges of the gray night sky pushed away by scarlet and saffron flushes of dawn. He was up before first light this morning, milking and feeding the few farm animals his family kept. Then, pulled almost irresistibly, he'd left the warmth of the small barn and tramped to the low stone wall that casually defined his property from his neighbor's to watch the last act of sunrise. The property rose to a little treeless knoll. From this vantage point he could both see and hear the rhythm of the Atlantic. Today the sea was flat and calm, hazy with morning mists. It was so quiet, so deeply quiet, he felt it inside himself, like a minor player in some huge drama.

He enjoyed watching the sky color at sunrise or sunset in a thousand hues. He liked to watch clouds forming over the sea, scuttling about by unseen currents. He would perch on the wall, keeping a lonely, solitary vigil with only the theater of dazzling stars—and the maker of the stars. The stars were like chips of crystal, like they made at Waterford. On clear nights he felt like a boy again and wanted to reach out and hold them. Sometimes he watched those stars and imagined that some young woman somewhere gazed upon them, too—and that they were destined to find each other, only separated by the breath of a prayer. But he kept those imaginings to himself.

He was the eldest, now 26. With his father gone, he had assumed the headship of the family. He sighed. It wasn't that he fully minded. He loved the sea, the pulling of your daily bread from the water. It was always a challenge. Was it his master or servant? He could never decide. But at other times, he wondered if things wouldn't have turned out quite differently for him if he hadn't been the firstborn. He wondered about things bigger than crops and the day's catch. Things that moved the compass from his little world to unknown perimeters. He had taught himself astronomy. What he wanted to know, and could not experience, he would study.

No one, save his mother and his little sister, knew this big fisherman's sensitivity. Few would suspect it in the the broad, unflinching shoulders and posture; the big hands and feet; ruddy, weather-chapped skin; keen, serious gray eyes.

A triangle of geese thrust across the pearl-like sky and interrupted his thoughts. He felt his stomach growl—he'd been up nearly two hours already. He turned abruptly and started back towards the farm buildings. It was time for breakfast.

Today was Friday. Friday meant hotcakes. Friday always meant hotcakes, for his energetic little mother was a sensible, predictable woman. He was glad it was Friday, his thoughts shifting effortlessly from the poetical to the practical. He loved his ma's hotcakes. He could eat a mountain of them. He was born with the proverbial farm hand's hearty appetite.

He knocked the mud from his ugly thick-soled boots with four swift kicks as he rubbed a mutt's silky head, a routine as predictable as the sunrise itself. He ducked into the doorway of the stone house, the silence that had enfolded him abruptly and unceremoniously unwrapped.

"And anyway...Jen's...this afternoon...and..." One of his brothers was talking with his mouth full.

He couldn't hear all the words as he thrust his face into the washbasin, rinsed in the cold water, then quickly dried off on the rough towel his ma held out for him. He was eager to attack those hotcakes.

His ma smiled, like she did most mornings. He was like a great big bull, she always thought, the way he washed his face, slinging water everywhere. She'd given up trying to change him. He'd been sloppy at his washing ever since he was as high as her apron strings.

"...Well, don't let Paddy know... He'll roar..."

His ma handed him a plate piled high with golden-brown, steaming hotcakes. "Don't be telling me what?" he asked as he poured the fragrant tea.

"Ah…" his brother Denny allowed.

He looked at the faces intently bent over their plates, at his mother who sat at the opposite end of the table.

"I'm going to be late, sure." His brother Rory hopped up, quickly kissed their mother and took the stairs two at a time.

"Pass the jam," said Pierce in his typical slow, deep voice.

"I'm asking again, don't tell me what?"

They all exchanged glances. Pierce, knowing his older brother's tenacity, finally spoke up.

"'Tis just that Jen's home this afternoon, on the two-thirty train." He took another bite. "You always get riled up, Pada, always do."

It explained nothing, and he appealed to his mother with an irritated look. His veil of patience was wearing thin.

His ma spoke up. "Jen is bringing home a friend, Padraic."

Everyone turned to stare, to gawk, to wait for the temperamental thunderstorm. Instead he defied them, stirring his coffee placidly, attacking the cakes again. They shrugged as one body and resumed their eating.

Rory was down the stairs again. He took one quick look in the mirror that hung in the huge kitchen. "Have you told him?" He ran his fingers through his hair.

"He knows," Denny mumbled through a mouthful.

"Wonder what she'll be, Paddy. The loud laughy type or somber, serious, ask-deep-theological-questions type? Bye, Ma!"

He was out the door with a slam. Another bad habit Ma was not able to change after 30 years of trying.

"I brought home a paper last night." Denny settled back in his chair.

"And well after midnight, it was, too," their ma interrupted pointedly.

Denny shrugged and smiled. "You know Kerry, Ma, she likes my…singing."

"If it was just singing, I should worry less, my laddie."

"Oh, Ma, there is nothing for you to worry about. Kerry is a grand lass, and—"

"And a perfect match for your angelic-ness," Padraic teased.

"Are you going to let me tell you about the paper or not?"

They all shrugged and continued eating.

"Well, Austria has served Serbia with an ultimatum—"

"Foolishess!" Pierce sputtered. "Utter foolishness! Such conditions! What proud country would agree to them? Sure, it's an insult to Serbia even if she did start the trouble."

"One of her citizens did," Padraic corrected. "Not the whole country."

"Austria is spoiling for a fight like a great, loud bully," Pierce continued with uncharacteristic vehemence.

Denny read the terms.

"Sure and it means nothing to us." Their ma calmly sipped her tea.

"Aye, it will if Britain is pulled into it," Padraic returned with equal calm.

Pierce finished his final bite. "The papers say nothing about Britain."

"I hardly think they're sleeping in London," Padraic said drily as he glanced up at the small leaded window that faced the sea. The sea was such a part of their lives. It was like a life vein. It was always there, always constant, when the world proved very uncertain.

But it had taken on a new complexion all of a sudden, the sea. It separated, but did not isolate, him and his family from the storm that churned on the European continent. The shores of Britain were a little over a hundred miles away. Still it was far away...too far to touch him? But if England was drawn into the conflict, wouldn't the young blood of Ireland be spilt again? He didn't like to think about that—not with three younger brothers at home.

"No politics at the table, your da never allowed it," their ma reminded them.

"Not politics, Ma. 'Tis what's happening out there." Padraic gestured to the window. "We can't ignore that exactly now."

He gave directions for the morning to Denny and Pierce in a tone that clearly indicated the facts about Jen's homecoming had not gone unnoticed. His ma knew he was irritated.

He stayed seated after they left; he was up early when they were still deeply tucked in warmth and slumber. He deserved this brief time. His ma poured herself another cup of tea and waited. She knew him, knew what was coming. Sitting like this was like sitting across from her late husband as she'd done for 35 years, so alike was her oldest son in looks and temperament.

"Well?" he asked after his last bite.

"Looks like a lovely day, it does," she returned evenly.

"Lovely," he snorted, but with a trace of a grudging smile. "Why does she do it, Ma? Better, why do you let her do it, I'm wondering."

"Now, Paddy—"

"Why does she have to bring a friend or roommate? Does she think we're keeping an inn or running a boarding house?"

"She's being friendly and hospitable, son. She enjoys people. She wants us to know and enjoy the people she does. There's nothing wrong with that."

"Maybe she should spend less time being hospitable and more time on her studies," the fisherman answered in a near growl.

His ma leaned her elbows on the table, smiling. "Sure, and is there any problem with your sister's marks?"

She fully knew the answer. He frowned. Jen was a high-mark scholar. Somehow that pretty head held socializing and academics in perfect balance. His frown deepened. Jen...he was closer to her than any of his brothers despite their near twelve-year age difference. He held a big, affectionate love for his little high-spirited sister. But this bringing home girlfriends...

"Ma, you know what happens! You see it right under your nose, just like a, a dime novel romance! She brings home this lass just like Rory said, flirty or serious, and your sons fall like dominoes. It happens every time, it does. Then they waltz off, never mind the heart they broke. First it was Denny, then Rory. Pierce nearly made himself sick over that last one. He was worthless working. He'd just stare at the ocean till a fish was flipping around in his lap! If you'd have seen him you wouldn't be as, as hospitable as your daughter!"

He had worked himself into a fine, very controlled rage.

"I saw him...I saw..." she soothed. These tirades were predictable and easily spent. She could handle them quite effortlessly.

"Well?"

"Well what?"

"Well, tell Jen to stop it."

"I certainly will not," she returned spiritedly. "You boys simply have to learn that flirting and romance are a part of life. "

"Sounds like experience," he said dryly.

He pushed back his chair abruptly, terminating the discussion. His ma rose also.

"You'll be kind to Jen's friend. No rudeness to a guest in this house, my boy. I simply won't allow it." Her voice was warm, but firm.

He pulled on his hat wordlessly as his ma took her napkin and dusted the crumbs off his shirt front.

"I might as well go over to Tom's right now and hire out his boys 'cause my brothers will be useless to me," Padraic mumbled.

"Twice bitten...I'm sure they'll learn until the right one comes along."

"I doubt it." His voice was still a growl as he patted his ma on the shoulder.

"Just the same, Padraic, mind your manners. They'll be here this afternoon."

By late afternoon Jen and her friend were well installed in Jen's old bedroom. The house now rang with Jen's laughter and the brothers' teasing. Everyone was more animated when Jen was home. But Padraic did not join in the enthusiastic welcome of Jen's guest. He took his dog and a small pack and went hunting, camping out alone. He would return Sunday, he told his ma in economical terms.

It was Sunday night and the household was quiet, lights extinguished, long in their beds when Padraic returned from his wanderings. He entered the kitchen, glad for the warmth and welcome of the kitchen fire.

Pulling off his coat and hat, his eyes roved the counter until he found what he was looking for. He smiled in the semidarkness. Lifting up the tea towel, he took one of the big scones the mistress of the house had left waiting for him. As he munched, his eyes grew accustomed to the dimness and he found he was not alone.

Jen sat in their mother's rocker, her head leaning on a hand, toward the fire. His smile broadened. She had waited up for him! Just like old times. She must not have brought *the friend,* after all. He went forward eagerly, saying her name.

"Jen!" He stooped down and impulsively kissed the top of her head.

The figure straightened, startled, having drifted off into a light sleep. It was not Jen. It was—*the friend.*

The young woman stood up, swaying with dizziness at the heat, her eyes adjusting. "Oh!"

Padraic stepped back, horrified, awkward, angry at his impulsiveness.

"You're not Jen. I thought you were Jen. My sister," he added dully.

Of all things, to kiss the top of the head of a total stranger!

"I couldn't sleep. I came down and the fire was so nice. I got sleepy."

Padraic backed up another step. Feeling wretchedly foolish, he drew his eyes away, freshly angry at Jen for bringing home this brown-haired stranger. In the firelight he could not see her well, assess her looks—or see that she had been crying.

Her smile was faint and cryptic. Padraic still stared at the mantel beyond her shoulder. Finally she spoke with returned control and a trace of amusement.

"You're Padraic."

Their eyes met.

"The lamps are going out all over Europe; we shall not see them lit again in our lifetime," the foreign secretary of Britain, Lord Edward Grey said solemnly. In the brief space of only eight days, Europe was armed, mobilizing—and ready to brawl. Even the most prophetic or militaristic could not imagine the length this misunderstanding would take. Alliances that ignored past grievances and suspicions were formed. It was time to take sides. Austria-Hungary, Germany and Italy became the formidable Central Powers—the Triple Alliance so steeped in military tradition. Russia, France, and finally Great Britain, or Triple Entente, became the Allies. The alliances were strengthened in those dramatic eight days.

Germany declared war on Serbia, then Russia, then France. Shock reverberated around the world when Germany invading Belgium, referred to the country's treaty of neutrality as a 'mere scrap of paper'. As the German offensive rolled through Belgium, the Englishmen across the

channel felt they had no alternative. They had pledged their national
honor to the defense of the neutral country. But more was at stake than
even honor. An overarmed, belligerent Germany would pose solidly on
the channel coast. With Belgium annexed, Germany would become a
menacing colossus. So, Great Britain signed the pledge of war that
sealed the conflict from the Irish Sea to the Mediterranean. Suddenly,
there was a chill in the summer air...

Chapter 3

New Orleans

♦♦ ♦♦ ♦♦

S he made a pretty picture sitting on the top of the seat of America's first sports car, the Stutz Bearcat, on that sunny and warm morning. Her white hat shaded her face, but did not lessen her concern that if Eddie didn't finish the tire soon, she stood an excellent chance of burning. And that would never do. She would be quite cross with Eddie if that happened. Her blonde-red hair came just to her shoulders. The hat was at once a shield against the sun, an acquiescence to fashion, and a crown that attempted to subdue the curls. But it was a vain attempt. Many times she tossed aside the hat with a laugh. This head of unruly curls was who she was, a badge as physically defining as any. The woman of 1914 wore her hair pinned and captured, lustrous yet demure. No riotous curls and windblown extravagance. Her ankle length dress was made from a peach-colored crepe de chine. Her legs were crossed, and her dainty pumps had slipped to the floorboard. A slender foot tapped to some inner music. Yes, she looked like a picture on one of the back roads of New Orleans, and occasionally the young man would look up from his work to enjoy the picture.

Obviously bored, she flipped through a magazine and frowned at nearly every page. *Woman's Home Companion* was clearly not the preferred periodical of this young woman of 18. It was far too tame, too domesticated with its advertisements for Keds, Wesson oil and Mennen talc. And patterns for baby rompers! That really was the limit. She tossed it aside and stretched luxuriously.

"How much longer?"

But the only reply was a groan and the clank of tools.

"Eddie, how much longer? It's warm out here!"

"Oh, pretty soon…"

"You said that 10 minutes ago!" she pouted.

"Patience, Miss Alcott, patience."

"We'll be late for the party!"

More clanking of tools. "That assures you of making a grand entrance. Every eye on you!"

She laughed at his frankness as she pulled the newspaper from the stack of mail on the seat. At least this would provide more mature reading. An article at the bottom of the first page drew her eye. War news from an American correspondent. The Belgian city of Brussels had fallen as the German army pressed toward Paris. Kate Alcott cared little for the war itself. Who could understand the motives and politics of war? But the article held her. She wanted to study the writing style.

"So, Eddie," she asked casually, "what would you do if the U.S. joined the war?"

"Huh?"

She repeated her question. She really didn't care about his answer, but she was tired of reading.

"What...war?"

"Oh, good grief, the war in Europe of course! With Germany!"

"I haven't any gripe with Germany."

"Oh Ed, that sounds—"

"Smart? Ol' Woody says it doesn't concern us at all. I'll trust his judgment."

She studied her nails. "I don't know about that. But let's say the U.S. did join. I mean, Britain and the United States are chums."

The young man stood up, dusted his cream-colored trousers, and smiled. "You know more about current events than I'd have—"

"Expected from a woman?" she asked archly.

"From a very pretty woman," he returned smoothly.

She blew him a kiss. "So you wouldn't enlist?"

Women liked men in uniform. He knew that, even if he didn't understand it. "If it came to that, then I would trust Woody's judgment. Yes, I'd enlist. But it certainly won't come to that. This whole thing will be over in six months or sooner. My dad says so."

She tossed her curls. "My grandfather said everyone thought the Civil War would last only six months."

"I need a drink," he said.

She reached into the pocket of his dress jacket that lay over the seat and withdrew a silver flask. "You look pretty dusty, Eddie," she said with a smile. "I'm not sure you're suitable to be at my side. Carolyn's party is a rather important event."

He took a long, satisfying drink. "Well, the fact is, Kate, we, uh, can't make the party."

"What!"

"Tire's shot. Spare's shot. We're stranded on a back road that you wanted to take. Sorry."

"Oh, Eddie! How could you?"

He came close to her. "I'm sorry, Kate. But at least we have this." He held up the flask. "And I'd rather be stranded with this and you than with anyone else."

She took the liquor, had one fleeting mental picture of her older sister's shocked face. She laughed and tipped up the flask.

"There, that'll make you feel better. You won't mind missing the party near as much now."

Her face was a teasing pout. "This is a new dress, Eddie. Just for this occasion."

"And a very lovely one," he agreed.

She pulled him closer by his shirt front. "When we're rescued, you'll take me to dinner at Antonio's."

"Of course. And a bottle of champagne to celebrate your new dress!" He fingered her curls absently.

"Then 'The Charleston Club' afterward," she pressed.

He pulled back. "Now, Kate—"

"No, you must promise."

"Kate, you're only 18. You have to be at least 20."

"You can slip me in, Eddie."

The 'Charleston Club' was New Orleans' trendiest speakeasy.

"Kate, come on, your father would have a fit if he found out I took you there. I wouldn't be able to get within a hundred feet of your house!"

"You've made me miss the party, Eddie."

"The car—"

Her finger danced across his lips. "So now you must take me to the Club after dinner." Her teasing eyes hardened. "And my father will survive fits. I'll deal with him."

Her arms wound around his neck, and he grinned broadly.

Peppercreek

When you stood at the top of the gradually sloping hill on the eastern boundary of the property, you looked at a local landmark—the once famous Peppercreek Orchard. Now, like all things famous, its season, its prime was over. Generations had come and gone, yet in the summer of 1914 the acres of gnarled apple trees remained—still generous, if not vigorous. The white stone house remained also. It had weathered every season, every storm, every harvest, every celebration, every feast and famine. It was once home to the now scattered flock of Alcotts—if not home, then a returning point to memories and tradition in a fast changing universe. Pepper Creek still flowed a quarter of a mile from the back door. It was an amiable little tributary, offering a quiet afternoon of fishing or wading, or a silver ribbon of ice for skating in the deep of winter. The town of Peppercreek was now a memory relegated to the old timers; it had vanished entirely, its foundations obscured by vast cornfields. So the old home endured with the new faces of youth and the indelible impressions of over a hundred years.

An old woman sat in front of one of the lower windows. It was warm on the broad front porch, and she preferred the cool dimness of the small parlor. Through the half open window, past the lazily stirring lace curtains, she could hear young voices. She wasn't reading, or writing letters, or shelling summer peas, or even knitting. Her hands were idle, but her mind was active. A stroke five years earlier had left her legs paralyzed. Typically she kept herself as busy as her age and infirmity allowed. But sometimes she just wanted to sit—to quietly think, or remember, or pray. And a grandchild or daughter-in-law or friend, young or old, found a wise and willing listener when they came to Grandma Sara who could listen from her wicker wheelchair. It always deeply pleased her to have them come—pleased that they would stop in their strength and youth, their busy lifestyle, to give her time, to show her honor, to open their hearts.

Her hair had become a soft, snowy white crown. Her skin was veined and splotched with age, but behind the silver rimmed glasses her eyes were still the bright cornflower blue that was once the beauty of her youth. Even her grandson Ben could see that. When he was a lad of six he had climbed into her lap and held her face between his chubby paws. "I bet you were a beautiful woman once, Grandma!"

She had taken his compliment with diplomacy and blushed like a schoolgirl. "Well, your grandfather thought so. And his opinion was the only one that mattered."

Her body was frail, but it was strong and vigorous years ago. She'd had the optimism of youth and an unending vista of big-eyed dreams. One of those dreams took her to Washington D.C. to serve as nurse when her country divided against itself. One of her dreams gave her the man she had loved since she was a skinny girl in braids. Out of their love and dreams had come four children.

She had lived through 28 presidents, one war, the expansion of the country to include 48 states, the advent of the automobile and flying machine and dress hemlines that revealed a woman's ankles.

"Aren't you shocked at the length of dresses nowadays, Grandma Sara?" her daughter-in-law Millie had asked.

"Just like the price of sugar, Millie, always going up. Let's hope they both stay fixed for awhile. Still, I admit this new length is an advantage if women want to bicycle."

Sara Alcott privately grieved that the stroke had stolen her chance to ever ride a bicycle.

She had survived her husband by ten years. Daily she missed him and felt the vacant spot that no thing or person could ever fill. She was a praying woman—as dependable as the trees in the orchard or the stone house itself. Her family knew she was often at His throne. It was part of her, like her vivid blue eyes. Each Alcott could quote exactly the words Grandma Sara used to end every prayer—it was like a scent that identified her.

'And even so, come quickly Lord Jesus...'

On this morning in late August, Sara Alcott was about the most important work left to her. Millie had read the entire front page of the paper to her earlier. There were rumblings of another war, even if off in faraway Europe. She had seen the penalty for the foolishness of war as a young woman in the crowded corridors of Carver Hospital in Washington. She had seen the blood, the stump legs and arms, the pain-filled eyes. Even far away she could imagine all too vividly the scenes. So she prayed for the soldiers and civilians—all were paying the same terrible price.

Leaning over the engine of the Model T, Ben Alcott whistled while he worked. Listening carefully, you could pick up the tune of "By the Beautiful Sea." His mind darted from one subject to the other. He frowned—maybe this was why he didn't do so well in his studies at the university. He found concentrating on one thing difficult. And so the engine repair claimed only a portion of his thoughts and competed with the vision of a young blonde named Alice whom he was taking to a dance that evening, and then the conversation he'd had earlier with his father.

He paused in his work to glance up at the house. His grandmother sat in her favorite spot by the parlor window. He gave her a big smile and waved. She smiled and nodded back. The tools clanked a little longer as he fussed to make the engine purr like a kitten. No distractions as he drove about with the lovely Alice.

This car represented three long, hot summers on a threshing crew. It also represented a thrift that had tested him severely since taking out girls could be a costly experience. He was tempted more than a few times to take his savings and throw a gigantic party for his friends. But when the used auto became his, he was glad he'd kept his resolve.

His younger brother David leaned over the car.

"How goes?"

"Almost...got...it."

"Just in time to take Sally to the dance."

"It's Alice, not Sally. Sally was night before last."

David laughed. "Good grief, Ben! How do you keep 'em all straight?"

"I don't have to. The girls do it for me."

Both boys laughed, and Sara Alcott smiled from the window. She loved the sound of their laughter. She loved to see them wrestling and teasing, defending each other at every occasion. David, fair and slim, reminded her of her eldest son Andy; Ben, broad-shouldered and dark, resembled her husband Ethan. She had watched them grow, seen that 18-year-old quiet-natured David admired Ben. Ben likewise was the protective and generous older brother. She knew she shouldn't have any favorites among her six grandchildren, but certain ones seemed closer to her heart. She loved David for his quiet, dependable ways, Ben for his charm and loyalty, Kate in distant New Orleans for her brash and boldness.

"You going tonight, Dave?" Ben asked.

The younger boy smiled and shook his head. He didn't have the finesse, the calm assurance with girls that his older brother had. So he'd stay home with his medical books.

"Want me to fix you up?" Ben offered generously. "I can, you know."

"Naw, you go ahead, Ben. Maybe another time."

Ben snapped a greasy rag at him. "You say that every time. You like girls, don't you?"

"'Course I do. I just don't have your way with 'em, that's all. I feel nervous around them."

"Hey, it takes practice, little brother," Ben replied seriously. "I was scared and nervous too, the first few times I took a girl out."

David's smile dropped. He could not imagine Ben afraid of anything. "You were afraid of girls?"

"Sure I was." Ben grinned. "'Course I didn't let them see I was. Now after a few hundred times, the only thing I'm afraid of is calling them the wrong name!"

David laughed again. "I don't want a few hundred girls. One is fine. But anyway, I need to study tonight."

Ben snorted his disgust. "You don't even go to college yet and you do more studying than I do! We'll go out on a double date night after next. I'll fix it all up and you won't feel nervous at all. No protesting. I go back to school next week and we won't have another chance for awhile."

"Okay, okay, I'll go. I heard you and Dad talkin' this morning."

Ben made a wry grin and closed the hood. "Yeah."

"So?"

"So, it's real simple. This is my last term if I don't get better grades. I'll be finished as the big man on campus."

"Gee, Ben, I'm sorry."

Ben shrugged as he wiped his hands. "It's all right. I can't really blame him for layin' down the law. He's paying his hard-earned cash for me to be up there, and he wants to see something for it besides a good time for me." He eyed his brother with affection. "You're the one who should be up there. You're the one with the brains."

David smiled. He would go to college when Ben was finished. The dream to be a doctor could become a reality.

"I'm in no hurry. I want you to have your time."

"Don't know what I'm doing there. That's my whole problem. I'm 21 years old and I don't know what I want to do with my life. So I guess I keep going till I figure it out...or Dad pulls me out."

"You're a hard worker," David ventured kindly. "You could get all kinds of jobs. Like working over engines or mechanics or something."

"Yeah, I know a bit about cars," he admitted slowly. Normally so self-assured, he felt confused when it came to his future. "So who's your date tonight? Miss Appendix or Miss Kidneys?"

Sara Alcott laughed from her vigil at the window as her two grand-sons wrestled in the yard.

Later Ben was cleaned, pressed, and freshly shaved. He stood before his mother and grandmother for final inspection.

"You look dashing, Ben," his grandmother said with a sparkle in her eye.

"Don't tell him that, Grandma," David warned from the doorway where he lounged. "It just inflates his ego. What's that cologne you have on, big brother, Essence of Romeo?"

"The fact that I'm all cleaned up saves you from having your nose rubbed again, Master Davy," Ben replied with a laugh.

"Boys, boys, stop it now. Ben, why are you dressed for your date so early when you don't have to leave till six?" his mother asked as she fussed with his collar.

"I want to take my wheels out for a spin since I did surgery on her, be-fore I pick up Alice. And Grandma's going to be the first beautiful gal to ride!"

He scooped the old lady up before she could protest. He carried her out to the car in his strong arms while Sara laughed.

"Are you ready to meet the Lord, Grandma?" David called cheerfully from the porch.

She waved her little straw hat. "All's in the Lord's hands, Davy boy! Off we go!"

New Orleans

Kate Alcott regretted missing the party at her friend's estate some 40 miles from New Orleans, but shrimp and champagne at Antonio's with the Charleston Club afterward made a respectable second. Eddie and Kate made a flashy couple—Eddie with his dark good looks and racy charm, Kate with her own fair prettiness, laughter, and friendliness.

The champagne flowed freely during dinner and made Kate more re-flective, more open and verbal about her family, than usual. Eddie

Palmer listened greedily. Here was a wealthy young woman—a suitable match from an economic point of concern, and fun loving as well. He wanted to know all about her and her family. He shrewdly assessed that such information could give him an edge over the competition. Kate had a flirtatious side, and he knew he wasn't her only beau. There were probably half a dozen boys strung along back at her school in Grambling.

With the Stutz back in perfect running order, they drove the streets of New Orleans after dinner, then parked on a shadowy lane until the speakeasy opened at ten.

Kate leaned her head back against the seat, her eyes on the stars without really seeing them.

"So, you see there was my father making his money designing troop transports for the Spanish American War. He even has some kind of citation Teddy gave him—"

"Teddy who?"

"President Theodore Roosevelt, Eddie. How did you do in history in school?"

"Depended who I copied off of." He grinned. "So that's how your pop got loaded."

"I've told him he was perfectly mercenary," Kate continued.

"But you don't wear rags or have a tin lizzie in your drive!" The young man laughed.

"Exactly. Mercenary or not, I appreciate Daddy's hard work..."

"I can see you do." He fingered the string of pearls that encircled her smooth, fair neck.

She did not feel like romance, and she gently pushed his hand away.

"My family is so, so odd!" she persisted irritably. "It scares me sometimes!"

"Aw come on, Kate, your family looks pretty normal to me. Besides every family has its oddballs."

She was exasperated with him suddenly. "Eddie, oddballs is all my family has!"

He laughed. "Okay, tell me about them."

"Well, there's my sister Melanie. You know what she's training to be?"

"I forget."

"Well, I haven't. It's embarrassing! She wants to be a missionary! Then there's my dear papa—"

"He looks normal, a regular Southern shipping magnate."

"Oh, he's rich all right, but ridiculously odd. Scandalously odd!"

"I thought you liked scandal," Eddie protested with a laugh.

"Oh, I do. But there's a right kind of scandal and an absurd kind. They are very different."

"Give me a right kind example, if you please."

She rubbed her hands together. "That will be fun! I'm only involved in the right kind."

"Of course."

She tapped her chin in thought. "Well, there are so many examples...Hmm..."

"Your poor father!"

"Oh, don't pity Daddy," Kate returned quickly, an edge in her voice. "He causes it all..."

"That statement would prove meaty for an analyst," Eddie suggested.

She ignored him. "Here's a small scandal. Barbara Winwood. She's a girl at my school and I thoroughly despise her. Absolutely no sense of humor. So, we have this one hour a week we may entertain gentlemen callers in the parlor of our suite. All very proper." She rolled her eyes. "So I'm coming in past the head matron's office and she asks me to go to Barb's room and remind her that the hour is nearly up. I can't imagine why a boy would want to go to Barb's parlor. Anyway, I, well, I conveniently forget the matron's message and go to my own room across the hall."

"I see no scandal in that," Eddie spoke up.

"No, not until the head matron in quite a huff comes up to Barb's room herself and finds..." Kate broke off, laughing.

"Finds what?"

"Finds a corset hanging on the doorknob!"

"Naughty, naughty, Miss Alcott," Eddie admonished with a smile.

"I know, but it was such fun to see Barb's horrified face from across the hall!"

"All right, so that explains your..."

"Naughty streak," she replied coyly.

"But we began with your father being odd."

"My father. He owned one of the largest plantations in western Mississippi. Called Tanglewood. It came from my mother's side. She married my father's cousin. Then he died, and she married my father."

"Well, I'm not sure if that's odd or just confusing. Was your mother odd?"

Kate Alcott had launched too far into this family dissection to retreat now. But she hesitated. The word mother was just that—a word. It conjured up an image, a picture in a frame of a smiling young woman. A woman that looked nothing like her, no different than a picture in a magazine of a complete stranger. When she was a little girl, sometimes she took the framed photo from her father's bedroom and went to some private place and studied the woman. Her little mind would beg for some memory—and come up with nothing.

"I don't know if she was odd or not. She died. Anyway, so there was my father and mother living at this big, wealthy plantation. They decide it holds too many memories for them, so they move to New Orleans, to 2121 Old Manor."

"I don't see anything odd about that," Eddie interrupted.

"That's because you think they sold it to some other wealthy planter or something for a tidy profit."

"Of course."

"Of course not, if you're Andy Alcott. He gives, emphasize *gives,* this plantation that was in one family for decades to...to a black carpenter."

"You're making it up."

"I wish I were. My father has very old-fashioned ideas."

"But, but a black carpenter? He gave it? Are you sure you got the story straight?"

Her voice was sharp. "Yes, I have it straight. You don't think I would mix up something like that, do you?"

"Well, it does sound pretty—"

"Odd. He's a religious fanatic like my sister. Did I mention that?"

"I think you did. But to give to a nig—"

"Don't say that word, Eddie. I'll have to wash your mouth out with soap. Daddy raised us to be very broad-minded."

"Your pop may be rich, but he's definitely somewhere between a hickory and a pecan!"

Kate burst out laughing. "Yes, that sums up dear old Dad. 'Course he doesn't think too highly of you, Mr. Palmer."

"Oh? How come? Ain't I showin' his little girl a good time?" He reached out and pulled her closer.

"Maybe too good a time. He thinks you're from a rough, fast crowd. Melanie thinks the same thing. She likes to remind me from time to time, 'Will the boys you go out with make good husbands, Kate?'"

Eddie groaned. He was glad the younger Alcott was nothing like the older. "And how do you reply?"

"I shock her. I say, 'I am not looking for a husband, dear Melanie, I am only looking for a good time!'"

They both laughed at this, and Eddie tightened his hold.

"So, with my father being the way he is, who can blame me for turning out the way I have?" She batted her lashes at him.

"Not me..."

"Mel and my father. Then there's my Aunt Meg and Uncle Barrett. They live near our former plantation in Mississippi. It's this mudhole in the road called Chisolm Crossing. More blacks around than whites. My aunt is their teacher and Uncle Barrett is their doctor. They could go anywhere in the world to live and work, and yet they go on living at that nothing little place. Aunt Meg is the most beautiful woman I've ever seen, a real stunner you'd call her."

"Like you."

She was known for her frankness. "I am not beautiful, Eddie. I'm attractive. But I'm more spoiled and outrageous than anything...according to the reports my father gets from school."

"Is there anyone in your family that you...like or respect?"

"There's my cousin, Ben, in Illinois. He knows how to have a good time. And...and my grandmother. She's an old lady I like."

"I can't figure out why you ain't your daddy's little girl."

Kate stared into the moonlit night. Suddenly she no longer felt like talking about her family. She had never fit in. Never been Daddy's girl. Her older sister had formed a bond with her father that she never had. She supposed it was because they had those times at Tanglewood, and she had only their shared memories. But more importantly, they had had a woman named Amy.

She glanced at Eddie. He was waiting for her to continue. But she couldn't. The champagne had done its work, then vanished. She knew Eddie Palmer only cared about her money, her looks, how nicely she would treat him. But she didn't hold it against him. She was an opportunist—and she recognized her own kind. All she cared about was an escort for fun.

"I've gone on and on about me." She pressed herself against him. "Do you really want to talk all night?"

Melanie Alcott leaned forward with a slight smile on her face. It was a bit amusing to see her normally dignified father asleep and rumpled-looking in a deep leather chair, his mouth parted and snoring.

"Daddy? Dad." She shook him gently.

He sighed deeply, and his oldest daughter wondered if she had pulled him from some dream he was reluctant to leave. There were times, like now, that she thought her father, always proper and in control, looked vulnerable and lonely. With the gray taking prominence in his brown hair, he was still handsome, but with the invincible touch of age taking its claim. She remembered the first time she had seen him 19 years ago. It was still a sharp memory.

She was nearly four years old. Of course, he was not her father then—only a tall, slim, bearded, stranger to the plantation home she shared with her mother. His smile and his eyes were kind. Gray hair and wrinkles would come, but that smile and the magnetism of his vivid blue eyes would always be the same. Shortly after meeting him, after seeing her mother's obvious joy and trust in the man, he had become her father. It hadn't taken long for her to come to trust him, as well. That hadn't changed in their years together. He was the best father in the world. Involuntarily she frowned and glanced at the ceiling.

"Daddy, did you sleep here all night?"

Andy Alcott pulled himself up in the chair with a groan. He yawned, finally focusing on his daughter, and smiled.

"Yeah, I guess I did."

"You want some coffee or a shower?" she asked.

He ran his fingers through his hair and frowned. "I want to know where your sister is!"

She patted his hand. "It's okay, Daddy. Kate's upstairs asleep."

He straightened up abruptly. "Up. . .when?"

"I heard her about four, I think. I was pretty sleepy when I looked at the clock."

"She woke you up?" he asked tightly.

Melanie sighed. The last thing she wanted was to bring more trouble to her little sister—or more aggravation to her father.

"No...not intentionally," she answered carefully.

"Not intentionally," he repeated stiffly. He knew what her words meant. Kate had come home drunk. It had happened before. "Did you talk with her?" he asked tiredly.

"No, I...didn't think she would...want to."

"Aw, Melanie..." He closed his eyes and leaned back in the chair. He half wished she hadn't woken him up.

"Dad, please don't..."

"Don't what?"

"Please don't be angry with Kate. She doesn't mean to—"

He stood up impatiently. "Doesn't mean to bring me grief? Was she held against her will somewhere last night? Couldn't get to a phone? You're a fine one to defend her, Mel. Didn't I hear her going at you yesterday before she left for that blasted party?"

Melanie sighed. "Well, yes, she was mad at me. She wanted to borrow my pearl earrings. I told her no...since she lost my last two pair."

"And I heard a few of the choice names she called you."

"Dad—"

"I should have forbidden her from going just for that reason alone! Not to mention I don't like that Eddie what's-his-name she went with."

"Palmer. Dad, I think when you try to forbid Kate from doing something, well, it seems to make her more determined to do the thing."

"So, I'm to let her do what she pleases?"

"Well no—"

He waved her words aside. He didn't want to talk about Kate. "Tell Mary to have my breakfast in an hour. I think I'll go see how your sister is feeling this morning...after her late night."

Left alone in the spacious library, Melanie Alcott closed her eyes and prayed for her father and sister.

. . .

He seldom entered either girl's bedroom. Melanie was rarely at home these days; Kate would never invite him. But when he did enter, he always felt he had taken a step back in time. The girls' furniture had come from Tanglewood, his late wife's Southern mansion. Very old and fine pieces—Melanie loved them, Kate scoffed and called them ugly and primitive. But Andy Alcott had not relented to her on that point. Amy had chosen the things years ago, and they would remain.

Rudely, he did not bother to knock on his younger daughter's bedroom door. He walked in and glanced at the bed where she was curled deep in sleep. He stepped over the stockings and lingerie, the slippers, the hat, the expensive dress. He crossed to the tall windows, pulled back the drapes, sat down at the window seat. Books, magazines, plates and cups, and laundry were scattered everywhere in the elegant bedroom. He shook his head.

The shaft of sunlight from the long window fell in a powerful beam across the figure on the bed. He went to stand beside her. She was curled on her side, a hand laying open on her pillow. He listened to her breathe. Deceptively peaceful-looking, he meditated. The curls were spilled across the pillow. Her creamy fair skin was blushed pink. He felt his own face softening, and he wondered why the only child of his love with Amy took no mark of her mother beyond the color of her eyes. Amy had wheat-blonde hair and was tall and slender. Kate was petite and lithe. And certainly the daughter took no temperament trait from her mother. He returned to the window seat.

He would try to calm down and think of reasonable things to say when she woke. It would be nice if they could have this conversation with no raised voices, or anger, or accusations.

Kate Alcott opened her eyes and immediately felt the dull throbbing in the back of her head. Why was champagne always so vicious after being so lovely? She sensed she was not alone in the room. She hoped it was the maid—who knew better than to disturb the spoiled young mistress of the Alcott home. It might be the maid, it might be Melanie—or it might be worse. She lifted up on an unsteady elbow—and looked into the eyes of her father. She fell back with a groan.

He was neither frowning nor smiling—simply looking like a judge, she thought.

Her voice was irritable. "I don't like sunlight this early in the morning."

He couldn't help but smile as he pulled the drapes partly closed. "How do you manage your morning classes at school then?"

She closed her eyes again. "I manage."

He conceded that must be the truth. Her grades never supplied him with complaint. He knew she loved the social side of life, so he could not fully understand it other than to think she must be an intelligent woman. He did not know her well, so he couldn't be sure.

"I really don't like waking up...feeling like a specimen under glass," she continued sourly.

"I don't like spending the night in a chair wondering where my child is," he countered.

A heavy silence. She wished she could drag herself to the bathroom for an aspirin.

"Where were you, Katherine?"

Katherine. Here it was. Predictable like the *New Orleans Gazetter* that landed on their front stoop with a thud each morning. Court was in session, and she was the criminal—Katherine.

"I called Carolyn's yesterday to make certain you had made it there all right," he continued in a moderate voice.

She raised up again. "I hardly need to be checked on like a six-year-old at her first sleep over!"

He shrugged. "When your actions are more mature..."

She could not fight on her back. She pulled herself up against the pillows, trying to ignore the room that was tilted at such an odd angle. She was disheveled and red-eyed, with very little dignity—but a surplus of fighting power.

"I don't feel like fighting, Kate," her father said, sensing her mood.

"I would like to go back to sleep," she returned with acid.

"I'm a little tired, too—"

"I didn't ask you to stay up and fuss over me!"

"Where were you, Kate? Why didn't you go to Carolyn's party like you told me you were?"

"Is this an, an inquisition?" she fumed. "I'm 18 years old!"

He said nothing.

"Eddie's car broke down. We were stranded until another motorist came along. He took us to town, then back out to Eddie's car. It took time to fix it, of course. Then Eddie got cleaned up and took me to dinner. There."

"Dinner till four in the morning?" he asked calmly.

She leaned forward as the throbbing in her head grew more intense.

"I can't wait to get back to school next week and not have to be treated like this! Maybe I'll go back early, maybe today even!"

"Where were you until four in the morning?"

Her arms were crossed, her eyes blazing. "I was at the Charleston Club having a wonderful time!"

She had slapped him in the face with the truth. No lies, no excuses, no games. Let him rage now.

But he did not rage. Andy Alcott did not know what to say. He had said it all before at times like this. He felt a quiet assurance that he should not say a word. But he could not keep the tears from his eyes and stood up quickly. He paused to pick up Kate's dress and drape it across the back of a chair. Then he laid her slippers on the bedside table. He did not look at her as he left the room.

He was nearly to his bedroom when he heard it. He had heard it before. It made the tears spill over before he could get to the privacy of his own room. His youngest daughter had thrown a shoe against her bedroom door.

For all her defects and misbehavior, Kate Alcott could be a generous and forgiving girl. Her temper and treachery could flare like a sudden tempest. She would put all her passion and attention to the conflict— whether between school chum, boyfriend, sister, or father. She could be a maelstrom of energy, anger or vengeance. But it would dissipate just as quickly. She was back laughing and friendly, amiable until the next storm.

A day of lounging in bed until late afternoon, lunch brought to her room, the memory of dancing at the Charleston Club, had put Kate in a steadier, benevolent mood. She wrote half a dozen letters to friends, read magazines, painted her nails—and basically forgot the fury she'd felt earlier toward her father. She had seen his tears and coldly dismissed them. He was, in her mind, an unfeeling, pious-acting judge, and Kate Alcott was far from opening her heart to him. How could one possibly get close to a man like that? Melanie had. But Melanie had something she didn't. And it was too difficult to determine what that something was.

Now summer vacation was over and her trunks were repacked. She was disappointed her father had not let her go to a friend's summer home in Florida, but it was a tolerable summer break. They had spent two weeks at her father's old home in Illinois. She had spent time with her grandmother, the only adult she truly respected. And there were Ben and David to have fun with. Two weeks at their summer place on the Gulf Coast beach. Then they had all gone to Tanglewood for one week—one boring week. It took six pages in her journal to describe just how hot and rural it was at her parents' first home. Melanie was in high spirits seeing the place she had loved as a little girl, and her playmates who had grown up but still lived in the area. It was a wonderful, memory-filled time for her sister and father—a painful endurance for her.

The remainder of the summer she'd spent at their New Orleans home, 2121 Old Manor. She chafed under the curfews and rules but managed to have fun with Eddie and his 'bearcat'. Eddie. She smiled. He had shown her a good time, and she had repaid him. The accounts were paid in full. And now it was time to return to school in Grambling. Freedom. Independence.

A knock at her bedroom door pulled her from her thoughts.

"All packed?" Melanie asked from the doorway.

Kate swung her arm around at the trunks and new white store boxes. "Yes, everything is all tied and tidy."

"You got a lot of nice new things for school." Melanie perched on a trunk.

Her sister eyed her with suspicion. Was that an accusation?

"You could have just as nice stuff, Mel," she replied tartly, "if you were interested in clothes." Kate presented her a box. "Here."

"What's this?"

"Open it up." Kate could not disguise her need for approval. Melanie opened the box. "Now, let's see if I missed anything. Three pairs of stockings, one pair of cream-colored pumps, one hairbrush, two pairs of pearl earrings, one bottle of Eau de Cologne."

"Kate, you didn't have to do this," Melanie said softly.

"I lost or used them up, didn't I? I knew you'd be too...wrapped up in Bible study or missionary lectures to replace them. So there."

"Thank you, Kate. This is very sweet of you."

Later they took her to the train station. She laughed and chattered the entire way. But Andy was silent, gazing out the window as he tried to think of something to say to his youngest daughter. He longed to convince her that despite all their differences, he loved her very much. But she always stiffened when he tried to speak with emotion, and he always felt awkward.

"So if my grades are good this term, can I transfer to Amherst like I've been wanting?" she asked suddenly.

He studied her a moment, and Melanie tensed. "What is wrong with where you're going now, Katherine?"

She sighed. "Nothing except that Amherst has a great journalism department."

He only vaguely knew about her interest in journalism and assumed her desire to attend Amherst was simply because she wanted to get further away from his authority.

"We'll talk about it when you come home for Christmas. If your grades are decent."

Fuming, Kate swung away from him.

"Dad, uh, you said that to Kate last term and her grades were fine," Melanie said gently.

"Is this a conspiracy against me?" he asked, half annoyed.

"No, I just think...you should consider her request...more seriously." Melanie leaned toward him, her eyes pleading. "Give her some hope, Dad."

Give her some hope. Had he forgotten already the passion he had at 17 to go to sea? Didn't Kate have a right to her dreams?

He sighed. "You can transfer to Amherst in January. If you still want to."

The girls exchanged an astonished look. This was far more than either had expected. Impulsively, Kate threw her arms around her father. His smile was faint—perhaps he had found a way to show her he loved her.

Peppercreek

"How can I pray for you, Benjamin, as you head back to school? Specifically, I mean."

Ben had taken his grandmother for one more drive before returning to Chicago for the fall term. He loved to take her driving. She didn't shriek or scold, or even grip his arm if she thought he was going too fast. In fact, it amused him to see that she really seemed to enjoy it when he pushed the car to its limit. No faint heart, his grandmother! Could there possibly be a gal with such sterling qualities for him some-where?

He pulled the car over to the side of the road, under the shade of a spreading live oak. His father's corn fields, ripening in golden brown waves, stretched before them.

"Let's see, how 'bout, figure out which girls for me to date from all there is to choose from at school?" he returned with a chuckle.

She jabbed him in the ribs. "Enough of your jokes, Ben Alcott. You leave in a few hours and I really need to know."

He searched the fields with his eyes as he carefully chose his words. "I know you want to know, Grandma. Well, I guess you could pray that I'd figure out what I need to learn up there, or leave and do something else. Grandma, I feel useless, or like I'm wasting my time and Dad's money."

"Have you prayed about this concern?" she asked gently.

He moved uncertainly on the seat. Depend on Grandma to be direct. "Sometimes I do," he admitted slowly.

She took his hand and squeezed it. "Benjamin, devote more time to prayer and things will become clearer for you. Life is like a map with all sorts of turns and choices." She smiled. "I've found it very helpful to know the mapmaker. It saves you quite a few wrong turns and can bring you priceless joy. You loved your grandfather."

"Yes, ma'am. He was a great guy."

The memory of Ethan, strong, tall and youthful filled her mind a mo-ment. His arms around her... "Your great grandfather was a man of faith and his father before him. You are of that line. And as I prayed for your grandfather, I pray for you. You knew him after he was already a man of faith for quite a few years. But as a young man, your age, he wasn't. He searched, he had many questions. He didn't know what to do with his life...until he turned to the one who gave him life. Think on that, Benjamin."

Chapter 4

*I*n three short months the war in Europe had stolen the peace of millions. With unquenchable greed, it demanded attention. The motives and sentiment varied, and certainly the languages—but generals and soldiers, mothers and fathers, husbands and wives, whether in Berlin, Paris, Vienna or London, lived, and sometimes slept, with war news. It entered into nearly every conversation—over a map in a muddy battlefield or government desk, in an open air market or in front of the home fire with a cup of tea and a bun. It was everywhere—in bold recruiting posters and newspapers, soldiers leaving or returning from the front at every train station, in restrictions and shortages at the market, in societies rolling bandages and knitting socks, in the postman bringing the dreaded telegram. Everywhere a grim presence measured in victories and losses, in a few feet of scorched earth captured, it was there.

In late October all of England turned anxious eyes toward the channel—that body of water, normally so benevolent, now seemed like a shield, a gigantic moat to protect them. The western front of the war stretched approximately 600 miles from the channel to the border of Switzerland, a line of death and destruction cutting across France's northern frontier. A critical battle raged between the Allies and the kaiser's army near the French city of Ypres. Like is common to war campaigns, it was an odd, indeed implausible battlefield, this little French village notable for its production of Valenciennes lace. But warriors, medieval and contemporary, seldom notice the beauty of a potential arena. If Germany was victorious in the struggle, it was an unmolested stroll to the coast and the channel. The German conquerors would then eye the near shores of Britain with anticipation. So London held its breath, and some prayed that the young men could hold the line firm, and the cost would not be too high.

London

From his third floor office, Thomas Fleming absently watched the boats chugging along the Thames River, their gray smoke mingling with the yellow green fog that hung over the water in the late-afternoon chill.

It was a great view of the river from his office at King's College, one of
the small but important pleasures in his quiet life. Yet today it gave him
little pleasure. His mind was not on how he could help those students
who struggled with their Greek translations. He wasn't even thinking
about the fight the newspapers called "titanic" and "vital" at Ypres.

He swung around to his desk and read the letter again. It was a short
missive, obviously written in a frail and unsteady hand, on lilac-colored
notepaper. It was from his French sister-in-law. She told him of the
sounds and sights of war that threatened and frightened her. He felt concern for her now. Forget asking her to come to London to live with Molly
and him. He could hear her now.

'France is my birthplace and here I shall die! Viva la France!'

'But Madeline, it's safer here. Stay until the fighting is over.'

'Safer in your London town, Thomas? Ha! One shell from the kaiser's
fat guns and poof, your city is gone!'

Thomas shook his head. Granted, they had had limited contact over
the years, but he loved this woman. She alone had approved of him, encouraged him, in fact, when he tried for her little sister's hand. He felt responsible for her somehow, though she would have smiled at the notion.
Still, she was too close to the war, too old for the stress. One plan presented itself to his logical mind. He dismissed it quickly and with annoyance noted its quick return. He glanced out the window, peering
through the gloom as if he could see the coast of France. He shook his
gray head again. No, it was simply too far.

Molly Fleming deeply respected her father. He was her best friend. So
when he suddenly and strangely raised doubts concerning Martin, she
filed those doubts carefully in her mind to consider. 'Have you and Martin ever had a decent row?' She meditated on that question quite awhile.
Was it a reasonable concern? Well, she had never known him to be anything less than reasonable. So…

She felt a trifle guilty as she dressed for the evening. She planned to
bait the guileless Martin into a row, see if it was possible—and what the
results might be. A deeper understanding between them? A flame of passion? She smiled. Passion. Was this what the girls at work so often talked
about? The desire to be kissed and pawed? She didn't think it was quite
that. And this wasn't the kind of question she could carry to her father
no matter how close she felt to him. Passion was a kind of longing,
wasn't it? As if everything she was and had was some precious and
unique gift—and only one man would treasure it. One man alone would
stir that passion in her as she stirred it in him. And somehow, Molly
Fleming would know the man to whom her passion belonged. She would
know without any questions, any hesitation, any doubts.

She peered critically into the mirror, demanding the truth and nothing less. She felt safe and comfortable with Martin—which was a nice feeling in itself. Comfortable! She cringed at the word. Martin certainly deserved better than that!

"Well, well..." Her father smiled over the rim of his glasses as she entered the room. Molly smiled in return. Those two words were her father's deepest compliment.

Martin, the victim, looked eager and happy. "You look great, Molly," he said as he pulled on her coat.

"A dish, perhaps?" she asked coyly.

Martin and Mr. Fleming exchanged a surprised glance. "A dish" was definitely not part of Molly's usual vocabulary.

"Uh, sure, a, dish," he stumbled.

Molly bent over her father and gave him a quick kiss. "Don't wait up, Dad."

They both knew he would. He patted her hand. "Have a nice evening."

Martin secured a cab and gave directions to the driver. But Molly interrupted. "We always dine at 'The Colony,' Martin. Do we have to eat there tonight?"

He looked bewildered only a moment. "Where to?"

"Oh, you pick."

"I'd pick 'The Colony.'" He laughed. "It's the only place in London I know I can afford!"

"Driver, please take us to Sherry's," Molly calmly instructed.

To the restaurant, and through dinner, Martin did most of the talking. His medical training was his favorite topic.

"Then Professor Thor slices through the abdominal wall and there's this huge abscess, just like he predicted. It was great. More coffee?"

"Martin, really. This isn't the best subject for dinner conversation," Molly said with affected annoyance.

"Hmm? Oh, yeah, you're right. I'm sorry. You know how I can get carried away. This is great veal, isn't it?"

"I wish we'd gone to 'The Colony'; theirs is better."

Martin took another bite and nodded. "You've been pretty quiet tonight. Anything up?"

She shrugged and gazed around the restaurant. What topic could she raise to provoke Martin? From their table she heard muted snatches of conversation.

"...Ypres..."

"...heavy casualties for our boys..."

"...a final offensive in the spring..."

War. Perhaps there could be a controversial note here. She took a deep breath. "Martin, have you thought of enlisting?"

"Enlisting? Not much. I'd hate to give up my studies just now."

"But they say there may be a general call up."

"It'll be over by spring, Molly."

"Well, that just may be unrealistic thinking. Some of the girls at the office...won't go out with a man...who isn't in uniform."

"Hmm...well, I guess that's their business. Remind them of that if they're left a war widow. Can you pass the salt?"

"You could join the medical corps."

"Yes, if I had to. But I still prefer Glasgow."

"Your loyalty to Great Britain might come into question."

"I know where my loyalty lies. I'm really not settled in my mind that we should have stuck our nose in this business anyway. It should have stayed between the Serbs and the Austrians."

"Think of Germany rolling through Belgium absolutely thumbing their noses at a treaty of neutrality!" Molly returned with real conviction.

"Who's to say how binding that treaty was really meant to be? But I will admit, it does look like a nasty piece."

"The point is, Martin, England did get into the fight and you're an Englishman!"

"Yes and a pretty stuffed one! Shall we take our dessert now or after the show?"

Molly sighed. "You choose."

On their way back to Molly's flat, respectably before the stroke of midnight, Molly Fleming raised her battle flags again. There might only be one topic that could elicit heat from her escort.

"Martin, do you think doctors know everything?"

He laughed and squeezed her hand. "Everything."

"No, I'm serious. If a patient came to you very ill and you had no idea what his problem was, would you tell him?"

"No, I wouldn't have many clients that way. You have to show authority to produce confidence and trust."

"Even if you don't have the answer?"

"Well, I'd do my best to find the answer."

"What if you gave the wrong diagnosis?"

"Depends."

"On?"

"On how critical it was."

"Don't you think doctors charge far too much? You know what happened to us when Dad got sick."

"Oh, they probably do," he answered mildly. "But think of the long hours they put in."

"They generally act very superior. I hope you won't get like that. You'd be hard to live wi—, I mean be near."

"I'd try to take off my crown when I came home," he said with a laugh. He yawned. "Did you like the play?"

"Did you?" she countered.

"Not too much. The plot was a bit thin. I think we've seen better."

"Really? I loved it!"

When Martin went to bed an hour later he thought nothing of Molly's unusual behavior. Women were moody and unpredictable; his medical training had taught him that much. But down the hall, Molly Fleming spent a restless night. A prize fighter without an opponent was a very frustrating thing.

Their second night out was Martin's last night in London before returning to Glasgow. Molly and Martin would not see each other until a brief visit over Christmas holidays. And as the night before, Molly prepared for the evening with more than just her brush and lipstick and pretty dress. Though she looked as lovely as she had the night before, there lurked in her mind a new strategy.

She had failed the night before to rouse Martin to even heated words or a raised voice. Could she fault him for being so even-tempered and good-natured? But tonight she thought of her father's words again. 'Do you thrill to see him when he walks through the door?' Was her father referring to passion? Now she tried to remember the ploys and phrases the girls at work used so effortlessly. She was nervous at the prospect of her new part. But perhaps she'd have better luck tonight.

In the darkened concert hall, she leaned against Martin's arm as she had never done before, entwining her fingers with his. Martin responded with a smile.

"You look lovely tonight, Molly," he whispered. "A real dish."

She leaned even closer, until her cheek brushed his.

"Would that be a stew or dessert, Martin?"

"Uh, definitely dessert. Is that a new perfume you have on?"

"Like it?"

"Yes, I do."

Then he returned his attention to the music for Martin was partial to concerts over plays. When it was over, Molly suggested a quiet cafe and a bottle of wine. Martin raised an eyebrow. Molly never drank anything stronger than tea.

One bottle of wine later, Martin started to give the cab directions back to Molly's apartment. He had to catch an early train to Glasgow— and with the sudden influx of soldiers, trains had become even more uncertain.

"Oh, have him drive around a bit longer, Martin," Molly said as she snuggled into the crook of his arm. "It's still early."

"It's a quarter till midnight," he countered easily.

"But it's so nice and cozy in here, don't you think? And this is our last night for a time..."

"You're right."

She closed her eyes in the darkened cab and hummed something she'd heard at the concert.

"Have a nice time tonight, Molly?"

"Um..." she returned dreamily.

"Sounds like that last glass of wine might have been a bit too much for you," he said gently.

"Why do you say that?"

He laughed. "Oh, just your voice, I guess. And you're more relaxed. In some ways alcohol is a stimulus, but for others it's a relaxant."

"I would think you'd like that."

"Like what?"

"To have me more relaxed."

"Why would I want you more relaxed?"

She curled around to face him, her hand laying lightly on his jacket front. "Because that would make me more...more defenseless against your advances," she replied with a little laugh.

"I think you've been reading too much war news! Advances, defenses!"

She gripped his jacket. "I am serious. The girls at the office say men want their girls to drink to make them more willing."

"Molly, I think you've been listening to the girls at work too much! When have I ever acted improperly toward you?"

"Never."

"As I said, I think perhaps you've had too much wine."

"Martin, would you define passion for me?"

Symptoms and diagnosis he knew...but passion? Martin felt edgy. Molly was definitely acting unMollyish!

"Molly, that's a bit, well, frank, don't you think?"

"That would depend. Is passion wrong?"

"Well, no...between...the right...uh, and in the right...circumstances."

Suddenly Molly Fleming felt as if she'd been slapped. Passion wasn't something you talked about! It was there or it wasn't, and if it was, you wouldn't need to define it!

"I'm sorry. That was a silly question."

He took her hand. "It's all right. Listen, I want to tell you this before we get back to your place."

"What?"

"I want to give you a ring at Christmas," he said softly. "An engagement ring. I think it's about time."

He waited. Of course, she knew this time would eventually come. So why didn't she feel thrills and breathless happiness? Why did she suddenly feel so tired?

"If you'd like to."

"Would you like it?"

He was right for her. He was a good man.

"Yes, that would be nice."

He gently pulled her closer. "And we'll seal it with a kiss."

"Martin?"

"Hmm?"

"A kiss that we'll feel till the holidays, if you please."

He laughed and thought of the wine again. "Whatever you say, Molly."

For the second night Molly Fleming went to bed feeling rather foolish.

The trees were leafless from Berlin to London and little islands of ice floated placidly on the Rhine. The mud was a frigid mire in the trenches, and the barbed wire that would come to symbolize the western front, cast up a hedge of ice-crusted thorns. So the first Christmas had come to the war, with a quarter of a million dead and peace no closer than it was in August. Perhaps in the spring...

Molly was unusually preoccupied of late. Thomas Fleming stirred from his world of Greek tragedies and conjugations and crossword puzzles to notice. Typically she made a decent show against him in an evening of chess. The last few weeks he'd won nearly every game. He speculated it might be something going on at work that she had not confided to him about. Perhaps the snippish girls there. He knew she edited her remarks about her working conditions so that he would neither fuss nor fume. But perhaps it was not the girls at work, at all. Perhaps it was Martin.

Martin was to spend a few hours with Molly the afternoon after Christmas, before returning to his family's home in northern England.

"One afternoon out of the entire holiday, Molly? Then back to school? That seems rather thin, don't you think?"

Molly shrugged, ever the diplomat. "Well, Mrs. Hampton has all sorts of family plans, you know. She, she misses him a lot."

Thomas returned to the book on his lap. Mrs. Hampton, Martin's mother. An autocratic woman. He glanced up at his daughter. The future mother-in-law thought her son's engagement to Molly was all sewn up, so why give the girl more than an afternoon? Thomas drew some queru-lous scribbles on the margin of his notes. He was startled when Molly suddenly spoke up.

"Why did you call Martin ambiguous, Dad?"

Fleming smiled. "You haven't forgotten that conversation?"

"Not a syllable," Molly said, smiling.

"Well, it's not easy to say…exactly. I don't want to offend you since he is your young man."

"I'd like to hear what you think," she countered calmly.

"He's a fine fellow and I always enjoy our chats. When I talk to him, however, I'm not quite certain how he stands on things. Is he agreeing with me on principle or because he's simply an agreeable chap, or be-cause I'm a prospective father-in-law? He's under the firm hand of his, well, his mother. And I don't know if he has his own mind or Mrs. Hampton's. Now—"

"Am I really any different?" Molly asked abruptly. "I think a lot like you. I weigh things by your scales. I always have. I can't imagine marry-ing a man you don't approve of."

"But you think on your own, don't you? I haven't brainwashed you, have I?" He was really horrified. To bring up a beloved child that didn't know how to think on her own!

"No, you haven't brainwashed me."

"You were nurtured on my faith, but I never forced it on you, did I?"

"No, of course not."

"It would be a shoddy, cheap faith if you only took it for my sake. And such an important decision as who you marry! If you loved a man, if you truly felt he was the Lord's choice for you, I would never stand in the way." He searched her face. "Molly, Martin will make someone a fine hus-band."

"Someone…" she murmured looking past him, and wondering if dreams weren't a bit like clouds and sticking to terra firma much safer for an English girl of 1914.

"Do you love him?" her father pressed gently.

"It's like you said. He's always been there. It's been him and no one else, as if there couldn't be anyone else. He's fine and steady and I do enjoy his company. I just…" She broke off and went to stand by the win-dow. Winter had frosted their windows in fragile ice lace. "He's bringing an engagement ring with him when he comes in two days."

"Ah…" Her father nodded. Now the preoccupation was explained. "Will you accept it?"

"I don't know, I just don't know."

"Well, my dear, perhaps now is the best time to tell you about this cor-respondence I've had with your Aunt Madeline."

"Aunt Madeline in France?" Molly asked, amazed that her father had seemingly made a huge jump in their conversation.

"Yes, Aunt Madeline in France." He sighed. "It is rather far, isn't it?"

When Martin Hampton, promising young medical student, presented himself on the Fleming doorstep, Molly generously admitted the young man looked very nice. His tweed suit was impeccable, his navy tie quite natty, his blond hair brushed to gleaming. He smiled broadly as he gave her a large bouquet of red carnations and a kiss. She loved red carnations and felt genuine affection as she returned his kiss. As he pulled off his coat and hat, he looked about for her father. "Where's your father, Molly?"

"Over at our neighbor's, Mrs. Crumple."

"Crumple?"

Molly laughed. "I know, she sounds like someone out of a Dickens novel. Grandmotherly, heavily built, sweet. She is sweet, but as tall and slim as Dad. She lost her oldest son at Ypres, so this is a very difficult holiday for her. But he'll be round before you have to leave."

He put his arms around her waist. "I'm sorry about not getting to stay longer. Mum has the grip on me. You know parents." He laughed.

Molly smiled. But she did not understand the tenacious, controlling hold of a parent. Her father had always treated her with respect.

They chatted over tea. He told her about his studies and certain operations he had viewed. But then his smile faded, and his voice became slow and thoughtful. "They say there will be a general call up by March. Unless I can get a medical exemption or get with a corp, I'll be in khaki come spring, Molly."

She knew she must choose her words judiciously. "What does your mother say about this?"

"I haven't told her," he replied gloomily. "It would ruin her holidays."

"I'm sorry. I know how much your school plans mean to you."

He set his cup down and took her hands. "It isn't just my school plans that are messed up. It's plans about us as well."

She looked down at his hands. Kind, dependable, talented hands.

"Well, since the powers that govern didn't consult us, I suppose we'll have to make the best of it." She laughed nervously.

"Of course, we could elope I suppose, but that would put Mum in a huff, and I don't really think you're the eloping kind of girl. And I'm not quite ready either. To support a wife, I mean. War is making a lot of things pretty darned inconvenient!"

Molly glanced to the window and thought of Mrs. Crumple—with her son's mess kit and a shoebox of photos to remind her that war was much worse than inconvenient.

Martin drew out a small velvet box from his jacket. "I brought this any-way."

She opened it to find a gold band with a single diamond. "It's lovely," Molly said holding the box, but not touching the ring.

"I didn't think you'd want anything terribly showy. Mum thought it was a sensible ring. Well, let's see how it fits."

It fit perfectly. A gold band, a trust of love on her slender finger—if she chose to keep it.

"You like it?" he asked eagerly.

"Of course."

"Well, we just won't set a date right now." His face darkened and he spoke hurriedly as if the truth were chasing him. "If I do get called up, well, it would be nice going with an understanding between us. And if anything happened, well—"

"Martin, actually, I won't be here in the spring. I won't be in London."

"What?"

"Yes, it's the most extraordinary thing because it's all so sudden. I'm going to France."

"France! Why?"

"My aunt lives alone there. My father's very concerned about her. So I'm going to go live with her awhile, see if I can do things for her and—"

"Molly, doesn't your father realize there's a war right in the middle of France?"

"Yes, he does, but—"

"You can read in the papers…are you serious?"

"Yes, quite serious. I'm rather…well, excited about it ."

"You're going to quit your position at Whitehall?"

She smiled. "Yes, that may be the best part."

"I thought you liked your job. This is a bit shocking."

"I'm sorry. I should have said something, before the ring."

He looked down at the ring. "Yes, the ring," he repeated dully. "What does this going to France mean to us, Molly?"

"Are you angry?"

"Well, not angry. Disappointed, I suppose. Surprised at the risk your father is putting you in. There's bombings and privations of all sorts. Why not bring the old gal here?"

"She won't come."

"Well, again, what about us?"

Molly took a deep breath. "Perhaps we should wait until things are more settled, you know, after I come back from France and you know what your plans are and—"

"Molly, I brought you this ring and I want you to take it," he returned with just the faintest touch of exasperation. "It gives us an understanding that even this war can't interfere with!"

"And what is that understanding?" she asked gently.

"Nothing more than we'll become engaged officially when you return. That seems fair."

Fair—it seemed an odd word to connect with romance. She did not want to hurt Martin, and perhaps after her time on the Continent, she would rush into his arms, all hesitation far removed.

"I'll take the ring as an understanding then."

He slid it onto her finger. "That's all I ask."

Kinsale, Ireland

It was an unusually mild Irish winter. Optimists believed it boded well—it would be a fruitful spring. The pessimists felt spring would come with an imposter's face and prove stormy and killing to early planting. Padraic Falconer was an optimist. He was glad for the temperate weather and did not analyze it. He only knew it meant he could be out of doors at chores or leisure without contending with the biting winds and rain from the North Atlantic. It allowed him time to work on his pair of vessels before the demands of the fishing season, come early spring.

The *Bluebell* and *Wanderer of Peel* were tied alongside a half dozen other fishing boats and steamers at the small harbour of Kinsale. Most fishing vessels that worked this coastline of County Cork were sheltered from the larger Queenstown port some 16 miles north. So the fishermen of Kinsale were a close-knit fraternity and good-natured rivals, glorying in a good catch equally for themselves or the boat that plied the wide waters off their bows. This affection and generosity did not extend to the Queenstown folk, of course. The Kinsale fishermen agreed that the *Wanderer* and the *Bluebell* were the finest two ships around, rivaling, in their minds, the Queenstown mariners.

Their opinion came from the two ships' well-painted sides, her scrubbed decks, her rigging, her mended and untangled lines and nets, her clean chugging engine and her simple, sleek lines. But in larger part their esteem came from the ship's owner, the Falconer family, and in particular, the skipper, Padraic Falconer. He set the tone for his crew—cheerful, loyal, helpful, generous. Every fisherman in Kinsale knew if the Falconer boats were coming in from a good catch, Padraic would be shouting from the deck where the prolific spot was. If he found a place in the vast waters already occupied, he would move away without complaint or challenge. It was these qualities that caused the fisherfolk specifically, and the townsfolk in general, to conclude the Falconer family was well off. They didn't suffer come a long, hard winter. Their larder was full, and their peats were neatly stacked for fuel. But Padraic would not have come to the same conclusion as his observant neighbor. In his own quiet way he would simply say, 'Aye, it's because the Lord is so good to us. He's the one that provides for our table, not me.'

Just like his father, Dennis Falconer, the neighbors would say. Like father, like son, they both held that same personal faith. Like they were on intimate terms with the Creator himself. Padraic Falconer was known to stretch out on the sunny deck of his *Wanderer* to read his Bible while the nets filled. If they didn't fill, he'd say, 'Another day, lads. If I had the whole of the ocean to swim in, I'd be just like 'em.'

He was known to pray, a practice most of his neighbors left to their more devout womenfolk. They would have thought him odd and superior to them if it wasn't for his good-naturedness. You couldn't separate his faith from his daily life any more than you could draw the blue from the ocean. He'd take a glass of stout on occasion to toast a catch or the arrival of a new Irish lad or lass, but he never hung on the pub stool after sunset telling tales and emptying mugs. He was off with his brothers to their home fire. The Falconer boys were good lads, and considered worthy prizes for their daughters by the womenfolk.

Padraic Falconer was in the cabin of the *Bluebell* one sunny December afternoon working on some carpentry chores that always got neglected in the prime of fishing season or potato planting. He sawed and hammered and measured and was glad of the quiet. At home every conversation seemed to begin and end with the unrest brewing in Dublin or the war in Europe. He heard a step on the staircase that led from the deck and looked up. A young woman, holding a basket, was watching him.

She had taken the name Anna Ruebens, but she was christened Marta Marie Schweiger. She claimed her birthplace was Salzburg, Austria, her childhood home, Antwerp, Belgium. But she was a born and raised Berliner—with the nagging fear that some day someone would discover all her claims were lies. She hoped she would rise highly enough in society that such revelations would not matter. For now though, she hoped Queenstown was far enough from the German city that no one would recognize her. If she could have fled to America and put the Atlantic between her and her past, all the better. But her money had only stretched so far, and the Irish town with its unobtrusive, unsophisticated quiet appealed to her. Only by constant and continual discipline was she able to minimize her Germanic accent.

She resented and rebelled against her mother's offer—but in the end she took it. She had reasoned cynically, we all use each other, we all become thieves at some time. If her mother was a thief, who could blame the daughter? So she took the generous deposit, tossed aside her conscience with her worries over money, and became a spy. Correspondence with her cousin Walther had supplied her with a piece of information even British intelligence would have coveted. Had he slipped it into the letter by accident or design, she could only speculate. It would be the middle of February before the rest of the world knew of the plans she had fallen privy to—Germany was declaring all waters around the British Isles a combat zone. This was unrestricted submarine warfare on any Allied vessel. Flour and sugar to bullets and blankets could be considered contraband, and those who pleaded neutrality were left to their own risk taking courage—or foolishness.

With charm and flirtations, with feigned ignorance, with eavesdropping and theft, she became quite knowledgeable of the goings on in the Irish channel and the port city of Queenstown. She knew there would be no sentiment for the Germans when their subs began their hunt in the water. Now she must determine what exactly would be their response, their defense.

Marta carefully cultivated her friendship with Jen Falconer when she learned the family owned vessels that worked the channel. When she learned that Jen had four unmarried brothers, she was smugly convinced she had found the right friend indeed. The talkative, friendly, innocent Jen was more than willing to answer every prodding question the older girl put to her. And when the invitation came for a weekend trip to Jen's home in Kinsale, Marta was pleased.

But, of course, Jen's information was limited. It was natural then, for Marta to choose one, or all, of the brothers for further confidences. If she would be a spy with a jaded heart, she would be a good one. Then, when her purse was full, she would take a liner to America. So, in the first hour, over the evening meal, she assessed the four in swift, calculating fashion.

The youngest was 19-year-old Rory who was tempered much like his little sister—fun loving and friendly. Rory was the local school-master. Twenty-one-year-old Denny was merely an older copy of Rory, but whose interest lay in fishing and not books and teaching. Pierce was the quiet brother, meditative, slow to speak, unmoved in emotion of any degree. She knew Pierce was useless to her purposes. Over that first meal, her eyes lingered longest on the oldest son, Padraic. She was not swooning or sentimental—that he was the best looking held little genuine interest to her. He mediated between the openness of Denny and Rory, and the reserve of Pierce. He would laugh and talk, and she reasoned, held more to himself the things that mattered. She had seen immediately it was this eldest son who held the controlling, deciding influence over the family. He made the decisions. He set the tone. So he was the one she chose. And even as she did, she recognized she had chosen the strongest, the one who would challenge her—and the one who perhaps held the power to unmask her.

"I brought your dinner, Padraic. Your ma thought you'd not want to take the time to come home for it." The young woman stepped into the hold of the ship.

He laid down his tools. "Then I'm thanking Ma for her thoughtfulness, and you for your kindness in bringing it."

She nodded and set the basket on the small wooden table. When she hesitated, he felt it only proper to ask her to stay. He thought it a wise idea to try and know better this young friend—for Jen's sake, of course. Sometimes his sister brought her friend home for weekend visits, and he watched her, chatted casually with her—and grew a little intrigued. She was different from the other girls Jen had brought home in the past. She seemed more mature. She asked questions, she was no brainless flirt! It pleased Padraic that she seemed not to have marked his brothers for conquest and treated them in an almost sisterly fashion.

"Care to stay, Anna? And share this." He examined the contents of the basket. "This mutton pie?"

"No thanks. I'll stay a bit, but I'm not hungry."

Padraic brushed aside the sawdust and tools and laid out his meal. Over the small oil stove, Anna made tea. She turned away when he bent his head to pray.

"And what are the lads up to?" he asked.

"Denny brought in the paper and was reading it aloud when I left."

Padraic shook his head ruefully. "About the war, I'm sure. Used to be the paper hadn't much more than advertisements and birthings and what was happenin' in Dublin. Now it is nothing but battles and casualty counts."

"You're not much interested in the war are you, Padraic?"

"Only enough to pray for peace. Europe being carved up like a mutton roast can't be good for anyone."

"And Ireland?"

"Ireland? Or Great Britain or Germany. Ireland had enough woes of her own without going to the Continent to spill blood."

"You're referring to the trouble in Dublin with the splitting from England unrest," she continued.

"Aye, I'm only thankful my brothers aren't infected with the political fever."

"You can't like being ruled by Britain, surely," she protested.

He smiled a moment. Jen's friend did have a thinking head on her shoulders.

"No, I don't like it much, but I can still catch fish. Seems rebellion isn't the answer. Think of the Jews under the Roman rule in the scriptures."

"I...I'm not much a student of the Bible," she returned smoothly and with a dimpled smile.

He mulled over her answer and found it created a few questions in his mind.

"But what would you do if the war came closer to your Ireland?" she persisted.

Your Ireland... "In what way, Anna?"

She looked out the small round window. "Oh...let's say the sea. St. George's channel goes straight to Liverpool. It's common knowledge America is supplying the Allies. I'd imagine Germany isn't too happy about that."

Padraic nodded. "Aye, she can be unhappy about it all she wants. But I'd imagine America would still do as she pleases."

"Well, Germany has a navy, doesn't it?"

"I don't know," he returned calmly. "It's likely."

"Well then, Germany could threaten with ships of her own. You know, warfare. You might go out fishing and have shells whizzing over your head!" She laughed.

He rubbed his chin thoughtfully. "Aye, and it would make a poor day for fishing, sure."

She seemed to want to talk of the war and his work. He wanted to talk about her. "So you don't feel as if the Emerald Isle is your home?" he asked.

She tensed. "Why do you ask?"

"Because you said, if war came to my Ireland."

"Well..."

"How many years since you came from Belgium?"

"Just four."

"Aye, long enough to love this island, then." He smiled easily.

She stood up abruptly and strolled around the cabin, running her hand over the smooth honey-colored wood. "What does the *Wanderer of Peel* mean?"

"It's the name of an old Irish ballad. One of my da's favorite."

"And the *Bluebell?*"

"A tribute to Da's first girlfriend. It was her favorite flower."

"I'd think your ma would have changed that when they married."

"Not Ma. It was a small matter to her. She got him, not that first girl."

He ate the remainder of his meal in silence, a dozen or more questions playing in his mind. He wondered about her family, her past, and most importantly, her faith. Yet, the big fisherman knew with some instinct he should proceed cautiously. This girl had a wall of reserve around her.

They talked an hour more. Then another hour passed as she watched him work in silence. Padraic noted the wind must have risen a bit, for the ship now rocked with more animation. Suddenly a terrific blast slammed into their quiet world. Anna jumped from the bench. "What was that?" she asked.

"A shell from one of those German boats you were talkin' about earlier, maybe?" he asked playfully.

She hurried up the steps, and Padraic watched as the small cabin door was ripped from her hand. The complexion of the morning had completely changed—its honest, peaceful face was gone. The sun was blotted from the sky. All was dark now in a fast falling veil of black. The wind was howling and the slanting rain held ice.

"Padraic!" she shouted fearfully.

He came up behind her and used nearly all his strength to pull the door closed.

"Aye, it comes up fast like that sometimes."

She was trembling. He held out a thick knitted sweater he had dug from a locker. "Don't be afraid, lass, we'll be fine till she blows herself out. We've food and fuel. We'll ride it out sure."

He kept his tone gentle and calm and Anna seemed grateful. She gave him a nervous smile.

Padraic had spoken the truth. The North Atlantic could churn up a storm without a polite and proper warning and hold all it touched in its fierce grip. The icy storm did not relent until early morning. By the time the young woman and the fisherman walked up the puddled path through the village, the fishing folk of Kinsale knew that Padraic Falconer had kept a woman on board his ship all night.

Chapter 5

*T*he events in Europe were served to the American plate with names like Ypres and the Marne, Kaiser Wilhelm, David Lloyd George and Winston Churchill, Czar Nicholas and his Russian steamroller. British soldiers were dubbed Tommies, Germans, Huns and Jerries. While most Americans were partial to the Allied cause from the beginning, there was no national sentiment to intervene or join the fray. It was a European conflict—without contagion. But that would change as surely as the seasons were changing on the western front.

The government and the people were basically in accord—staunch neutrality. Some voices, like that of former President Roosevelt, spoke out that the U.S. must enter the fight, but they were muted, dissident voices. When the first German soldier stepped across the border into peaceful Belgium, the sentiment against the Central Powers increased. Those Americans of German heritage suddenly began to hear ugly whispers of 'Hun' and 'Kraut' behind their back. Schoolchildren took up the taunts on the playground at those with whom they had played peacefully the day before. The suspicion, the violence, would not grow in proportion to what the Japanese would suffer 30-odd years later, but as the conflict progressed in Europe, the ugliness against Germans grew in America.

New York

It was proving a good theatrical season for managers and producers, actresses and actors, playwrights and audiences. The sober news from across the Atlantic seemed to have little effect. New York theaters, which begat shows for theaters across the country, were producing a colorful, vaudevillian menu—acrobats and dancers, singers and comedians and drama troupes, and for the less discriminating, even talking dogs in tutus. A young escape artist named Harry Houdini was amazing audiences with his performances. Nickelodeon houses offered flickering films with everything from bathing babies to airplane flights, for a hard-earned nickel. Vern and Irene Castle, Buster Keaton, Charlie Chaplin and Mary Pickford were the reigning illuminaries of the New York stage.

It was an especially good season for Lilly O'Hara. A 'plum role' had fallen to her that many insiders had expected her rival, Ethel Barrymore, to claim. Her personal manager, George St. John, was ecstatic, and not above a little gloating.

"Some champagne, Miss O'Hara?" he asked, fully knowing the answer.

"No thanks, you go ahead."

The manager poured himself a liberal measure. "Poor Ethel is surely home weeping," he said without pity.

Lilly laughed and stretched from the sofa where she was writing a letter. "Oh, Georgie, don't be silly! I hardly think she's home weeping. More likely she's reading another script, like I'd be doing."

"I tell you she's lamenting the loss and calling down curses on her manager! Think of the nasty things Maude Adams said to the paper when you beat her out of *The Little Millionaire*. I tell you, Ethel is wringing her hands!"

Lilly yawned. "Well, no one should get that wracked about it. There are enough parts for all of us."

St. John eyed his glass and shook his head sadly. This woman had no ambition whatsoever! He'd known her for years, been her manager for 20 years. He'd seen her go from performing and singing her heart out in a mission hall dining room, to off Broadway acting houses, to the grand lights of New York's finest theaters. And in her zenith climb, St. John could not remember one evidence of pretense or zealous plotting or temperamental fits in the redheaded actress. She was as hard working as any, and when she saw a part she really wanted, she tried for it with all of her energy. But there was no scheming or clawing in Lilly O'Hara. It was one of the things that set Lilly apart from the rest of the theater crowd. Like her strong voice, she was unique. Success had changed her address, but not who she was.

Her manager also now lived in a fashionable apartment, rubbed shoulders with the stars and haggled with the producers. But when the final terms were presented, everyone agreed, Lilly O'Hara had the best voice in Broadway. Now the hit of Broadway, this winter of '14 was 'High Jinks' starring Lilly O'Hara in the title role.

"Well, the producer clearly saw the superior talent," St. John said in one final effort.

Lilly was drifting off for a prerehearsal nap. She tapped her throat. "It was the pipes, Georgie, the pipes."

St. John rolled his eyes and poured a final prerehearsal drink.

Lilly O'Hara had arrived at a toleration of New York winters, as most New Yorkers had. You railed and complained and wondered why you didn't move come spring, but in the end you endured every year as the East coast settled into a worthy imitation of the Arctic regions. Lilly's easygoing nature made her philosophical of the hardships, and besides, she would make her exodus when summer came and turned the concrete city into a broiler. The theater season would slip into a predictable lethargy, and Lilly, like other fortunates, would flee to her home in the Adirondacks in upper New York state, or one of the summer residences of one of her many friends across the country.

Outside the theater a light snow fell, like scattered bits of cotton. Lilly O'Hara was alone in her dressing room. She preferred to do her own makeup and hair. Outside in the hall, she could hear the rush of activity that preceded a Broadway performance. Forty minutes till the curtain went up. The dressing room table framed in lights was balanced on either end by two huge vases of roses. Lilly smiled, then laughed out loud. The vases were appropriately symbolic—one of red roses, the other white, competing in beauty and scent as the two competing suitors who had given them. She bent over each and took a long breath. The white were delicately perfumed. She glanced again at the card. 'I will be in the third row, watching the most beautiful woman in the world. Karl'

She sat back down to brush her hair. Karl, straight and tall, soft spoken and kind. He was a handsome man as well, with his silvering hair and magnetic smile. Lilly had known him almost a year as his diplomatic duties called him between Washington and New York City. Yes, a gentleman—and growing to love American theater because of a certain vivacious redhead. And he was a believer. She knew it was only a matter of time before he would look deeply into her eyes and tell her he wanted her to marry him.

She smiled as she brushed her hair and tried to imagine what life would be like as Karl's wife. The thought of a little Karl and little Lilly running around made her smile widen. Did it matter she had just passed 40? There were times she still felt she was a girl of 20. There lay the one 'plum' Lilly had always yearned for and never reached. She loved children. But as the years had gone by, and the men had passed through her life, only one had ever claimed her heart. One morning in early spring, she held his hand as he died in a New York hospital bed. He was never able to receive the full measure of Lilly's love. There was never anyone else, though there were dozens of hopefuls. Until Karl.

She imagined them in her home in the mountains raising their children. She could leave the glitter and allure of New York theater and success without a backward glance. She'd exchange rehearsals and scripts for diapers and learning to cook. She could see pouring herself into such a life as she had this one. Given a little more time to know Karl better and to pray, Lilly O'Hara could make another monumental change in her life as she had 23 years ago when she boarded the train from New Orleans for New York. New Orleans...

She laid down the brush and went to the small sofa. She ignored the laughter in the hallway, the hurried steps, the slammed doors, the distant tuning of a violin. She really should be thinking of her part. She'd slip into it as she slipped out of her silk dressing gown. She would be another woman for two hours and not Lilly O'Hara. She'd raise her voice and sing half a dozen love songs, but in her heart they'd be raised to the One who had given her song.

So, instead of running over her lines, she picked up the newspaper St. John had left lying there. It was almost buried on the last page, in a story one column wide and two long. She couldn't imagine how she managed to notice it, except that it was just below the continuation of an article she'd begun on an earlier page. Somehow, her eyes had picked up the words, "New Orleans shipbuilder," then, "Andy Alcott." Her heart raced at the black printing of those ten letters. She hadn't heard from him in years, never seen his name in print. Suddenly here it was, a simple article describing the British government's interest in New Orleans shipbuilder, Andy Alcott, designing troop transports and such as he had done in '98.

A knock came at the door. Without looking up, Lilly knew it was 30 minutes till showtime.

"Come in!"

A young man named Tim stuck his head in the doorway. "Thirty minutes, Miss O'Hara," he said with obvious pride at this ritual honor. It was the closest he came to the stars.

"Thank you, Tim," she replied predictably.

And just as predictably he entered with a tea tray. Lilly O'Hara always took a cup of peppermint tea before a performance.

"You look great tonight, Miss O'Hara," Tim ventured as he left.

Most nights she would look him in the eye, smile, and say, "Thank you very much, Tim. It's always nice to start the show with a compliment."

He loved her radiant smile—as most men did. And he always looked forward to the few words she gave him before a show. During rehearsals, she'd ask about his family or something going on in his life. She was a pleasure to work for, not like some of the egos with a star on their door. But tonight she did not glance up from her newspaper. She gave him an absent 'thank you' and Tim had gone off a bit disappointed.

She returned to her table and managed to apply her makeup though her thoughts were far from the task. Andy Alcott. The name conjured up so many memories. And so many questions. She leaned back and sipped her tea. If only the article had given her more information. Personal information like "Andy Alcott shipbuilder, devoted husband, father of..." A photo would have been priceless. She thought of him as he looked on her last day in New Orleans. She had traveled widely with her success since then but steadfastly ignored any offers from that Louisiana city. It was a part of her past that was painful, and she had no desire to return to it. But she could not help but wonder about Andy. He was her first real friend, a man who had not threatened or tried to use her. She shook her head and studied herself critically in the mirror. She thought of him as he looked nearly 20 years ago. She could hardly imagine him any other way. But if he saw her now, would he think she had aged terribly?

"You're not the girl he knew," she whispered.

A sharp rap at the door. "Come in, St. John!"

It was always 15 minutes till curtain when her manager came to her dressing room. He looked impeccable in his tuxedo. He was nervous as he always was until Lilly was on stage. He came up behind her. "Full house even with the snow. You are an irresistible draw, Miss O'Hara."

"Um..."

He rocked back and forth on his heels, his hands jammed into his pockets, then paced the length of the room. He told her the condition of the stage, the audience, the orchestra pit, the fussy director, her fellow thespians. Lilly listened with half attention as she always did. St. John expressed his nervous energy through talking. She stepped behind the screen to slip into her costume.

St. John glanced at the flowers, then read each card without guilt at such presumption. One bouquet was from a fellow actor, the other was from the German. He frowned. This Karl fellow was spending a lot of time with Lilly, and he could tell she was mutually interested. It didn't look good. Oh, he didn't mind Lilly having a private life, goodness knows, she was entitled to it. But her manager also suspected that Lilly would put into a marriage the time and commitment she put into her career. This Karl fellow could be stealing one of the glittering talents of Broadway!

Another knock on the door. "Enter!" St. John commanded.

It was the costume designer. "Any problems, Miss O'Hara?"

Lilly stepped from behind the screen and twirled around with a girlish giggle. She still loved the dressing-up part.

"Perfect!" the manager and designer cried in unison.

She ran through her scales while St. John paced. Then she sat down and finished her tea. "St. John, I'd like you to look into renting a hall for me on the lower east side."

"The east side!"

"Yes, St. John."

"Miss O'Hara, that is the poor, German section of our city and certainly not—"

"I want to hold a concert there. Proceeds to the Belgium fund for orphans. Patriotic songs. I've got a few people in mind to join me."

"People?" he asked with suspicion.

"Some wonderful singers I've met over the years who happen to be German Americans. Even Harry said he would pitch in."

"Houdini said he'd share the stage?"

She nodded. St. John scowled at the flowers. "Does this have anything to do with Mr. Von Bulow, may I boldly inquire?"

She smiled affectionately at her shrewd manager. They were different in so many ways, yet so devoted to each other. She loved him. "It has nothing to do with Karl, beyond that he might attend. It has everything to do with the war and this unpleasant hostility I keep reading and hearing about toward German Americans who are loyal citizens and not, not spies from the kaiser!"

"I applaud your noble motives, Miss O'Hara, as I always do. However—"

Another sharp rap at the dressing room door. "Five minutes, Miss O'Hara!"

St. John stopped his speech. Even without the interruption he seemed to know it was futile. Miss O'Hara was a determined woman when it came to these...these 'causes' she sometimes took up. Typically he fussed, she countered and smiled, he fussed some more, then gave in.

"Like a great lump of clay in her hands," he muttered.

He stood up to leave. Lilly insisted on being alone the final minutes before she went on stage. Yet another tradition like the tea.

"You're lovely tonight. You'll do fine, Miss O'Hara."

He always said that.

She kissed his cheek and patted his shoulder. "Thank you, Georgie."

He glanced at the flowers again. "Going to dinner afterwards with the diplomat?" he asked gruffly.

"Uh huh," she replied as she dusted his lapels.

St. John muttered and frowned as he left. The actress smiled as she sat down and bowed her head.

Five minutes later the audience erupted into thunderous applause as Lilly O'Hara took the stage with a dazzling smile.

After the applause and the autographs, Lilly wanted an hour or two of quiet, an antithesis to the excitement, the lights, the crowd of her partying theater friends. Tonight she wanted to be alone with Karl, the man who was becoming part of her life—and perhaps her future. He seemed subdued when he appeared at her dressing room after the production. His eyes were smiling and kind, lingering on her beauty.

"You were wonderful tonight," he said as he bowed over her hand. "As always."

She smiled into his eyes. "Did you make reservations somewhere?"

His grin was guilty and shy and she laughed as she linked her arm in his. Karl had developed a distinct taste for the humble fare of the American diner. A little cafe near the Manhattan subway that specialized in mammoth hamburgers and greasy fries. Lilly did not mind that her escort did not take her to one of the elite New York night spots.

"You're quiet tonight, Karl," she said as they waited for their food. "Is something wrong?"

The tall man stared at his folded hands, then into the lovely green eyes across the table from him.

"My work with the German embassy has become...more difficult these days. I...I do not always agree with the policies coming out of Berlin."

While the Wilson administration held fast to its neutral position in the European war, philosophically it laid the fault more heavily with the Central Powers. They were the aggressors and seemed stubbornly deaf to appeals for peace negotiations. Yet Woodrow Wilson was equally determined the channels of communication between Washington and Berlin remain very open. Therefore, the German embassy was open and active, with both sides displaying frigid respect, courtesy—and unveiled caution. It was a time the two governments could afford courtesy but not foolishness. The United States was neutral now, but how long could it remain so? The possibility was very real, despite Wilson's diplomacy and propaganda, that America might at some future point swing heavily into the Allied camp and pick up rifle against the young men of Germany.

Even in his lowly position on the embassy staff, Karl knew this. Everyone in diplomatic circles knew this. And it was dispiriting to him. He suddenly felt lonely and isolated. Men he had known for years were suddenly acting like strangers. They eyed him warily. It was disturbing to the kind-hearted German. He had hated the war from the first tragic shot in Sarajevo that had caught his beloved country in a terrible current. He could not extricate himself from his native Germany just because he disagreed with it. His family remained there, marching to the piper's hypnotizing tune. He had prayed that when his hour of decision came, he could be obedient to the Higher One he served. His time in this country that had been his home for 14 years was drawing to a close. And it made him treasure every moment with the lovely, vivacious American actress.

"Have you been harassed, Karl?" Lilly asked kindly.

His laugh was shaky. "Oh, not much. One of the places I like to eat in Washington asked me not to come back. They politely told me some of their customers were complaining about them serving a German, or rather, a Hun." He shook his head. "Some threats were called into our office, but nothing has come from them."

"I'm so sorry, Karl." She took his hands in hers. "I wish it wouldn't get like this."

"Lilly, I think…it may get much worse, before it gets better. 'They' are concerned with the American government as a neutral, selling munitions and even food to the Allies. The shortages are growing worse in German cities."

Lilly did not know what to say.

His smile was faint. "I am sorry, I did not mean to be so somber this evening. I wanted only to please you."

"Don't apologize. It pleases me that you can talk to me about something that is bothering you."

He put her hand to his lips. "You are as generous as you are beautiful."

She rested against him in the darkness of the cab later. She felt tired and drained now, yet she was enjoying the comfort and strength of his nearness.

"Sometimes lately, I desire to close my eyes and wake up in another place that is far away from the newspapers and telegraphs and…just somewhere to plant a garden and read good books and do a little painting and not…live as if this…hand was looming over me. It is in this dream that I see you, Lilly, you with me."

"It sounds like a nice dream, Karl," she replied softly.

"I return to Washington in the morning. There is a strong possibility my duties will keep me there for several months before I can return to your city. But when I come back I would like to make that dream…real."

Lilly smiled in the darkness. Spring was the time to fulfill a dream.

New Orleans

The Christmas decorations were all in place at 2121 Old Manor. The tree was trimmed, the yule log laid and the gifts wrapped. The fresh greens fragrantly spiraled down the bannister. These were only outward displays of the holiday season, however. In the hearts of the mansion's two occupants, it seemed a contrived, sometimes cold and artificial celebration. Kate Alcott rarely looked forward to the season. And her father always seemed more withdrawn, almost morose. That was when he was home. Often, he put in long hours at his waterfront office, while his two daughters decorated and wrapped and tried to bring some warmth and tradition into their little family.

But Kate was a big girl now, and the bitterness left little room for sentiment. This Christmas would be even more difficult with Melanie absent. Melanie was spending most of the holiday with her fiance's family.

Melanie engaged to a missionary! How perfect, Kate had moaned. No more Melanie to act as mediator and interpreter. Just she and her father. But Kate Alcott was a determined young woman and was on her best behavior lest her father in a fit of irritation, change his mind about her transfer to Amherst. It was all Kate dreamed of.

Andy Alcott felt a touch of nervousness with Kate home from school, as well, and no Melanie to act as a buffer. He did not realize until she was gone, how much he depended on his oldest daughter, and how much he missed her. He wanted no trouble between he and his youngest. He would try his hardest to keep peace.

In the library, he stood beside a parlor table where Kate had placed the creche. He was grateful she took the time to decorate. He must remember to thank her. He picked up the porcelain figure of Mary. It was his favorite piece, so delicate, her face so content and serene. He and Amy had chosen this nativity set together their first Christmas.

Kate came to the open doorway and paused. She watched as her father held the figure, then gently replaced it. He continued staring at the table, but in profile she saw his face drawn in lines of sadness. She instinctively knew where his thoughts lay—and they weren't with her. Always in the past... She sighed louder than she intended. He swung around.

She wore a new party dress of royal blue and silver. Andy frowned at her, making her feel awkward.

"What's wrong? You knew I bought this dress, you said I could," she began defensively.

He shook his head. "There's nothing wrong and yes I knew you got that dress."

"Well, you were staring and frowning like..."

"Oh, well, I, I...somehow when I looked up, you made me think of your mother."

They seldom mentioned her. She came between them, neither healing or divisive.

Kate did not soften her tone. "That's because it's Christmas and you're feeling nostalgic. You were looking at the creche and she's in your mind."

He gave her a tired smile. "No, Kate, it wasn't that. You did remind me of her, with your hair pinned up like that, and your dress. You did look like her for a moment."

In the awkward silence that followed, Kate did not know whether to feel flattered or offended. She took a brusque tone to cover her confusion.

"You're looking pretty sharp, too. Going out with Mrs. Hollins?"

He turned back to the fire. "Yes, Virginia and I are going to dinner and a concert."

Kate perched on the edge of a chair, watching him. He had courted so few women over the years…and Kate had never approved of a single one. "You know, Dad, I've heard that Frank Hollins left quite a few debts when he died."

"You shouldn't listen to gossip. But what if he did?"

"If he did, then that would leave Mrs. Virginia Hollins in a pinch."

"A pinch," Andy returned cautiously.

"All right, I'll speak plainly—"

"Please do."

"She's after you, plain and simple. It's your bank account."

He calmly poked the fire. He did not turn to face her. "Do you really think that?"

"Yes I do."

More poking, more silence. Finally he turned around, the sadness again in his eyes. Instantly, Kate Alcott regretted her words.

"Then you think she couldn't be interested in me, for me?"

Kate squirmed on the chair. "Well…I just hate to see you taken in by a designing woman!"

"That's very considerate of you."

Again their time alone had dissolved to sparring. They could not seem to talk. Kate stood up abruptly. "I'm going to finish dressing."

"Who is your date tonight?" her father asked.

"Clark."

His face offered no clues. He looked at her as if trying to read her mind.

"Does Clark Benton meet your approval?" she asked stiffly.

"Clark is a nice boy and a long time family friend. Are you…really interested in him or is this just a friendly date?"

"My motives are entirely honorable, Dad." And she turned and left.

Andy sunk to the chair with a sigh. "And she calls Virginia a designing woman!"

The Alcott family had hosted Christmas Eve dinner for their friends, Clark and Dorothy Benton, for the last 20 years. They had been Andy's friends from the time he took up permanent residence at 2121 Old Manor. Over the years the friendship had held firm with every family triumph and tragedy. They knew Andy when Amy was at his side. Dorothy Benton thought Andy Alcott had been different back then. The older woman knew well the father and his struggles as a single parent. She had been outspoken and blunt, her husband consoling and companionable.

She knew the two Alcott girls as if they were her own. She knew Melanie as calm, responsible, devoted, but Kate sailed in a far different orb—high-spirited, independent, and strong-willed. Dorothy didn't mean to be judgmental, and she did love the girl, but she wasn't sure she liked the thought of her only son courting the young Alcott. She had watched the temper tantrums, the stormy silences, the extravagant dressmaker's bill. As the children grew up together, young Clark was always easygoing with Kate's spoiled ways. Dorothy thought Melanie Alcott was a much more palatable choice for her son. No, she wasn't comfortable with the idea of Kate Alcott as a possible daughter-in-law.

Yet Mrs. Benton was comforted by the fact that neither her son nor Andy's youngest had shown any special interest in each other besides family friendship. They had done things together over the years and held a wide circle of friends. Dorothy took security in that.

Andy was relaxed and smiling. It was hard not to feel the influence of the season with good friends and family gathered around a beautifully laid table. A fire snapped in the background, symbolic only against the mild warmth of a New Orleans winter. Even Melanie had arrived at the last moment. So the long table was set for seven—the three Alcotts, the three Bentons, and Andy's date, Virginia Hollins. Dorothy with her continual flow of chatter, Clark with his unflappable manner, young Clark with his teasing and laughing, Melanie with her kindness, and Kate. He smiled at his youngest at the end of the table. She had done all the work to make the evening a success. And now she was acting as the perfect hostess. He must credit her for that.

They were well into the meal when he spoke up suddenly.

"The beauty of the table this evening and the fine meal is due to my youngest daughter's hard work. She arranged everything. You did an excellent job, Kate."

Kate was flustered by the unexpected praise. There was hearty clapping as she stood to take an extravagant bow.

"Take note, Clark. You always say I haven't any domestic skills!"

Dorothy could hardly eat for talking. She was one of those warm, generous women, who thrived on knowing everything about everybody. As she glanced around the table, she knew of course, that Andy Alcott was courting Virginia Hollins. But more importantly, she knew that Virginia Hollins was hoping that the relationship would become more serious, very soon.

"We're going to London in the spring," Dorothy boasted.

"But Dorothy, there's a war going on over there," Virginia pointed out.

"Oh pooh. It might all be over by then, and if it isn't, it will not affect our plans in the least. Clark had promised me the trip before the whole business started and I always make the man keep his promises. Now let me tell you about our trip to New York last week."

She launched into an extensive and detailed monologue of the Bentons' recent trip at one end of the table, while her husband Clark and Andy talked business, politics, and war at the other end.

"The highlight of the trip was going to the theater. We saw—"

"Even above shopping?" Kate interrupted.

The women laughed. "Yes, that was the best part. But it was a wonderful night at the theater. Clark managed to get tickets to—"

"Was scalped," her husband said sourly with that ability that mates have to monitor each other's conversations—without appearing to do so.

"We saw *High Jinks*!" Dorothy continued. "The theater was full to overflowing. Oh, to see Lilly O'Hara was a treat!"

"Best voice I think I've ever heard," Clark interjected.

Kate Alcott glanced up at her father's face at the mention of the famous actress's name. She smiled—he was trying to appear uninterested. "You saw Lilly O'Hara?" she asked.

"Oh, yes, she was wonderful!" Dorothy enthused. "She's a great actress. But afterwards came the real thrill." The older woman leaned across the table dramatically. "We went to the stage door like a bunch of youngsters! Of course, Clark was fussing the whole way, but he got very quiet when she came out."

"I did not want to appear as a silly, giddy autograph seeker," the husband replied pointedly.

"Which was exactly what you were!" Kate laughed.

"Oh, don't listen to him. He got quiet because he was as impressed as the rest of us. Several men around her tried to brush us away, but Miss O'Hara just laughed and smiled and signed every paper that was stuck under her nose. You should have seen the fur she had on! Oh my!"

"Small fortune..." Clark mumbled. "But it did look sharp on her."

"Tell them, Clark," Dorothy squealed. "Tell them what she said to us."

Clark smiled. "She signed our paper and asked us if we liked the show. 'Course we said it was wonderful. Then she asked us were we from New York or visiting. When we said visitin' from New Orleans, she said she hoped we enjoyed our visit."

Andy Alcott was the only one at the table whose eating had not been suspended by the tale. But when he heard of the actress's kind words, he could not restrain a smile as he studied the table linen. He remembered the Lilly he had known years ago.

"Lovely voice even when she wasn't singing, too," Clark added, now enjoying this captivated audience.

"Dad would know about her lovely voice," Kate Alcott said firmly.

The dining table grew still a moment before Dorothy Benton erupted. Andy looked up at his daughter and gave her a thin smile.

"What's this?" Dorothy asked. "You've heard her?"

Andy kept chewing.

"Oh, he's more than heard her, he knows her," Kate continued impishly.

"Kate," Andy returned in a warning voice. For some reason he did not feel like taking up this teasing, confessing tone.

"What!" Dorothy echoed again.

All eyes were on Andy Alcott. He finished chewing, dabbed at his mouth and carefully rearranged his forks.

"I knew Lilly O'Hara years ago, before she was a famous actress." He took up his glass.

"Andy! Are you serious?" Dorothy asked in a breathless voice.

"He appears most serious, my dear," her husband said calmly.

Dorothy leaned toward him now. "Well, Andy, tell us all about it. Don't act like a perfect clam!"

"There isn't much to tell, Dorothy."

He looked Virginia in the eye. She smiled at him. "You'd better satisfy her, Andy, or she won't let you eat."

"Indeed I won't. To think we've known each other all these years and you never told us," she huffed.

"They were practically sweethearts," Kate spoke up.

Melanie shot her sister a look, but Kate ignored her. Andy's frown deepened. "Katherine, you do not know what you are talking about. That is untrue."

She was not nettled by his tone. Instead she batted her eyelashes at him. "Tell them then."

He sighed. "As I said, there isn't anything to tell. I met Lilly O'Hara over 20 years ago here in New Orleans when I was first mate on a British clipper. I became injured and she helped take care of me for a few weeks. Then she went to New York and I went back to sea. We exchanged perhaps two or three letters. I haven't had any contact with her in years. That's it. Sorry, Dorothy." He turned back to Clark, clearly revealing the subject was closed. "So, where were we in our discussion?"

"Is that all?" Dorothy asked in a plaintive and disappointed voice as she appealed to Kate. They all laughed and Andy smiled. Dorothy was a hopeless snoop and gossip.

"Like all of us, Dad has his own secrets, I suppose," Kate returned coyly.

Andy ignored his daughter and hoped Dorothy would, as well.

But in the end it was Andy who could not dismiss the subject. It stayed in his mind through the evening though he engaged in half a dozen different conversations. Finally, he could stand it no longer. With the women cloistered at one end of the room, Andy drew Clark aside under the pretense of another business discussion. His eyes were alert lest anyone come close and hear his question. He watched the women as he spoke, imagining they were still drawing inferences from his comments—thanks to Kate.

"Clark, I need to ask you something. Confidential, of course."

"Sure, Andy, what is it?"

"Well, it's confidential because of...well, you know how women can get carried away with...things."

"Things? Like what?"

"Like what I said about Lilly O'Hara. You know every woman at the table was thinking there had been something...romantic between us."

The older man leaned forward. "Yeah, was there? I won't tell Dorothy."

"Clark!"

"Well, come on, Andy, it wasn't what you did say, it was the way you didn't say what you didn't say."

Andy shook his head. "Clark, look, we were friends and that's it. Now, can you answer a simple question and not repeat it to Dorothy or magnify it in your own mind?"

"Okay, okay."

Andy Alcott felt a sudden nervousness, as if he were a young boy trying to work up the courage to speak to a girl. He leaned forward.

"Tell me, Clark, tell me about how she...looked, what she seemed like. I'm just asking out of curiosity, of course."

"Of course. Well, she wore a costume most of the time and in one act she had on a wig. She—"

"No, no, I mean when you saw her at the stage door."

"Oh. Well, like Dorothy said, she laughed and smiled a lot, didn't seem put out with the fans pressing all around her. Seemed real friendly for a star." Now he leaned forward. "Was she that pretty 20 years ago?"

"Yes, yes she was."

"Well, then she got into a cab with a tall fellow."

Andy looked down at his polished shoes. He felt foolish somehow.

"She's a beautiful woman," Clark said softly. "That red hair..."

"Still very red?"

"Yep."

"Green eyes?"

"Green eyes with long lashes. What you call a knockout. One of those women who..." He cast a furtive glance toward his wife. "Who get prettier with age, you know." He laughed. "Not like us with spreading middles and gray hair!"

"Um..."

"Think Lilly O'Hara is married?" Clark asked cautiously.

Andy shrugged "Could be. I don't read the variety page much."

"Maybe you should," Clark suggested with a lifted eyebrow. "She's an old friend, like you say."

Andy relaxed and smiled. "Yes, an old friend."

Chapter 6

Chicago

◆ ◆ ◆ ◆ ◆ ◆

*B*en Alcott was stretched out on his narrow dormitory bed, reading. Unfortunately for his academic career, it was not a textbook. He would squeeze in English Lit, or Chemistry, or Philosophy 101, as an afterthought to all the events of his day, and only when an exam loomed ominously. He lay on his unmade bed in rumpled clothing, needing a shower and shave, and growing hungrier with each minute. But Ben was completely absorbed in the volume propped up on his chest. He lay in the quiet dorm room in the luxurious and contented state of one in the hold of a good book. It was a new book on aviation, his fifth volume on the subject. He had shoveled snow after classes for three weeks to earn enough money to order the prized book. He glanced up at the little crudely made shelf beside his bed. Four books on flying and airplanes stood there—testaments of the young man's passionate interest. He treasured his personal library above anything else he owned.

The door opened, but he did not bother to look up. Someone entered humming a tune and tossed a wrapped sandwich onto the bed beside him. Without taking his eyes from the book, he held the package to his nose and sniffed.

"I asked for bratwurst, not polish sausage," he grumbled.

Across the room a young man prepared to shave at the little wash bowl. "They were out."

Ben laughed. "They're never out, Marty. Admit that you got my order wrong."

The young man lathered his face.

"I didn't get it wrong. They were out and they will be from now on."

Ben lowered his book. "What? They have the best bratwurst in Chicago!"

"Had Ben, had. The old man behind the counter told me too many customers were complaining about the German food items on the menu. So…" He slid a finger across his neck.

"That's crazy," Ben growled as he returned to his book and ignored his lunch.

"Yeah…it's crazy all right," Marty agreed. "Say, aren't you and Carolyn supposed to go skating at two?"

"Uh huh…"

"Well you must not care that you look and smell like you need more than 30 minutes to get ready." He waited for a reaction. "You know, I think it's mighty convenient you and I having girls who are roommates."

"Uh huh…"

"Yep, mighty convenient."

Nothing from Ben.

"'Cause it makes me privy to knowing what Carolyn thinks about you."

"Hmm…"

"Puts me in possession of some very interestin' info. Yep."

Nothing from the man behind the book.

"Like for instance that your Carolyn told my Helen that she thinks you are on the verge of askin' the question."

The book lowered to allow Marty to see the dark eyes of his roommate. "Asking the question?"

"Yep."

"What question would that be?"

"The age old, 'Will you marry and enslave me?' question."

"What?" Ben raised up on an unsteady elbow.

"Yep, she thinks you are ready to tie the knot, buddy. And she's waitin'."

Ben sighed. "Where in the world did she get that crazy idea?"

"Somethin' you said maybe?"

"I would say nothing even close to the subject of marriage. Are you kiddin'?"

"Marriage is just not for you, huh?"

"Nope, not for a long time, a couple of decades at least. I have a lot of living to do."

"Aw, Ben, that's just because you haven't found the right girl yet."

"There is no girl on this planet who could tempt me to marry her," Ben said with boyish arrogance. He returned to his book. "So I guess it just won't be convenient anymore, Marty."

"You're dumpin' Carolyn?"

"I wouldn't call it dumping. But yeah, desperate times call for desperate action."

"Helen will be riled at me!" Marty said in an injured tone.

"A hazard of dating roommates, I guess. I need a girl who knows how to laugh and have a good time, and let me spoil her, and how to kiss. A lot of girls out there fit that description. I need a girl who has no…no domestic urges."

Marty eyed the book with annoyance. "You and your airplanes! A fine thing to cuddle up to!"

"Hmm…"

"Here I have to go and explain to Helen to explain to Carolyn that you prefer airplanes to girls!" Marty fumed.

The book lowered again. "Girls with matrimonial designs, definitely." Ben yawned and reluctantly put his book away. "I like airplanes and girls, Marty. In that order."

Peppercreek

The Christmas holidays were celebrated in a wealth of sights, sounds, and smells at the old Alcott home in Peppercreek. It was a time of nostalgia, a season with a unique, almost reverenced complexion in the mellowing twilight of a year. A time of family traditions, when hearts were knit closer together from the holiness of celebration.

Most Alcotts tried to return to the white stone house during some part of the season. So it was that beds were shared, and the feasting board was expanded, and voices and laughter rang like pleasant music from dawn until the high rising of the moon. Ben loved the season as a man of 21, as he had loved it as an eager-eyed boy. He loved the house filled with cousins, aunts, uncles, and friends. As he and David hadn't any sisters, it gave him great pleasure to have girl cousins to talk with and tease. They were spirited playmates as children, and now they proved enjoyable as young women. There was sledding, skating, ice fishing, and sing-alongs around the piano.

But even Ben's good nature was taxed by his mother's request. "Ma, it's a dance, and David and I both have dates! You don't take too gawky kids along on a date!"

Millie Alcott planted her hands firmly on her hips. It was his mother's resolute, unflinching combat posture. "Just yesterday I heard you say Emily and Elizabeth were great girls, not gawky kids!"

"B—"

"And is Marilyn too selfish to understand your need to entertain your cousins from Mississippi who come but twice a year?"

"Ma—"

"Ben, it's okay. Marilyn will understand and I'm sure Bess will, too," David interrupted laconically from the edge of his parents' bed.

"There you are!" his mother flashed triumphantly. "Besides, Elizabeth and Emily think the world of you two boys and they are very well behaved and I'm sure you won't even know they're there."

Ben rolled his eyes and threw up his hands. Not even know they were there, ha! Two young cousins were fun to sled or play cards with, but to take along on a date? He had wanted this to be a time alone for the two couples. Through the fall David's letters to Ben at school were full of a certain young woman named Bess Hoffman. Ben was eager to meet this girl who had seemingly swept his little brother from his isolation and captivated him completely. Now they would have along four extra eyes and four ears...hardly romantic!

The conflict was overheard by Aunt Meg. "Really, Millie, the girls don't need to go with the boys."

"That's true, Aunt Millie," Elizabeth spoke from her mother's elbow. "We don't need to go to a Christmas dance. We can stay here and play cards...or something."

In the heavy silence every eye in the bedroom turned to Ben. He sighed. His amiable disposition reasserted itself. He waved a warning finger at the girls. "Just be ready when it's time to go!"

He couldn't help but chuckle at their squeals.

Strains of 'Alexander's Ragtime Band' filtered out of the upstairs room of the Elks lodge like the lights that cast golden geometrics on a softly purpling snow. Cousins or tag alongs, by whatever epitaph, David Alcott was enjoying himself hugely at the Christmas dance. The room was packed with excited young people and a few mature-minded adults, who tried to refrain from tapping a wayward foot to the music. They were community guardians whose chief role lay in keeping a strict surveillance of the punch bowl that tempted some young men to make additions from the silver flasks they carried in their dress jackets.

David, looking carefully groomed and manicured, was pleased with his older brother's reaction to his first and only girlfriend. Behind her back Ben had flashed his brother a big grin and an upward thumb.

"Guess you didn't need my help, after all," he whispered.

Ben's date was a vivacious blonde who warmly appreciated the attention of one of the local "catches." Ben was good-looking and knew how to show a girl a good time. Both boys danced with their Southern cousins with great fun. The girls were not obtrusive.

It was a perfect evening from the dancing and laughter to the passionate kiss on the front step under a luminescent moon. But then a shadow crept across the moon, not brought on from the presence of the two cousins. A group of friends gathered around the refreshment table, resting between dances with laughter and a dozen orbiting conversations that no one was really listening to. David stood with Bess, Emily, and Ben's date. "Having fun?" he asked his young cousin.

He need not bother to ask. Emily's eyes were sparkling, her cheeks were brushed pink. She nodded eagerly. From the floor they heard Ben's booming laugh as he danced with Elizabeth.

A young man and woman left the dance floor and joined the group at the table though they were strangers.

"I think I know you." He pointed at Bess. "What's your last name?"

The girl glanced apprehensively at David. Then she spoke up firmly. "My name is Hoffman."

"Yeah, yeah, I thought so…" He took an exaggerated sip of his punch.

"Ready to dance, David?" Bess asked. "It's time for you to take Emily out."

"No…not just yet."

Another boy joined the table, his arm loosely around the shoulder of a smiling girl. These were not local boys. David felt uneasy leaving Bess unattended until Ben returned from the floor. He had noticed the two couples earlier in the evening, both for their big city sophistication and their frequent trips in and out of the room—each time they came back from the hall, they were more jovial and red-faced.

"Say, Adam, look there." He nodded at Bess. "They let a Kraut into this shindig!"

An instant silence fell on the group around the table, like a needle was abruptly lifted from a phonograph. David carefully set his glass down. He felt every eye on him. He did not look at the newcomers.

"A Hun at this dance? Tsk, tsk. She looks pretty enough, it's hard to tell. You a German, sister?"

Bess's chin came up. "I am of German heritage."

David turned to face them directly. He felt his pulse racing. The two antagonists stared at each other, then they burst out laughing. The adult chaperons across the room smiled; everyone was having such a jovial time.

"In Alton we don't let Krauts into our dances," the boy called Adam spoke up.

"In Springfield we aren't as rude." Emily Browning spoke up hotly. "Why don't you go back to Alton?"

David laid a quieting hand on her.

"You a Kraut lover, little girl?" Adam sneered. "Or is it you?" he directed at David.

David Alcott seethed inside, but he was a strategist more than he was a fighter. He was carefully assessing the best plan in this volatile situation.

"You fellows have a nasty mouth," he said coldly. "Why don't you leave. You're not welcome here."

"We paid our two bits."

"I don't like Krauts or Kraut lovers talkin' to me like that," the young man hissed.

His girlfriend was no longer smiling. She pulled on the young warrior, saying, "Come on Bill, let's shake this hick town."

Ben Alcott and Elizabeth came off the floor, laughing. When Ben saw his brother's face, he stopped as if he'd run into a wall. He swiftly glanced at the others who were all looking alarmed and tense. Bess's eyes were pooled in tears, Emily and his date were red-faced, David was pale.

"Hey, Davy, what's the matter?"

"He called Bess some rude names." Emily pointed haughtily at the two interlopers. "He's been very insulting. He's what we'd call a bigot back home."

Emily was relishing the drama with youthful enthusiasm.

Ben relaxed his stance and crossed his arms. His head was cocked, as if he were trying to determine what type of species the two men were. "Well, Emily, we'd call them bigots here, if what you say is true. You fellows were being rude to my friend?"

His voice had lost that friendly edge, replaced with something tougher and biting.

"Ben, please, it's all right," Bess whispered anxiously.

The most belligerent of the two was well fortified with whiskey to make him foolishly and arrogantly bold. The thin, scholarly-looking David had seemed like an inconsequential opponent. This broad-shouldered fellow with flashing eyes might be more of a challenge!

"The gal is a Kraut, a Hun. Probably has a cousin in the kaiser's army!" he spewed.

"What do you care if she does?" Ben returned with icy calmness.

"I care! Everybody cares! It ain't American...to...to like Germans!"

David stepped up to his brother's shoulder. "Ah, Ben, I think we should go outside with them...you know..."

Ben ignored him. "You haven't got your facts straight, buddy, but even so, I always believe in giving a man the chance to repent. How 'bout an apology to Miss Hoffman? Then we can all go back to having a good time."

The man snorted as his fist came up.

David suddenly remembered his brother's best fighting asset—his quickness. It was uncanny how Ben could stand there so easy and comfortable one minute, and the next moment his arm would come up like a churning piston. David hadn't seen the reflex in a few years, so he was nearly as surprised as everyone gathered around the table.

Ben parried the man's blow with his left arm, while smashing his right fist into his nose. The man flew backwards in a cacophony of breaking dishes, splattering blood, shouts, and high-pitched screams. But the friend standing to the side took advantage of Ben's moment of inattention as he regained his balance. His first punch landed solidly in Ben's stomach, and the other glanced off his left eye. David was on top of him and the crushed table in an instant.

The chaperons were horrified. Hadn't they been vigilant to their task? Oh, the gray-haired matrons would howl when this little episode was circulated. The two young men were given rags for their bloody noses then politely escorted to their fancy jalopy. And while the broken glass was swept up, David and Ben became sudden celebrities with slaps on the back, and requests for details on the incident. It certainly livened up the country dance. But the Alcott brothers no longer felt like dancing, or even staying in the charitable atmosphere, even though their dates were commendably solicitous over their injuries and affectionate as well. Ben turned to his young cousins as they all climbed into his model T.

"So, you two have a good time?" he asked with a wry grin.

"Wonderful!" they chorused together.

The two brothers sat in the darkened bedroom they had shared for 18 years. They did not bother to turn on the lamp, the only light emanating from the hissing orange glow of a small coal heater. They sat facing each other in their shorts and socks on the edge of their single beds.

"I feel like I did that night we ran home after painting the school outhouse pink." David laughed.

Ben nodded. "Yeah, remember the tannin' Pa gave us when he found out?"

"Think we're too big for that now, Ben?"

Ben shrugged and yawned. "I don't know. Ma did tell us to show the two E's a good time."

They both laughed. Then David sobered. "Sorry about the black eye."

"Your cut lip and knuckles look worse than mine. Hurt much?"

"Naw, it's all right, I think." David glanced down at his bandaged hand, a dull gray in the darkness. With his dreams, he could not let anything happen to his hands. "I hope I didn't look like a coward to Bess," he said quietly. "I was just trying to figure out what to do about those two clods, when you came up."

Ben tossed a sock at him. "The way she was cuddled up against you on the way home, I don't think she was thinkin' like that!"

David looked past his brother in the darkness, his voice dreamy. "Yeah..."

"You really like this girl, huh?"

"I think she's the one."

"Come on, you have to go out with a lot of girls before you find the right one. How can you know she's the right one that fast?"

"I just know."

"Sounds scary to me..."

"Haven't you ever felt like that even a little bit for a girl?"

"No, I haven't. But I figure there's one out there. Just a matter of finding her...someday."

"How will you know it's her?"

Ben wasn't accustomed to such personal confessions. "Well, I, I think I'll look into her eyes and I'll see something there that I haven't seen in any other girl, something that tells me this is the one. But that's a long way off..."

He climbed into bed. They both lay staring up into the ceiling, held by the claims of their own thoughts. David smiled into the darkness as he thought of the fair-haired German girl named Bess.

"I have a friend at school who left to join the French foreign legion," Ben said slowly. "They take Americans."

David waited a moment before he spoke. "You thinkin' about that?"

Ben yawned loudly. "Just thinkin'...Bess is a real nice girl, pretty too."

"Yeah..." David leaned over a moment later. "You told Ma and Pa your plans yet?"

Ben was drifting off to sleep. "No...I'd sooner tell them I caused a fight at the Christmas dance."

Millie Alcott was slightly annoyed with her oldest son. Whenever Grandma Sara was ill or infirm, if Ben was at home, he hovered and was anxious for her well-being. He could not do enough for her. It was contrary to his normally independent, fun loving, unemotional manners. So, now here he was suggesting all sorts of remedies and propositions when Millie Alcott thought she had Grandmother Sara's health care well in hand. He had always had a strong attachment to his grandmother. Still a boy in so many ways—Millie frowned. And this latest scheme of his...

Sara Alcott looked queenly in the huge four poster. She wore a soft gown as snowy white as her hair. She sat propped up against a small fortress of pillows, the counterpane of her bed an undulating sea of bright colors. Ben brought her breakfast on a tea tray. His quick glance took in the healthy tone of her skin.

"Ma says your fever's gone," he said cheerfully.

She nodded, unable to speak a moment. He saw her blue eyes fill. He sat down quickly and took her hand.

"What's the matter? Are you hurting somewhere?"

"You, you look more like your grandfather each day, Ben. When you came into the room you made me think of him. After each baby, he made me stay in bed a week. He'd bring me meals on a tray."

"You miss him, don't you?"

"Oh not as much as I did." She smiled at Ben's surprised look. "I mean, I'm enjoying all of you so much, watching...watching the designs of your life unfold like a...a tapestry. And it gives me such joy to think I'll see Ethan soon."

"Not too soon," he said, wagging his finger at her.

She smiled. "And we'll have eternity to be together!"

He began arranging her food.

"Now, tell me, is there any girl in your wide acquaintance that makes you feel like that?" she asked.

He smiled and leaned back in his chair. "Everyone's concerned for my romancing lately!"

"Choosing a life mate is very important. Nothing to be flippant about."

"Oh, I know that. I'm just not ready to choose."

She leaned forward, her eyes sparkling. "I don't think I really need worry about you. I think when you find the right young girl, you won't turn her loose!"

He laughed.

"Now, tell me, when are you heading back to Chicago?"

"After dinner."

"And has the storm subsided?"

Ben grinned. "I guess so. Ma made me breakfast, though it did feel a little frosty in the room. Pa was kind of frowning at me." He scratched his head. "I don't get it. I'm not wasting his money at school anymore. I'm on my own, paying my own way!"

"Parents want the best for their children. They just don't always see eye to eye on what is best."

"Yeah…"

"And aviation is such an uncertain profession, Ben, not to mention dangerous. Now tell me again, you are just going to be a mechanic?"

He felt his face glow with excitement. "It's a new airfield outside of Chicago. There will just be me and one other fellow as mechanics. It's a small outfit. I'll live there at the field and get paid for working on planes."

"No flying?" she asked.

"Grandmother, you're the fearless one in the family! You don't mind when I drive fast."

"But that is on the ground!"

"Look, I promise I won't fly until I learn. This is a great opportunity. I feel like I've been let out of jail!"

She patted his hand. "My responsibility as a grandmother insists that I say this. Don't be foolish with your freedom, Ben."

"Okay, okay." He laughed.

She pointed to her dresser. "Bring me that package there, will you?"

He could tell her frail, unsteady hand had wrapped the tissue covered parcel. It endeared her to him even more.

"What's this ?"

"It's a late Christmas gift. Open it."

"You gave me socks and shorts!" he protested.

"Socks and shorts! Humph! And this is just as well that it was late. I couldn't be certain your mother and father would appreciate my gift to you." She shrugged and gave him a guilty smile.

The tissue paper revealed a sage green book. *Bennet's Book of Flying.* It was like the *Gray's Anatomy* of aviation.

His eyes were wide. "Grandmother, I know this was expensive."

"It's the one you wanted, isn't it?" she asked eagerly.

No one else in his family acknowledged or gave credence to his passion for the new invention.

"It's the sixth book. There aren't any other books on aviation. This gives me the complete set." His bronzed hand caressed the cover. He lifted his eyes to her. "You understand, don't you?"

She smiled.

Amherst College, Massachusetts

Kate Alcott surveyed the new campus with the look of a general planning his campaigns. She stood in the cold January morning in an expensive woolen coat, hat and scarf. Here was the place she had set her sights upon, a new field of dreams—a step forward in her journalism career, and of course, a new harvest of suitors. She turned to her father's secretary who stood quietly and unobtrusively beside her.

"Well, here I am!" she exclaimed brightly.

"Yes, Miss Katherine, here you are."

Despite his years behind a desk, Collins was a man with a functioning eye for beauty. He saw, and not for the first time of course, that his employer's daughter was indeed lovely. The long train trip had not flagged her spirits or paled her looks.

She smiled at him. "Isn't it exciting, Collins! I'm starting a new adventure!"

He smiled and nodded but did not say a word. She looked back to the red brick buildings of the campus.

"I really believe this is just the place I need to polish up my writing and start my career!"

"Of course, I'm happy for you, Miss Katherine," he allowed with a nod.

"I've already talked on the phone with one of my professors. He was telling me about the journalism department and the Clifford prize that is given each spring."

"The Clifford prize? I don't believe I've heard of that."

"It's like a contest that the journalism department holds. Students submit an essay on a specific topic and the best writing wins the Clifford prize!"

She was nearly breathless as she gripped his arm and leaned toward him. "Guess what the winning essayist receives this year. Just guess!"

He was flushed by her close proximity—as he always was.

"I, I can't guess, Miss Katherine."

"The winner of the prize receives an expense-paid trip to...to England as a war correspondent for the school paper! Oh, Collins, can you imagine?"

Inwardly, Collins could not imagine. He could not imagine Andy Alcott allowing his young and impulsive daughter to go to Europe, near a war zone—prize or no prize! It was a 'war' just getting her to this new college.

"Uh, yes, that would be...something, Miss Katherine."

She searched his face with sudden intensity. "Collins, I know Father has no faith in my writing, but do you think I might have a chance?"

"Yes, I do, Miss Katherine, I do. And if I may be so bold—"

"I like boldness," she interrupted with a teasing smile.

"I'm confident your father is aware of your, uh, many talents."

"Oh pooh. You know him as well as I do. He is aware of ships." Her voice became biting. "And Mrs. Hollins."

The secretary opened his mouth to speak, then thought better of it. He could point out the father had finally allowed her to transfer. That was no small victory.

"Collins, do you really have to be so formal? Miss Katherine? That's what my father calls me in his severest tone. Kate is much cozier."

"Uh...well..."

"What is your given name? All these years you've just been my father's right-hand man named Collins."

"I was christened Albert."

"Albert...when is your train back to New Orleans?"

"This evening."

"We just got here! I think you should stay overnight at least."

"Well, uh, your father does need me, especially since he's been ill."

"Oh, Dad is fine. I've never seen him ill."

"Well, uh, he was ill enough to send me with you in his stead."

"He did want you to see me settled in. That should take a few days at least, don't you think?"

She stood close to him now.

"I, I suppose I could stay a few days."

"Perfect. We'll go to dinner tonight." Her gloved hand slid into his coat pocket.

Emden, northern coast of Germany

Walther Schwieger at 30 years of age held two principal passions in his life—submarines and classical music. From a fine old Berlin family, he was the fair-haired, intelligent, healthy picture of Aryan genetics that would be of great importance in the Fatherland some 30 years later. He did not smoke or drink beyond an occasional ceremonial toast. His governing interests in life kept him unattached.

Clinical, dispassionate, logical, he felt submarine warfare was the perfect, in fact, only solution to the Allied blockade which was already putting a strangling grip on Germany. Letters from his mother and sisters described shortages at the markets in beef and butter, luxuries and fuel. War came in a host of ugly faces—hungry children, underfed troops. And men tried to 'even the score' whenever possible. Such was the drive and commitment of Walther Schweiger.

He was a Kapitanleutnant for two years, and by the time his career ended at 31, 149 sinkings could be credited to his resolve. His area of patrol extended some 3,000 miles from Germany's northern coast, past Scotland, and finally around the southernmost tip of Ireland into St. Georges' channel. It was not a dull patrol.

On each mission, Walther took a stack of letters. There was always time to reread them, and write long replies. He felt a duty in this, as well. Letters from his cousin Marta Marie were most interesting. Other submarine captains had information from German intelligence on Allied activity in the war zone, but who had a cousin sitting on the coast observing things first hand? It gave Walther an added feeling of confidence. Marta was always a headstrong, unconventional girl, Walther mused. He liked her well enough. But she was the kind of girl you had fun with, not married. She was an opportunist and he couldn't help wondering what poor Irish bloke was getting soaked and not knowing it. Just like the German fellow she had strung along then stolen from to finance her sudden flight from her family and homeland. Yes, Marta was a deceptive sort, but this time Walther did not mind.

London, January, 1915

She stood on the station platform at Charring Cross, one hand gripping a leather satchel, the other thrust deeply into her steel-blue wool coat. She wore a matching woolen tam. She had been to France as a little girl, but that was years ago. And this time, she was going alone—stepping off into that uncertainty called adventure. Perhaps it would be nothing more than caring for a maiden aunt in a foreign country wholly minus of any drama, but perhaps it would be more, it almost had to be with four major countries quarreling within a few miles. In London, she felt the war by painless, impersonal waves; in France, she would feel it nearly at its fiery center. Molly Fleming hoped it would be a challenge—and that she was up to every minute of it.

Her father stood beside her choking on the lump in his throat and scolding himself. He had suggested this plan, after all. Would he be cowardly about it now as it unfolded? He felt a calm certainty this was the right thing for his daughter, but how he would miss her!

Molly knew how he felt. He had been especially quiet all morning. She felt both the thrill and the sadness of leaving him. They avoided each other's eyes as they glanced at the few soldiers and nurses who also waited for the train.

"They'll be lots of men in uniform about, Molly, and you'll be like a magnet to them, pardon such an unpoetic comparison, my dear."

She laughed. "Well, I do have a ring on my finger if they get too friendly."

His eyes narrowed with professorial scrutiny. "It's a ring, not a contract. I don't think you should feel bound by it, in the event you should meet someone over there."

"Dad, I'm going to help Aunt Madeline, not fraternize with the Allied army!"

"Just the same, you're an unattached and very lovely woman."

She ignored his implications. "The one drawback to this plan is leaving you. I mean, I won't be there to look after—"

He patted her arm solicitously. "We've been over this before. Mrs. Crumple is more than willing to get my meals and tidy up. She welcomes a purpose in her life now."

Molly cocked her head. "She welcomes seeing you more. Yes, she's willing."

Her father burst out laughing. "Oh, Molly..."

"And we're talking about me and your worries with all those soldiers about. I don't think it's me we should be concerned about!"

"I'll try to be careful."

The porters began their call. The train hissed and heaved in its ritual ceremony of departure.

"Molly, you must be careful. Front lines can change in a matter of hours. If you have advance warning, you must get yourself and your aunt out. I'm sure I look foolish to be letting you go, but I, well, I feel it's the right thing."

"I do, too. And I'm not afraid."

He sighed and lifted her cases. They had never been separated before.

"I think I better get on now."

But he had to look in her eyes. They were so beautiful. "I will miss you very much. Come back to me...happy."

"I'll miss you, Dad."

He watched the train until the last car curved out of sight. Thomas Fleming was praying—praying the fire in France would be a refining fire, and no worse.

At the time, of course, it was simply called "the war." In the States, "the war over there." Some years later when the history pages were written, it was called "the great war," by virtue of its magnitude. Certainly there were tribes in central Africa or Australia who did not know, and would not care, about the continental war. Because it was so far reaching in its peripheral influences, it created a vast theater of human drama—from palaces to trenches, battlefields to hospitals. To that vast stage, the players now converged.

Chapter 7

Chicago

◆◆◆◆◆

*I*t looked like a patchwork quilt from the air, scattered geometrics in earthy shades of gold and yellow, copper, and emerald. And the landmarks, natural and manmade, had utterly lost their proportion in size. Everything was now in miniature. Everything except the sky. The sky! So blue, so vast and open. It was incredible! Ben Alcott let out war whoops and shouts until he was hoarse.

"I feel like a giant!" he yelled.

When the pilot in the seat in front of him began a slow spiral preparatory to landing, Ben immediately protested.

"Don't go down! Not yet! Please, a little longer!"

The pilot smiled and pointed a finger to the fuel gauge. They must go down. Ben sat in the cramped seat a full minute after they stopped before he climbed out. His first plane ride! It was as thrilling as he had hoped—and more.

He climbed down and ran his hand along the fuselage.

"When can we go back up?" he asked eagerly.

The pilot punched Ben on the shoulder. "You were hired to work on 'em, Alcott, not be a passenger all day long! We have paying customers for that!"

Ben walked reluctantly to the hangar. But he turned at the edge of the grass and looked back at the 'bird' so still and silent now waiting on the strip.

"There's kind of...a, a magic about it, isn't there, Jimmy?"

Jimmy the pilot shrugged. "Yeah, I guess. I'm kind of used to it now."

"I'd never get used to it," Ben whispered in awe.

The pilot smiled and shook his head. He left Ben alone gazing at the plane.

Tonight before he went to bed he'd write David. He had to try to describe what it was like soaring hundreds of feet above the earth. Perhaps though, he couldn't describe it. Davy would have to experience it for himself. Ben smiled. That was it. As soon as he could fly, he'd take his brother up. Turn one of those loops that made crowds gasp and passengers lose their stomachs. It'd be great, he laughed to himself.

He turned back to the hangar. It was time to work. Ben Alcott had never been happier. Life had suddenly become a banquet, a feast for him to enjoy and savor in every detail. It wasn't just the flying. It was working over sputtering engines until he made them purr. Then watching Jimmy glide through the skies without a sputter. It was oily rags and tools and humming tunes and daydreaming. Staying up late and eating bad. He loved every minute of it. And his conscience was clear. He had not flown like he'd promised Grandma Sara. But he'd been up there, and he'd never be the same again.

Nehi Field was one of the first airfields near Chicago. It was postage stamp size in a surrounding ocean of corn. Jimmy Weed, pilot and owner, chose to name the field after his favorite drink. Nothing sophisticated about the long-limbed, affable Weed or his operation. At 45 years of age, the bachelor had left his machinist job in the bowels of Chicago, and plunked all his life savings into this enterprise three years earlier. He'd hauled out a big, old tin barn to serve as a hangar and apartment. With a pair of mules and log drags, he'd smoothed the dirt runway. Finally, he bought a shiny new biplane. Twenty acres were his—Nehi Field with wave after wave of cornfield encircling him.

"Why didn't ya' cut down more of the field, Jimmy, at the end of the strip?" Ben asked.

Weed nodded and smiled. "Just so any pilot of mine would have to learn his stuff, and learn it right the first time. Learn to lift up and drop down in a specific space or else he'd crack his plane up."

"Maybe get a corn stalk through his head," Ben added skeptically.

"Exactly the point. When you learn to take off or land in a tight spot, a tight spot won't be much of a threat. Makes a man more careful when he knows what his boundaries are."

Weed's enterprise was a success with Saturday afternoon stunt shows and sight-seeing trips and jaunts for prosperous and adventurous Chicago businessmen. It was such a success, he bought another plane and hired a mechanic.

Ben had heard about the airfield at school. It had distracted him from his studies. He approached Weed with enthusiasm and determination—and an impressive knowledge of airplane engines. Weed liked the young man on sight and jerked his greasy thumb toward the hangar.

"That's home, Alcott. You're mechanic and cook if you prove better than me. Pay ain't much and we're pretty remote out here. Can't be galavantin' into town every night." He shrugged. "It ain't much."

Ben's grin was wide. "It's enough."

It was Friday night. And as much as Ben loved his work, his camaraderie with Jimmy Weed and the whole little world of Nehi airfield, Friday nights were meant for dancing and a pretty girl. Even with the seclusion of the field and the demands of his work, Ben had managed to get a girlfriend in short order. David had mentioned the talent years earlier.

"What is it about you, Ben? They seem to find you like a magnet!"

Ben had pulled a long face. "Yeah, it's a real trial for me..."

Young women who came for the Saturday afternoon show could not miss the broad-shouldered mechanic with the appealing smile. Never mind he wore oily overalls!

So it was a girl named Paula in Jimmy's borrowed jitney for a hamburger and shake at a little cafe between the big city and the field. They had great food and a phonograph that played the tunes that Ben liked best. Paula didn't seem to mind the simple evening. She smiled, appreciated his humor, and smelled good. It was all Ben asked.

"You sure look great tonight, Paula," Ben said as he bit into his burger.

The girl across the table smiled sweetly. "Thank you. So, did you go up today?"

Ben frowned. "Nope, we did housekeepin' all day. Cleanin' the hangar and the plane."

"A show tomorrow?"

"Nope, a young fella from Chicago is comin' out. He bought the whole afternoon. Name's Melvin, or Martin Meyer, I think."

"Martin Meyer?" Paula asked eagerly.

"Yeah, maybe."

"Ben, Martin Meyer is only the son of one of the richest families in Chicago. Ever heard of Meyer meats?"

"Nope." Ben shrugged as he dropped another onion ring in his mouth. "I don't know if it's the same Meyer or not, doesn't mean much to me, though. He's just payin' the groceries. Come on, let's dance!"

It was a perfect day for flying. The windsock hung limp, the sky was brilliant blue and cloudless. Jimmy Weed was in an untypical jovial mood. He donned clean clothes and insisted Ben do the same.

"We don't want to look like slobs today, Ben," the pilot said after breakfast. "We need to look competent here."

Ben couldn't see how slightly less greasy overalls would make them look more competent, but he was silent and trusted Jimmy's judgment. The young Meyer arrived punctually at 12:30, his Stutz Bearcat stirring up a comet's tail of dust from the country road to Chicago. He climbed out, smiling, eager, and friendly.

Jimmy waited for the gregarious Ben to introduce himself to their customer. But Ben hardly noticed the young man. He was wholly distracted by a blonde head with a pert white cap perched on top—a woman sat in the passenger seat of the sports car.

"Uh, Ben, Ben," Jimmy nudged.

"Oh sure, welcome to Nehi Field, Mr. Meyer!"

"Hey, I'm not ready for that mister stuff. I'm Marty."

The mechanic and the customer shook hands.

"We're ready when you are...Marty," Jimmy interrupted.

The young man turned back to the car. "You sure you want to stay? I'm gonna be up there for a while."

He turned back to the flight crew and smiled. "She came out to watch and make sure I come back in one piece. Protective little sister, you know."

The young woman stepped from the car and came around to the trio of men. She looks so clean and fresh, thought Ben.

"I don't mind staying, Marty." Her eyes traveled over Ben and Jimmy. "Is this safe, gentlemen?"

Ben smiled. "Sure is, Miss Meyer. This is Jimmy Weed and he's the best pilot this side of the Mississippi."

"And Ben here is my mechanic and a virtual wizard with engines. Why, Ma'am, your brother is as safe in this plane as he is in that machine you drove in here."

She gave her brother a sidelong glance. "Actually, Mr. Weed, this is the third Bearcat. Marty wrecked the other two."

"Now Ellie—"

"Miss Meyer," Jimmy soothed, "We're just going to let him look things over from up there. I'll do the drivin'."

The men laughed.

"Let's get going! Bye sis!"

When the plane was airborne and Martin Meyer, heir to a fortune in beef, was waving wildly at them, Ben stood watching till they were out of sight. He knew how the young man felt in his first ride. Now he was oblivious to the young woman watching him.

"You'd like to be up there with them," she said simply.

He turned around. She was leaning against the running board. How could he have forgotten her?

"Yes, Ma'am, I would."

"I'm Ellie."

His grin broadened. "I'm Ben. Like to pull your car over there in the shade by the hangar?"

"Ever driven a Bearcat before?"

He shook his head. "No, Ma'am, no...Ellie."

She tossed him the keys. "You can if you like. We could go for a drive."

He looked at the sleek car, and glanced quickly at the girl. A fast car and a pretty gal—it was a tempting combination.

"I...thanks, but I have to hang around, you know, in case they come back soon."

"Then I suppose you could drive it over in the shade and we could just...chat."

She showed him a bulging picnic basket. It would be a much more interesting afternoon than he had imagined.

"What about Paula?" Jimmy asked between mouthfuls of cold pork and beans.

Ben tried hard to swallow the flat, very salty biscuits Jimmy had attempted. He'd be wiser to stick with flying and stay out of the bachelor kitchen. "We need to hire a cook, Jimmy. I think you forgot the baking powder and tripled the salt."

"Can't afford to."

"My ma is gonna throw a fit the next time she sees me," Ben moaned. "Call me a skeleton or something."

"Now, about Paula."

"What about her?"

"Thought you were sweet on her."

"She's a real nice girl. So?"

Jimmy leaned back and began picking his teeth. "But she's been replaced."

"Who said? I never said that," Ben protested with a laugh.

"You're going out to dinner with that slaughterhouse queen."

"Jimmy, that isn't very flattering! Ellie's a nice girl. And her brother is paying our bills, so what's the problem? I can go out with two girls."

"They know about this little two for the price of one arrangement?"

"Aw, you've been a bachelor too long! You know nothing about romance!"

"Maybe, but do they know?"

"Well, no...but it doesn't matter."

"Dangerous situation, Benjy boy, dangerous situation."

"Aw, Jimmy..."

"I'd rather be up there with my landing gear broke and my tank empty than be in your shoes, fella. I've seen cat fights before!"

"Jimmy, it isn't gonna be like that."

But the pilot was merciless. "Sure hate to see Paula hurt."

"What have you got against Miss Meyer anyway?"

The pilot's eyes narrowed. "She's rich."

"Well, so?"

"Rich women make terrible wives. They buy you, or you end up buying them. Stick with Paula. May not be as pretty, but she's a sure sight safer."

Ben laughed and shook his head. This was one time he'd not heed the pilot's advice. Jimmy knew about planes—Ben knew about girls.

Amherst

Kate Alcott was like a bright constellation with a collection of friends and admirers orbiting around her. She was likable in her confident and friendly way. Many other girls envied her position of popularity and power, but Katie Alcott hardly seemed to notice it. She was busy—too busy to pay much attention to her social zenith at the college. Yet the truth was, in a few short weeks, this newcomer on campus had created quite a stir. She pursued her academic life with as much zeal and energy as she did her social life. How could her father complain about the money she spent or curfew violations when she kept a top grade average? In this way, Kate Alcott trusted she held just a little power over her father.

The established sorority types on campus weren't quite certain how to take the rich girl from New Orleans. She could be blunt and provocative in her speech and manners, disarmingly generous and affable. She wasn't the beauty of the campus, but she possessed a certain charm and was the kind of girl you didn't leave your boyfriend alone with.

Kate was rarely alone outside her private dormroom. But one early spring morning, she managed to slip away from the dormitory unnoticed. She walked quickly to the piece of campus she had privately christened her "sanctuary," a small tree-covered lawn between the back of the cafeteria and the maintenance building—a spot few coeds had cause to notice. But strolling with a boyfriend one moonlit night, she had discovered it. It was secluded and quiet with only staff along the path. She had a favorite spreading live oak to sit under. She laid aside her hat, ran a hand carelessly through her curls, and sat chewing on the end of her pencil.

She loved school, the friends, the parties. She was convinced all along this was the place she was meant to be. So far it fulfilled all her expectations. But Kate Alcott possessed one fascination, one goal, one objective. Everything else was secondary. Everything else revolved around this in her mind. She wanted to win the journalism department's Clifford prize. She wanted to win it desperately. She had won a concession concerning it, but it was not hers. Not yet. And now, this unsettling rumor that had caused her to cancel a tennis game for time in her "sanctuary."

The Clifford prize was only open to an upperclassman, junior or senior. So it was for 35 years. Kate was a sophomore and did not want to wait to enter the competition next year. Outraged, she had stood up in journalism class and boldly denounced the injustice. She hadn't pouted or scolded or thrown a hysteric. Very calmly, logically, reasonably she had presented her appeal. Few in her class could disagree. She was right. It was unfair.

"...So sir, it seems to me good writing, excellent writing, is not created by, or should be limited to, a person's class ranking. That would create the appearance that skill is secondary to position in the school. Writing is a craft, a talent to be encouraged through equal and fair participation. The Clifford prize should be open to any student of Amherst."

The students around her clapped while the professor tugged at his gray fringe of beard. He liked the spunky sophomore and liked also her riotous red curls.

"I will present your appeal to the journalism officers, Miss Alcott."

Two days later the Clifford prize was opened to the collegiate community. An important first victory.

The topic of the essay was posted. Four weeks to write it, polish it, submit it. Kate continued her schedule of parties and social life without interruption. But late at night or early in the evening she labored at her little writing desk. She piled small mountains of paper and perfected every sentence till finally she presented the essay with her head held high and a smile on her lips.

Now rumor was circulating that from the 17 applicants, three were chosen for final consideration. Katherine Alcott and two others.

"But how did you hear this, Carol?" Kate demanded.

"Betty Jo is Professor Davies' student secretary. She saw the list on his desk. Your name was on it."

A finalist for the Clifford prize! But a mere finalist was not good enough. She could close her eyes and imagine the triumph of accepting the award, the excitement of going to Europe! What would her father say? Wouldn't he be as proud of her now as he was of Melanie's missionary fervor?

So Kate sat under the oak tree chewing her pencil and revolving a new question in her mind. How could she insure the prize? How could she eliminate the competition?

Nehi Field, Chicago

"So, what do you think about the war, Ben?"

Ben worked over a tire that had blown on landing while Jimmy took an afternoon nap curled up in the shade. Spotless in his linen suit, Marty Meyer sat on a crate nearby, peeling an orange. Ben was greasy and sweaty in a pair of stained trousers and undershirt, his suspenders hanging down off his shoulders. His hair was shaggy and in need of a cut. Regardless of such opposite lifestyles, seemingly symbolic in their attire, the two young men had forged a quick friendship. The friendly red-headed Marty Meyer was a congenial sort, more interested in adventure and thrills than learning the meat packing trade. Marty was profoundly grateful he was the youngest of two sons, and that his older brother Mike was his father's pride. He loved the business. So Marty hung around the Nehi Field at his leisure. Ben enjoyed the friendship, paying no attention to the disparity between them. Or in his dates with Ellie Meyer. She was as polished as her brother. And she was friendly, too.

"What'd you say?" Ben straightened up and tossed a tool aside.

"What do you think about the war?"

"I don't know. I guess just what I read in the papers." Ben shrugged. "It's a war."

"That's it?"

"Well, yeah. I feel sorry for French folks. It sounds like a lot of the fighting is on their soil, and they didn't even start the squabble."

"Read this," Marty said angrily as he thrust a paper into Ben's hands. "This should make your blood boil."

It was a front page story on the Chicago *Times,* but it could have been the front page of any paper across the country. Indeed, this horror story was circulating from London to Nairobi. The Germans had unleashed a vicious new weapon in the European war. Bullets and bayonets, shells and shrapnel were not enough. The arsenal must be added to. Ben quickly read the grisly story.

On a drive to the French city of Calais on the channel coast, now called the second battle of Ypres, the German army had attacked the defending French, British and Canadian forces in a novel way. Soldiers peering from the relative safety of their trenches found a greenish white mist floating toward them. It was eerily quiet, and almost ephemeral in its slow moving tide. Deceiving in its advance, deadly in its purpose, soon the front-line troops were gagging, gasping and vomiting. Some stumbled a few meters and pitched headlong into the trenches that instantly became their graves. Others managed to run back into their own lines and were blinded as a badge of war. Gas warfare had entered the arena of conflict. While the Germans did not press their advantage and gain much ground, they opened up new possibilities—a pandora's box of horror. Only quick action by British and Canadians sealed the breach and thwarted a German onrush. The city of Calais was saved at a terrible cost.

Ben handed back the paper without a word. Marty was pale and tense. "The Krauts are madmen and murderers!"

"Yeah," Ben agreed. "Sure sounds like it. Seems cowardly, this gas business."

Marty walked to the open hangar door. Ben followed him. Heat waves trembled across the airstrip. It was quiet. Butterflies darted above the grass, a hawk circled then disappeared. A war of such proportion and devastation seemed a planet away.

"You ever heard of the French foreign legion?" Marty finally asked.

"Sure. I knew a fella at school who quit to join them. You...thinkin' about that?"

"Yeah, I'm thinking on it. Can't quite get it out of my mind. The Germans are just...just wrong! And I..."

"You get hassled much...about being German?" Ben asked carefully.

"Not much. There's all my money, you know. Folks swallow their bigotry most of the time when they see a dollar sign. But I see them look at me and I know they're thinking, 'He's just another Kraut.' But I'm not! Good grief, I'm as much a red-blooded American as they are!"

"Sure you are, Marty," Ben soothed.

"So, I just feel sometimes this is one American of German heritage who'd like to go over there and fight alongside those poor Frenchies and kick the Krauts back across the Rhine where they belong!"

"What does your family think about—"

"They don't think anything right now, 'cause I keep it to myself. So don't say a word to Ellie, okay?"

"Sure."

"So, you like my kid sister, huh?" he asked as his humor returned.

"Yeah, she's a nice kid."

Marty laughed. He really did like the mechanic of Nehi Field.

New York

Broadway directors knew the strengths and weaknesses in their casts—actors and actresses were a temperamental lot, full of personal quirks. While audiences saw the blazing talents, the directors saw the sometimes shadowy side, the unvarnished private lives of the famous ones. They knew their skills—like perfect oratory, comedic timing or dramatic intensity. Or a great singing voice like Lilly O'Hara had. She was great in comedy, flawless in tragedy.

Directors knew whose marriage was stable and whose was shaky, who drew stimulus and solace from alcohol, and who, away from the bright lights, was really shy and withdrawn. Some had minor habits like wearing certain jewelry or colors for luck, or having particular flowers in the dressing room or a certain meal before opening night. Success allowed the dramatists the luxury of such eccentricities that minor players were not permitted. Directors knew they could not approach Lilly O'Hara five minutes before a performance—her dressing room was off limits. They knew she would not play cheap roles that compromised her 'religion' or rehearse or perform on Sundays. The same applied for

Thursday. She was immovable on these points, and because she was so popular, they did not challenge her.

Thursday mornings, Lilly spent as she pleased. She slept late, perhaps, then read for a few hours in the huge city library or strolled alone through a museum. By early afternoon she was at the mission house working with the choir and drama troupe she had formed. She had done this for years. All of her students were neighborhood children. This time with them was as much of a highlight in Lilly's week as was a Saturday night performance in the packed house of the Empire Theater.

This Thursday at the mission house she turned and found Karl waiting for her. She was shocked to see him so suddenly. She had not seen him in three months. He stood up as she approached, a jacket hung casually over his arm.

"Miss O'Hara." He bowed politely over her hand.

His calmness masked how glad he was to see her.

She took his hand and led him to the front hallway. It was deserted. She stretched up on her toes and kissed him on the cheek.

Finally, he smiled.

"You surprised me," she said cheerfully.

He nodded. "Yes."

They searched each other's face for some clue to feelings. Had anything changed in the months since they had seen each other? He was tired looking, drawn and pale. Lilly inwardly hurt for him.

"How 'bout dinner?" she asked easily. But she did not feel easy. Karl looked too tense and reserved.

"That would be nice."

"An omelette? My place?"

"Sounds…perfect, Lilly."

Lilly O'Hara's apartment was modest by the standards of a successful Broadway actress. It had a view that Lilly treasured—a statue of a lady far in the distance, barely discernible between the miles and the tall buildings. But a glimpse of a monument that had meant so much to the actress since she had first seen it 23 years ago.

She swept into the living room, tossing off her hat and kicking off her shoes. She plumped the sofa pillows for Karl.

"You sit, I'll make coffee."

"Don't go to much trouble. I am not so hungry."

"I make a great omelette. You won't be able to resist it!"

He could easily believe she could make a great omelette. He could easily believe she could make anything she said she could—and he would, could not resist her. This German diplomat with impeccable manners and decorum wanted nothing more in life than to make this beautiful woman his wife.

She slipped on an apron, calling from the kitchen. "So, how long do you have in New York?"

He hesitated as he stared at his hands. "I...have moved to New York, Lilly. I have an apartment here."

She came to the doorway. "You've moved here?"

He smiled and nodded. "I have an apartment near Central Park."

She came to sit before him. He took her hands.

"Are you pleased?" he asked gently.

"Yes. Are...you?"

His answer was a warm kiss on each palm. "Will you marry me, Miss O'Hara?"

It was the prerogative, indeed the duty of George St. John, to worry and fuss over his client's private life. An actress was really an illusion on stage, another person with different clothing, speech, motives, mannerisms. Off stage, a real person emerged—one that often required careful 'managing'. Lilly O'Hara was George St. John's only client, and her personal life typically afforded him little concern. Her success alone sustained and made him comfortable. Few in the theater could boast of such a magnanimous and talented client. But now St. John was worried. So worried, in fact, he did something he had never done before—he went to Valentino's Italian restaurant without Lilly. He had never gone there alone.

So when he entered the restaurant on a Thursday afternoon, Valentino looked up from his pasta board with alarm.

"Is she all right?" he asked quickly.

"Yes, yes, she's fine," St. John replied with annoyance. The big Italian became flustered too quickly. St. John must be calm for the two.

"She's not with you," Valentino continued in a worried tone.

St. John tossed down his hat and sunk wearily onto a stool.

"And you didn't come to dine," Valentino prodded.

"No, I certainly am not hungry. Tea, perhaps?"

Valentino quickly filled a cup. He set it before the manager, then took a stool beside him. His eyes were ferret-like. He was like a child, nervous and without tact. What was Lilly's manager doing here?

"If nothing is wrong with Miss O'Hara, then why are you here, Georgio?"

St. John did not like to be called Georgio. His scowl deepened. "I did not say nothing was wrong, did I?"

These two men were Lilly O'Hara's first New York friends when she came to the big city years earlier. They were different in their temperaments, yet completely alike in their paternal love and protection of the actress. George St. John had come because he knew only Valentino could understand his anxiety.

"So tell me!" Valentino exploded impatiently. "Tell me what brings you here without Lilly, in the middle of the day. You're giving my poor heart...palpitations!"

"Calm down, Valentino, calm down."

Valentino held his tongue but bit his nails.

"When was the last time you saw Miss O'Hara?" St. John questioned.

"Sunday night, of course."

"And was she alone?"

"Miss O'Hara is greatly loved, Georgio. She is never alone! She was with her German friend."

"Von Bulow..." St. John returned in a dry voice.

"She looked very happy," the Italian said eagerly. He lowered his voice suspiciously. "She was happy, wasn't she?"

St. John shrugged. "She may be too happy."

"What? Too happy? You talk in riddles, George St. John!"

"Have newspaper people been around here asking questions?"

"About Lilly? No."

The manager leaned forward. "The papers found out she's engaged."

Valentino's face reddened. "She has not said a word!"

"No, well, I had to pry it out of her. I'm sure she's waiting for the proper time to surprise you. But somehow the press got wind of it and there you are. Not exactly the kind of publicity I'd like for Miss O'Hara."

"There is a ring on her finger?" Valentino asked.

St. John shook his head. "Not yet. But she admitted Von Bulow asked her to marry him, and she has accepted." He took a long drink of tea. His voice was sorrowful. "And that's that."

Both men were silent a full minute.

"We don't like this, St. John?" Valentino asked in a near whisper.

"We aren't sure, but we think we don't like it because of him."

"Him...hmmm...he seems so considerate to Miss O'Hara. He has paid my pasta extravagant compliments. He must be a good man."

St. John turned away and rolled his eyes. "I don't mind her getting married. Why should I mind? Everyone has a right to marry, don't they? Of course, of course. So the theater loses a great talent, so I lose a job. So I become a pauper on the streets. What is that to a man of 65?"

"She would leave the stage?" Valentino whispered hoarsely. "No more Sunday dinners? Would she leave New York?"

"Of course! She might leave everything! She'd want to become a proper wife with...with...those babies and things," he said with distaste.

Valentino smiled broadly. "Now, now, Lilly would be a wonderful mother. What you call a, a natural for the part!" He poked the manager in the ribs. "You want every happiness for her, don't you?"

St. John shook his head angrily. "Valentino! You miss the point!"

Valentino's smile dropped instantly. "I do?"

"Yes, you do."

"What is the point, as you say?"

"The point is, is Karl Von Bulow the right husband for our Lilly?"

"Oh."

"Oh, Valentino? Oh? The man is German!"

"I am Italian!"

"We are not at war with Italy!"

"We? We are at war?"

"Valentino, the United States may not always be neutral about the war in Europe. If we did enter, do you think we would side with Germany? And Von Bulow is a German diplomat! Which side would he be on? Hmmm?"

"Oh, Miss O'Hara would be horrified to hear your suspicions!"

"I know," he replied flatly. "That is why I am talking to you." His voice dropped to a mumble. "A lot of good it's doing..." He turned to the Italian. "Do you like him? Do you think he will make her happy? Do you think he is the right man for Lilly?"

Valentino held up his hands, then placed a beefy arm around the manager's shoulders and squeezed. "Well, it seems it does not matter my opinion in this, or yours. It is, what does Miss O'Hara really think? Hmmm?"

Lilly O'Hara wakened to the soft sound of rainfall. She closed her eyes a moment because she so enjoyed the sound of rain—and to see if she could recapture her dream. But it was gone. Still, she smiled in the darkness. She laid there a moment longer, then slipped from her bed and went to stand at her bedroom window. Lilly watched the light rain falling on the city. She always thought such a rain as this beautified New York, somehow softened the harsh, angular lines of the city. And quieted the noise with a music all its own.

Lilly was a grown woman. She'd learned some stern realities as a young girl in New Orleans and from the often seamy side of theater life. She was always honest with herself. And standing there at her window, she honestly wished she was not sleeping alone. She wished she could waken a man with a kiss and invite him to the window to watch and listen to the rain. She was lonely tonight. And there was that dream.

She had not said Andy Alcott's name in years. She had not dreamed of him since those early days when she'd first met him. But tonight she had. Tonight he was there—so real as he walked along a stretch of beach with his arm around her. They sat on a hillock of sea grass and laughed. Then he grew quiet and still and—he cried. She could not understand what had hurt him so. All she could do was kiss his eyes and hold him.

Lilly smiled and shook her head. Why hadn't she dreamt of Karl? Karl was reality. Karl had asked her to be his wife. Karl would be the man she could wake up, the one with whom she could share the rain.

She crawled back in bed but did not fall back to sleep easily. She faced facts as she always did. She was tired of living alone, and sleeping alone, and making plans alone. Tired of having no one to share pain and pleasure with, tired of a life that revolved around her career on stage and its peripheral glory. She wasn't greedy, but she did want more. Karl could give her more—and she could give him herself.

New Orleans

With both his daughters away at school, Andy Alcott could spend even more time at his office. He could work longer into the evening. He could practically live in the second story office that fronted New Orleans' busy harbor. He could accept the interference of a few well-meaning friends like the Bentons and Virginia Hollins. The widow was finding it difficult to conduct a romance with a man so involved in his work. She wondered if marriage would change him—or if, in a way, she'd still be a widow.

He finished dictating several letters to his secretary. Only one remained now—a letter to Kate's dormitory matron.

Your daughter defies our curfew rules almost nightly. I cannot allow such violations to continue…

Andy tossed the letter aside. "Where's the paper, Collins?" he asked abruptly.

"Paper, sir?"

"The *New York Times,* remember?"

"Oh…oh, yes. It's on my desk. I'll go get it."

The secretary hurried to his outer office. Andy shook his head. This usually efficient man was so absentminded lately.

Collins returned with the paper. He might have wondered why his employer was suddenly subscribing to the eastern paper. But he didn't ask. "Here you are."

Andy took the paper and began to read. Collins stood waiting. Andy could hear his breathing. He lowered the paper.

"Yes?"

"Are we…uh, finished, sir?"

"I thought we were."

"Well, uh, actually there is that letter from Mrs. Hoover about Miss Katherine."

Andy laid the paper down reluctantly. "Yes?"

"Well, I, I think she is waiting to hear from you...about this problem."

"I don't know what to tell her," he replied, mildly exasperated. "Surely she's dealt with girls who stay out late before Katherine came along. Let her handle it." He ruffled the paper.

"Well, uh, I think she has tried, sir. She's appealing to you."

"I haven't had much success with making Kate follow the rules. She's appealing to the wrong person."

Andy tilted his head. When had his secretary become so concerned with his private life, or rather, his daughter's?

"You seem to know a lot about this, Collins."

The secretary colored. "Well, I would hate to see Miss Katherine expelled. You don't think they would do that, do you?"

Andy shrugged. "I don't know. Depends on how naughty she is."

"Yes, well, her grades aren't suffering. They're excellent—"

He stopped and his color deepened. Andy had not showed him a grade report. How could the secretary know? Andy stared at him, a slight smile on his face.

Collins gathered up his pens and paper. He straightened the desk, his chair while Andy watched him with some amusement.

"Yes, Kate's grades are good," he admitted.

"She...she would appreciate hearing you say that," he stumbled. Then he turned and hurried from the room.

Andy did not return immediately to the paper. Collins was a predictable man, rarely showing emotion, confining his conversations to Andy's profession. Now these sudden, unexpected comments about Kate's grades. And the man was so preoccupied lately...ever since he'd delivered Kate to her new campus.

Andy shook his head and thumbed through the paper, past international news, domestic news, business and finance, sports. The arts. He glanced up guiltily at the door. He did not want Virginia to come in suddenly. He flipped to the theater page as he had done ever since that Christmas evening dinner party when that name from his past was suddenly spoken. He could not seem to dismiss Clark Benton's words. 'Best voice I've ever heard.'

He felt silly ordering a New York paper then perusing it as if it could really offer something significant to his own life and future. But he wanted to see her name in print. Only twice had he encountered it so far. Once merely as the star of a new production, another time in a society news piece about a benefit concert "given by the lovely Lilly O'Hara." He hunted through the paper each day, chiding himself as he did so. Now he read, he scanned, he was about to toss the paper in the trash when he saw it. "Miss Lilly O'Hara, star of *High Jinks,* now playing at the Roxy is rumored to be engaged to Karl Von Bulow of the New York office of the

German embassy. Miss O'Hara will not comment, nor will her manager... This would be the first marriage for the talented and lovely actress..."

Andy Alcott slowly folded the paper.

St. Charles Park, New Orleans

He had not gone to this park in years. Other changes had come to the city, of course, but the old park was still the same—mellow, dignified, quiet. It was nearly deserted when Andy strolled in. Twilight was falling with cabbie horns and voices muted in the distance. He walked past the rose garden just coming into bloom. He found the stone bench he'd sat on two decades ago. He sat down tiredly. Past the fountain, across from his bench, was another bench. She had sat there. It was empty now.

He sighed deeply. He felt lonely. He knew why he'd come here, why he'd left work early. He'd come, pulled by Lilly O'Hara's name, like he could turn back to the past—and find some comfort. Why was he thinking so much of the actress lately? Why not Amy? Amy he had loved. Lilly was only a friend once—like a sister.

She had sat on the bench wearing a red dress. Of course red. Her face was heavily painted, and her shoulders sagged under some invisible weight. She was so young, so innocent looking despite the revealing red dress and heavy make-up. She'd watched the children wistfully, like she wanted to join them for a game.

Andy watched her, not lured by her beauty, but drawn by her pain. A woman hurrying past her had hurled some ugly taunt, and the shoulders sagged even more. Andy stood up then, decisive, and walked right up to her. He couldn't remember his first words, but he did remember she grew agitated at his approach. But instead of a proposition for her flesh, he offered her a question for her spirit.

'Do you know Jesus?'

That was the beginning for Lilly O'Hara and Andy Alcott. A friendship made quickly, then tested. They had parted, each on a course that did not seem to intersect with the other's at any point. Years passed—Amy, Melanie, Kate, Amy's death, years of work. Lilly struggling in New York, her career, success, Karl.

He sat on the bench for another hour or so thinking of his youth—and Amy. He thought of the years of failure with Kate. There in the twilight, the father cried.

New York

It was a difficult morning for George St. John. He'd overslept, spilled coffee on his shirt and stepped on the cat's tail. It was raining and his arthritis was bothering him. St. John did not like rain. It was too messy. It made people hurry and splash and get soggy. Coming up the slick back steps of the theater, he nearly lost his footing. And it would have been an ungraceful fall. He fumed as he stepped into the hallway where he shook out his overcoat and umbrella like a wet dog. This morning, the noise of the place grated on his nerves. Music, shouting, doors slamming. In the distance he heard Lilly laughing. Well, at least she was in a sunny humor. But then, when wasn't she?

"Good morning, St. John," a stage hand called as he hurried past.

"What's good about it?" the manager growled.

"Hey, everybody! St. John is out of his den! Be careful!"

Lilly emerged from the crowd, smiling and soothing. She patted his arm. "Georgie, you're scowling terribly!"

He wagged a warning finger in her face. "Don't start telling me how lovely rain is, Miss O'Hara!"

"You need a cup of coffee," she calmed.

"I need something stiffer."

She laughed as she led him down the hallway. She returned then to the stage with the cast and director, and George took a seat in the dimly lit first row. He sipped his coffee, mopped his face and finally calmed. Rehearsal was well under way when St. John realized someone had come to sit behind him. He did not bother to turn. But an unfamiliar voice spoke over his shoulder.

"George St. John?"

The manager turned slightly with annoyance.

"You are Miss O'Hara's manager?"

St. John turned all the way around in his seat. Not one, but two men sat behind him. They looked like bookends, he observed sourly, with their identical dark suits and hats and unsmiling, emotionless expressions.

"I am Miss O'Hara's manager," he replied in a clipped tone.

"We would like to speak with her."

"As you can obviously see, Miss O'Hara is busy with rehearsal."

Still no emotion, no moderation in the voice. "We need to speak with Miss O'Hara. We are with the United States State Department."

"Government men?" St. John blurted.

Both men nodded in unison.

"Why do you wish to see Miss O'Hara?"

They were silent. St. John sighed and stood up. The morning was getting worse. "I'll show you to Miss O'Hara's dressing room," he said impatiently.

He was flustered as he led Lilly from the stage.

"They wouldn't say what they wanted?" Lilly asked.

"Like the Sphinx and the brother of the Sphinx, those two!" St. John sputtered. "Lilly, I don't like this."

She smiled. "You worry too much. They probably just want my autograph, hmmm?"

The two men looked awkward and out of place in the extravagant dressing room. They made their introductions curtly.

St. John mopped his brow and paced the room nervously, interrupting and spouting. "Miss O'Hara is very busy, gentlemen."

The government man heartlessly ignored the manager. "We have some questions for you, Miss O'Hara."

"I'll be happy to answer your questions as well as I can," Lilly said with a smile.

"Do you know a gentleman named Karl Von Bulow, Miss O'Hara?"

St. John stiffened.

"Yes, I know Mr. Von Bulow."

"Can you tell us the nature of your relationship with him?"

"We are friends."

The two men cast each other a quick glance. "The papers suggest that you are more than friends."

Lilly did not like the phrasing but replied calmly, "You gentlemen should know you cannot trust the papers on everything."

Another exchanged look. "Miss O'Hara, you are aware that...your friend is employed by the German government?"

"Yes, I am aware of that."

"Have you ever met any of Mr. Von Bulow's associates with the embassy?"

"No."

"I really think these questions have kept Miss O'Hara away from her work long enough. Now—"

"Do you know why he has moved from Washington D.C. to New York City, Miss O'Hara?"

"No, I don't. I assumed it was connected with his work."

An eyebrow was raised. "You indicate you are a good friend and yet you have never met any of Von Bulow's associates or know why he has suddenly moved to New York." The bland voice was tinged with accusation now.

"I suppose I'm flattered to think he may have moved here because he loves...the theater. Now, gentlemen, I think it is time for fairness. Why are you questioning me about Mr. Von Bulow?"

"Miss O'Hara, there is a war in Europe. Which side do you favor?"

"Why do you ask?"

"A business or...marriage relationship with a German citizen would imply loyalty to Germany."

Lilly was no longer nervous. Now she was curious. These men were intent upon gaining information about the man she was engaged to marry. She must know why. She strolled about the room, keeping her voice casual.

"If I was loyal to the German government, why would that interest the State Department?"

"She didn't mean that!" St. John blurted.

She gave him a gentle and patient look.

"It would matter," came the evasive reply.

There was a silence in the room with no room for compromise.

"The State Department is interested in all German diplomats, Miss O'Hara. The Allied cause is of great concern for our government. You would do well to consider the risks friendships place your...loyalties in. Good day, Miss O'Hara."

St. John was in a ferment. He paced and ranted until he slumped into a chair with exhaustion. Lilly sat quietly, looking into space. She had given up trying to calm him.

"I don't like those men, Georgie."

"I don't like it at all. They were giving you a warning."

"But why?"

St. John leaned forward, his face flushed, his eyes beady.

"I think you'd better ask Mr. Von Bulow that, Miss O'Hara."

The ring was one of the most beautiful Lilly O'Hara had ever seen. An emerald surrounded by diamonds.

"An emerald is a beautiful stone, but nothing in comparison to your eyes, Lilly."

He gave her a huge bouquet of roses and a bottle of vintage wine. He looked so pleased, so humble, she did not have the heart to ask Karl Von Bulow, her fiance, why the American government was suddenly so interested in him. Not tonight, not when they were so happy with each other...

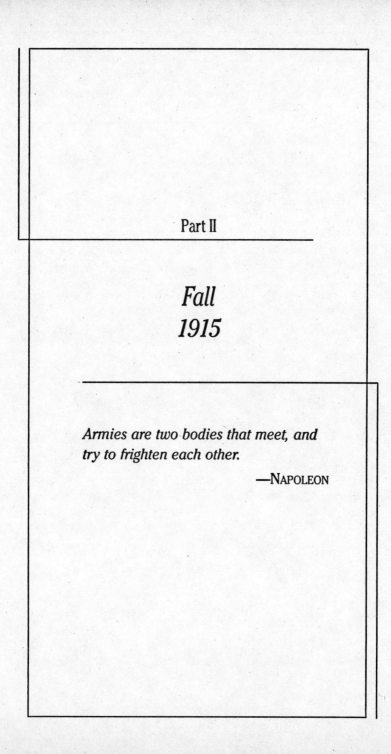

Part II

Fall 1915

Armies are two bodies that meet, and try to frighten each other.

—Napoleon

*A*s the armies across the western front became deadlocked, neither side gaining nor losing their lines of combat, it seemed natural for strategists to look to the navies to alter this balance of power. And too, embargoes were having a telling effect in Germany. While no extensive or detailed plan for warfare on the high seas was in place at the inception of the hostilities, the potential could no longer be ignored. The time had come—the seas must share with the land some of the burden of war.

Kinsale

A full moon was suspended in the clear Irish sky. A million scattered stars twinkled, and lights from the cottage windows mixed with them. Light poured out from the open pub doorways. The sound of an off-key piano playing and slightly slurred and sentimental singing, a dog barking, a horse and rider clip-clopping through the cobbled town square, a door slamming. The lone figure on the road that paralleled Kinsale heard it all—and heard nothing specific. Her mind was not on night sounds or the balmy springtime loveliness of the evening. The moon's brightness made her way along the rutted cart road without treachery or shadow. She walked as confidently as if the sun were at its zenith. She was a Kinsale girl, born and raised, and with no plans to depart this earth from any other spot. At 63 years old, she was well known by the inhabitants of the small fishing village, respected and liked by most. She had no need to feel threatened though it was just after midnight.

Who would ever trouble or raise a hand against Maggie Falconer? Not Kinsale folk, and a stranger with criminal designs would find a stout and fearless opponent. Strong and determined but with an equal leaven of gentleness and love. That was Maggie Falconer. She was walking home now after a four-hour labor and delivery some two miles down the road. Maggie Falconer was the Kinsale midwife—another factor in her undisputed affection and respect. Her place of honor was just below the village priest.

But her mind was not rejoicing as it usually did on the new Irish lass she had eased into the world, or the jubilant parents. She was thinking of her own child, or at least thinking of him indirectly. Four sons and one daughter—her man had passed away nearly 13 years earlier, and it was enough to challenge the strongest of mothers. And Maggie Falconer was that. She loved her children with a fierceness only rivaled by her daily commitment to praying for them. She felt it her obligation, her privilege to pray for them as much as it was to feed and clothe them while they were under her roof.

Although it caused remarks from her neighbors, Maggie Falconer was not overly concerned that not one of her four sons had yet married. Why should she be eager for the absence of their love and laughter from the Falconer cottage? And she would not hurry them into any marriage that was not the absolute best and the one the author of marriages had intended.

"There are four Irish lasses out there, with my son's names written on their hearts. The lads will find them in good time, sure," she would reply to her more vocal and gossipy neighbors.

The neighbors would wag their heads. Oh, the Falconer boys were good lads and that was the truth, but still at home? Maybe they didn't like girls. But that was absurd and made Maggie Falconer throw back her head and laugh when she heard it. Denny brought home a different girl nearly every week. Rory kept up a steady correspondence with a girl in Dublin he'd met on a school outing a year ago. That left Pierce and Padraic. Pierce might be the one to take in hand, might need a little maternal push, she admitted to herself. He was quiet and intense, concealing his emotions. His girl would have a task. But she was out there. Jen was too young but already had a line of suitors that kept her brothers busy. Padraic. Padraic, the townsfolk agreed, was the best looking of the Falconer lot. Congenial and hard working too. Should have been married ten years ago and made Maggie a grandmother.

Padraic was the child on her mind this moon-bathed night. He was showing uncustomary interest in Jen's Queenstown girlfriend, and Maggie Falconer was convinced this was not the girl with Padraic's name on her heart. A recent bit of information had given her cause for more than a little concern. Did she hold it quietly to herself and let her son find out in his own painful way, or did she tell him—and perhaps spare him?

The road curved and dipped slightly and she could see the dark shapes of the few outbuildings on her property. And the stone wall where a figure leaned casually. His sudden appearance did not startle her. She smiled.

Her voice was as brisk as her step. "You should have been in bed hours ago."

He uncrossed his arms and came forward with a smile, as well. "And should a good son go to bed when his ma is out and about in the late hours?" He put his arm around her. "But you're not the least tired are you, Ma? You're as lively as you were at six this mornin', and I'm about rubbed out."

"Aye, I could walk a mile or more on such a night as this. You know, bringin' a new life in always flits away my weariness. Perhaps I'll be bringin' in my own grandbabes in this decade. *Perhaps...*" They both laughed. "You'll be ready to leave in the morning?"

He nodded. "The *Bluebell* is ready, the boys are ready and you've filled the galley so we'll be off for four or five days. We'll get a catch, I can feel it. I'll miss seeing Jen when she's home."

They reached the gate to their cottage. Maggie stopped and faced him. Her hands were on her hips. He was waiting for her when he could have gone to bed like his younger brothers. She interpreted that as an answer. She would tell him.

" 'Tis the truth you'll not see your sister this time, but is it Jen you'll really miss seein', Paddy?"

Padraic scratched his head. "Well now, Ma—"

He stopped. She looked at him earnestly, with concern. All jesting was gone.

He took a deep breath. "I'd be sorry to miss visitin' with Anna," he admitted slowly. "I've come to enjoy our conversations. She's a bright lass."

" 'Tis true you're showing more enjoyment of her than any other girl I can recall in a long time," Maggie replied pointedly.

"I suppose you're right. She...interests me."

"Why?"

"Why? Well...Ma, don't you like her?"

Maggie Falconer had felt an unexplainable uneasiness toward Jen's new friend from the first weekend she had brought her home. She smiled wryly. And Padraic had reacted so irritably to the idea of Jen bringing home a girlfriend because he was worried about his brothers! The girl was guarded, that was one thing Maggie sensed. Friendly enough with the boys but tense and cool to her. As if they were two opponents circling each other in the ring.

Maggie was alarmed at her first feelings. It wasn't like her to make a quick and indeed, unfavorable judgment. She was typically more generous. But this girl...no, she couldn't explain it...until now perhaps.

They were silent a moment. Maggie did not pass through the gate but leaned against the wall. She faced the sea hammering below the cliffs. She could smell it and hear it—like an insistent knocking, not threatening, but never satisfied or quieted.

She looked at Padraic standing tall beside her—waiting for an explanation. "Padraic, I'd never mean to hurt you."

"Sure you wouldn't, Ma. Now what's the trouble with Anna?"

"You know, I hear things as I'm in and out with bringin' babes in. Most doesn't go past my lips. Most isn't worth the breath to repeat. But I was with the Flanigans three days ago. Sean's older brother was home."

"Dan."

"Aye, Dan. He's been in Queenstown for over a month or more working on something. He didn't want to tell me. I had to pull it out of him, the big lug. He was fearin' your wrath."

Padraic chuckled. "And why would Dan Flanigan be fearin' my wrath?"

"Because he knows you're takin' with the Queenstown lass. Everyone knows, Pad," she continued. "Ever since…"

The darkness concealed his blush. Was there no privacy in this village? Every action and word were examined for motives. It wasn't really a vindictive or ugly kind of nosiness, merely an amiable interest in *everything*. It had never really concerned him in the past—it was part and parcel of life in a small town. It never concerned him, until now. Caught in a sudden squall with a girl on board the *Bluebell* had proved impossible for the wagging tongues of Kinsale to ignore. He had always known it would be this way. When you courted a girl you courted her with a crowd of smiling, nodding Kinsale folk at your elbow.

"And what did Dan not want to tell you?" he asked with unmistakable crispness in his voice.

Maggie laid a hand on his arm. "Don't be angry with Dan, or—"

"His gossip?"

"Dan recognized her going into a tavern along the Queenstown harbor. She was with a skipper of the fleet there. He…he asked someone about her. He was told she goes there most every night…I don't know why Jen didn't know about this."

"Ma, Jen wouldn't know since she's in her room studying every night and at least not…not down on the waterfront. But…but you're assuming that what Dan said is true. He could have seen a lass that looked like Anna."

"Aye, but he asked her name."

"Sure and it looks like Dan Flanigan took great pleasure in this little detective work of his."

"Padraic, now don't be a mushhead! Dan has no reason to spite you."

"*If* it was Anna, then…then is that what troubles you about her?"

"I'll be honest with you, Padraic. I'd rather cut my own flesh than see you hurt. I don't trust the lass, I can't say why. She makes me uncomfortable. And now this. It seems to me there may be another…side to her life in Queenstown that she's neglected tellin' ya' in your conversations."

Padraic couldn't look at his Ma now. He felt oddly embarrassed, frustrated and confused. His arms were crossed and his chin set. He did not want to talk any longer.

"Paddy, don't be angry with me."

"I'm not angry, Ma."

She sighed and opened the gate. Now she felt tired.

"You coming?"

"I'll be in in awhile."

Queenstown

Padraic hitched a ride from Kinsale to Queenstown on a farm wagon to make the appointment on time. His brothers and Ma were suitably impressed with the fact that a member of the Falconer family was summoned, via the phone at the pub, to the admiralty office in Queenstown. Padraic was more curious than impressed. He'd planned to wear his work clothes since he was taking the *Bluebell* out on his return to Kinsale—after he answered everyone's questions of course. But Maggie Falconer was firm, assuming an imposing posture of authority though she was a full six inches shorter than her son. Hands on hips, slightly red-faced, she would broach no argument.

"You'll not be walkin' into the admiralty office smelling of fish and looking as if you've slept in your clothes with the cows for a month!"

"Seein' as I'm a fisherman, and they know it—"

She poked him in the chest. "Aye, and not to be confused with Joe Fitzgerald, will you?"

Padraic had to laugh. Joe was the local loaf, shabby but good-natured, content to sit in the sunshine rather than do an honest day's labor. Padraic lumbered up the stairs to bathe and change.

"We're not ashamed of being fisher folk are we, Ma?" he called over his shoulder.

She snorted. "Your da was the hardest working fisherman in the channel for 30 years and was ever sweet-smelling when he came to our—" She shook her head and reddened. "He was a gentleman."

Shaved and cleaned, he presented himself for her exacting inspection later. She smoothed his hair.

"And why are the Brits looking at the likes of us, son?"

Padraic glanced at his father's pocket watch and reached for his cap. "Won't know if I can't stop this primpin' and get on my way."

Her hand restrained him a moment at the door.

"Will you drop in and see Jen?"

But of course, that was not who she really meant—and they both knew it. "If I've a mind to," he answered shortly.

The admiralty office was small and unpretentious, occupied more by dusty books, ledgers and maps, than furniture and humans. With the bigger ships landing at Liverpool far more often than Queenstown, the staff was reduced to three. Even though it overlooked the cobbled town square with a glimmer of sparkling blue and the busy harbor, still Padraic could not imagine how a man could spend his daily eight hours of wage earning in a cubicle as this. The dignified, silver-haired Sir Coke, who would conduct the interview, measured Padraic with keen gray eyes as the fisherman took the chair offered. It was a direct, ferreting, yet impersonal scrutiny. Padraic was suddenly glad of his tidy countenance—though it wouldn't do to confess such to Ma.

"I will try to be succinct and frank with you, Mr. Falconer. I know you are a busy man as I am. Time forces me to be direct. What are your feelings concerning the present war in Europe?"

"Well, sir, it is an unfortunate thing to be sure. I'm not certain of all the particulars, but it appears Germany and Austria have acted very boldly, bitten off a big chew, you know, and men are losing their lives because of it."

"Then I would understand your position as pro-Ally?"

Padraic shifted in his chair. Where was this leading? "If I must take a...position, Sir Coke, then yes, it would be as you say."

"The admiralty in London is eager to establish patrols along the Irish coast."

"Patrols for what, sir?"

"Our information is very reliable. German submarines will become active in this channel. While the war seems stalemated along the western front, the kaiser seeks a new theater of attack. It is also true the Germans are feeling the effects of the embargoes and supplying of Allies by neutrals. They are confident in their navy to change these facts." He pushed a map across the desk for Padraic. "This channel is busy as you well know, offering many targets for submarines. Patrols must be formed to counter this threat."

"We don't see the British troop ships this far in, sir," Padraic pointed out.

"The Germans are interested in anything they perceive as sympathetic to the Allies."

"Including passenger ships like the White Lines and Cunard or fishing fleets or ferries or, or merchant cargo vessels?" Padraic asked incredulously.

"We can only hope they will...discriminate, Mr. Falconer." He leaned back to light his pipe. "But my personal opinion? Germany will take as many trophies as they can...war, you know."

Padraic was shocked. He knew the channel. He knew a hundred or more ships that plied the waters in trade and pleasure. Innocent and uninterested in the war for the most part. The channel would become a war zone! He looked up to find the man studying him intently.

"As you can understand, the German submarines in Irish waters can affect all of us."

"Aye, I can see that." Padraic nodded slowly.

"Our plan is simple. Patrols from Queenstown south along the coast. Reporting submarine activity, acting as escort under extreme situations. We want a patrol from Kinsale, and our inquiries of the local fishing fleet have led us to conclude you are the man we want to act as leader. Very simple."

Very simple, he had said with calm authority. Well, not so simple. Apparently he didn't know the intensity of anti-British feeling on the Emerald Isle now, that men might not like the idea of taking orders from the admiralty of a nation they had little respect and affection for. Still, they would be incensed by this invasion of their waters. Perhaps the patrols could keep the coastal waters quiet, the only raging battle the one between a shrewd mackerel and a sweating and determined Irish fisherman. But the man would have to be a mediator, a leader.

He sighed. "Aye, Sir Coke, Kinsale will sail."

He stepped from the office torn with the desire to hurry home and take the *Bluebell* out for its afternoon run, or to find Anna Ruebens. He hadn't seen her in weeks. And she was so often in his mind—more so now with his ma's troubling words to consider. He turned and headed for the business where she worked.

"Good morning, Anna."

She looked up from her desk, startled at the deep timbre of his voice, coloring and glancing at the other secretaries around her. They gawked at the plainly dressed man standing there smiling and confident. So typical of the aloof Miss Ruebens not to partake in office gossip and tell them she had such a handsome beau.

"Hello, Padraic. This is a surprise."

"Aye, I was in Queenstown and thought I'd…drop in."

She shifted nervously. "I…you can see I'm working."

"Thought perhaps I could take you to eat on your off hour."

She stood up and led him to the hallway. "I really don't think I can get away, Padraic, but thank you."

"Not eating?"

"No, just other plans."

Another secretary hurried past, calling over her shoulder and giving the fisherman a brief, teasing smile. "If you don't want to go, Anna, I'm available."

They both looked away embarrassed.

"Why are you in Queenstown, Padraic?" she asked after an awkward silence.

"Up to see Sir Coke."

"Sir Coke in the admiralty office?"

"The same. Well, do you think you might be coming down to Kinsale soon? With Jen, I mean."

It was hard work, this courting, Padraic decided. A man should only have to do it once. All night fishing on a choppy sea was easier than this!

He looked at her closely. She looked tired. His mother's words swept through his mind. They were tired eyes, yes, and eyes that did not reflect happiness.

She seemed to feel his scrutiny. Her face brightened and she squeezed his arm. "I don't care about those other plans, Padraic. I'd like to go to lunch with you."

Kinsale

Padraic Falconer stood silent while the group of men fussed and sputtered and argued around him. A few had stopped by the pub before the meeting; most would make a sojourn there when the meeting broke up. At various times, one would tap his pipe, then his fist on the table in an attempt to bring some organization to the Kinsale men. It was comically futile. All were angry. The sea, their sea, was meant for fishing, commerce, travel—and nothing more. The role it was now forced to play offended their sensibilities.

Padraic walked to the front door and stepped out into the night air. Forming the local fishing fleet into some semblance of a patrol might take all night. He sighed deeply and closed his eyes. If only closing one's eyes would make this ugliness go away. German submarines had been spotted in "his channel." They were stalking out there in the cold North Atlantic.

But Padraic wasn't thinking entirely of the menace in the channel. He was thinking of Anna, thinking of the meal they had shared in Queenstown, and the walk they'd taken afterwards. Her reserve and caution, her guarded looks, were gone when they left her place of work. She had become animated and eager, listening and laughing at his humor. She was interested in his visit with Sir Coke. Padraic was pleased the girl had a sharp mind. They had talked for over an hour about the problems of German submarines along the coast and what could be done.

"You're the perfect leader for the Kinsale patrol, Padraic. You know the water better than anyone."

He smiled in appreciation of her praise. "'Tis true it won't be easy. The lads are an independent lot."

"They may balk, but they'll listen to you. They respect you."

He rubbed his chin. "Well, I don't know about that."

"What does one do to spot an underwater vessel? Wouldn't that be like trying to see the mackerel under the *Bluebell?*"

"Aye, but Sir Coke has ideas from London. He said he would come to Kinsale and give us the information when we were organized."

"I'm sure it will be interesting work," she continued.

Padraic had smiled. "I'm just hoping those...big fish don't get as close to the *Bluebell* as one of my mackerel."

So here they were trying to organize. He would let them jaw awhile longer before he went in and firmly told them the time had come for action and muscle now, not mouth. But he had to let them harangue for a spell, it was the Irish way.

He looked out at the night landscape. Such a night of beauty was a pleasure to be shared...Anna. He knew so little about her. He must change that. Go to Queenstown more often and spend time with her as he had done a few days earlier. Then the unexplainable uncertainty, the hesitancy he felt about this young woman would float away like the wisp of clouds that variegated the dark heavens. There would be no doubts about her if only he could get to know her. In time, she'd explain her presence at the waterfront. Then there would be no uneasiness. Nothing to trouble him or his ma.

She was good at this. Who would suspect this friendly young woman of more than a liberal measure of interest and curiosity? So many lasses just babbled about fashion or gossip. How many really wanted to know the details of a man's daily work? It made men feel important—and it didn't hurt for her to thread her leading questions with comments such as, "How hard you work!" "You're very brave to sail out there with the danger of German subs underneath you!" "The Allies should be very proud of your efforts." In six weeks, Anna Ruebens knew as much concerning the Queenstown patrol as the local admiralty office did. She knew every ship, every skipper, when they sailed, their efforts at spotting subs. Learning about the amateur patrol from Kinsale was not difficult. No, in fact this entire service was painlessly and childishly simple. Enduring a few hours with talkative, affectionate sailors was enough to fill her letters to Captain Walther Schweiger, via a woman in Liverpool.

She had never had a close girlfriend before. Her life was spartan in close and healthy relationships. Alone and independent, she used people for her designs. To her, Jen Falconer was only a silly, impressionable and sometimes gullible girl. Of little value—except for her brothers.

She found the oldest Falconer son as interesting as he found her. He had not wanted to tease or flirt or be chummy, and somehow in his courtesy she felt his respect. It was the first time she could recall a man really respecting her. Well, perhaps cousin Walther. His disapproval at her Berlin scandal had been mild. In his own proper, aloof way, he'd forgiven her. So Marta Marie was a bit wayward.

Now she detected a slight change in Padraic's attentions. He was still attentive when she visited with Jen on an occasional weekend, but now that attention seemed more...personal. She wasn't certain how she felt about this—excited or flattered. She had never felt pretty or attractive. She liked Padraic well enough, but she hoped his foolishness wouldn't prove embarrassing, or jeopardize her plans.

In the big, noisy Falconer kitchen she sometimes looked up and found him watching her. He'd give her a faint smile, as if they shared something private, then turn away flustered. Perhaps the look went undetected by the rest of the brothers and Jen. But Anna knew Maggie Falconer missed nothing—not a sniffle, joke, or look. She was wary of the older woman—something about her cordial manner made the Queenstown girl cautious. A few times the German spy felt that Mrs. Falconer must know about the double life she led and her use of the Irish family. Surely, she was only biding her time before she exposed her, Anna thought bitterly. But the surprise would be on Mrs. Falconer. By then, Anna would be gone.

And if the big fisherman's heart was broken?

London

It glided over the channel, silent and ominous, yet ungraceful, almost comical in its dimensions. In daylight it would have cast a huge, sausage-like shadow. But it only visited England at night, a nocturnal creature, slipping between clouds, evading the moonlight. Tonight was perfect for its surreptitious sojourn; the sky was purple-black, heavy with layers of clouds that promised rain on the British coast by morning. While the weather was ideal for the ship, it created some strategic problems. The targets could be obscured by the same concealing clouds. So it sailed quietly above the sleeping English countryside like a giant, predatory bird.

Thomas Fleming had trouble sleeping in the humid summer nights of London. It made him long for the open, fresh air of the rural hamlet he had known most of his life. He theorized that the crime he read about in the morning papers or the raucous noise that sometimes filtered into his open window from the neighborhood, were in part the result of other Londoners restless from the night heat. But the quiet man did not turn to crime or gaiety in his insomnia. Often he sat on the darkened roof of the apartment building, hoping for a vagrant breeze to punctuate the stillness, until exhaustion overpowered him. He would think briefly of his students; so many had left now to become British soldiers.

"We must do our bit, Mr. Fleming," they would say cheerfully. Most would not come back.

He would think of Molly, missing the jokes they shared, missing the companionable silences. What was her daily life like on the war-divided continent? Was she meeting lots of soldiers...and forgetting Martin in Scotland? Was she as contented, indeed happy, as her frequent letters portrayed? She had written him immediately upon her arrival at Aunt Madeline's home in France. But convinced as he was of the rightness of Molly's presence there, it did little to assuage his loneliness for her. It reminded him of the pain those first years after her mother died.

He gazed up into the storm-painted sky now, the spires of London only slightly darker than the city's background. Then, fleetingly he saw it—quickly enough that he doubted his own tired eyesight. A dull flash of silver. He stood up and stared hard. There again! Just behind the edge of a cloud—large and sinister. The German Zeppelin had found London.

Like the other major players of the Great War, France too held the tragically ignorant optimism that this conflict with Germany could be decided in a matter of weeks. Many young men marched off to war thinking it a grand, and perhaps remotely cruel, adventure. A month or two away from home, returning by Christmas, the grape harvest at the latest. But by the autumn of 1914, the disappointing reality was evident for the people of France, both civilian and military. The illusion of a quick victory was shattered for Germans, as well.

Now the challenge fell to both nations of surviving in the absence of a significant portion of its male population. Every country who fought on one of the fronts had inadvertently created another theater of courage and fortitude. It was called the home front.

From her second-story bedroom window, Molly Fleming looked down on a garden. Untidy as it was, she found it lovely. Chestnut trees and lemon trees, old rose bushes, meandering ivy, scarlet delphinium, and sprawling lilac bushes were enclosed by a crumbling brick wall. A goldfish pond like a dusky mirror fringed with moss, a cream-colored wooden bench peeled and chipped—that was the garden, small and unpretentious. In its own way it was dignified and beautiful, rather like the entire property and the mistress who lived there.

Molly loved the view and was grateful her aunt had chosen this bedroom for her.

"I know it is not much, cherie, very plain and small. But..." She rolled her eyes at the ceiling and shrugged.

"Aunt Madeline! I love this room already!" Molly hurried to the window. "You don't know what my view in London was like!"

Past the walled garden, she could see the fields where flax was growing. On a sunny day, she could push open the shutters, and the breeze would bring her the scent of warm earth and hay and best of all, lilacs. She could close her eyes and imagine she was back in England with her father in their country cottage. But France was not England—from language to culture, to the very real presence of war. When she crossed the channel, she left behind academic discussions of the conflict. Landing at Le Havre, she encountered a country in the grip of a demanding master called war.

The trip from Le Havre to Amiens should be a half day's journey by train. Instead, it had taken nearly two days. But despite the inconvenience and discomfort, the crowds and uncertainty, Molly was not unduly bothered. The longer journey gave her more time to inspect the country—and prepare to meet her mother's older sister. She had not seen her since that bleak day the hearse had carried her mother to the old cemetery. It was her sixth birthday. Her aunt had looked dignified and unapproachable then in her black silk dress with the high collar. But just before she climbed into her carriage to return to France, she bent down and smiled into Molly's eyes. Molly had glimpsed tears in the warm brown eyes. That was over 15 years ago, and besides a birthday card each year and a handful of letters for her father, there had been no further contact.

Molly didn't fear this woman—certainly her father would not send her off to some dominating shrew! And Thomas Fleming had always spoken affectionately of his sister-in-law. Yet Molly did not know what to expect. Aunt Madeline was so firm in her letters about not leaving her home—even if a shell, courtesy of the kaiser's army, landed in her kitchen lettuce bed. Molly knew she must prepare for the possibility of a polite but unenthusiastic welcome.

Amiens was a city of history as so many French cities were—cities that had seen Roman, Prussian, and Celtic conquerors, cities paid tribute by extravagant kings and queens who toured their country in gilded carriages. Lying a little over 80 miles north of Paris, Amiens' boasts went beyond the lovely geography of fertile fields and the undulating Somme River at its doorstep. France's largest church, Cathedral Notre Dame was built in the heart of the city. Impressive and soaring above the other surrounding nondescript buildings, it was one of northern France's most important attractions. And now in the early summer of 1915, Amiens was unknowingly preparing for an even larger role in French history.

Molly was glad when she finally arrived at Amiens. She was eager for a bath and bed that did not sway. The small French villages of the countryside the train had spiraled through revealed little evidence of

the war, minor or grand, miles in the distance. Despite the train irregu-
larities, it was a trip of pastoral beauty. But that changed abruptly with
the wheezened halt of the train in Amiens. The German army had
tramped these streets in their resolute march to the French capital the
summer before, and the citizens had not forgotten. Their gratitude was
enormous for the French and Allied forces who pushed the kaiser's men
back across the Somme. Amiens had become a city of old men, women
and children—and the constant presence of military men in transport. It
was a quiet city, but for the rumble of artillery just past the horizon.

Molly decided to walk to her aunt's home. It was such a beautiful day,
and after being on a ship or train for what seemed like a week, she was
eager to walk.

"Monsieur, where is rue de lilac?" she asked the station master.

"Through the city, a little way into the country. A pretty street."

"And the lines? How far are they?"

He pulled at his eyebrows. "Perhaps 15, 20 miles, mademoiselle. Perhaps closer." He yawned, stretched and pointed to the east that was
hazy in the sunshine. "And the escadrille is stationed here. Not far from
the city." He winked and pulled at his suspenders.

"Escadrille?"

"Flyers." He stretched out his arms and glided in imitation.

"Oh, yes, I see."

"They come to town, a sociable lot, yes." He winked again and tilted
back his head to mimic drinking.

Molly had to laugh. The friendly French... "Yes, well...can you have
my bags sent round to rue de lilac?"

He nodded thoughtfully. "You are English."

"Yes, I...I've come to live with my aunt Madeline Chaumont for
awhile."

"You are Madame Chaumont's niece?"

"Yes."

"Ah...you have come to help her then! A kind lady your aunt, and to
be doing what she does at her age. Very kind, yes."

Molly hesitated. "What she's doing?"

The loquacious Frenchman had turned to another passenger, and forgotten the young English woman. So Molly began walking. She would
look closer at the city of brick streets when she was established. Still she
walked and looked with interest. This was her mother's childhood
home. She found the street easily. It was lined with ancient elms, a leafy
canopy and every home boasted a hedge of lilacs. Old two-story homes
with mellowed and peeling paint faced each other across the road in stoic
silence uncompromising of the challenges of war. Rue de lilac, no. 10 was
the last house at the end of the lane. It fronted a small, enclosed park.

Molly smiled. It looked positively British. Its courtyard was enclosed in a black iron fence. The house itself was faded rose, tiled, with many mullioned windows. A large, vivid green hedge bordered the street and made the house even more remote looking.

"What a lovely house," Molly murmured as she came to the gate. She drew a deep breath and approached the wine-colored door. It opened almost immediately at her knock, and she was face to face with Madeline Chaumont. She was in black silk. Was it the same dress? The face was more lined, the eyes that deep, penetrating brown.

"Bonjour, Aunt Madeline, I'm Molly."

The French woman studied Molly—a young woman in a dark skirt and white blouse, hat in one hand, a small leather bag in the other, eager eyes.

"Oui, you are Adela's daughter, Molly. You look as she did."

Molly shifted nervously under the direct gaze.

"You did get my father's last letter, that I was coming?"

"Non, I've had no letter from Thomas for months. The mails are uncertain as everything is these days."

"Oh, I...see..."

She glanced past her aunt's shoulder into the cool, shadowy hallway. Her aunt was standing so...so rigid and formal. Molly set her bag down carefully.

"Well, I suppose I should tell you what my father's letter said." She smiled weakly.

Still Madeline said nothing, her hand still on the door, her face completely masked of emotion.

"I—" Molly began, but somewhere behind her aunt a door was suddenly thrust open, then the sound of running feet, a scream and a squeal.

"Mademoiselle Chaumont! Madame Chaumont!" It was a boy of eight or nine. "Pierre has stolen my top! He's taken it out to the garden and won't give it back! Make him stop!"

"Rupert!"

The boy was instantly still and quiet, his eyes wide as he finally saw the young woman at the open door.

Molly looked into her aunt's face for an explanation. But the woman's face was impassive, a mask of perfect control.

"Will you step in, Molly? Rupert, I will deal with Pierre later. As you can see, I have a guest now. Marcel and Louise?"

"They are watching the mowers behind the garden, Madame."

"Then you will join them until I come for you."

The boy gave Molly one final, quick look from under his cap of dark hair.

Molly's aunt led her down the deeply carpeted hallway, past closed doors, to a small sitting room. It was pretty with its brocade wallpaper and floral chairs, enamel fireplace, vases of fresh-cut flowers, stacks of books and dull reprints by the masters in heavy gold-leaf frames. They sat opposite each other.

"This is a lovely room, Aunt Madeline," Molly ventured.

"They have not taken it from me, at least." The voice was bitter. Molly smoothed her skirt with a hand she willed not to tremble. She felt the penetrating eyes across from her would miss nothing.

"You have traveled a long way," the older woman said finally.

Molly nodded. "I left London three days ago." Already it seemed much longer and half a planet away.

"Then you would be very tired."

"A little perhaps." Molly drew a deep breath. "Aunt Madeline, I was counting on your receiving father's letter explaining my coming. He was concerned for you, with the reports of fighting so near Amiens. He, well we, thought I could be of some...help."

The silence stretched; it was so quiet Molly could hear a bee in flight outside the open window over her shoulder.

"What kind of help, Molly?" The voice held no warmth, but no edge, only the leaven of curiosity.

"Well, to help you around your home, and with shopping...and anything else you needed."

"That was kind of Thomas, but it wouldn't be a holiday for you here. There is a war on," she returned crisply and with a level look at the younger woman.

Molly Fleming was taken slightly by surprise at the tone. It would be so easy to take offense at the challenge. But she saw a flicker of something in the eyes of the older woman, and somehow she knew then.

"I came to help you, Aunt Madeline. War or not, I really want to help."

Madeline Chaumont leaned back against the wingback chair and closed her eyes. There in her aunt's vulnerable posture Molly could see the lines of graceful aging—and the stronger lines of fatigue. Molly waited in the stillness of the little parlor.

Finally her aunt resumed her dignified, very straight position. "I have children here, Molly." The tone contained a trace of warmth.

"Yes?"

"Northern France is occupied by the kaiser's servants. A most impossible situation. You can imagine what it has done to entire families, the innocent children. When this dreadful war began, it quickly became apparent to me I must do something beyond sacrificing my cream and eggs for the French army. Something for my fellow countrymen who were paying a greater price than I merely because they happened to live a few kilometers closer to Belgium than I! So there I was. What to do?" She shrugged. "A large house, well, it only seemed natural. These children are orphans, Molly. They have been smuggled out of the upper towns. Today I have four, last week I had twelve. Next week?"

"Twelve children! Are you alone here, Aunt Madeline? Besides the children?"

"Oui, I am alone," she replied with great dignity.

"But where do these children go?"

"There are connections farther south. The village priest arranges everything. Amiens is merely a temporary stop for them. They are smuggled about. Some, like Marcel and Rupert who are brothers, were smuggled out because their parents did not want them to suffer through the dangers of the occupation. For now, they have a family to return to." Her eyes traveled to the window. "My world was very well ordered one short year ago..."

And mine too, Molly smiled to herself. Work at Whitehall, the girls, Dad and evening tea, Martin. She felt a sensation she had never experienced before, as if a veil were suddenly pulled away, or the pieces of a puzzle fell into perfect place. This is why she was in France—even with the obvious risks and privations. No holiday, or girlish whim—a real purpose. Molly could not wait to write her father.

"So you cook and care for the children all by yourself."

Madeline avoided Molly's eyes but lifted her chin. "Oui, so far I have had the strength."

There was no appeal for sympathy. This woman was doing what her hands were given her to do.

"This is why you would not come to London," Molly continued.

Her aunt's head inclined slightly for an answer.

"I am here to share your work with the children, Aunt Madeline."

Still the regal tone. "I dared not hope..." she whispered.

And so, Molly Fleming's French adventure began.

Chapter 9

Peppercreek

◆ ◆ ◆ ◆ ◆◆

*S*he decided it was another true sign of aging when everyone gathered and made a big celebration of your birthday. In early April, when the old apple orchard was a redolent orchestra of pink and white blossoms, Sara Alcott turned 75. And so she asked her grandson David to wheel her to the middle of the orchard one morning.

"Want me to stay, Grandma Sara?" he asked.

She smiled and squeezed his hand. "No, David, thank you. Come back for me in an hour. I'd like to be alone awhile."

She gazed at the trees in the northwest corner. She had helped Ethan plant those trees, one for each anniversary, one for each child. So many years ago... She sighed. The orchard was older than she was—and more beautiful. She smiled wryly. Tomorrow they would hold a birthday celebration for her on the broad front porch of the white stone house. All her children would be there—Andy, Meg, Matthew and Daniel. And her grandchildren, Ben and David, Melanie and Kate, Emily and Elizabeth. A few friends from town. Another birthday without Ethan...

She turned and looked toward Pepper Creek though it flowed out of her sight. She could still remember a certain summer day as beautiful as this one when she and Ethan had walked through the orchard to the creek. He was home only one week from the war between the States, nervous, uncertain, almost shy—and sensitive about his empty sleeve. Then he opened up his heart.

"I can only hold you with one arm, Sara, but I will hold you with all my heart forever."

Sara enjoyed that she could speak aloud now with only the wind to hear her words. "And I have held you forever. Oh Ethan, how I do miss you!"

She was glad to be alone—her family would be alarmed at her emotions. Wasn't a grandmother too old to remember the tenderness and passion of romantic love?

She breathed deeply of the scented spring morning air and smiled. Even with missing Ethan, life was as beautiful as the old orchard. She pulled a book from beside her lap. She opened the cover.

War Remembrances by Ethan Alcott
A personal diary of the war years, 1860–1865

Ethan, who made no pretensions to writing skill, wanted to record those years he had served in the Union Army, then as a personal aide to President Abraham Lincoln.

"Maybe...maybe, our children will enjoy these stories, like a companion to their history text. Maybe they'll gain some wisdom...avoid some of the mistakes I made..."

He'd begun the project shortly after they were married. She pulled another book onto her lap: *Our Lives Together, Ethan and Sara Alcott.*

When the first baby came, Ethan began this second journal.

"We've been so blessed, Sara, we have to write it down so we don't forget. So *they* will know..."

She looked in the direction of the white-fenced plot, though like the creek, it was out of her view. A cross marked where Ethan lay.

"But you're not there, of course," she said aloud. "You're with Him, waiting for me..."

She closed the books and began to pray, for Ben, David, Melanie, Kate, Emily and Elizabeth. "So they will know..."

New Orleans

The young woman was asleep on the library sofa. She was up late unpacking and repacking, then with the tension and excitement of the last few weeks, she was exhausted. She had decided on a quick nap before she, her father, and older sister caught an evening train north. A middle-aged man stood watching her sleep. He felt guilty, but she was so still and quiet—she looked childlike and innocent and very lovely. He sighed. It was enough to waken her.

She sat up, hair tousled, cheeks flushed, rubbing her eyes. "Oh hello, Collins..." She yawned. "I fell asleep a minute." She stretched, then smiled. "Looking for Dad? He's over at Mrs. Hollins'. You know, a good-bye luncheon, or something." She rolled her eyes.

He had watched this woman since she was a child. He knew her misadventures and crimes. He knew her as well, and probably a bit better, than her own father. But lately, her presence disturbed him.

"Welcome home, Miss Katherine."

"Thank you."

"Has Miss Melanie arrived?"

"Yep, she's upstairs packing or something."

He shuffled.

"Did you need to leave a message for Dad?" Kate asked.

"Uh, no, uh, I actually...came to say congratulations on winning the Clifford prize, Miss Katherine."

Her eyes brightened and she smiled widely.

He pulled a bouquet of roses from behind his back. His normally placid face was beaming.

Kate hopped off the sofa. She wore a silky, floral lounge suit. Collins tried hard not to stare.

"Oh, Collins, how sweet of you!" She gathered up the flowers in her arms. "This is so kind of you…"

"Well, I hoped you'd be pleased…"

She lingered over the flowers, not looking at him. Only then, did her father's secretary see the touch of sadness in her smile.

"Miss Katherine, I…you did win the Clifford prize, didn't you? I know how badly you wanted to win."

She arranged the flowers in a vase. Yes, she had wanted to win the Clifford prize, very badly…

Finally, she faced him. Her voice was edgy. "Dad won't agree to my going to Europe. I'm surprised he hasn't told you."

"Well, he, we, usually confine our conversations to business, you see. But I do know he was pleased you had won this journalism award."

"Oh yes, he did seem happy enough," she conceded softly. "Said he was…proud. But who knows with Dad…"

Collins knew his boss, and his boss's daughter. He stayed prudently silent.

She plopped back on the sofa. It was quiet a full minute as Kate stared absently at a pillow.

"Your father doesn't want you to go to Europe?"

Her face became animated, her voice crisp again, as she pushed aside the pain. "Can you imagine? Here I've won the prize and my journalism department is fully expecting me to go on the trip to England. They've made all the arrangements, paid the expenses. But Dad says while we're at Peppercreek, he'll decide. He's going to discuss it with the other adults there. Just like he has a jury and I'm on trial!"

Collins raised a hand to interrupt, but Kate was not finished. "Should a girl of 18 be allowed to sail to Europe and be near a war zone? That is what he'll ask them. Who is the girl, they'll say, Melanie or *Katherine?* Then he will resurrect any of my past offenses and I'm sunk." She tossed a pillow aside and looked at the man who waited nervously in front of her. "He thinks I'm a child!"

"Oh, no, you're hardly a, a child," Collins managed with difficulty.

"Well, don't you see how mortifying and humiliating it will be if I have to turn down the prize after all I did?"

A blush came suddenly to her cheeks, and she stood up impatiently. She looked at him, smiled, and came to stand before him.

"Perhaps since you're with Dad so often...perhaps you might say something to him, explain how much this means to me." Her face clouded a moment. "I can't even get Melanie on my side this time. So..." Her slender finger ran up the lapel of his jacket. An artless Eve at work...Collins swallowed hard.

"Well, uh, uh, Miss Katherine, I—"

"Kate," she reminded sweetly.

"Kate, I just don't know that speaking to your father on this is just the thing to do. I—"

"You don't want to help me? You don't want me to go? I thought you believed in my talent! Your letters said so."

"I do, I do, of course. You got my letters then?"

"Yes, of course. Didn't I write you back?"

"Uh, no."

"Well, I'm sure I meant to. You know how busy I was with school and working on the essay."

"Yes, I know you were working hard." His voice was eager and shy. "But, but, you did like my letters, didn't you?"

She smiled. "Of course I did. They were fun. Now, Collins. Do you know what liner the school has reserved for me to sail on? Did Dad tell you?"

"No, I don't believe he mentioned it."

"Only the—"

"Ahem!"

Her father stood in the doorway, unsmiling. But Kate managed a smile anyway. She shrugged. "Thanks for the flowers, Collins." She gave him a quick kiss on the cheek and quickly brushed by her father.

Young Clark Benton whistled as he hurried up the walk to 2121 Old Manor. He felt like he had a prize in his pocket. Actually, he had a wonderful idea in his mind, and like the dutiful son he was, he already had his parents' approval. He was happy that Kate Alcott was home from school. That alone was enough to put him in a jovial mood. But that he could please her, give her something she really wanted, well, he could hardly contain himself.

He was shown into the library where he rocked back and forth on his toes in anticipation. Four months had passed since he'd seen the youngest Alcott daughter. He knew her well enough to know her months at school were not cloistered or lonely ones for her. He knew she had boyfriends waiting for her return. And that was fine. He would wait. He was cheerfully optimistic that someday young Kate would see past the crowd of boys—and see just him.

As much a campaign to win her was to win his mother to the idea of an Alcott/Benton alliance. Mother and son had never spoken directly to the issue, yet Clark knew his mother's feelings. Kate Alcott was too flighty, impulsive, headstrong and not a proper candidate for a Benton wife. But Clark saw things in Kate that his mother didn't. He entertained a vision that perhaps few people had for Kate. It started about four years ago when he was 17. Before, she was just a family friend, like a little sister—always into trouble. But one winter afternoon he found her alone in the Alcott library crying with a passion and brokenness he had never seen before. At first, in her embarrassment, she was haughty and rude. But Clark, ever good-natured, was unoffended. Finally she told him she'd had a terrible fight with her father.

"Over what?" he asked.

"Oh, just that Sophie Hamilton and I got into her father's liquor cabinet. We mixed a bunch of stuff together. It was awful! I was sick all night! And we spilled some scotch or something on the carpet and the Hamiltons are furious and called Dad...and, and said I...was a bad influence on Sophie and we can't see each other for an entire month!" She broke down in sobs. "Oh, Clark, why do I do these things! I'm always in...trouble!"

Clark boldly put his arm around her and let her cry on his shoulder. And that was the beginning. He had seen her generous, loyal, caring side dozens of times when no one else had. And then he began to see Kate Alcott in a different way. Some day she would grow up—and a part of her never would, and he would love her.

"'lo Clark!" she said brightly as she sailed in, towel-drying her hair.

"Gee, you look great, Kate!"

She stopped and gave him more than a cursory look. "Thank you kindly, Mr. Benton."

They eyed each other, Clark appreciatively, Kate carefully.

"Packing for Peppercreek?" he asked finally.

"All finished. What brings you here in the middle of the day away from your dungeon of cold facts and figures?"

"Well, you, of course."

She had the feminine courtesy to blush.

"I wanted to congratulate you on that prize you won at school."

"The Clifford prize, and thank you. So Dad told you about it."

"Yep, he's still at lunch with the folks and—"

"Mrs. Virginia Hollins," Kate interrupted in a flat voice.

"How come you don't like her? She seems nice enough to me."

"Would you want her for a mother?"

"Why would I want her for a mother when I have a mother?" he joked.

"Oh, Clark, the woman is...is insipid!"

"Insipid! How?"

Kate ignored him as she rearranged the vase of roses.

"Whose are these?" he asked as he came to stand beside her.

"Mine. Collins gave them to me. Sweet of him, huh?"

"I think he's sweet on you, Miss Alcott."

She rolled her eyes. "He's my dad's secretary."

"So?"

Her voice dropped slightly as she turned back to the flowers. "So he knows me too well to be sweet on me. Besides, I can always recognize when a man is…is infatuated with me."

"Oh you can? Hmm…"

"They're transparent! Well, I've got things to do so I can't play tennis with you this afternoon. We leave on the 7:00 train. Now—" She stopped. "You look like you've swallowed a great big secret!"

"You use three-dollar words, Miss Alcott, but you don't have a very good memory."

"What are you talking about?" she demanded with a smile.

"You forgot that my folks were supposed to go to Europe this summer."

"Yes, now I remember…"

"Well, Dad isn't going right now, so I am." He grabbed her hands. "Kate, Mother says she'll go now so we can go with you. You won't have to cross alone. She told your dad at lunch. Isn't it a great idea! And, well, I…thought of it."

"And what did my dear father say about this?"

"He said he'd think about it. But it looked like a yes to me."

She threw her arms around his neck and laughed. "Then you may be my hope, Mr. Benton!"

His arms went around her. Her hope—it was enough for now.

The Alcott family left New Orleans and boarded the train north. In two days they would arrive in Springfield, Illinois, where family would meet them and drive them to Peppercreek. The three began their journey wrapped in their own private thoughts. Melanie Alcott was thinking of her fiance, and the impending visit to her father's boyhood home—and of the tension between her younger sister and father. Well, the tension was not entirely confined between the two; Kate was obviously irritated with her also. She was frigidly polite, answering in monosyllables and a forced smile.

"I'm sorry, Kate, I just think Dad's right this time. You're only 18 and a trip to Europe with a war and everything. I just don't think it's wise."

"I'm almost 19!" Kate sounded disgusted. "You'd think I'm in bloomers the way you and Dad sound. I am very mature for my age!"

"Kate—"

"Do you want to hear some of the mature things I've done, Missionary Melanie? Shall I shock you?"

"Oh, Kate, please!"

"Your arguments are perfectly ridiculous, Melanie. I'm not going into a trench with shells buzzing around me. Do you think I'm that foolish?"

"Still, Kate..."

"The journalism department gave me the award for the best essay. They knew my age and I guess they've heard of the war! So, they have much more faith in me than my own family!"

"Kate, I know you worked hard for that prize and yours was the best paper, but—"

Kate's eyes narrowed. "To come home and get this treatment!"

"He hasn't said no yet!" Melanie exclaimed.

"He listens to you. You're the daughter he respects and you're voting no."

"Well..."

"You're jealous, Melanie Alcott! That's what it is!" And Kate stormed from the bedroom.

Melanie Alcott did not know how to soothe her stormy sister any better than her father did. So here they were heading for a family gathering, a time to celebrate, with this fuss between them. Melanie shook her head. What would happen at Peppercreek besides Grandma Sara's birthday?

Andy sat looking out the train window at a landscape that changed dramatically from hour to hour—from delta marshland with cypress to forest woodlands to croplands to a prairie of waving bluestem. The track paralleled the Mississippi, a winding river bisecting the country and bringing so many memories back to Andy. A love of ships and sailing began here years ago when he was a boy. But each click of the wheels along the track reminded him of the present, like the train that had obliterated Mississippi riverboat travel. He must think of today. Today was Peppercreek and his mother's birthday and his family. Today was Virginia Hollins in New Orleans waiting for him to return with a ring and a future together. And today was Katherine across from him looking at a magazine and occasionally sending him sullen glances.

Andy Alcott was an organized man who thought on each conflict in careful fashion. He smiled. Virginia would hardly care to be referred to as a conflict. Yet...Virginia Hollins was good for him. He could recognize that. She brought a wholeness to his life. She was a charming hostess, gracious, efficient, loyal. He glanced up at Kate. Perhaps she could bring some peace and stability to his relationship with his daughter. Was that possible?

Now this trip to Europe. It throbbed in his mind like a dull headache. He was proud of his daughter's success in journalism. He'd read the essay and was impressed. But reality superseded even an award or prize. It was too far, too dangerous, and she was too young. Her high spirited personality led her into mischief so often. He could imagine Kate flashing her inviting smile to some man, foolishly persuading him to take her across the channel for a closer look at the war. He suddenly thought of his secretary back in New Orleans. Collins knew about those curls and tempting smile. Andy knew the man was infatuated with his daughter, and it irritated him. She's irresponsible to toy with a man like Collins, never seeing she could build up his hopes then destroy them in a moment with a casual shrug of her shapely shoulders. Even with the Bentons, he didn't feel at ease with the idea.

He rubbed the back of his neck. No, she shouldn't go on this trip to Europe. But he knew how much she wanted it—and how she would despise him if he denied her. He sighed. Perhaps at Peppercreek he could find the courage to refuse her, or the peace to allow it.

"You don't trust me," Kate said abruptly, her voice untypically sad. "That's why you're not letting me go."

Andy leaned forward. He took her hand and was surprised when she didn't pull away. "Katherine, it isn't that. I...I told you. It's such a long way and you're young and there's a war. I don't feel it's safe for a young girl."

"Dorothy Benton is willing to go with me. That should satisfy you," Kate returned coldly.

"Well, I admit that helps, but—"

"Then you could go. That way you could keep your fatherly eye on me. You could keep me safe from any shipboard romances or falling in a shell hole or, or tumbling into the Thames!" Her voice rose with a shrill edge.

"I thought of that, but I'm in the middle of an important project right now. Men are waiting on me."

"Of course, work." She looked away from him to the window, pulling her hand away. "I understand, Dad. Perfectly."

The train glided through the darkness, bringing a father and his daughters closer to their destination—but no closer to each other.

"...Pa was thinking of the apple harvest and all I could think of was war. Each day was a race to town to see what the papers could tell me about it. I knew Pa was against it, worried, though he was silent. 'A house divided against itself cannot stand...' and Henri and Wyeth agreed with him. I felt like we'd created our own small armies, they on one side, me on the other, yet looking at the very same conflict. But I did go away. I left to join the Union Army, proud, eager, and sustained at later times only by the youthful hope I could show them their fears were in vain. It seemed a far off battle, in Virginia, and unconnected with my life in Peppercreek, Illinois. Yet somehow this feeling persisted that I was to be a part of it..."

Sara closed the volume carefully, then looked up at her two grandchildren with a smile.

"You're gonna give us a hook, then stop?" Ben asked incredulously.

Sara chuckled. "It isn't ready yet. I told you that, Benjamin."

"Oh no, she's using your full name, Ben. Watch out! When I hear 'Katherine,' I run for cover!"

The three laughed as they sat on the lawn under a shady elm. Laughter and noise came from the house, but these three had pulled away, drawn by a mutual affection and respect.

"It sure is good to be home." Ben sighed in contentment where he lay stretched out.

"I've been here two days and you've eaten more than I do in a week!" Kate prodded him with her foot.

"I don't eat anything but beans and biscuits up at Nehi. Can you blame me?"

"A shameless diet!" Sara interjected. "Have you flown in one of those dangerous aeroplanes?"

Ben rolled over and smiled up at her. "I've ridden as a passenger. It was great! Ever flown, Kate?"

She stretched lazily. "Nope." She looked toward the house where her father sat with his brothers and sister. "I'm still trying to be a passenger on an ocean liner! I haven't gotten very far on that, however."

An awkward silence then. Of course, everyone knew of Kate's prize—with the troubling string attached. Another battle line formed, the cousins all firmly and enthusiastically with Kate. She must go. It was the chance of a lifetime. The adults formed the opposition—reluctant and cautious, supporting Andy in his parental concerns. Except Grandma Sara. She, Kate noticed, sat silently with her hands folded while the controversy swirled around her. No one bothered to ask her opinion—perhaps assuming her age guaranteed a negative vote. But Kate couldn't help but wonder. She wanted to ask her boldly, but respect for the old woman softened and restrained her.

Sara reached out suddenly and laid her wrinkled, aged hand on the red-blonde head. Kate looked up, surprised. It had been...well, a long time since anyone had touched her with tenderness.

"Katherine, you look very much like your mother sitting here," Sara said softly. "She was a gentle, loving woman, your mother."

"I'm not a bit like her." Kate bristled but did not move away.

Sara's eyes filled. "How can you judge since you never knew her, granddaughter? You are precious in my sight and so much more in the Lord's."

Kate glanced nervously over at Ben who appeared to be sleeping, his cap pulled over his face. She did not know what to say. Her grandmother always seemed to tug at something in her heart, demand a softness from her.

"Why do you want to go to Europe beyond claiming it as a reward, Kate?"

Kate cleared her throat and looked directly into the deep blue eyes of this woman who so openly loved her. If she knew the truth, surely she would be filled with loathing for her granddaughter. "I want to see things, you know, new places. And I want to write about them," Kate said easily.

Sara stroked the young woman's head. "God has given you a gift, and I'm very proud of you."

Kate smiled though the tears spilled out. "I want to go on this trip to prove that I can do it, that I can be safe and responsible... You understand don't you, Grandma?"

"Yes, child, I do. I wanted to go from Peppercreek to Washington D.C. to become a nurse during the war. I was a girl only a little older than you. In my way, I wanted to prove something, too. And you heard what I read earlier about your grandfather. He had something to prove, also. Youth is like that..." Sara looked to the pasture, yellow-green and hazy in the sunshine. She saw with the vision of a prophet. "I think you'll go to Europe and, like my trip to the capitol and Ethan's in the army...He will use it to change your life!"

There were many pleasures to Andy Alcott in coming home to Peppercreek. Apples, riding, sleeping with the window open in his boyhood bedroom, walking along the creek. It was a place to draw deeply from peaceful reserves, to lean on family ties, to sit quietly and think. And one pleasure was to spend time alone with his younger sister, Meg. He was always closer to her than either of his brothers.

They had walked down the road from the house and he had told her everything, all about Virginia and his most recent conflict with Kate. Since they had a history of turbulence, it was nothing new to Meg. She listened in silence, offered few comments. Andy finally stopped walking and leaned against a fence post.

"Do you love Virginia, Andy?"

"I think I should...marry her."

"That is hardly the same thing, you know."

"Well, I think we could be good for each other. Certainly I could grow to love her in time."

"I cast a no vote," Meg said bluntly.

Andy laughed. "Meg! Come on!"

"I know you're lonely. Believe me, I understand that. I know you haven't loved since Amy. But you have to be with the right woman, not just one who's convenient."

"Good grief, you make me sound mercenary!"

"You know what I mean. You have to have that love that you can't explain, can't ignore, you feel like you'll die if you can't be with the person. You know."

His smile faded. "Like I had with Amy. You only get that kind of love once. I had mine."

"I'm sorry."

"Can you imagine loving another man as you've loved Barrett?"

"Well, no...I can't imagine that."

Andy turned away. The night sky was softened in moonlight, a beautiful night that could punctuate loneliness and longing. He turned back to his sister. "Okay, you've delivered your verdict on Mrs. Hollins. My daughter?"

Meg smiled. "She's a lot of rough edges, isn't she? She always has been."

He nodded. "But I've made a lot of those edges even sharper over the years, you know. I..."

"She has always been cool to me. I think it's because she knows you and I are close and she doesn't trust me. But she's a jewel underneath that roughness. Do you know that?"

"I do sometimes."

"I think you'd better let her go on that trip. It could...it could smooth those rough edges."

"Maybe a few of mine too..." he said quietly.

Even Kate could be forgiving and generous on Grandma Sara's birthday. She cast her father and older sister no dark glances. She smiled and laughed, and seemed to forget herself and enjoy those fleeting times of pleasure with her family.

Twelve Alcotts were assembled on the shady front porch on this special day. Pots of red geraniums and pink petunias were clustered around the white wicker furniture, and a long table was laid with fried chicken, potato salad and lemonade. A huge pink frosted cake sat proudly in the center. Beside it, a smaller table was piled with presents.

"I love presents!" Sara laughed.

But more, so much more, she loved the sight of her family gathered. When Andy stood and prayed for her, she heard the earnestness in his voice that she had heard when he was a boy of 12. Then, moments later, when it seemed appropriate, he went and stood before his daughter. The porch grew quiet. But Andy smiled as he pulled a small envelope from his pocket. "Here, Kate, this is for you."

Kate looked embarrassed as she opened the envelope. Sometimes her father was strangely unpredictable. Inside was a thin yellow slip of paper—a telegraph receipt from Cunard lines in New York. It confirmed cabin accommodations for Miss Katherine Alcott of New Orleans. Departure noon, May 1.

"Congratulations on the Clifford prize, Kate," Andy said.

"And three cheers, hip hip hurrah and bon voyage!" Ben shouted.

"What was your present to Grandma, Ben?" Emily asked her cousin later on the porch.

Sara patted the young girl. "You're all here; that's present enough."

"He spent it all on the bolgna queen, most likely—nothing left," David said as he pulled out his own empty pockets.

"Bolgna queen?" Kate laughed. "Who is that?"

"Miss Ellie Meyer of Chicago, heiress to the meat packing empire. Ben's snagged a wealthy one this time."

Ben was on his third plate of food and enjoying himself too much to mind his brother's teasing.

"I could have loaned you some money for a gift, Ben," cousin Elizabeth spoke up.

Ben held up his hands.

"You all leave Ben alone." Sara laughed.

"It's okay, Grandma. I'm used to David's jealousy. And they're all wrong. I do have a gift; it just isn't ready yet. Sorry."

"Ben, you know that doesn't matter to me."

"When? What is it?" Emily demanded.

Ben laughed. "You'll see it before we go, and you'll agree it was the best gift Grandma got!"

"Did Grandfather Ethan want to be a writer?" Kate asked her grandmother. It was their last time alone together before Kate returned to New Orleans.

Sara smiled. "Oh no, not in the sense that you want to write. He wanted to record...or capture things that were important in his life and in our lives together. He hoped, he prayed they would be helpful to generations of Alcotts after him."

Kate eyed the journal in her grandmother's lap. She wished she could take it home with her to read, to gain something from the past, though she wasn't certain what it was she was looking or hoping for.

Sara seemed to read her granddaughter's thoughts. "It isn't ready yet. I'm still reading them, adding a few of my own thoughts."

"But I can read them some day?" Kate asked eagerly.

"Yes, of course you can. I want you to very much." Sara leaned forward in her chair. "But I don't think you're quite ready."

"Not ready? Why not?"

Again that feeling of some future event in Kate's life challenging her swept over Sara Alcott.

"I can't explain it exactly. Except I'm trusting Him to tell me when you're ready."

It was the day they must all leave Peppercreek.

"Anybody seen Ben?" Andy asked. "We need to say goodbye."

David pointed to the garage by the barn. "He's in there workin' on Grandma's birthday present. Won't let anybody in."

They were all on the porch again. Sara was as eager as a little girl. Then the shed opened and Ben came out, beaming as he rode a new two seater bicycle up to the front porch. He wore a clean white shirt, bow tie and straw hat.

The family laughed and clapped. He had removed the second seat and constructed a wider, more secure seat for Sara. The pedals underneath were stationary.

He cleared his throat dramatically. "As you can see, a little added comfort." He pulled a lever and an umbrella rose over the second seat. "While riding in sunshine or caught in a sudden summer storm, you will be adequately protected." He came to the bottom of the steps and bowed deeply. "Mrs. Alcott, your bicycle awaits."

So at 75 Sara Alcott finally rode a bicycle. She loved her grandson even more for he had remembered her longing. He knew what so many often forgot—the temple was old and crumbling but the spirit inside was young and alive. It reminded her of something Ethan would have done. She remembered that golden afternoon long after it was past. They all did. They all remembered how Grandma Sara had giggled like a girl on her first bike ride. It was a day that would be treasured in Alcott family history—and the last time they would all be together.

Chapter 10

New York

♦ ♦ ♦ ♦ ♦

*L*illy was having trouble sleeping. Normally, she was tired enough to drop quickly into a sound sleep. Now she stared at the ceiling each night, for hours, then slipped into a shadowy, confusing world of dreams. Tonight she had dreamed of Andy Alcott again. But tonight it brought her no pleasure. Tonight she was in New Orleans singing in one of the city's largest churches when the men in the congregation suddenly stood up and began yelling at her—ugly things. They accused and condemned her. They shouted she had sold her body to them, and the people around her looked horrified. Even Valentino and St. John were there; they listened, then looked to her for a word. But she couldn't say anything—somehow her voice was frozen. Then they joined in the abuse.

Another man in the crowd stood up. He smiled and reached out his arms. It was Andy Alcott. But the crowd turned on him with a vengeful wrath. He struggled, but he couldn't reach her. He couldn't silence the crowd; he couldn't protect her.

She woke up perspiring and sobbing, then sat on the edge of her bed shaking. Never had a dream seemed so real! She flipped on her bedside lamp to steady herself.

"Jesus...please comfort me," she whispered hoarsely. "I'm afraid..."

Lilly O'Hara's past was like a haunt to her, one she thought of infrequently but one that remained real enough to terrify her in her dreams. For in her youth, she had sold her body in desperation to survive. It was a brief time in her past—it seemed the youth of another person entirely and so different from her life now. But it was there. And there were times she wondered if some man from those days would stand up in an audience where she performed on a New York stage to declare her sordid beginnings.

Thirty years ago Andy Alcott had saved her. But tonight he could not save her from her dreams, or reality. But there was a better savior for Lilly O'Hara. She reached for the small Bible on her bedside table.

New Orleans

"Dad, you really don't have to make this trip to New York with us. I mean, with Dorothy and Clark, I'll be fine. I—"

Andy held up his hand. "I want to go. I want to see you off safely."

She toyed with the pen set on his desk. "But you're so busy at work."

He leaned back eying her speculatively. In her crisp linen skirt and navy striped blouse, she looked pretty, young, and vulnerable...and flirtatious. He sighed to himself.

"Thank you for your concern, but I think I can manage a week off."

"Well, you could send Collins in your place if you needed to." She smiled and hopped off the edge of his desk. Her father was getting that...fatherly look. Time to clear out... "Since we leave in two days, I really do have more shopping to do. See you later."

But his voice stopped her. "Katherine, you have to stop doing that."

She whirled around, her arms crossed. "Doing what?"

"What you're doing to my secretary."

"And what exactly do you think I'm *doing* to your secretary?"

"You know exactly what I'm talking about. You're too old to play these games. You're flirting with the man, leading him on, like—"

"Leading him on...oh, Dad, really, that sounds so, so..."

She avoided his eyes by studying her nails. He came from around his desk. "Collins is a fine man. You have him muddled and confused and imagining you might be serious about him."

"Oh, you're silly! I think you are the one imagining things."

"Kate—"

"Uh, Mr. Alcott, sir?" Collins stood in the open doorway. He carried a stack of files. He was pale, his eyes riveted on his employer. "I, I have those records you wanted."

"Thank you. Just put them on my desk here."

With one scathing look at his daughter, Andy left the room.

Kate sighed. It wasn't wise to antagonize her father now, with the trip up ahead. Her father was a man of his word. He said she could go to Europe and he would not go back on that. But he might include some foolish, totally fatherish restriction—like dragging proper Melanie along.

Collins arranged the files in precise stacks, adjusting each corner to just the right angle. Kate watched him a moment with amusement.

"Collins?"

The man turned reluctantly.

Kate's voice was soft. "Collins, did you hear what my father was saying?"

He could have saved them both some embarrassment by lying. But he was a man of integrity. His voice was low, his head hanging.

"Yes, Miss Katherine, I did."

"Everything?"

"Well, yes. I'm sorry. I know eavesdropping is abominable. I don't know what came over me."

"Oh, I understand. You heard your name."

He shifted uncomfortably.

"My father, well, he has silly, old-fashioned ideas. He imagines things. You haven't misunderstood our friendship have you? We've known each other for years!"

He swallowed hard. "Yes, for years."

"We'll always be friends, won't we?"

"Yes, of course, friends."

She patted his arm happily. "Well, I have a lunch date, better run."

He seemed not to want her to leave. "It's exciting for you, I'm sure, sailing to London."

"I can hardly sleep at night. To see New York!"

"There is a lot to see there. Will you take in a Broadway play?"

"A play? Well, I don't know. We'll only be there two days before I sail. A pitiful amount of time to try to see a city like New York."

Collins sighed. "I thought with your father's interest, he'd be sure to take you."

Kate laughed. "His interest? In theater? Since when?"

"Well, I, I only thought..." Collins became noticeably flustered.

Kate pounced. "Collins, why do you think Dad has an interest in theater?"

"Well, simply that he's been ordering the New York paper the last few months and discarding everything but the theater page. But I'm sure there is a simple reason, or no reason or..."

"That's very interesting. Very."

Collins looked alarmed. "Perhaps I shouldn't have spoken. Your father might—"

Kate smiled roguishly and laid a finger across his lips. "I won't say a word. Dad's secret is safe."

Collins was sweating now as Kate stood close to him. He cleared his throat and clutched his hands behind him. "Miss Katherine, I wonder, if before you go, I might ask you a favor...since it will be months and...."

"Of course. What would you like?"

"Well, remember when I brought you the flowers some weeks ago?"

"Yes, they were lovely."

"You, kissed me on the cheek that day. Very briefly and, and friendly."

Kate Alcott saw Albert Collins then. She saw him shy and hesitating. "You are a dear man, Collins," she said as she kissed him.

They left New Orleans two days later—Andy and Kate, Clark Jr. and Dorothy Benton. Clark declared Kate's small mountain of steamer trunks would certainly sink the liner.

"A woman must dress to travel, Clark," his mother defended. "And no references to sinking, please."

"Kate will be stylish," Andy grinned. He had put aside his fears and gloom. He wanted nothing but happy memories with his youngest daughter before her big trip.

"Dorothy, nothing can sink our ship," Kate declared stoutly. "She's too fast and too big and—"

Dorothy leaned forward to clutch Kate's hand. "Don't say that. I do wish there was a train from New York to London! Floating palace or not, there's so much water to drown in!"

They all laughed. Dorothy Benton was experiencing a case of pre-sailing jitters.

"Dorothy, you know I was a seaman as a young man. The oceans are generally very kind. I don't think you should worry," Andy consoled.

"It's an adventure." Kate squeezed Dorothy's hand.

"I plan to sleep in my life vest," the older woman insisted.

"Aw, Mom." Clark shook his head.

"Times are different even if the oceans are the same, Andy," she continued, ignoring her son.

"Ships are much safer now though. Steel hulls and radio and—"

"But there's a war on," she reminded them quietly.

New York

Sunday night was the highlight of Valentino's week—the night Lilly O'Hara came to his restaurant. If she came more than once, he was ecstatic—and tended to babble. He would navigate between kitchen and dining room with tornado-like energy.

"Watch the sauce!"

"Yes, that is Lilly O'Hara, the best of Broadway. Don't stare!"

"More water? Tea? What is your pleasure tonight, Miss O'Hara?"

"Clean off that table, you lout!"

"The bread is burning!"

"Another slice, my dear Miss O'Hara?"

If she came alone, which was seldom, he was in a state of total delight to have her all to himself. He would prepare her plate personally, serve her with utmost dignity, then sink into the seat opposite to watch her eat. She would smile a lot, relate the events of her day and ask about his daughters. She seemed to enjoy his zealous attention. But if she came in with friends or her manager he assumed correct and formal behavior. He would watch her nervously and covertly. She would laugh with her friends, then look up to catch his eye and wink. Invariably, he would blow her a kiss and wave.

Lilly was not alone this mellow spring evening. She was with her German friend—the one St. John was so agitated about. Valentino seated them, chatted briefly and with great restraint, took their order, then hurried across the room to polish glasses with unusual vigor.

She was with the fellow who'd given her a ring. Marriage. Valentino sighed. Would Miss O'Hara leave New York? But tonight they did not appear so much like happy lovers over a romantic dinner. The German, Valentino decided, looked sad in his eyes. He toyed with his silverware and hardly looked at the lovely actress across the table. The actress, Valentino viewed with growing alarm, looked pale and unsmiling. She would lean forward to hear the German's words. Twice she took his hand as if trying to comfort him. And Valentino was disappointed—Lilly had not winked at him the entire evening.

Her visit to the restaurant ended abruptly. They rose from the table after barely touching their meal. Valentino could hardly have been more horrified unless she had thrown down her fork and declared his pasta uneatable! The Italian was at their side instantly. "Something is wrong? The sauce? Has it grown cold? Oh my poor pasta!"

Finally Lilly gave him the first smile of the evening.

"The food was perfect, Valentino, as it always is. We just weren't as hungry as we thought we were."

She gave him a reassuring kiss on his expansive pink cheek.

"Not hungry?" It was difficult for the Italian to fathom.

"Thank you, Valentino, and goodbye," the German said with a dignified bow. "I have enjoyed your creations greatly."

It sounded final. He looked quickly at the pale Lilly. Yes, he saw sadness in her eyes as well. This German was hurting her! Valentino opened his mouth to speak.

"I'll see you Sunday night, Valentino. I'll be ready for the minestrone." She waved gaily. "Goodnight!"

Then they were gone.

In the cab, Karl Von Bulow sat rigidly looking forward. Lilly leaned back in the leather seat and closed her eyes. It all happened too fast, too suddenly. She was very busy the past month with her work which left her little time beyond Sunday afternoons to see Karl. But he was occupied with his own affairs. Now, now this. During most of their visits lately he was withdrawn and subdued. But a few times he'd relaxed and let Lilly O'Hara infect him with her vibrancy—like a splash of color on a gray canvas. The night he had slipped a ring on her finger he had forcibly pushed work from his mind. That night had belonged to him and his dreams.

Then early this evening he looked like he was crumbling—and she was powerless to help him.

"Lilly…I can't keep this…it is slowly killing me."

"Tell me, tell me what is happening to you," she pleaded with tears already in her eyes.

And so he had. It was a strange narrative of a good man caught in a web of evil. The things he had worked for, the principles he held were being snatched from him. And a far different set of designs were given him in their place.

"Your President Wilson has tried valiantly to keep America neutral in thought and deed toward the war. There are some in my government who have seen that. Still, others are…angry, very angry."

"Angry at Wilson? Why?"

"He allows Americans to supply the Allies—munitions, food, clothing. But they are not selling to Berlin. They have appealed, but it has not stopped."

He paced the living room of Lilly's apartment.

"My position for so many years has been strictly diplomacy between Washington and Berlin. We have had times of, of disagreement in the past, but these problems we have smoothed out. We still could work, at least speak together. But now…" He lifted his hands in appeal.

"And now that has changed?"

"Lilly, I have always followed what my employer has told me to do. Yes, that was my life's work. If they say go to New York and buy an apartment, I go. If they say sell oranges on the corner of 15th Street, I sell oranges."

"I'm certain you have been the best diplomat they have had," Lilly encouraged. "Two state department men came to see me a few weeks ago. They asked me about you. Does this have anything to do with what you are trying to tell me?"

He stopped pacing and looked at her with agony in his eyes. "I am sorry that you were bothered with this. They suspect all government officials now. Yes, they suspect me."

"Why?"

He slipped to the sofa beside her and began to cry.

"Because…because they know Berlin has run out of patience with this supplying the Allies. I was sent to your city, to no longer serve between our two countries with peace, but with, with revenge. I must act treacherously with yours, to be faithful to mine." He took her hands in his to steady himself. "There are German spies in this city. I, I have met with them. Many are working along the waterfront to watch the great ships that go to Europe. They are to sabotage these ships in every possible way. They are to find useful information for Berlin. They are to take their orders from…me."

"Oh Karl, I…I am so sorry."

"Do you know what they want me to do now? In my apartment safe there is a serum. My...agents are to slip along the waterfront where they are loading for Europe. They are to...to inoculate the horses with this serum. By the time the ship lands in France or Britain there will be a cargo of dead horses. Then there will be explosions." He stood up again. "I did not agree with my country when they went into this war, but I tried to serve them. Now?" He perched in front of her. "Lilly, I should never have told you these things...but I thought I would die if I did not...I could not go and not tell you, not look into your eyes and hope with my life that you would understand."

"You must go?" Lilly asked in a broken voice.

"Lilly, I cannot do these things. I will not!" He drew a deep breath. "I must leave. I must leave you. I have been recalled to Berlin. Please, don't cry. Please, I would never mean to make you cry. But you see I must go. I have my aged mother and sister in Germany to think of...I cannot leave them."

The cab pulled up in front of Lilly's apartment, but Karl did not move. Lilly felt numb with shock. She was engaged that morning when she lay in bed. She had stretched out her arm lazily to admire the ring. Now...wordlessly she slipped it off and into Karl's pocket.

He could not look at her. He could not say goodbye yet. "There is a small dinner party Saturday evening. It was planned weeks ago and I cannot change it. Will you come? I can say goodbye there among others, not...here. You could sing perhaps if you would."

She nodded. "I'll come, Karl...and sing."

If George St. John was concerned with Lilly's involvement with the German at the beginning, it was nothing compared to his anxiety now. Even the director of *The Beauty Shop* noticed. Her performances during rehearsal were flawless, but she moved mechanically, without the vibrancy she was known for. She was quieter, withdrawn. Something was very, very wrong. With one swift, hawklike glance at her finger, he saw that the diamond was gone. Von Bulow. St. John gritted his teeth.

She was painting her nails when his frustration boiled over.

"Miss O'Hara, you are obviously sorrowing. Is there nothing I can do?"

She steadied her voice. "Mr. Von Bulow and I are no longer engaged, Georgie. He must return to Berlin."

St. John masked his relief. He came to stand behind her, patting her shoulder awkwardly. "Perhaps it is better this way. You won't have to learn German," he added feebly.

"Perhaps..." She grabbed his hand and began to cry.

St. John was horrified. Lilly weeping, no, sobbing!

"Miss O'Hara, now, now..."

"Aren't you ever lonely, Georgie?...Desperately lonely?"

He blotted her eyes and cheeks. "Well, of course, I get lonely, but I manage, you know..."

She searched his face. "Well, I don't want to manage anymore. I don't want to live alone! I want a husband and children. I..." She broke off crying.

"Oh, this German fellow wasn't for you. He hurt you! That proves he was unfit!"

"Why wasn't he for me? Tell me why?"

"Well, think of this. He would be wanting German food all the time, and...well, you do make a lovely omelette, but..." He spread his hands out.

"Oh, Georgie." She managed a weak laugh.

"And if there were children he would want them to speak German and you would want English, of course. And not to mention he would want you to leave New York and all your friends and I have heard Germany is very cold. So. No, it could have been difficult."

Not to mention war loyalties, the manager thought grimly.

"Georgie, you are delightfully ridiculous sometimes," Lilly said with the beginnings of a smile.

"Don't be lonely, Miss O'Hara. So many love you!"

She shook her head sadly. "So many, Georgie, except one..."

When St. John retreated to his fashionable apartment that evening, he was not thinking over the business side of his day. He was thinking about the woman he had known for years—the woman with the stunning voice, luminous green eyes and vivid red hair. She was lonely. He must do something.

Emden, Germany

The weather was perfect for launching—as sinister as the purpose of the gray submarine tied by steel cables to the dock. Cold, drippy, windless, the ocean and sky blended in melted gray. Wraiths of fog shrouded the visibility, still the ocean seemed flat calm. Of course, that mattered little to Walther Schweiger. Once his vessel slipped quietly below the water's surface, he was in another world void of unpredictable weather. Choppy currents were a concern, but for launching and beginning a voyage, it was a minor consideration. He did, however, prefer bright sunshine for launching. A saboteur or spy could work unseen under the cloak of fog.

Schweiger stood on the dock breathing deeply of the moist, crisp air. He considered it a tonic against the ship's fetid atmosphere that he would have to endure for two weeks. Forty-two men filed from the barracks down the wet dock and onto the sub, each wearing a heavy woolen jacket with its collar turned up against the chill. They did not look much different from their 'brothers' who filed into trenches all along the western front. There was little noise beyond the creaking of the submarine against the lines—no man spoke. None called a cheery greeting to the captain. They knew he did not like such familiarity. Captain Schweiger believed a launching a solemn affair.

In such limited space they each carried only one small bag of personal belongings. One man carried the precious gramophone. Another crewman carried a blanket-wrapped bundle under each arm. He had hissed a stern 'Quiet!' as he left the barracks. The sub's two dachshunds were brought on board each patrol without ceremony, official permission or objection. They were the resident pets of the U20. It was one of those leniencies of Schweiger which bonded his crew to him. The last man in line swung past and picked up the captain's personal satchel. The captain carried his leather case of classical records. He trusted no one else with them.

He shook hands briskly with his commander who stood beside him.

"For the Fatherland!" the commander said in German before he returned to the warmth of his office.

Walther tapped his breast pocket and felt his written orders resting there. Against Marta Marie's latest letter. He knew the great Cunard liners of Great Britain were slipping up St. George's channel to Liverpool unmolested and without escort destroyers. Arrogance of those Englishmen—Walther smiled to himself. Ferrying passengers, and troops, and munitions for the Allies—thinking themselves indestructible and immune from attack. He spoke to a crewman waiting for him on the bridge.

"All in order?" he asked crisply.

"Yes, Captain."

Schweiger glanced at the sea that was muffled and veiled. "And our...passengers?"

"The ladies are resting comfortably, sir," he said with a wide grin. But the captain did not return the smile.

Seven torpedoes which the crew had affectionately named, lay in their racks—ready to serve Germany if needed.

Five minutes later, spray swept over the narrow deck and conning tower of the gray-bodied sub. The German national anthem played on the gramophone. The U20 and Walther Schweiger had an important appointment...with history.

New York

The Grand Astoria Hotel was as posh and impressive as Kate Alcott had hoped for. A grudging gratitude formed in her heart for her father—he was trying to give her a special time. She was the proverbial wide-eyed country girl who had come to the country's largest, most spectacular and cosmopolitan city. Maybe she would sleep after they sailed but only after she had seen every inch of the mammoth liner.

This was New York! From the moment the train pulled into Grand Central, she did not stop pointing, chatting or pulling her father or Clark to another sight.

"You sure you won't come to dinner with us, Dad?"

He smiled wearily. "I'm just going to order something up here, then turn in. I'm pretty worn out."

She twirled around in front of a full length mirror. "Well, I'm not! I could stay up all night!"

"Kate, you sail day after tomorrow. You keep this speed up and you'll be exhausted. That's no way to start a trip."

He was shifting into that fussing tone. She had to divert his attention. "How 'bout a play tomorrow night? Then dinner. Just you and me."

"I doubt we could get tickets to anything decent this late," he returned absently.

"You could...if you really tried." She smiled.

"You want to see one that badly, huh?"

She looked persuasive perched on the low table. She wore a dress of creamy yellow and a string of pearls. Her excitement had highlighted her cheeks and eyes.

"I thought *you* would want to see one," she said pointedly.

"A play? I'm hardly a theater buff."

"Well..."

"Well what?"

"Well, only that a certain actress of your former acquaintance stars in *The Beauty Shop* at the Empire each evening at 8:00."

He closed his eyes, laughing. "Oh, Katherine."

She punched him playfully. "You are going to look her up, aren't you?"

"Why should I?"

"You're old friends!"

"Kate, that was years ago. I'm sure she's forgotten."

"Oh, really. Your thinking process is positively frightening sometimes."

"Thank you."

"She's not performing at the Empire tomorrow night. She's at some mission across the city." She leaned forward dramatically. "And no tickets required."

He regarded her with amusement. "What have you been up to?"

"Only a little checking around, you know. Innocent inquiries about Miss Lilly O'Hara, star of Broadway."

"I hardly think there's anything innocent about the things you do...and I'm sure Clark is waiting for you."

She ignored his taunt. "Goodnight, Dad. You might think it over. I would like to meet her even if *you* don't care to."

The hotel room was quiet, a faint perfume lingering where Kate had twirled in front of the mirror. Andy stared up at the ceiling. Though he had read the papers in search of her name, he made no plans to seek out the actress, this long ago friend. But now he was in the very city where she worked and lived...

He forced his thoughts to the woman in New Orleans—who was waiting for him. It was an awkward parting with Virginia expectant and Andy reluctant. Somehow the words seemed to stick in his throat. He couldn't say anything—and he felt guilty and embarrassed. Virginia was cool.

"Andy, I hardly want to pressure you."

"No, I understand. I guess I'm still a little...concerned about Kate leaving and everything," he said lamely.

"You want to settle this when you come back from New York?"

He laughed. "Uh, that sounds like a business deal or something."

"Yes, I was hoping for more than that."

So when he came back, he would slip a ring on her finger or gracefully say goodbye. He yawned and thought of Kate. Kate, so eager and animated—and scheming. He frowned. But deep down he had to admit he was grateful for her bit of detective work. He could buy a ticket and sit in the darkened theater, a face among many—and be reintroduced to Miss Lilly O'Hara.

If Kate was determined to win the Clifford prize and go to Europe, she was equally determined her father would see Lilly O'Hara before he left New York. She'd prefer to be there for the meeting and she had one day to pull off her plan. As usual, her father was being difficult.

"Why isn't Clark coming sight-seeing with us?" Andy asked the next morning.

"Taking Dorothy for one final shopping tour. Let's go, Dad, the cab is waiting."

"How many clothes can you wear at one time? The stewards on the liner are going to give you a fuss about your luggage. You'll need a mule train to get your gear on!"

"Come on, we have a full day."

"Where are we going?"

"A few sights and shopping. Dinner here at 7:30 with Clark and Dorothy."

At nearly 4:00 Kate directed the cab to Clarion Street. After seeing the usual city sights, the cab driver raised a quizzical eyebrow. "You say 'street,' lady?"

She consulted her paper. "Yes, Clarion Street."

"All right, lady."

"What's the problem?" Andy asked quickly.

Kate sent the driver a scathing look.

"It's just that it ain't like up town, kind of, see?"

"Yes?" Andy prompted.

"Rough, mister—it's a rough neighborhood."

"I see. Why do you want to go there, Kate?"

"One last sight, I promise."

When the driver pulled up to the Clarion Street mission hall, Andy understood. "Katherine."

She laughed. "I knew it would be Katherine and not Kate. Come on."

"Look, I don't think we should go...in there. Not like this."

"Come on, we'll slip in the back. Look how crowded it is! You're not afraid, are you?"

"Afraid?...Yes, I think I am." He shrugged and smiled weakly.

Kate softened a bit. Her father afraid?

"But isn't your curiosity bigger than your fear?"

Lilly had a wonderful day at the mission hall. It was the tonic she needed and now she felt she could breathe again. She would think of Karl less for what they had lost together, more for the tragic price the good man was being forced to pay. She could see now, they were not meant to be together—not because he was German, as St. John suggested, but because he was not the man the Lord intended for her. Calmly and rationally she knew she would live alone.

At the mission hall she could serve. She could see other needs beyond her own. The long lunch hour was over, the tables were cleared. Now it was time for 'her' choir of children to sing. The ragged crowd listened with starved attention. The children and the pretty redhead with the infectious smile gave them something nothing else could. Even the tall slim man in the farthest row could see the love the crowd had for the woman on stage. And the love she had for them—it was a mutual, intangible exchange. He was spellbound. He did not see the looks of amusement the young woman at his side gave him.

The children finished their program, and the crowd clapped enthusiastically. Then a voice called out, "Sing one for us, Miss Lilly, just one."

She smiled. It was always the same. The same request each Thursday. But if it brought them joy in their cheerless lives, she would gladly give it. They deserved far more than those who took the top-dollar seats at the Empire.

A young black boy brought her a stool and she placed her arm around him. "Sing with me, William."

She sang clear and without accompaniment. And no one in the mission hall stirred. But unlike other Thursdays, tears slid down her cheeks as she sang.

Kate Alcott had never seen a more beautiful woman, certainly never heard a better voice. Then the crowd was clapping and whistling and Lilly was smiling again. But suddenly she felt the oddest sensation—like an urgent concern toward someone in the crowd. So many in the audience were old familiar friends. The crowd was dispersing, the children crowding around her for hugs. But still she looked for something she could not name. There was nothing that could account for her feelings. She did not notice the tall man who slipped through the crowd to the door.

Kate was brazen in her designs, but now when she stepped into the dressing room, she was seized with a panic that nearly caused her to shake. Her eyes quickly scanned the room—the posters, the flowers, the dressing screen, the scattered costumes and hat boxes, the lighted mirror, the actress. The actress! Lilly O'Hara was quietly assessing her. Kate clutched her purse and felt perspiration clamming her skin.

She nervously cleared her throat. "I'm Katherine. I'm called Kate."

"Hello, Kate. I'm Lilly O'Hara."

She was, and she wasn't what Kate expected now that she stood only a few feet away. The famous woman wore a crisp white blouse and a navy skirt. She could pass for a shop girl on 5th Avenue. But the red hair...

"Yes, you are!" Kate blurted, then crimsoned.

Lilly laughed and Kate smiled. Lilly glanced at the note in her hand. "Your note says you're with a friend of mine from New Orleans. I don't know of any friends in New Orleans."

"I'm Kate Alcott, Miss O'Hara."

Kate was determined to boldly gauge the woman's face, to see the expression that would surely come from hearing that name. But the woman stood perfectly still. Kate had not reckoned with the talent of Lilly O'Hara.

Finally she spoke. "Alcott," she said evenly.

Kate felt a panic. "Yes, Alcott. You do remember my father, don't you?"

Lilly took a deep breath, then a smile spread slowly across her face. "Of course, I remember Andy."

Kate exhaled loudly and sagged against the door.

"You're his daughter," Lilly continued.

"Yes, his daughter." An unexpected, unexplainable note of pride had crept into her voice.

"Is, is he here?" Lilly nodded past the door.

"Dad? Oh, no. He's back at our hotel. Too silly or nervous."

"Too nervous?"

"To come see you."

Lilly's smile deepened.

"He saw you at the mission hall yesterday afternoon though."

Lilly's smile dropped. "Yesterday? He was there?"

Kate nodded vigorously. "I was all for coming up and saying hello. What has it been? Twenty years? We got there late and sat in the back. When it was over he was all in a rush to get out. Got very cross when I tried to persuade him. I really haven't ever seen him act so, so un-Dadish."

Lilly looked like she was only half listening. "I wonder why he was so nervous," she said almost to herself.

Kate perked up. "Oh, he told me later at the hotel, after I'd gotten him put out enough about it. That's the way Dad and I communicate, mostly with intensity. Anyway, he finally exploded and said—"

Lilly held up her hand. "Kate, I think if your father was...was upset, he spoke to you privately and wouldn't want his feelings explained this way."

Kate felt a bit deflated. "Oh."

"So, was your entire family at the mission hall?"

"Just Dad and me. My older sister Melanie is in school."

"I see..."

A moment of silence followed as they both felt their way about.

"And your mother?" Lilly asked carefully.

Kate's eyes were sharp and probing. "My mother died when I was a baby."

"I'm sorry."

"You didn't know?"

Lilly shook her head. "The last contact I had with your father was in a letter. He was engaged to a woman named Amy."

"That was my mother."

A sharp knock sounded on the door. "Lilly." The door swung open. "It's time for—oh!"

"Max." Lilly smiled and shook her head.

"Sorry, my ma didn't teach me proper, okay? Didn't know you weren't alone."

"Kate, this is my director, Max Allen. A marvelous director but quite absentminded when it comes to knocking on closed doors. Max, this is Miss Kate Alcott of New Orleans."

"Hi ya, kid. It's about time to start, Lilly."

"I'll be there in a few minutes."

Lilly stood up and began removing her shoes for a pair of dance slippers. "I'm sorry, but I have a rehearsal, Kate."

"Oh, I understand. I'm just thrilled I made it past the...well, that I was able to see you and...everything."

Lilly smiled. "And how did you manage to get past Jerry who watches the door?"

Kate Alcott smiled and batted her eyelashes. Lilly wagged her finger at her and they both laughed.

"Your father obviously doesn't know you were coming to see me."

"No, he would have tied me up and sent me back home!" Kate laughed. "I have to be careful, best behavior and all that, you know. I sail for Europe tomorrow!"

"How wonderful for you. Your first time?"

"Yes. But it's just me and some family friends. *Dad* isn't going. I suppose he'll just go back to New Orleans, with that woman waiting for him. He cares nothing for her, of course. A pity you won't get to see him..."

Their eyes locked. Lilly finally looked away. "Does your father plan to come to a show, Kate?"

"Couldn't get tickets."

"I...see..."

"Miss O'Hara, will you come to him?" she asked almost impatiently.

"Kate, I...you said he was hesitant about coming."

"He wants to see you, Miss O'Hara! I *know* he does! It's just that shyness, you know. We're at the Astoria Hotel and having dinner there at 7:30 tonight. Goodbye!"

Kate Alcott left, and the actress went to her rehearsal. It was the first time in years Lilly O'Hara had trouble with her lines.

She couldn't remember being this nervous before—not even at her first Broadway opening. She tried on a dozen gowns before she was satisfied. Never before had her wardrobe seemed so, so matronly. She surveyed herself in the mirror critically, then laughed out loud at her vanity. She paced her apartment. She would go to him. No, she couldn't. Of course, she would. He was a good friend from the past. No, if he was reluctant to see her...She stopped and stared at the New York landscape. Andy Alcott was there, only a matter of a few city blocks away, a ten-minute jaunt in a cab. She would go. No, she couldn't...

Kate Alcott paced in the suite she shared with her father. She glanced at her watch and frowned. She was not coming. Andy looked up from the sofa where he sat reading a newspaper and studiously ignoring the society pages. No need to read them—and give Kate more cause on this campaign to go to Lilly O'Hara. He had seen her...yes, he had seen her on the stage, and in his dreams that night.

Twenty years ago she was a young woman suddenly in his life, a woman in need. He had thought of her as his younger sister and rescued her. But in the mission hall, he found a mature, confident woman that dazzled him. He wasn't prone to superlatives or flashy adjectives, but dazzled was the only word to describe how he felt when he saw her. She hadn't any need now. It had startled him seeing her like that, and stirred up a strong desire to meet her again. He wanted to be silent, but there was Kate poking and prodding him.

"Dad, you act like you're afraid of her!"

He smiled to himself. Yes, maybe what he felt did contain a shade of fear.

"Kate, you're going to wear a track in the carpet if you keep that pacing up. What are you so energetic about?"

"Tomorrow," she answered distractedly. "Tomorrow..." She stopped before him, planting her hands on her hips. "Dad, you need your tie on."

"Why? Dinner isn't for another 30 minutes."

"Still you'd look...sharper with it on *now*."

"A tie chokes me." He laughed. "Why don't you sit down and relax?"

She sat down, then popped up 30 seconds later.

"I'm going to Dorothy's suite and help her dress or...something. Be back soon."

The knock at the door came ten minutes later. Maybe Kate had forgotten her key.

"Kate," he began in his scolding tone, "you have to remember... your...key."

She wore a cream-colored dress with violets at the throat. Her hair curled around her shoulders in soft waves and made Andy think of shining copper. Her voice, so trained for control, was momentarily unsteady. "Hello, Andy." Then she relaxed and gave him the famous O'Hara smile. "How's your foot?"

Twenty years ago he had taken a terrible beating at her expense that nearly crippled him. Twenty years...

'We'll meet again someday and laugh over my run in with Max Hawk,' he had said. He had said goodbye then to a young girl, and now he was saying hello to a lovely woman.

"Lil," he said finally, with a note of relief—and unmistakable tenderness.

He had called her Lil those years ago when they'd first become friends. Tears welled up in her eyes now. He stood there, so slim and handsome as he struggled with his tie. She reached out and knotted it for him, not meeting his eyes. It seemed the natural thing to do. A mundane task but suddenly intimate between them...

"Lil," he said again, now smiling, and if felt like they were back in New Orleans so many years ago…

"Now, I…I see where my young daughter was off to this afternoon," he said slowly.

Lilly smiled. "You have a delightful daughter, Andy."

"A bold one," he added.

They looked at each other directly, smiling and appraising…

He took her hand. "And now I'm grateful for her boldness."

The Astoria Hotel dining room was accustomed to wealthy and notable patrons. Still, staff and guests alike couldn't help but gawk and whisper. Lilly O'Hara was in the restaurant. Her vibrant good looks were well known, and by the end of the evening, so was her laughter. Dorothy Benton chatted with the famous actress as easily as if they were chums from college days. But as she did so, she also watched Andy Alcott. They *were* old friends. He toyed with his food, smiled faintly, only speaking when addressed. And when he looked at Lilly O'Hara, Dorothy Benton felt she was intruding upon something personal, even for her frank sensibilities. Andy was like a man gazing upon a treasure. Later, in the suite alone with her son, she delivered her verdict with an all-knowing chuckle and bluntness.

'Poor Virginia. I think she'd better go hunting again!'

Kate was disappointed in her father. He was too quiet, too preoccupied. Lilly O'Hara would certainly go home thinking age had dulled her friend from the past and she wouldn't think any more of him. So Kate exerted herself to be wittier than usual, resulting in the actress's frequent laughter.

When the conversation lagged, Kate turned to her father with a coy smile. "So, Dad, are you hurrying back to New Orleans and your work after we sail tomorrow? Or will you take in a few more…*sights* of New York?" Her face was a mask of innocence.

Every eye was on him.

"I don't know quite what my plans are, Katherine."

But she was pleased to see him finally rouse from his lethargy as the dinner ended and turn to Lilly.

"Would you…I mean, if you're not busy or…would you like to come with us in the morning to see Kate off?"

"I would love to."

Andy and Lilly stood in a sea of waving hats, handkerchiefs, and tiny flags. Several thousand were gathered on the spacious Cunard pier 54 that bisected 14th Street. A holiday-like atmosphere prevailed amidst the confusion. Bands were playing, streamers were flying, everyone was

excited. A Cunard liner was sailing—it was a social event in a city measured by events. Everything was on such a grand scale; indeed it was a
farewell party for the fortunate 1300 passengers. Many turned out to
enjoy the send off vicariously. Cabs and coaches dropped off passengers
who streamed aboard from three different levels of gangways—third
class, second class, first class. Bellboys and porters in beige uniforms
with gold braids hurried along with baggage and shouts of telegrams. The
crowd parted respectfully at the arrival of a gleaming black brougham.
Millionaire Alfred Vanderbilt stepped up the gangway with a wave and a
shy smile. It sent off a chorus of cheers. Other celebrities were on the
passenger list, including Broadway producer Charles Frohman. Policemen on horseback threaded the crowd. Their presence was token—they
could do little in a jovial throng such as this. It was a sunny holiday at
pier 54, the herald of a pleasant crossing.

Like an open mouth the cargo hold was still receiving late baggage
and supplies, though it was only 15 minutes until departure. Already
delayed by two hours, Captain Turner on the bridge was fuming. It was
a costly delay, though it seemed insignificant at the time. The cargo
was as varied as the swarm of New Yorkers dockside. The freight and
crowd were similar beyond diversity—an ominous element was
present in both. German spies mingled at the gala occasion—and car-
tridges and shells entered the hold beside huge rounds of cheese and
sides of beef.

Andy Alcott was thinking neither of the war or German threats as he
squinted into the sunshine. Of course he had read about the famous
liner and seen her photograph in the journals that came to his office.
But still he was unprepared for her overwhelming size. This was the
largest, fastest ship of her kind—a 'floating palace'. He knew her dimensions by heart—785 feet long, 30,000 tons, 7 decks above the water
line, 3 below, 4 mammoth funnels, mastheads rising 216 feet in the air.
For a man whose life work was about sailing vessels, he eyed it critically—and with a sense that the sailing days of his youth were centuries, and not decades, earlier.

"What are you thinking of, Andy?" a voice asked softly at his shoulder.

He had momentarily forgotten Lilly O'Hara standing beside him.

"Well, I..." He laughed. "I was wondering how many *Ivanhoe's Dream*
or *Magnolia Remembrance* would fit inside that boat. It's a colossus!"

The boats of his youth. Lilly smiled. "She is impressive. I sailed to
Europe on her a few summers ago when we did *The Little Minister* over
there. It's like sailing in one vast hotel!"

"Nothing like I've ever known," he said quietly. "Only the port and
starboard, stern and bow are the same." He searched the promenade
deck. "Kate looks small up there."

Kate waved a sailor hat from where she stood pressed against the rail. Even from this distance, Andy could see she was smiling.

They had all gone aboard to see Kate's cabin. And to satisfy Andy that she was close to the Bentons.

"I'll watch her like she was my own, Andy," Dorothy had whispered.

"Don't worry about a thing, Mr. Alcott," Clark had said cheerfully. "She's a treasure, you know."

"Yes…"

Kate had rolled her eyes and grown exasperated with the attention. They treated her like she was one of the children who were dashing around the decks with a frantic nursemaid in tow!

The mournful 'All ashore' gongs sounded. It was time to leave.

"Goodbye, Dad. I'll be a good girl, I promise."

He smiled weakly. "Have a good time, Kate."

"Don't get…sentimental on me. I'll be fine."

He took her hand. "I know you will."

Kate looked to Lilly who stood chatting with Dorothy. "She's a pretty woman."

"Hmm? Oh, yes…"

"Going back to that big project in New Orleans right away?"

He looked her in the eye. "I may stay a few more days…a few more sights couldn't hurt, you think?"

She gave him a quick kiss on his cheek.

"I love you, Kate. Goodbye."

Half a dozen tugs chugged and darted about the great liner as it slowly eased away from the pier, its propellers churning up the Hudson in a brown foam. The band that remained began playing 'God Bless You 'til We Meet Again' and the crowd finally began to thin. The party was over until the ship returned in two weeks.

Andy and Lilly stood watching until only a handful of dock workers remained. Lilly was silent, completely content to stand in the sunshine with this man. She knew he was hurting for the daughter who was sailing away.

"Beautiful day to begin a voyage," he said finally.

The alphabet flags fluttered from the liner's masts. She was picking up speed, her bow shearing the water, her trail of smoke becoming a mere smudge of gray against an intense canvas of blue. The sunshine glinted off the foot-high gold lettering on the port side. The *Lusitania* was heading for open seas.

Chapter 11

Voyage of the Lusitania
Atlantic Ocean

◆◆ ◆◆ ◆◆

*F*ew among the 1,257 passengers of the *Lusitania* could be indifferent or nonchalant about the palatial grandeur of this "transatlantic hotel." Perhaps Alfred Vanderbilt, one of America's wealthiest bachelors, accepted the rich appointments casually, but most did not. Even 3rd class travelers in the more utilitarian cabins considered this voyage on the famous Cunarder the trip of a lifetime. Though their cabins and dining room were clearly defined, unspoken democracy ruled on the ship, and 3rd class passengers had the freedom to explore, perhaps even mingle with the wealthy and famous.

Those aboard were prepared to enjoy those amenities that made the ship well known, and to ignore, or discredit any threat posed by sailing on a British liner. A feeling of smugness prevailed from captain and crew to passengers, despite the fact this ship was sailing into hostile waters, in fact, a declared war zone. This was the *Lusitania*—large enough with her many watertight bulkheads to withstand a sinking attempt and too swift to even give a German sub a respectable target. For those few less confident, however, there remained the theory that such a large passenger ship would be adequately warned before attack.

She sailed away from New York under sunny skies and typical fanfare. The seas and weather were travel-book perfect for the seven-day crossing. Only occasional early-morning or late-evening fog obscured the visibility. A pleasanter trip could not have been arranged.

For months, Kate Alcott had dreamed and imagined what it would be like aboard the world's most famous ocean liner. And reality surpassed her expectations. She was amazed by the opulence and elegance, the luxurious quality of the ship. This was the reward for her efforts in writing; this was the prize she had striven for. She should do nothing but enjoy it in every detail. Yet...

She had stepped on board as wide-eyed as when they had first arrived in New York. Her mind raced to observe, then contain all the sights and sounds so she could record them. She didn't want to miss one inch or one minute. Yet when she had stepped on board something else, something totally unexpected happened. It came subtly at first, yet persistent—some mixture of sadness, thoughtfulness, sobriety. It hung on her like a heaviness she couldn't shrug off. It disturbed her at first, then frustrated her completely. She was to be having a gala time, not a moody and introspective one. She didn't want to look closely at herself or her feelings or any serious thing. But yet it nagged her—like a painful exposure of herself. She laughed and explored and danced—and inwardly cursed this feeling of melancholy.

Moonlight on a glittering calm sea, a ship slicing silently through cobalt blue waters—it was an unrivaled romantic setting. This their first night aboard the *Lusitania*—music from the orchestra played in the spacious grand dining room while couples strolled leisurely along the decks. Clark Benton felt like a shaft of moonlight had filled him, like he was glowing inside. To be alone with Kate...

She was wearing an evening dress of icy blue and borrowed jewels from his mother. She looked like many of the other eager-eyed young women on board—but the loveliest of all in Clark's eyes. As they walked along the deck now, Kate grew unusually quiet.

"Kate? You've been so quiet all evening. Anything wrong?"

"I feel fine..." She sighed almost listlessly.

Clark was disturbed. She was so excited and animated all day. She'd pulled him along the entire length of the the ship several times.

"Seven hundred eighty-five feet, Clark!"

"Yes, I see."

Up to each deck, then down, a look into each salon and public room. "Look at the carpet!"

"Makes me want to take a nap."

The domed and sculptured grand dining room had left her speechless and hoping she could describe it accurately with her pen. They toured the captain's bridge. "Look how far you can see!"

He thought her curiosity and energy endless.

They came upon the first and second class nursery. Kate intended to pass the scene, but she lingered. Toddlers and infants in rompers with their nannies and nurses. Very efficient. She scribbled down some notes. A boy with unruly blond curls and unsteady steps approached her and clung to her skirt. Clark knew she had no fondness for babies. But she leaned down and chatted with the little boy.

"So what do you think of the *Lusitania,* young man?" She looked up at the supervising matron. "How many infants are on board this voyage?"

"Thirty-nine, ma'am."

Clark was not certain if this subdued Kate was an advantage in romancing or not.

"You're probably just tired from being girl reporter all day," he said gently.

She shook her head, and turned away from him.

He came to stand close to her. "Feel like dancing?"

"Too crowded in there." She motioned. "And it's so nice out here."

He took her in his arms before she could protest. "All right, let's dance out here."

She laughed. "Clark, people are looking."

"And what will they see? A beautiful young woman dancing, no, floating in the moonlight with a man who—"

He stopped abruptly and colored. Kate gazed into his face a moment, then moved to the rail. Clark stood beside her silently, scolding himself that he had nearly spoken too soon. He looked at her from the corner of his eyes. She was crying. He pulled her shoulders around. "Kate, what's the matter? Can't you tell me?"

"Oh...I..."

"Let me help you."

She took a deep breath. "Do you like me?"

"Do I like you? Well, of course I do. You know I do."

"Can you like me in spite of, of anything?"

"Anything. Now tell me. Something's been bothering you since we've sailed. I can feel it. You're like, like a tightly strung wire."

He knew her. He knew her better than anyone. He would understand...and forgive her.

"What a good friend you are. I don't deserve you," she said without coyness or flirtation. "I don't know exactly how to put this in words, what I feel..." She shook her curls. "Guilt."

"Guilt?"

"It isn't supposed to be like this. This, this sadness that I can't shake. I can't even tell what I'm sad about! I'm supposed to be having the time of my life, not, not moping about inside. I feel like a weight is on me." Her chin came up defiantly. "I didn't win the Clifford prize, not honestly anyway."

"You what?"

"Have you ever wanted something so badly you were willing to do nearly anything to get it?"

"I..."

Her eyes were flashing. "Of course, you haven't. You're the honorable son of Clark and Dorothy Benton. But I'm not like that! I was willing to do what I had to do to make sure I won."

He looked out at the ocean, not knowing what to say.

Her voiced lowered. "I wanted to win. But I didn't win. A senior girl named Carolyn was going to win. She should be here on the *Lusitania* this evening. She should...she should be hearing the orchestra and sleeping in my cabin. She should have a room in London waiting for her.

War essays should come back to the college with her name on them...
not mine."

"What happened?"

"What happened? I...I became a spy. I schemed and lied until I
found out the contest had come down to Carolyn and myself. Only one
English professor was left to make the final decision." She closed her
eyes. "He was flustered at first, then he liked the...attention, you
know, perched on the edge of his desk with my legs crossed and...so
he tells me sweetly that as good as my writing is, Carolyn's is better
and the next morning he will tell the committee that. I keep chatting
with him..."

"Kate, you really don't have to tell me this."

Her voice was hard. "Oh yes, I do. Maybe...maybe confessing will, will
get rid of this, this thing! I flirted with that old man, without shame, as
Melanie would say. He said, 'You have great promise as a writer, Miss
Alcott.' Then he pinched my cheek. 'You really shouldn't be in here. You
could get us both in trouble.' 'It could be a nice kind of trouble, don't you
think?' I asked as I leaned close to him. He shuffled his papers and tried
not to look at my legs. I very firmly told him I wanted the Clifford prize.
He was fidgety and blushing. He told me he always favored redheads,
so..."

Clark did not want to hear any more. He felt stricken. But Kate was
not finished, the purging was not complete.

"So I hugged him and toyed with him and..."

Clark closed his eyes.

"The next day he presented the decision to the committee. Miss
Alcott has won the Clifford journalism prize this spring of 1915."

Then she was silent, pulling a silk shawl around her bare shoulders.
They heard laughter and looked up to see a couple stop in the shadows
of the lifeboats to kiss. They looked away.

"Do you thoroughly despise me now, Clark Benton?"

"I would never despise you," he said tenderly.

Tears filled her eyes again. "Everything should be perfect," she whispered. "Here we are on a wonderful ship, the sea like, like jewels on rumpled velvet..."

"You know, perhaps that professor just said he was going to choose
the other girl, maybe he really was going to choose you before..."

Kate's smile was sad. "Before I wove a silky web around him?" Her
voice was bitter. "Well, we'll never know, will we?"

She spent a sleepless night aboard the luxury liner. But at morning
she awakened just as the sun, dusky red and gold, rose above the calm
Atlantic. She gripped the rail, her voice fierce in her determination. "But
I am here!"

the U20

Walther Schweiger's cabin aboard the U20 was not much larger than the submarine's radio room. The recent arrival of a litter of dachshunds made the room even more cramped. But the captain of the U20 was not unduly annoyed with his spartan quarters. He knew privations were part of one's service to a greater Germany. His zeal and dedication could rise above personal comfort.

His mission was direct and simple. British troop transports would leave Liverpool for the Mediterranean; they were being sent against German forces massed there. It was obvious—the submarines of Imperial Germany must see that such ships never reached the front. The course was a round trip of 3006 sea miles from his naval base in Emden around northern Scotland and western Ireland into the Irish channel, then up into the Mersey River that led to Liverpool. The waters leading to Liverpool were busy ones—with a multitude of opportunities for a prowling German sub.

The underwater currents gently lulled the steel tube as Schweiger rested on his bunk, once more reading his cousin's latest letter. He dwelt only briefly on how his ingenious cousin had obtained these instructions to Cunard captains. Clearly they originated from the British admiralty in London.

'...Cunard liners are instructed to avoid headlands along the Irish coast, like Galley Head or Old Head of Kinsale. They are to steer mid-channel on a zigzag course, operating full speed past harbors such as Queenstown...'

It was useful information for an ambitious captain—the best he'd received from Marta Marie. He would consider these instructions as he plotted his course up the channel.

the Lusitania

Kate found herself a chair on the sun-drenched promenade deck, slightly apart from any passenger who might be inclined to strike up a chat. A light, salty breeze blew in from the starboard side. She was too busy just now to talk. She had work to do—writing and recording all she had seen and experienced in these first few days at sea. Recording these impressions was important, she must capture the spirit of them while they were still fresh. So she frowned when Clark plopped down beside her. In spite of her desire not to notice, she had to admit, Clark did look handsome in his tennis whites.

"Girl reporter hard at work, huh? How 'bout a game of tennis for a break?"

"The girl reporter *must* work. Sorry."

"Oh, come on! You're always writing or interviewing. I bet you've crawled all over this ol' tub!"

She laughed. "I have! Yesterday they showed me the boiler rooms. Those poor men who work down there! They were positively black! They constantly feed the furnace to keep us chugging along our merry way. Six thousand tons of coal are needed!" She leaned forward. "I bet you didn't know we aren't using our full boiler strength. One of the four boiler rooms is shut down. One of the stokers told me, and in a very confidential tone. They shut it down to conserve coal for the war effort."

"That would mean..."

"Exactly! That means our top speed is only 21 knots when Lucy's been advertised at 26, and our cruising speed is only 18 knots."

"You've worked long enough—let's go play tennis."

"Do you know how many eggs the kitchens brought?"

He sighed. "No, how many?"

"Sixty thousand, Clark! Can you imagine?"

"That's a lot of chickens."

"This afternoon I'm going to watch the first-class chefs prepare lunch."

"Kate—"

"Can you imagine a dining room that can serve thousands at one time? It's, it's—"

"Hard to imagine." Clark laughed. "Kate, how do you get these privileges? You know more about the *Lusitania* than—"

"Than Captain Turner? He is a dear little man. He's been very helpful. He says we should see Ireland tomorrow and he'd let me up on the bridge with his own glasses! I should ask him about this boiler business though. Like can we still outrun a submarine?"

"I doubt he would like that question very well. Better stick to how many cheeses are on board."

Her eyes narrowed. "You're teasing me."

"No, I'm not... So, you don't want to play tennis?"

"Sorry." She tapped her notebook. "I have to get everything down just right, you know. Amherst must be glad they sent Kate Alcott. They'll get back such a report on the Lucy they'll think they were on board themselves! They'll hear the orchestra, and the children scampering on the deck. They'll feel themselves gliding through the Atlantic and feel the spray on their faces..."

He took her hand. "Well anyway, I'm glad you're feeling happier."

It was the wrong thing to say. Kate did not want to be reminded of the heaviness that dogged her unless she kept herself wholly distracted and busy. It was like a reflection of something inside, something nameless that reminded her of how she'd won the Clifford prize, and her family, her future, who she really was. She was never like this before—and it frightened her. The feelings came at night, when she tried to fall asleep. Perhaps when they landed at Liverpool the melancholy would flee with the new excitement. She didn't want to be reminded of her confession.

"Clark, I, I'd rather we didn't mention what I told you the other night, about the prize. It's in the past, you know, and I don't want it to come up again."

"Sure." He stood up. His face had lost its eager and happy look. "See you later."

"Yes, this afternoon."

She watched him walk away before she returned to her writing. His shoulders sagged and she knew she had hurt him. Before, it wouldn't have bothered her—but now it did. She chewed the end of her pen thoughtfully. Clark was beginning to act like...no, this would complicate their relationship. They were only friends. And really, she didn't have time for any other emotions.

the U20

It was an uneventful voyage for the U20 through the Scottish passage. The seas were choppy, the weather clear and cold. But rough seas had not impeded the vessel's progress. Patrol and destroyers were sighted, but Schweiger was cautious. The flotilla of ships were too distant or the ocean too turbulent to favor attack. The well-trained crew became restless in their confinement of steel.

The fourth day out, the submarine found a solitary British steamer to attack. But the torpedo jammed in the firing tube. Schweiger cursed his luck and slammed down the periscope angrily. He couldn't afford such failures again on this voyage.

the Lusitania

"Tell me again, Kate, how many lifeboats?"

Kate smiled at the older woman. "There are 22, and half a dozen more collapsible boats."

"Who would feel safe in a boat called collapsible!" Dorothy fumed. "But still, that isn't near enough for all the passengers and crew. And why haven't we had any lifeboat drills?"

Dorothy Benton had enjoyed the trip these fine days at sea. The ocean was benevolent, no churning or chopping, no inclement weather. But as the ship approached the Irish channel and its final destination in

Liverpool, the old anxiety reasserted itself. Over a game of bridge in the salon one day, she gossiped, chatted and listened carefully. Some passengers were calling the voyage boring thus far. Others pointed out that their arrival in the channel could change that. "It would be fun to try a run at a sub or be chased by one!"

"The kaiser would be foolish indeed to fire on a ship of Americans!"

"A British ship none the less. And the Americans chose the risk."

"Perhaps the Germans would be so kind and take the Americans off before she attacked!"

These comments were greeted with bantering and laughter, but Dorothy lost her concentration on the game. She didn't appreciate shipboard teasing such as this. It did nothing to steady her nerves and gave voice and substance to her fears.

"Of course, we all know the kaiser is aware of the *Lusitania* and that she may carry munitions."

"She carries passengers!" Dorothy declared forcefully to the stranger. "Innocent men, women and children."

The card player shrugged and the game resumed. But he would not be contained by one nervous middle-aged woman! He lowered his voice as if spies lurked behind the potted palms.

"The kaiser could say he warned us, if he tries anything."

Dorothy was completely exasperated. "What are you talking about?"

He carefully produced the *New York World* newspaper. Dorothy read the advertisement in mounting horror.

"This is audacious!" Dorothy exclaimed. "And, and ridiculous! They wouldn't try, they wouldn't!"

A sip of wine and a shrug. "And if they did? She's too swift for any German sub. It would be fun to see a periscope peeking out of the water, don't you think? Rather thrilling...I pass."

"Did you bring this on board just to go around frightening people, sir?"

"Well, I, I actually thought it would make a—souvenir," he admitted sheepishly.

Dorothy grabbed the paper. "I am taking this so you won't alarm anyone else. Good morning!"

Now Kate strolled about the cabin brushing her hair.

"So why haven't we had lifeboat drills, Kate?" Dorothy asked again.

"I will ask the captain at dinner tonight. Now, really, Dorothy, you're acting nervous again."

"Nervous is one word...and what about the lifevests? They haven't given us instructions about them either!"

Kate went to the closet and pulled a life jacket on over her evening dress. "See? A strap here, a buckle there, and you're bobbing like a cork with the little fishes tickling your toes!"

"Katherine! Please don't talk like that!"

Kate became gentle. "What's the matter?"

She didn't want to frighten the girl, she really didn't. Here she was supposed to be the responsible guardian, not the one inciting hysterical fears! But she must say something.

"This, look at this."

"What is this?"

"Last Saturday's New York *World.* I...I borrowed it from a man at the card table this afternoon. See, the Germans placed a warning."

Kate read quickly. "Dorothy, really, it's just a hoax or something, a prank."

"You don't really think that! This is a British liner and Germany is at war with Britain! Oh, I do wish Clark Sr. were along with us."

"Dorothy, we're a passenger liner."

"Tell that to some overeager, nearsighted German sub captain!"

Kate placed her arm around the trembling woman. "It'll be all right. We'll be there day after tomorrow. They say the Lucy can't be attacked, you know, unsinkable and fast and—"

Dorothy Benton's smile was wry. "Didn't they say something like that three years ago about the *Titanic?*"

the U20

Sighting Fasnet Rock from his submerged submarine, Schweiger now entered the Irish sea. Now his business became more challenging and perilous—more destroyers, more patrols. The channel could be heavy with traffic. He was more than ready.

the Lusitania

It was not uncommon for the captain to bring a passenger up to the bridge, and it was obvious to the crew that Captain Turner was enjoying the enthusiasm and interest of the collegiate "reporter." It seemed like every time they turned around the petite coed with red-blond hair was there smiling and scribbling furiously in her red notebook.

"Miss Alcott, all this work, your writing, have you had time to enjoy my ship?" the captain asked as they toured the marconi room together.

Kate laughed. "Oh, Captain Turner, I've had plenty of time to enjoy Lucy! I'm in the music room till the orchestra plays the last note and I've had time for at least three shipboard flirtations!"

The grizzled little man joined her laughter. "I can see how that would not be difficult, Miss Alcott."

Then the wireless began its clicking—the world was trying to reach the *Lusitania*. The operator took the message in absorbed silence.

"How exciting!" Kate whispered. "You're getting a cable now."

The captain's chest swelled. "Perfectly routine, Miss Alcott."

The operator finished the message then handed the paper to the captain. But he eyed Kate skeptically.

"Oh don't mind me." Kate smiled breezily.

"It's from the admiralty, sir," the operator spoke in a low voice.

Turner tugged at his chin as he read. Kate knew she must not look over his shoulder as she wanted to do. Her mind raced. She took a guess. "About those pesky German subs," she said confidently.

"Submarines sighted off the southern coast of Ireland," Turner read aloud while the crewman turned hastily to his instruments.

The captain leaned forward. "You musn't write that." He pointed to her paper.

"Of course not."

"Or speak of what you heard," he continued with visible agitation.

"Not a word, Captain Turner."

"It could only cause…unnecessary concern among some of the passengers," he said as he steered her from the cabin. "We swung the lifeboats out this morning. All in perfect order, of course."

"Yes, we saw that. It pleased Mrs. Benton whom I'm traveling with. But Captain Turner, there was no actual drill. And there haven't been any drills for putting on lifejackets."

He hurried her along, trying in his mind to remember what he might have said to this inquisitive young woman that he wished he hadn't. "Drill for life jackets is planned for tomorrow. The first mate will see to it." He stopped and attempted a confident smile. "But really, Miss Alcott, do you think those drills necessary? You can see for yourself this is a modern vessel. Can you imagine a submarine catching the *Lusitania?*"

Kate was silent. The captain watched the blue, white-tipped swells a moment. "A torpedo can't get the *Lusitania*. She runs too fast."

Another wireless message reached the captain as he sat down to dinner later. It too came from the admiralty in London. It was a repeat of the earlier message with only one word changed.

Submarines *active* off the Irish coast…'

But this was the *Lusitania*…

the U20

The U20's second target was not as fortunate as her first. The British schooner *Earl of Latham* sunk from a surface attack in a matter of minutes; her cargo of bacon and potatoes bound for Liverpool sunk quickly in the dark Atlantic. The following day the U20 found two more targets—one at midmorning, the other just as the evening mists settled in. Two British steamers went down without challenge and Schweiger returned to his cabin well satisfied—two firings, two hits. Three torpedoes remained: Bertha, Mary and Emma. He could make only one more attack in the Irish sea as orders required him to save two torpedoes for the return voyage.

He called his first officer into his cabin as he began his diary entries. "We are changing our plans, Raymond," he said crisply as he tapped the charts.

"Yes sir."

"I feel it would be senseless to continue toward the coast of Britain. We must conserve our fuel. We shall change course southward, remaining in these waters eight hours more." He poured himself a cup of Turkish coffee. "We shall find something bigger than a mere fishing boat, I am confident."

the Lusitania

It was a cool May night as Kate walked alone along the promenade deck of the *Lusitania*. She had said goodnight to Clark at her cabin, then made her way to the deck. She needn't feel nervous on the shadowy deck, a situation even her father could approve of, for the ship was hardly asleep as it steamed through the Atlantic. Poker games were still in progress in the smoking rooms, she could still hear snatches of laughter and the clatter of china. She knew from her tours in the subterranean regions of the great liner that someone was always working— the laundry crew, the three different shifts of boiler stokers, the kitchen staff in preparation for the following day's feasts. A handful of couples, young and old, sauntered along the deck, their voices muted. Various crew members were stationed at various positions along the ship as the nightwatch. But what could they really see in the vast, moving, inky darkness?

For such a large liner cutting the waters, she gave off little light. The thinly scattered stars seemed to be far more luminary than the shrouded, gliding ship. Europe and the war zone came closer with each white-tipped swell. Beyond this night, Kate had only one more night aboard, until her return voyage to the States. Tomorrow night she would be with Dorothy and Clark; tonight she wanted the solitude.

She wondered again if she could enjoy herself fully once she landed on the British Isle and shook off this silly and useless introspection. That sort of seriousness was more in line for her sister Melanie or her father—not her!

"But still you can't ignore it, can you, Katherine Alcott?" she whispered to herself. And the tears welled up in her eyes. Tears!

It seemed more than just the deception of the Clifford prize. It was more...it was serious and unexpected thoughts of her family. She thought of her father as he had looked watching Lilly O'Hara at the mission hall, shy and awkward. As he looked at Peppercreek when he'd given her the news she could go to Europe. And as he looked standing on the Cunard pier beside the actress, frail and vulnerable. She frowned—likely he was back in New Orleans now, poring over ship plans with ever-faithful Collins at his side. And Virginia Hollins waiting.

She remembered the last few words they had said to each other. "I'll be a good girl," she said flippantly.

"I love you, Kate," he returned seriously.

She hadn't told him she loved him. When was the last time she had said those words? Probably as an energetic little girl years ago.

"That long?" she said to herself now. "That long..."

The sea gave her no answers. Maybe she didn't even love him. When was the last time she told anyone she loved them? A beau? Melanie? The tears continued and she hated them. She thought suddenly of Grandmother Sara, her grandmother who had always loved her in spite of anything she did. What if...what if something happened to the old woman before she returned from Europe? She had never imagined life without her grandmother—she would live forever. But could there be life without Grandmother Sara sitting almost regally in her wheelchair dispensing advice and encouragement? And listening.

Why hadn't she ever told her how she felt about her? She gripped the rail tightly. "Maybe I can't love!" She took a deep breath; she had to stop thinking like this.

Sara had come into her thoughts earlier that day, over lunch. They were eating when Kate caught the snatch of conversation from a nearby table. Some middle-aged woman was pointing to the domed ceiling of the richly furnished dining room with one hand and dipping a silver spoon into a dish of ambrosia with the other.

"Oh, this is divine! This is what Heaven will be like!"

Her companions tittered, but it caused the young woman at the next table to grow pensive. What a silly comment. Her grandmother came to her mind. Sara would have rolled her eyes and smiled at the woman's words. Kate heard her voice, lilting and careful in her mind.

"Eyes have not seen, nor ear has heard all that God has prepared for those that love Him."

The scripture had come unbidden to her mind. It was one her grand-mother quoted often. She was surprised it had stayed in her mind when she did not even know it. Grandmother Sara would be pleased in her old-fashioned way.

'...prepared for those that *love* Him...'

She knew nothing about love, she decided bitterly. She turned away from the rail.

"Can you capture moonlight with your pen as so many poets have attempted?" a suave voice asked from the shadows of the stairway.

Kate was never without her pen and notebook. She jumped.

A man stepped forward with a slight bow. "I beg your pardon, I did not mean to frighten you."

"I...you didn't frighten me. You startled me."

"Ah..."

"You...you're Mr. Vanderbilt."

He stepped closer, his voice teasing. "Ah, a man must have an iden-tity even in the middle of the ocean! Do you think they'd know me at the pyramids in Egypt?"

"Well, if you traveled with the entourage there as you have here, then yes, probably." She laughed, marveling at her composure as she chatted easily with the famous millionaire. Here was a story! "The gossip says you are going to England to race your horses, not Egypt."

"The gossip is true...for once."

"I met Lilly O'Hara before we sailed a few days ago," Kate exclaimed proudly.

"Ah, yes, Lilly and I are old friends."

"Really?"

"Yes, I've asked her to marry me many times over the years. But she's always turned me down."

"Were you...married at the time, Mr. Vanderbilt?" Kate asked mis-chievously.

He laughed loudly. "That might have been the trouble. I notice your little notebook there. Are you a very pretty reporter or a very lovely casual diarist?"

"I'm a writer, I mean, I'm trying to be one."

"Anything published?"

"No, not yet. But I will some day."

"I'm sure you will, and I would buy your book having seen the au-thor!"

"You can't judge a book by its cover or a writer by her looks, Mr. Van-derbilt. I may not have any talent at all!"

"I'm sure that is not true." He stepped up beside her at the rail. "Even a corrupt soul like me finds beauty in a moonbathed ocean. So serene, no demands..." He shook his head. "But a young woman is even lovelier. What color exactly is your hair, my dear? In this light..."

She stepped back, suddenly nervous. "Do you think they are out there, Mr. Vanderbilt?"

"They? Oh, you mean the Germans. Well they may be, but I wouldn't be here if I really thought so. I have ponies waiting for me in London. Are you worried, Miss—?"

"Alcott. I have heard people talking about it, as we get closer, you know. Did you know of the advertisement in the New York paper from the German embassy?"

"I heard of it." He waved his hand as if German subs were nothing more than annoying flies. "The Germans wouldn't try anything. They wouldn't do that. It would move America from her neutrality and they don't want another fighter in the schoolyard tussle."

"So, you think there's nothing to it then?"

"Right, and you may quote me, Miss Alcott. Think of it like this. If I was going to grab you as you came around a corner in order to punch you, more likely kiss you, would I advertise it before I did it?"

She laughed. "Well, no."

"Don't worry about Germans. Your concern should be for prowling millionaires like myself," he said lightly.

She took another step of retreat. "Thank you for this interview, Mr. Vanderbilt. Goodnight."

It was time for the captain of the *Lusitania* to make his customary speech of farewell. His tone was gruff as he addressed the crowd, his smile awkward. It was evident that the captain was much more comfortable steering a ship than making a speech.

"I thank you for traveling on the *Lusitania*. I hope your voyage has been a pleasant one. We have had warnings of submarines in the war zone, but there is no cause for alarm. We shall arrive in Liverpool early Saturday morning." He tugged nervously at the edge of his blue uniform jacket, as he wet his lips.

"Are we in any danger, Captain?" a man called out from the audience. "What about curtaining the portholes and the lifeboats swung out?"

Turner's brow was beaded in sweat. "Mere precautions. In wartime...there, uh, is always danger, but I must repeat there is no cause for alarm." He attempted a broad, comforting smile—which to Kate looked very Cheshire-ish.

"I will make one final request to those gentlemen who are fond of cigars—please do not light them on deck. I bid you a pleasant evening." He nodded to the orchestra to continue. He did not want the tactless man in the crowd starting a volley of questions.

The orchestra played Strauss's "Blue Danube" and Kate was in rapture. She loved the music. It made her feel happy, and beautiful and ephemeral. She was floating, only lightly tethered by Clark's hand upon her waist and hand. With such beautiful music she felt everything must be equally beautiful and peaceful in the world. She could ignore any tidings of fear or apprehension Turner's little speech might bring. Others might be thinking of the Atlantic as sinister, but she could ignore it. Often she waltzed with her eyes closed, letting Clark lead her. She hoped they would play all night—this final night on the gracious *Lusitania*.

Clark gazed down at her and smiled. "You love this music, don't you?"

She nodded. "There is nothing like Strauss..." she replied dreamily.

"I'm glad you're having a good time. You're certainly the loveliest woman in this room."

He waited. He couldn't speak now in the brightly lit music room, but he must speak soon. This could be the perfect time with Kate in such a benign mood from the waltzes. She wasn't defensive or teasing or scribbling in her notebook. This was one of the few times she didn't have it with her. Tomorrow night she'd be packing or helping his mother pack or scurrying about the liner for final observations. It had to be tonight.

He studied her profile, the rich luster of her hair as it curved away from her neck. Kate and her riotous curls—they defined her. The little pearl earrings, the thin gold necklace around her slender neck... She flashed him a contented smile and he almost groaned aloud in his desire to speak to her and tell her his heart. He glanced up at the orchestra as they began "Tale from the Vienna Woods." It was nearly midnight, and while he enjoyed the music, he hoped it was their final piece.

Later they were on the deck and Kate was humming. The moon was full, glowing gold, casting a luminescent path across the water. They stopped near the rail. The ship was running smoothly and effortlessly.

Kate sighed. "It's beautiful," she said looking up at the moon. "You could almost reach out and touch it. Think it would make you glow if you could?"

"It is beautiful," Clark said not even giving the moon a glance.

She heard the low and gentle timbre of his voice.

"Kate..."

She knew what was coming. "Clark..."

"Don't protest, Kate Alcott, let me speak," he said earnestly. "It isn't the music or the moonlight, so don't say that."

"Clark, please."

"You know how I feel, you...must know." He took her hands.

"I, I—"

He put a slender finger to her lips. "You talk too much. You have to listen, you have to. I may not get another chance."

"What do you mean by that?"

"I just—"

"Are you worried about the submarine warnings? Are you?"

"No, I just know when we land you'll dash off with that perpetual notebook and pen! Please let me say this."

She softened, though dreading the thought that she must surely hurt him.

"You know I love you. I love you, Katherine Alcott."

She couldn't ignore or protest or minimize. The longing was too tender in his eyes. "Clark, I value our friendship."

He groaned aloud and turned away.

"I know how cold that sounds. I'm sorry, I really am! I wish I could...love you like...you love me."

They stood silently for several minutes.

"Some day you'll feel about some man the way I feel about you." Clark turned to face her.

She shook her head as tears came to her eyes. "Something's wrong with me. I don't know if I can really...love anyone."

His smile was tender as he drew her into his arms—like a brother comforting his little sister. "You will, Kate, you will."

Dorothy and Kate took a late breakfast their last full day on the *Lusitania* before their arrival in Liverpool. Though approaching the noon hour, the liner still laid a sumptuous brunch table.

"You look tired this morning," Dorothy said taking a sip of coffee.

"I didn't sleep very well, but I'm fine."

"Well, I slept wonderfully until early morning when the captain began sounding that dreadful horn every five minutes! What a way to treat passengers at five o'clock!"

"Well, it was for safety, the fog."

"But it lets everyone know where we are! Even a blind man could find this ship!"

Kate shrugged. "We'll pick up escorts this evening and that will be that. Now, guess who I met the other night? I haven't had a chance to tell you."

"I can't imagine. Haven't you interviewed everyone on board?"

Kate smiled patiently.

"Good morning, nearly noon, ladies! Great looking day isn't it?" Clark came up to them with typical energy and enthusiasm.

"Bon jour!" Kate returned happily, glad that Clark was too magnanimous to brood over her rejection.

"Now there you go again with those French phrases." He pulled up a chair. His expression had become serious. "I've noticed the last few days you've been using them. Why?"

She batted her eyes and assumed an innocent pout.

"Mon cheri, I'm just brushing up on the French I learned at school a few years ago. It isn't something I want to forget."

"Uh huh. Why now?"

Kate daintily cut her food. "You're sounding suspicious with your silly questions."

"I think I have reason to," he replied soberly.

Dorothy leaned forward, her fork in midair. "My goodness, it sounds like you two are about to quarrel!"

Kate ignored Clark. "He's doing a very good imitation of my father this lovely morning. After such a lovely night."

"Kate, I'm serious—"

"That's the problem. Dorothy, which is better: the plum marmalade or orange?"

"Kate, I told your father I'd watch over you and I will."

"Orange."

"Clark, you are being annoyingly—"

"You're brushing up on your French because you want to cross the channel and get closer to the war!"

"France? Kate isn't going to France. She's going to London," Dorothy said firmly.

"Ignore him, Dorothy. He's being an alarmist…like the man with the paper."

"Kate, you can't go to France."

Kate Alcott had never liked being told what to do. She flared instantly. "You have no place to talk to me like this. I'm a grown woman, Clark Benton!"

"Children, children!"

Clark stood. "Well, I think I'll go find a game of shuffleboard or something." He gazed into Kate's eyes, regretful they had argued—and remembering her as she was the night before. "I'm sorry."

She looked up, still angry, but cooling under his gentleness. She never wanted to quarrel with Clark. He was her good friend. "We'll talk later."

He nodded and left.

"My son cares for you, Katherine," Dorothy said.

Kate looked up nervously. "You're calling me Katherine. I take that as a warning."

Dorothy's smile was fond. "Perhaps it's my son I should be warning. You know, it really is a lovely morning. More marmalade?"

Kinsale

The telegram arrived just as the Falconer family finished breakfast. Maggie and her sons watched silently as Padraic opened the envelope.

He sighed wearily after reading. He felt as if a cloud had passed over the sun, and it had promised to be a lovely spring day.

"Padraic, what is it?" Maggie had seen the change come into her eldest's eyes.

"It's from Sir Coke in Queenstown. Three ships were sunk in the channel in the last two days…by German subs." He went to the window.

"They're on our doorstep," he said softly.

the Lusitania

It was nearly one in the afternoon as Kate walked along the port side of the promenade deck. Like so many others, she enjoyed watching the distant Irish coast glide by.

'…We have sighted the coast of Ireland,' she jotted in her notebook. 'Gray rock promontories and cliffs in some places, a smooth, inviting line of green in others…I would like to travel there some day…the Emerald Isle…'

With no boats in sight, the island seemed remote and wildly beautiful. Kate hugged her journal. She didn't feel like writing anymore. She just wanted to enjoy the sunshine and beauty. It was such a lovely day…

the U20

The submarine submerged mid morning to find the weather had cleared completely. The ocean was a smooth blanket with no ships of any kind visible for miles. Walther knew Irish fishing smacks would be out soon. But he would not waste a torpedo on a dingy fishing boat. He would be disappointed if he did not see something bigger soon. He glanced once more at the fuel gauges and made a mental calculation. His order came swiftly—they would begin the homeward trip.

Two hours later, while still submerged, the shout came that always electrified the crew.

"Ship!"

Schweiger hurried on to the slippery deck, his glasses trained southward. Four stacks, two masts of a large steamer, approximately 13 miles distant. Cunard liners took this course…

"Diving stations!" he shouted.

In four minutes the sub had dived, running at top speed in a course directly toward the great ship.

the Lusitania

As two o'clock approached, Kate noticed fewer children scampering on deck. She knew they were below decks with the napping hour. A passing crewman pointed out the whitewashed lighthouse with black bands that stood like a sentinel on the coast.

"So, do we know where we are?" she asked.

He smiled. A crewman could never admit he didn't know where the vessel was. "That's a true navigation point, Ma'am. That's the lighthouse off the Old Head of Kinsale."

In her deck chair, she grew sleepy. She should go find Clark and try to make amends for their quarrel that morning—and the pain she had caused him the night before. She would assure him in her typical friendly way that they were still good friends. She closed her eyes for just a moment, feeling the fatigue from the sleepless night before.

the U20

The superstructure of the liner seemed to fill the periscope. Schweiger, so typically cool, could hardly contain his excitement. This was incredible good fortune—the ship had turned perpendicular to his own. He ordered the U20 up, then down slightly, in perfect position for attack. The atmosphere was tense, the crewmen knew they were stalking a great prize. The voyage had come to this encounter in the placid Irish sea.

Schweiger's voice was clipped. "Stand by!"

A young quartermaster responsible for relaying orders to the torpedo room stood rigid and pale. He remained motionless, the speaking tube limp in his hand.

"I will not attack a ship with women and children aboard." His voice rang metallic in the confines of the sub.

The crew eyed each other nervously. It was unthinkable to disobey orders. It meant certain courtmartial. One of the dachshunds whined in the eerie stillness.

Schweiger, intent upon his prey, ignored the disobedience. "Stand by!" he shouted again.

Another crewman hastily took the speaking tube. "Torpedo ready," he said calmly.

the Lusitania

She woke up with the jolt of someone who had fallen asleep when not intending to. It was a panicky feeling, making her dizzy. She took a deep breath of the clean, crisp air. What had made her afraid? Was she dreaming? Gradually, she grew calmer. The sea was still as shimmering and placid, the sky as cloudless. She stood up. She must find Clark. He would steady her out of her fears.

the U20

Captain Schweiger of the U20 gripped the periscope handles tightly. He calculated the ship's speed. Seven hundred meters.

"Fire!" he barked.

Sixty seconds to target.

the Lusitania

Clark Benton was walking toward Kate Alcott when someone at the rail near him shouted. For an instant, he ignored it. Kate was wholly in his mind. Her smile had told him he was forgiven for the morning's heated exchange. But then he turned and walked calmly to the rail to stand beside the man and woman. The man had shouted. The woman was now covering her mouth, her eyes wide with fear. A white streak of foam was headed toward the ship. Clark glanced up quickly when someone on a higher deck shouted also. Clark looked back to the sea, so sunny and bright. The line of foam was closer—like a line of white across a chalkboard. His mouth went dry. A porpoise perhaps? But there was no leaping fish in sight. The man beside him pointed. His voice was strangely calm. "It's a torpedo."

It seemed to have hypnotized those that rushed to the rail. Under the opaque sea, the steel torpedo could be clearly seen. The *Lusitania* could not swing away quickly enough. What was discussed so casually was suddenly, starkly real.

the U20

There was complete silence in the U20 after the firing of the torpedo. Schweiger stood transfixed at his periscope. He had watched the missile streak toward the liner. He knew he had met the target somewhere between the third and fourth funnel from the spray of sea that shot up. A perfect, clean shot. Ten seconds, twenty, thirty seconds. A second explosion, more powerful than the first, shook the great liner.

The submarine rocked heavily from the explosion. Typically the sub must dive to avoid attack. But there was no need now. On this clear, sunny May afternoon, no rescuing ships were seen on the horizon. Schweiger watched fascinated. Finally, he turned to the crew who stood tensely near him.

"The ship is sinking," he said in an emotionless voice. "Take a look if you like."

Several crew members crowded forward. A gasp! "It is the *Lusitania!*"

the *Lusitania*

The deck was already beginning to tilt slightly as Clark ran to Kate. "Kate!"

"Clark! Clark, what's happened?"

He felt shocked that he must say the words. "We've been hit."

He gripped her hands. There was no shouting, or running, no disaster unfolding. He looked into her green eyes, suddenly calm. "I've got to go get Mother. She's in her cabin."

But Kate would not turn him loose.

"Please don't leave me," she whispered hoarsely.

"She'll be terrified. I have to get her for the lifeboats."

One last smile. He kissed her quickly on the cheek. He was gone.

the *U20*

Schweiger returned to the periscope after the crew had taken their look. They had sunk the *Lusitania,* pride of Great Britain, but the cheering died away to stunned silence. The ship was sinking far too quickly. Lifeboats dangled, then crashed into the sea while passengers jumped into the ocean. She should have taken hours to sink, letting the passengers get away safely in the boats.

"Another look?" the captain asked curtly. All could see he had gone pale. A thin line of sweat dotted his upper lip.

No one moved. No one wanted another look.

Schweiger slammed the periscope down with finality. His mouth was drawn into a hard, white line, and his voice was steely calm.

"Take her down 60 feet. We are going home."

the *Lusitania*

It was a bizarre sensation—as if she were suddenly caught in an ocean whirlpool. Life became a vortex of sound, distant yet clear, her vision spinning and hazy. She felt panic as she knew she was seized by something undefinable. The day was at once pristinely clear and bright, vivid blue—the muted landscape of Ireland parallel to the liner. Now all of that vanished and was replaced by a mural of stark terror. Everything was unfocused and unreal.

After Clark left, slipping through the wave of frightened people surging up on the decks, everything became fragmented. And as long as she lived, it was always that way.

'... There was shouting, without clear words, and screams, and crying...and the sound of wood breaking and the deck chairs sliding, then pitching over the rail like chips...running feet and someone shoving a lifejacket in my hand, I don't know who...there were no faces...the deck was leaning, and I didn't know which way to turn...an old woman grabbed my hand, said words, but all I could hear was screaming and yelling, then she was gone...the dining room...the crockery and china was sliding and shattering and no one was stopping it...the chairs were piled up against the wall...the beautiful glass was shattering...I was stumbling down the steps...'

"Ma'am, you can't go down there."

"What? Where am I?"

"Corridor to the public rooms, Ma'am. You gotta get back up on deck to the boats, Ma'am. They be lowerin' the boats soon."

"Yes..." But the young woman couldn't move. She sagged against the wall, her breath in short gasps. Clark?

"Your knee is bleedin', Ma'am. You gotta get up on the deck."

"But...Dorothy, I came with Dorothy, she's..."

The steward pulled gently on her arm. "Lifeboats be waiting for women and children, Ma'am. I'll stay with you and help you."

"Children? Children!" She grabbed at his jacket. "There are children, infants, 39 infants in the nursery and they need help with the jackets. We must go for them."

The steward drew a long, ragged breath. His eyes turned back to the hallway where the water was already a foot high.

"Ma'am, I thought of them too...I...I come from there and, and it's done under water, Ma'am."

"Under?...No...No!"

"Come along, Ma'am, I'll help you. We got to hurry, though."

Kate Alcott was sick all over the expensive carpet of the *Lusitania*. The steward waited.

"I'll get you in a boat, Ma'am. It'll be all right."

She leaned against him. "Are you Clark?"

He cried then—she was too young to go mad. "I'm Clark, now let's hurry."

She lay on something cold, hard, and wet. The motion made her feel sick. Her mouth was painfully dry, her eyes were clamped shut. There was a pain somewhere, but she was uncertain if it was a part of her. If only it would be still and quiet. But she heard distant screaming and moaning near her, and the pungent smell of smoke and salt.

"Look...she's going...she's going." It was a flat voice beside her.

A searing, burning pain filled her eyes as she opened them. But she wanted to find the voice. Was it her own? Another odd sound, like breaking. She lifted up on an elbow, and her vision cleared for one vivid moment.

The *Lusitania* hit the ocean floor, her stern upright like a tower, the rudder spinning lazily. Those who remained alive in the water would never forget the sight. The liner hung for fifteen seconds before its slow slide into the Atlantic. Then there was nothing but the debris, human and unliving scattered on the sunny waters.

Kate Alcott, still clutching her journal, closed her eyes. She didn't want to ever open them again.

This was the *Lusitania,* sleekest, fastest, 785 feet long—gone in 18 minutes.

Chapter 12

New York

◆ ◆ ◆ ◆ ◆ ◆

*T*hey watched the ship slip over the horizon. Then Andy turned and found Lilly looking up at him with a smile.

"Hello," she said.

He laughed and bowed. "Miss O'Hara."

"Welcome to New York."

"Thank you."

It was there, undefinable, unexplainable—a connection that had never been broken. Two people alone and conscious of no others.

"You were quiet at dinner last night," she said. This was their first time alone together.

"I...I was surprised and...delighted to see you. It's been a long time."

"Yes, it has."

"Do you have to be anywhere soon?"

"I have a small dinner party to go to this evening. Will you go with me?"

"Sure. But do you know what I'd like to do now? I'd like to walk, just walk."

They walked the beach of Long Island. Anyone who observed them saw two people with their heads close together, laughing frequently. The man, somewhere in his early 40's, looked closely at the woman at his side as if he could see nothing else. The woman with the broad white hat looked at the man as if no one but this man could really make her happy.

A question pulled at Andy while they walked that afternoon. She had told him of her struggles and finally her success in the theater. But as he listened he wondered about what he'd read in the paper.

"I read something about you in the papers recently."

"Oh?" She laughed. "You know you can't trust everything you read in the papers!"

"I know. The piece said you were engaged."

"I was." It was easy for her to talk about Karl. She told him everything except the violence he had been ordered to perform. "He returns to Berlin tomorrow."

"He sounds like a nice man," Andy said sincerely.

"He is. He's a good man who only wanted to live honorably. You'll get to meet him tonight."

It was a small dinner party of Karl Von Bulow's friends from the diplomatic circle. They only knew the German embassy was recalling Karl to Berlin—only Lilly O'Hara knew why. She had gained his confidence where they had not.

She was slightly nervous—saying goodbye to Karl and introducing Andy. But the evening progressed smoothly. She hoped Andy felt comfortable. She hoped, too, that she could convey to Karl what their relationship had meant to her. The sadness in his eyes haunted her. With Andy in conversation with another guest, she stood apart with Karl. "You leave in the morning?" she asked.

"Yes, very early...I leave."

Her eyes scanned the room. "Your belongings?"

"They will be sent to me later. Berlin is anxious, you see."

"Karl, I...I'm so sorry...for everything to end like this."

His eyes traveled across to Andy. "Lilly, I did not want to say anything earlier when I was talking with your guest..." He looked away from her, and she sensed his hesitation.

"What is it?"

"Lilly, did I understand that Mr. Alcott's daughter sailed today?"

"Yes, on the *Lusitania*."

Again the hesitation.

"Why?"

"Did you see the newspaper yesterday?"

"No, why?"

"There was a notice in the paper, in many papers across the country from the German Embassy concerning transatlantic travel. I...I was ordered to place it. My last duty, you see."

"What did it say?"

"Simply that passengers of transatlantic vessels are reminded that a state of war exists between Germany and Great Britain and her Allies. They are sailing into a, a war zone, Lilly. They sail at their own...risk." His voice had become tired.

"But the *Lusitania* is a *passenger* liner!"

He ran his hand wearily through his hair. "I know, I know. But she is still British."

"This can't be. It's a passenger liner. It..."

He took her hands. "I don't know anything specific."

Her voice was barely above a whisper. "But you would not have sent a loved one on it."

He shook his head. "I am so sorry. If it was in my power..."

"I know."

She scanned the room for Andy. Karl understood. "I saw him wander into my library."

Lilly suddenly felt cold, as if the warmth and gaiety of the evening was slipping away like a shawl from her shoulders. She wanted to stand close to Andy, to draw strength from his presence. She found him alone in Karl's library.

"Andy, there you are. Ready to leave? Tired?"

But he did not answer. He stood very still, his arms limp at his sides, his face white.

"Andy, are you all right?"

A word, a fragment, a suggestion, a texture or odor—it could draw the mind back into the past where memories were always kept, yet often forgotten. He wasn't standing in a German diplomat's library in New York, 1915. He was 28 years old and in Mississippi at the home of his cousin Patrick Cash. Patrick Cash the artist. Patrick Cash whose last painting was titled *Magnolia Remembrance.*

Magnolia Remembrance, a painting of a young woman seated under a bower of magnolias and roses. A painting with a young sailor standing in the sun-dappled corner. A stolen painting thought lost at the bottom of the muddy Mississippi years ago.

"Andy?" Lilly gently touched his arm.

"Do you like this work, Mr. Alcott?"

Von Bulow stood behind them.

"Yes, I do. It's beautiful."

"It is also one of my favorites."

"Do you know what it is called?" Andy asked his host.

"No, I'm afraid I don't. Its origin is unknown to me. As you can see the artist's signature is obscured by water damage."

"How did you come by this painting, Mr. Von Bulow?"

"I purchased it from a dealer years ago when I first came to the United States."

"Andy? Is something wrong?"

"Wrong? No..."

He remembered as if it were yesterday. Amy was at his side. Now he could look on the painting—and see her again as he had first seen her. He drew a deep breath. "This painting is called *Magnolia Remembrance.* It is the last work of Patrick Cash...my cousin."

Lilly and Karl exchanged a look.

"The young woman became my wife...Amy," he continued slowly.

A silence. "Then this is your painting, Mr. Alcott," Karl said kindly.

"Mine? No, no it was never mine, really."

"But I will give it to you, surely it belongs—"

Andy smiled and patted the German's arm. "No, Karl, it is yours. It is a part of the past."

He took one last look at the painting, this testament of his youth.

Later, as they said goodbye, Karl looked at Andy across the room.

"Will your Mr. Alcott return to his New Orleans soon?" he asked the actress.

"Well, I...I don't know. In a few days most likely."

The diplomat leaned forward conspiratorially. "Without you?" Karl asked with a smile.

Lilly felt silly for the color that rose up her neck. She did not know what to say under Karl's piercing gray eyes.

"I do not think he *can* leave you," the diplomat continued. "He holds you with his eyes."

The blush intensified.

"And you. I think you will be very happy. You love this man."

"Karl..." she began helplessly.

He bent over her hand and kissed it. "You gave me my dream for a time, Miss O'Hara, and I thank you for that. Now will you do this one last thing for me? Would you sing for me? Let me carry your song in my heart."

Lilly O'Hara sang for the guests of Karl Von Bulow. She stood beside the piano singing, and Andy looked on with pride and Karl with tears. She sang 'Keep the Home Fires Burning' which she'd made popular for its sentiment in the face of war. And she sang 'Auf Wiedersehen' for Karl alone. Andy looked at the tall diplomat and knew this man had loved Lilly O'Hara and a part of him was dying from losing her.

They were both quiet in the cab that night. Lilly wondered if the man beside her was thinking of the young wife he had lost. And Andy had seen the sadness in Lilly's eyes when she said goodbye to Karl. Did she love him still?

The next day was Sunday. They spent the entire day together. They went to the mission hall where Lilly attended church ever since she'd come to the big city. Andy was silenced when she raised her voice. No Broadway comedy or drama, no patriotic tribute could stir him as she lifted her voice. Andy closed his eyes.

'Turn your eyes upon Jesus, look full in His wonderful face...'

Afterwards she took him to Central Park for a picnic.

"It's a beautiful park and a beautiful day," he said, not trusting himself to look at her when he spoke—lest he look too long. He sighed in contentment. "Right now, I'd rather be here with you in your Central Park than anywhere else on earth."

He was instantly furious with himself as he reddened. Certainly he had embarrassed her with his forwardness. He dared not look at her now. In the awkward silence, he finally pointed across the park to a small duck pond.

"You remember we met in a park, Lil."

She loved it when he called her Lil. No one else ever did—it was like a personal, intimate name he had given her.

"That is a day I'll never forget," she said. "I was tossing crumbs to the ducks and you walked up to me."

She had worn a cheap and gaudy wine-colored dress on that day. Her makeup was heavy but did nothing to conceal the despair and hurt Andy saw from where he sat. A woman had hurried past Lilly, spewing some curse, and Andy had gone to her then.

"And you said?" she prompted with a smile.

"Something about ducks." He chuckled.

"'Ducks are greedy, aren't they, Miss?' Then you asked me a question."

He looked into her eyes now, as he had then. They replayed that first meeting. "Do you know Jesus Christ?" he asked.

She tilted her chin up as she had those years ago. "I know about the Bible."

"No, Miss, about Him. Do you know Him?"

She was defiant in her fears when they'd first spoken. Now, Lilly had not forgotten her tone or her words.

"I've heard of God!"

There in Central Park they laughed together.

"I was a bit tart with you!" Lilly laughed. "Then you said, 'Knowing *about* Him isn't *knowing* Him, Miss!'"

Andy nodded. "You remember that little conversation very well."

She glanced away from him a moment and studied the fleecy clouds that drifted over the spires of New York. She turned back.

"It was the most important conversation of my life."

Their eyes held. He quickly scanned her face. She gazed at his mouth a moment and the sunshine on his beard.

"I suppose in some ways, 20 years isn't that long," he said quietly.

She smiled her agreement.

When Lilly and Andy stepped through the door of Valentino's the Italian was ecstatic, nearly upsetting a waiter in his path, as he reached for her.

"You are back! You are back! Oh, Miss Lilly!"

Even Lilly was surprised at her friend's welcome.

"I was so afraid, Miss O'Hara! It has been days of misery!"

"Why, Valentino! Why didn't you think I was coming back?"

"You were so sad when last you were here and you could not even eat your favorite veal parmigiana! Then your German friend was saying goodbye, and I feared, oh I feared you might go with him! It's been agony, Miss Lilly, agony!"

Smiling, Lilly kissed the big Italian's cheek. "I would never leave without really saying goodbye. But look! I'm here and hungry!"

The cook covered her hand in kisses. The other diners were spellbound, both by the presence of the famous actress and Valentino's extravagant and emotional performance. Then he straightened up, dried his tears and tried to recapture some professional dignity. But when he saw Andy, his dark brows elevated, and his face froze. Another man at Lilly's side!

"Valentino, I'd like you to meet Andy Alcott. Andy, this is Valentino, one of my very first New York friends and the finest Italian chef in New York!"

"Mr. Valentino," Andy said as they shook hands.

"I am Valentino alone," the cook said with obvious approval of the slim, bearded gentleman.

He seated them at the table that was always "Lilly's," no matter if occupied or not. Lilly was a little embarrassed with the Italian's arduous attention. "Valentino, is…well, he's very attentive as you can see. Spoils me…" She shrugged. "He can be fatherly at times, but he's very dear to me."

"I think he loves you," Andy said as he leaned back and regarded her. "In fact, Miss O'Hara, I have this observation."

"Yes?"

"Everyone we've met loves you," he said warmly.

Lilly colored under his gaze. "When I came to New York, he was there for me when I needed a good friend. I'm grateful for that."

There were years and their lives to share.

"…When Amy died…I died in a way. The doctor told me she was getting worse, that the cancer was advancing, but I…still, I was shocked and I didn't want it to be true. You know, we'd only had two years together. And then, she was gone. There was Melanie and Kate to raise. Kate was only a year old. I hadn't planned to raise them alone. It was supposed to be Amy and me together…" His voice drifted off.

Lilly did not know how to hold back her feelings. It was like trying to hold back the tide. He was as kind now as he was when she was a girl in pain. The tender heart was still there.

"I was afraid, Lilly, I don't know why. Fear made me a coward, drove me from my own children. I've never really talked to Kate about her mother. And there was my work. I could do that competently. The harder I worked, the better I got at it. Now I had a name in shipbuilding."

He looked up from his hands at Lilly across the table. "Do you think Kate is all right tonight?"

Lilly refrained from taking his hand in hers. She could not worry him with Karl's chilling words.

"I'm sure she's fine and having the time of her life. Probably dancing in the music room!"

"Perhaps I should have gone with her, even though she wouldn't have liked it. I...I've made so many mistakes with Kate. I know you can see that we...aren't very close."

"I can see that you care and love her deeply."

His eyes filled suddenly. "But love her enough? Or love her in the right way?" His voice was hoarse. "She's gone now and I feel...I feel like she's lost to me. I've lost the chance to make things right with her."

"She'll come back," Lilly said softly. "And you can love her again."

Later, they stood on the steps to her apartment. It was early morning in a city that never slept.

"I've kept you up too late, but I've had a wonderful day, Lilly."

"Me too," she said with a calmness she didn't feel.

He was so tall and handsome. They lingered in the shadows and finally said goodnight—though it was the last thing they both wanted to do.

"I have rehearsals and fittings most of the day tomorrow," Lilly said reluctantly. "Sorry."

"Oh, I'll be all right. I can't monopolize all your time."

"What will you do all day?" she asked casually, trying not to sound too intense or tender—as if she had some claim on him.

"I'll probably just hang around the hotel, do some work I brought along. And wait for you."

He looked embarrassed. But those four words kept Lilly O'Hara smiling all the next day.

St. John was too agitated and preoccupied to notice Lilly was humming and smiling. She was trying on costumes behind her screen while the manager paced the dressing room. He was sweating a bit around his stiff white collar. He glanced at his pocket watch—twenty minutes until curtain time. This wasn't the best time to bring this...this thing up, but if he didn't do it now he felt he would collapse from the strain.

"Uh...Miss O'Hara, I've thought over the...problem."

"Hmm?"

"The problem we talked about."

She peeked from behind the screen. "You mean Albert? Oh Albert was fine in rehearsal."

"No, no, not that. What we talked about the other day, you know."

"What did we talk about the other day? The critic from the *Sun?* Well, we just can't expect everyone to like the play. He was tactless but—"

"No, no, not that problem," he returned with exasperation.

She came from behind the screen and patted his arm. "What is it? You're acting jittery. You know that isn't good for your heart."

"Listen. The problem was your being lonely."

"Lonely? When was I lonely?"

Georgie sunk into a chair. Women! Didn't this prove his anxieties perfectly?

"Oh yes, now I remember. That seems so long ago."

"It was only a few days ago, Miss O'Hara. I have a suggestion, a plan for your loneliness. I have spent many long hours on this, and well, I think it could be a mutually, uh, mutual. It need not be complicated or distasteful. I've stayed awake long, ponderous hours..." He readjusted his tie. "I feel this is an imminently practical solution. Such arrangements can be, uh, messy but ours need not be. We respect each other—"

A sharp rap at the door interrupted him. "Ten minutes, Miss O'Hara!"

"Dear Georgie, what are you talking about?"

"Your loneliness, Miss O'Hara, your loneliness!" the manager nearly shouted. He had no idea proposing marriage could be so difficult! Certainly he expected it to be uncomfortable. But he was willing to be uncomfortable for the actress. He had gone over this problem carefully, finally arriving at a painful conclusion.

'We will live our lives as we have been...only together,' he had rehearsed in the privacy of his apartment. 'I will be your husband. No baby things...you will have to get over that. Perhaps we will buy a puppy...'

Another knock on the door. St. John knew it was time to leave. Miss O'Hara must have her pre-show privacy. He would try his proposal after the show. Surely it could go no worse than what he had already attempted. He opened the door.

"Miss O'Hara will not be bothered before a show!" he barked.

A man stood in the doorway with a huge bouquet of roses. Lilly brushed past St. John. "Andy! Come in, come in!"

"Hello Lil, I brought you these."

They were ignoring him entirely. St. John gave the stranger a scathing, head-to-toe scrutiny. Who was this man barging in? And Lilly! Actually fussing over him!

"They're lovely. Thank you."

The manager cleared his throat loudly.

"Oh! St. John, this is an old friend, Andy Alcott. Andy, this is my manager, George St. John."

They shook hands, with St. John suddenly stiff and suspicious.

"I'll see you after the show, Lilly." And then Andy was gone, leaving Lilly smiling into her flowers.

"He did look so...handsome in a tux, didn't he?" she asked absently.

St. John's lips pursed with disdain. What was happening to his normally levelheaded charge?

"Who is this man?" he asked icily.

"I told you, an old...dear friend."

"Dear?"

Lilly turned from the flowers to face him. "Yes, Georgie, *very* dear."

Lilly did not look lonely. In fact, she was radiant. He hadn't seen her look this way in months. He sighed deeply, relief flooding over him. As much as he loved Lilly O'Hara as a friend, he felt a little like a man whose execution was just commuted.

She wore silk and a string of jewels, and he was debonair in his tuxedo. They stepped from the theater looking like a couple enjoying a night on the town—a night of Broadway theater, and she was the star. But tonight she was more radiant than usual. Lilly and Andy were laughing—and Lilly O'Hara felt she was in a separate, private world with him. Just the two of them sharing memories and laughter. Intimate.

Then someone was at their shoulder, like the casting of a cold shadow. Two men.

"Miss O'Hara?" from a flat voice.

Lilly turned around slowly. These were no eager autograph seekers. It was the 'bookend brothers' as dubbed by St. John.

"Yes?"

"We'd like to speak with you for a few moments."

Four eyes traveled to Andy, measuring him. Andy turned toward Lilly, a question in his eyes. She gave him a quick smile.

"These men are from the State Department."

Still they hesitated, uncertain with Andy's presence.

Finally, "Miss O'Hara, we would like to ask you a few questions."

"You questioned me several weeks ago. Neither one of us learned much from that interview," she returned calmly.

"We'd like to change that."

She smiled. "Then please be as honest with me, as you expect me to be with you."

The government man who was silent now spoke. He was not as patient or as diplomatic as his partner.

"I suggest you cooperate with us, Miss O'Hara. A little item in the newspaper about the New Orleans background of a famous actress might not..." He let his words drift off significantly.

Lilly paled. She dare not look at Andy, though she felt him stiffen at her side.

"You are threatening me," she spoke hoarsely. "Why? Why?"

Andy's voice was firm. "Lilly, I don't think you have to answer these men, if they are indeed from our government."

"Please, Miss O'Hara, it's only that we want your cooperation with Karl Von Bulow."

"What do you want with him?"

"We want to question him. He's under suspicion and he's disappeared. We know you and he—"

Lilly held up her hand. "I saw Mr. Von Bulow two nights ago. We…we said goodbye. I understood he was leaving for Berlin the next morning. That is all I can tell you. Goodnight."

They slipped back into the shadows, and Andy and Lilly climbed into the cab wordlessly. Lilly gazed out the window. She was trembling. They had broken in on her lovely night like a discordant note in a symphony of perfect music. They had threatened and bullied her. They had brought up the ugliness and pain from her past—in front of Andy. Of course he knew it all; he had been there. But now it seemed she was cruelly exposed, and reminded of her sin.

Slowly his hand covered hers in the dimness of the cab. "Lilly?" he asked gently.

His voice opened the vault of tears.

"Lilly, Lilly, it's all right. They don't have to spoil our evening."

But she could not stop weeping. "It's…it's so…ugly," she sobbed.

He seemed to understand then. She was like a young girl of 18, trembling and ashamed in front of him. Tears came to his eyes, too. He slid his arm around her, pulled her against his chest.

They went to her apartment instead of a trendy New York night spot, and by the time she had the coffee going, Lilly was singing softly. She made them French toast and her 'famous' omelette. They were talking again, laughing and smiling. When he looked into her eyes as they sat on the sofa and ate, she felt that warmth she thought was stolen from them. The lights of Broadway, the war, espionage…that was another world. She and Andy were alone in her apartment sharing a meal.

They grew quiet after a time, their past real between them, their future a question mark.

"Andy, why were you nervous about coming to see me after you came to the mission hall?"

He glanced away then back to her. He fidgeted a moment under the gaze of her green eyes.

A blush crept up into his cheeks. "My daughter talks too much." He smiled weakly.

"She told me you were agitated and nervous. But I wouldn't let her tell me why. I wanted you to tell me."

"I…I planned to come up to you after you finished…but then I saw you…"

She leaned forward. "Yes?" She was completely charmed by his boyish, humble, hesitating manner.

He looked at her directly. "When I saw you, I thought the years had only made you more beautiful. But to me, they were less generous. Suddenly, I felt...old." He shrugged and smiled guiltily.

She knew then what in a way she had always known. She loved this man. She had loved him over 20 years ago. She had never stopped loving him. He was why she had never married. He had claimed her, even when he didn't know it, even when years had separated them, even when it had seemed he would never have her.

Tears suddenly spilled down her cheeks.

"Lilly?"

"I'm sorry. I keep getting soggy on you." Her laugh was shaky. "I'm just glad to see you...happy you came to New York."

An hour later he stood at her door to leave. "I had a nice evening, Lilly." She nodded.

Now she was nervous. She was holding herself back—from throwing herself into his arms. The strain was killing her. His daughter had implied there was a woman in New Orleans waiting for this man...

"Dinner was great, better than anything I've had in New York so far," he said with enthusiasm.

She laughed. "Valentino would be miffed, but thank you."

His hand rested on the doorknob. They stood only two feet apart. They both looked back into the lighted room. It was quiet, inviting, homelike. He shouldn't be leaving, going back to that lonely, impersonal hotel room.

"Well, good night," he said cheerfully.

"Goodnight, Andy." She smiled.

She leaned against the closed door after he'd left. Now that he'd come back into her life, letting go of him was even harder.

They were together each day that week for as long as they could be. Lilly's rehearsals were the only demand upon their time. Lilly dreaded the moment Andy would say he must return to New Orleans, but he made no mention of it. Still, Lilly knew it would come.

She felt as if some softly played music had begun the moment Andy Alcott opened his hotel door. It played in her mind, weaving around her heart—and the man from her past was a part of it. He was in the muted melody, in the lyrics they had not spoken.

She showed him the sights of New York from the Woolworth building to Carnegie Hall, to Wall Street and Trinity Church and Battery Park, and the Brooklyn Bridge. They worked beside each other serving sandwiches at the mission hall.

"Say Sal, ain't Miss O'Hara lookin' bloomin' this spring day?"

"Pass the pepper. She looks bloomin' every Thursday, Pete."

"But today she's more 'n usual. Must be that fella with the beard beside her."

"Must be."

She took him to the New York street where she'd come as a young girl for voice lessons.

"I couldn't afford lessons, so I'd stand there on the corner and I could hear everything from the open window. I was coached by one of the best and never paid a penny!" She laughed. "A true New Yorker!"

She showed Andy the sight that had stirred her heart the most of all the sights in the vast city. She showed it to him as she had first seen it— from a ferry deck on the Hudson River one early morning.

"Please humor me, Andy," she said apologizing for the early hour, "but she's really best seen with the sunrise behind her."

He smiled.

Liberty Enlightening the World stood clear and majestic in the early spring sunshine.

"When I came to New York, I had never seen anything so grand before. I still haven't. She seemed...she seemed to represent all my big dreams. And I remember wishing you were there to see her, too."

He gripped the rail as the towering statue came closer. Her copper skin was turning green from the continual assault of the Atlantic, but she was no less magnificent.

"You were right to be impressed," Andy said.

They climbed the 189 steps to the observation deck. New York in hazy splendor, the Hudson curving with tiny barges and tugs, the Atlantic stretching out in an endless vista of blue.

"I remember before I left New Orleans you told me that my dreams weren't too big." She looked up at him.

He smiled. "It looks like you got all your dreams, Lilly."

She turned away from his gaze back to the panoramic view.

"No...not all," she whispered.

"So..." He stood nervously juggling his hat from one hand to the other.

She stepped closer, but he did not seem to notice. "Yes...so..." she agreed.

"It's been, I mean, I've had a wonderful week, Lilly."

"It's been wonderful for me too."

"So...so I suppose, however, it's time to get back to...work."

Lilly gazed at him, not saying a word. He pulled at his ear.

"Back to New Orleans and...work and things."

And that woman, she thought. She had restrained herself, with some difficulty, from touching him, from being forward in word or gesture. But he was leaving. Leaving. She didn't want the music to end. She couldn't hold back any longer—never mind if he was shocked or embarrassed. Her hand went to his cheek, slid down the line of his jaw.

It totally flustered him. He turned red. But Lilly did not, could not stop. Hers was a pure love. As full as her life was, physical affection and intimacy were absent. It was like a well waiting to overflow.

"And of course you have your work to return to," he continued.

"Hmmm..." Her right hand caressed the back of his neck, wove into his hair. Her left hand toyed with the buttons of his jacket.

"And...I suppose we...could write...if you wanted."

Her eyes were closed. "I suppose..."

Her hands slid lightly across his chest. Then she held his face in her hands a moment, fingering the softness of his beard.

"I'm sorry, Andy, but I can't really seem to...stop myself."

Her arms slipped around his neck.

"Lilly..." he whispered. "Lilly, why didn't you ever marry?"

She smiled. "I was engaged years ago. And then there was Karl. But really, there has only been one man all these years that I really wanted to give my heart to."

He stared at her in complete surprise. "I never thought...I'd get to love again," he said softly.

"I never thought I'd get the man of my dreams..."

"Lil, I've told you about Amy...and what a mess I made with Kate, how I've lived for work, lost sight of the important things..."

Her finger brushed lightly across his eyes. "Maybe I can help you get your sight back, Andy. Let me try."

Tears rolled down his cheeks. "Could you want a failure like me?"

"Could you want a girl that once belonged to Max Hawk?" she asked, smiling through her own tears.

His arms went around her. "Are you real, Lilly O'Hara?" he asked huskily.

"Kiss me, and find out how real."

His arms tightened. "I think...there's only one thing left for us to do," he whispered into her hair.

"I think you're right," she answered softly.

"Is tomorrow too late?" he asked smiling.

They were married the next afternoon in a little chapel outside the city with only Valentino, his wife, and George St. John present. Immediately after, they slipped away to Lilly's summer home in the mountains. But not before Andy dispatched a telegram to Mississippi.

Meg, I was wrong. There can be more than one great love in a lifetime. I have been given the gift again. Andy

St. John was happy for Lilly, despite the uncertainty it cast upon her career.

"I would say yours was a very unconventional and brief courtship, Miss—pardon me, Mrs. Alcott. But I trust it will be a, a forever one."

Lilly smiled and kissed his cheek.

"Oh no, Georgie, this wasn't a brief courtship at all." She looked across the room at her husband. "This is a love affair that started 20 years ago."

Chapter 13

Kinsale

◆◆◆◆◆◆

*P*adraic Falconer thought he would never sleep again without seeing the floating bodies in his mind. He had never seen anything equal to it in his 27 years. Something like a groan twisted inside each time he viewed another victim of the *Lusitania*'s last voyage. He drew deeply on the tangy sea air he had breathed since he was a lad, and tried to focus on the miserable, but living victims that now filled his decks. He could take on no more, Pierce had come to the tiny wheelhouse to tell him, or the *Bluebell* would flounder. He nodded curtly and turned his craft back toward the Irish coastline. Hopefully the other rescue ships were as full of survivors as his was.

It was a good morning of fishing for the Falconer brothers' *Wanderer of Peel* and *Bluebell*. The catch of mackerel was prolific. By noon, the duo of ships had returned to Kinsale to unload. With such success, Padraic decided it was wise to return to the flat calm for an afternoon try.

The weather was balmy, the boats lulling gently in the cradle of the sea. Padraic had sent young Tom Wood below decks to fix tea for the crew of five. He glanced up at the smooth line of the horizon, momentarily stunned and transfixed by what he saw. A ship was in distress. Four stacks, a huge liner then. The morning's telegram came back vividly. In the beauty and work of the morning he had put it to the back of his mind, hoping the German subs had left the channel.

'Aye, and be helpin' 'em out there, please Lord.'

He shouted up at Pierce who held the wheel. "Swing her around!"

The crew vaulted to the rail. An incredible sight, a ship going down bow first. Padraic rushed to the port side, yelling and pointing to Denny who captained the *Wanderer* some yards away.

"Go to her!"

Three miles to the horizon, and never had three miles seemed so far to the captain of the *Bluebell*.

It was late afternoon when the *Bluebell* eased into her berth in Kinsale's little harbor. The docks were crowded with townsfolk. It looked to Padraic as if all of the village and surrounding farms had turned out. The constable bristled with sudden importance, directing the ships as they unloaded their human cargo and trying to marshal the curious, eager-to-help crowd.

And already the tide was bringing in the unfortunates. They would drift into the Kinsale coastline for weeks to come. Padraic shook his head—no, not many would forget the sights they'd seen this spring day. But he could not dwell on that now. The living were just below him, shaking in the coming evening chill, moaning and crying out for loved ones, injured, staring with vacant, shocked eyes. Pierce came up to him again after the ship had docked.

"Aye, and you know I'm not a drinkin' man, Paddy, but I feel I could use something...after...this..."

Padraic nodded in understanding. "But our work isn't over. Let's get to it."

The constable and his 'deputies' tried to sort through the confusion, taking names of the survivors who could speak. And the Kinsale doctor was giving orders as he quickly assessed the injuries.

Constable Speight came up to Padraic and Pierce. The three looked into each other's eyes briefly, then turned away. Words could not express the horror. "Falconer, we've about unloaded your boat. 'Tis a good thing you were in the harbor when...'tis true you saved a lot of souls this day."

But so many more I was too late for, Padraic spoke into himself.

"Where are the injured going, Jim?" Pierce asked.

"The admiralty has sent that bus there to take them to Queenstown. Others will stay in our homes tonight and be moved in the morning."

They turned as the final rescue ship chugged in. A woman cried out her child's name in an eerie wailing. Padraic turned away, his throat tightening. He suddenly felt like Pierce—a stop at the pub was what he needed to help him sleep tonight.

"We've unloaded all," Pierce said with a gray face, "except those poor souls." He pointed to the six lifeless bodies covered by a fishing canvas on the *Bluebell*'s deck.

Padraic sighed and looked to the docks. The constable hadn't any help to spare. "We'll put them on the wagon there, Pierce. Come along then."

Together, silently and gently they carried three men, and two women to the hearse. Padraic was relieved there were no children on the *Bluebell*. That would be too much.

A beautiful, tranquil evening was slipping over the harbor, and still the crowd lingered. Padraic felt tired as he knelt by the last figure. He could carry this one alone, the figure was so slight. He had not looked at their faces, but he felt drawn to look at this one.

'Look Padraic,' a voice seemed to demand inside him. 'Look!'

Wet hair that curled, a fine oval face, an angry red slash across the lower jaw, eyes and long lashes as if closed in exhausted slumber. He glanced at a hand, fine and delicate, gripping something. He carefully pried the fingers open, as if afraid he could cause further pain. The fingers clutched a broken pencil.

"Padraic, son."

Padraic looked up to find his mother standing beside him. He was so glad to see her. Her graying hair was loosened as if she had been running, her red sweater clutched at her neck, her eyes wide.

Padraic nodded. "Aye, Ma..."

They looked back to the body. Maggie Falconer knelt down on the wet, fish-smelling wood.

"Ma, this one is...is so young!" Padraic sobbed. His tears overflowed then. Never mind if his fishing cronies saw the big fisherman kneeling and crying on his deck on this awful day. He pulled the limp body to him, hugging it and crying. The wrist fell against Maggie Falconer and her midwife skills were instinctive. She held the slender wrist. "Paddy! There's a pulse!"

"What?"

Maggie felt the throat. Yes, a faint but true pulse.

"Son, this one is alive. She's alive! Get a blanket. We must get her warm. Pierce!"

He laid the body down quickly. "You sure?"

And then the eyelids fluttered open just an instant—green eyes that made Padraic think of the sun on the Irish sea.

She woke up cold and wet. She was 12 again, swimming in the Gulf when her father had strictly forbidden it. She shook her head slightly and sighed. It wasn't like she couldn't swim. In fact, her father said she was a fish. But he didn't like her swimming alone, or with her young friends. The tide could be dangerous. She had disobeyed and now she wondered in a disoriented way what her punishment would be.

She did not open her eyes, but she knew someone was caring for her.

"Dad?" she whispered weakly.

"Aye, you are all right now, you're safe. We are taking you home."

It was a strong, smooth voice—with something else, an odd lilt that she couldn't identify. Well, it didn't matter, whoever it was would take care of her, she could feel that. She was safe now, and Dad wasn't scolding. She felt that heavy blackness coming over her again.

"Dad..." she moaned.

The Falconer home was strangely quiet. Darkness had fallen, and all the brothers were at home and gathered in the kitchen. The fire was lit, but dinner had not been laid, and no one was thinking of eating now. Pierce sat in a rocker, his head back and his eyes closed. Tired as he was, he was not asleep. Denny sat at the long oak table, staring at his hands. Rory was pacing. Padraic stood at the fireplace, one foot on the hearth, poking absently at the logs.

Maggie Falconer was in her bedroom off the kitchen with the doctor and the survivor Padraic had carried up the long path from the harbor.

"We can take her in the cart here," Maggie had pointed out.

But Padraic shook his head stubbornly, and his ma knew better than to argue. "You ride, Ma."

He had felt that somehow the girl depended upon his protection and strength. And besides, the body was so light, it felt almost weightless in his arms. He could walk up the path as quickly as the donkey cart Rory and Denny had brought down.

Denny started the tea. "How old, Padraic?" he asked in the stillness of the big kitchen.

"Hmm?"

"How old do you think she is?"

Padraic shrugged. "I didn't look close—a young girl, maybe 14 or so." He turned back to the fire. He did not want to answer any questions.

The bedroom door opened and the doctor emerged. He glanced briefly at each boy.

"A cup of tea before you go, Doc?" Denny asked respectfully.

The medical man shook his head tiredly. "I'm thankin' ya, Denny, but no. I've…others to see about, you know."

"What can you tell us about…" Pierce nodded toward the bedroom door.

"Only that she's a young girl in a state of shock and exhaustion. In the morning, I'll know more."

Padraic did not look away from the fire. "There was a red welt on her face," he said quietly.

The doctor nodded as he pulled on his hat and coat. "Probably hit by something in the…confusion. May have had to jump overboard. Well, goodnight boys."

The kitchen was quiet save for Denny stirring a pot of soup.

"Knowin' Ma, she'll want to stay in there all night. She'll get worn out. We'll have to take shifts. And we need to get her to eat."

Padraic looked at his younger brother and smiled tiredly. "Your soup, Den? You want us to eat *your* soup?"

The brothers chuckled, and it eased the strain.

"Go on and fetch her in here, Pad," Denny shook a spoon at his big brother. "And you can eat with the pigs if you have a mind to."

Padraic stepped into the little bedroom off the kitchen. He closed the door quietly and stood rooted in the shadows a moment. He rarely had occasion to enter his ma's bedroom, but when he did he was always and immediately struck by its smallness and sparsity—it reminded him of a chapel. Smooth, whitewashed walls and two small leaded windows that faced the sea, a sturdy bed, a rocker, pegs driven into the walls for her clothes. Such a plain room without ornament.

"Ma, you could take a bigger bedroom and fancy it up," his sister Jen had said.

"There are other rooms for that," Maggie said without looking up from her bread board. "I want no distractions."

Jen had rolled her eyes without understanding. But Padraic knew. He knew his ma prayed in this room as much as she slept. Simple, plain and peaceful, that was Maggie Falconer, and that was her room.

He came to stand behind his mother and laid a big calloused hand on her shoulder. "Dr. Ellis didn't say much," he said quietly as he watched the face of the young girl in his mother's bed.

Maggie nodded. "Aye, and it's a short tongue the man has, you know, Paddy."

"How is she?"

Padraic trusted his ma's wisdom and experience as a midwife more than he did the taciturn village doctor with his black bag of ancient arts in dusty brown bottles.

Maggie sighed deeply. "She's a young one, Padraic, and I'm hoping that's where her strength lies. She's fighting a fever from exposure. Look here, the doctor and I did not agree." She pushed back the coverlet and exposed a slender arm to her son. Padraic winced. The arm was mottled with bruises. The hand was bruised, swollen, red and raw.

"What does the doc say?"

"He looked it over and says it's a bad sprain and no more. But I think the hand is broken right here. Looks and feels the way Rory's did the time he fell from the tree. I need to set it." She looked up. "I know you're tired."

He watched the girl's face. "No more than you."

"I can ask Rory to help me. I know such sights…"

Padraic flushed at the reference to his notorious aversion and weakness at the sight of blood.

He shrugged. "I think I can manage this time," he replied gruffly. "Has she spoken?"

"Nay, she is in and out of a deep sleep. Best to set her hand now."

So young-looking and vulnerable…

"Jen's age maybe or younger?" he offered.

Maggie nodded, thinking the same. Someone's young, tender daughter had lived through this horrible tragedy.

"She'll be frightened when she wakes up in a strange place," he said.

"Aye, I'll be stayin' the night with her. When she wakes, I can calm her."

"We can take turns," he said easily. "No need to wear yourself out."

Maggie stood and looked into the face of her oldest son. Here he was showing more...interest in this 'situation' than she would have expected. He must be feeling this protection that she was feeling.

"To think if you hadn't held her close, Paddy, someone might not have discovered, and she..."

She couldn't finish. Even the practical, steady Maggie Falconer was chilled at the thought. The young girl could be lying in the cold morgue in Queenstown.

But he had held her—and his ma had felt the slowly ebbing warmth of life. Yes, this one, from so many, he was able to save. He smiled then in the dimly lit bedroom. Like a chapel, this was a good place for the survivor.

"Let's get to her hand, Ma, 'fore she wakes."

"Aye, son."

This was the loveliest sleep she'd ever had. Something like a baby must feel tucked in its mother's arms. Before, she had always felt sleeping was a waste of time, but this was different. Nothing could tempt her from this delicious rest. She felt weightless, somehow suspended, without any feeling in her body. Like she was drifting...just drifting. And not having to think.

Four lifeboats rocked quietly against the rough wooden dock. They were tied together, a grim testament, the stunted offspring of a mammoth parent. Only four, from the world's largest passenger liner. *Lusitania* was painted a deep blue upon their smooth sides. Tied there in the Kinsale harbor, they would demand attention and photographs from the crowd.

So the admiralty officials worked quickly in the paleness of dawn. The boats would be towed on to Queenstown. But first they must be emptied of the assorted collection that lay in the few inches of muddy water at the bottom of each. They held the items that passengers had clutched in their escape, but were separated from in the rescue. Items to be boxed up and sent to Queenstown. The workers were silent as they gathered up the pitiful reminder.

Six mismatched shoes, three lifevests with *Lusitania* emblazoned on the backs, one broken deck chair, one leather belt, two soaked gray sweaters, a crushed watch, a beaded purse. The workers did not meet one another's eyes as they picked up the toy doll. And one red leather book. A journal. The fly leaf was waterstained, obscuring the name of the owner. The worker flipped through it casually, noting the fine hand, then tossed it into the box. Any of these items, especially the lifevests with the liner's name, would command a premium from the hunters. Already that was happening along the beach. Well, not these. These were bound for Queenstown.

"They've counted over 700 dead," Pierce said in a dry monotone as he came up the path from town. His brothers were lounging in the sun-shine outside of the cottage.

"Seven hundred," Rory repeated, shaking his head. "That's more than Kinsale folk."

"And a black day it is for Germany!" Denny added fiercely as he tossed down the garden tool he was sharpening. "America will be in by tonight."

"Hard to say," Padraic said. "The men in government are not a pre-dictable lot, Denny. Who would think the kaiser would allow his navy to act so?"

The town was congested with strangers, and while the pub and hotel keepers had plenty to keep them busy, there was not much for the broth-ers and most of Kinsale folk to do. Rory had closed the school.

"What's the use?" he shrugged. "They are all at the harbor, or along the beach or hanging around the market."

It was unspoken, but no one, not even any of the local fishing fleet, wanted to be out in the water just now, no matter how the fish were run-ning.

They had gotten all their meals and cleaned up after themselves, their ma appearing sporadically. The girl's hand was set, and now the brothers heard a low but discernible cry from behind the closed bed-room door off the kitchen. They eyed each other nervously. Denny kicked at the ground with his boot.

"I can't stand this. Can't Ma do anything for her?" he asked as he jumped up.

"She's trying, Den, she's trying," Padraic soothed with false calmness. The pathetic cries tore at him too.

Maggie appeared suddenly at the door. Her hair was straggled, her face pale. "She's wakin'. Run down to the apothecary's, Denny. Fetch this back to me. Hurry!"

Her strength was feeble as she fought against the intrusion into this delightful sleep. Persistent, worse than just annoying. She didn't want to wake up, not yet. But something was pulling on her...pulling on her...hand! Making it hurt. No, no...stop, this is hurting me. On fire, and so thirsty. More than just her hand, her whole arm. Now there was definition to her, the drifting, weightlessness was abruptly, harshly gone. Now her arm hurt, and her hand throbbed. She felt pain when she breathed, a burning across her face. Please, please stop, stop pulling me...

Maggie Falconer was rarely agitated. Like the gray cliffs along the coast that weathered the ferocity of the North Atlantic winds, she stood against the storms of life with unwavering calm. The brothers rarely worried about her. They laughed about how the cottage could burn down around her and she would just continue darning.

"Aye, 'tis true it's a little warm in here, but I'll just finish this sock, then we'll look for a new place," they could imagine her saying.

But now she was a little concerned and nervous. Padraic watched her with amusement.

"What is Lydia thinkin' to be startin' at a time like this?" she sputtered as she gathered her shawl and changed her shoes.

"I suppose I could go over and tell her and Burt that Maggie Falconer said she needs to wait," Padraic teased. "Tell the little one inside, too."

Maggie frowned. "I knew it would come in the middle of the night like this. All the McHans have been unthinkin' about other folks' sleep. Middle of the night babies, every one of them."

Padraic glanced at the clock on the china dresser. "'Tis only nine, Ma, hardly the dead of night."

She shook her head, unmoved by his words. "I was afraid this would happen. I don't like to leave...her."

They all knew who 'her' was.

She pinned on her hat. "Now, Pad—"

"You've told me, Ma, a dozen or more times already. Give her the dosage if she gets too frantic. Sponge her down if the fever goes up, try to keep givin' her water."

She took his arm and peered up at him. "Can you manage, Paddy? She's wakin' from it and she may get rough."

"I can manage."

"You'll send one of your brothers if you need me?"

"There's two upstairs in their beds and Pierce snoring in his chair here. I'll send if I need you."

"I'll be back soon." And with another shake of her head she was gone.

Padraic took a deep breath and stepped into the bedroom. He was confident in front of his ma, but now...he approached the bed cautiously. She was moaning and beginning to thrash. He was afraid she would hurt the arm and hand that was swathed in bandages. And so he carefully held her arm, and she grew calm. He pulled up the chair, slowly relaxing. Perhaps she'd do no more than sleep until Ma returned.

· · ·

She was humming the "Blue Danube" to herself. Strauss was so lovely. Maybe if she kept humming she could fall back into the soft grayness. Then she wouldn't feel this sharp, burning pain. If only the waltz would last...

It was past midnight and Padraic had fallen asleep. Something woke him, some movement or noise. He woke groggy then became instantly alert as the figure in the bed woke. Her back arched, and her arms flailed out. When she threw her head back in a scream, Padraic jumped up, sending his chair over backwards. She was thrashing and screaming. Padraic was terrified. His ma had not prepared him for anything like this.

The bedroom door flew open and his brothers entered in their night-shirts. They were wide-eyed and pale.

"Do something, Pad!"

"Where's Ma?"

"Help her, give her something!"

"Go on now, go on all of you! I'll be takin' care of her." Padraic waved at them sternly.

They retreated skeptical and shocked.

"Glad you're the oldest tonight," Pierce muttered as Padraic slammed the door.

She sat up, wild-eyed, her face flushed and perspiring. He stood beside her uncertain. He didn't want his presence to frighten her further. He knew from the look in her eyes she was seeing past him, seeing those terrible things he had not seen. He lowered himself carefully onto the edge of the bed and slowly put his arms around her. She did not fight him.

"'Tis all right now, lass. You're safe, easy now."

Panting like an animal caught in a trap, finally she relaxed against him. "There now, there..."

Her eyes were closed, and her breathing grew easier. Padraic wiped her forehead, her lips with a warm wet cloth.

"Now try a bit of water, lass, aye, that's it."

Still she wouldn't open her eyes, but she took a sip of cool water.

"Dad?" Her voice was tentative.

Dad. That was the American word for "father," wasn't it?

"No, lass."

There were tears in her words. "Clark, please?"

"No...lass, but you are safe."

She slowly opened her eyes.

Padraic saw her face in a new way. Those green eyes he had only glanced at, the delicate oval face, a pretty mouth, the angry red slash against the jaw. She was looking at him, her eyes frozen wide. She backed away.

"I won't hurt you, lass...never," he said.

The tears spilled out. "Who, who are you? Where am I?"

"You are in the Falconer home. I'm Padraic. My ma is caring for you."

She couldn't stop shaking. "Where's my dad?" The tears continued to spill.

"I...I don't know, lass. I'm sorry."

The eyes clamped shut. "Where's Clark and Dorothy?" she whispered.

Padraic twisted his hands. If only Ma were here.

"Can you take another drink?" he asked gently.

She shook her head violently.

"Please don't be afraid, lass."

Kate Alcott was a proud girl in her own way. Confident. And if she was ever afraid, she was careful not to show it. She was terrified now, terrified because she couldn't think clearly. Suddenly the past and present were muted and mixed together. She didn't know how to begin to understand. And this stranger.

Thirty minutes passed in silence. She lay very still. Then she finally drew a deep breath. "Where am I?" Her voice was hoarse.

"Ireland. You're in Ireland."

Ireland? The Emerald Isle...Ireland. How...

Screams and pushing. The black steward forcing her to...to jump to the lifeboat. Jump. Then she couldn't see his face at the rail. There were no faces. Only the cold wetness and the sudden pain in her hand.

"No, no..."

The *Lusitania* was sinking. The blissful, welcoming darkness came over her like a soft blanket against the chill. She was glad it was back.

Queenstown

Anna Ruebens was shocked at the dramatic changes that had come to the port city seemingly overnight. The streets were choked with crowds, and schoolchildren were everywhere with the unexpected holiday. The fishing fleet was in. The local police force with its new recruits stood at every corner. Even while there were crowds, a somber, rather than festive atmosphere prevailed. Churchbells tolled, slow, deliberate, almost ominous. American flags hung at half mast from the consulate building. Three public buildings, including the town hall, were turned into temporary morgues. Horse-drawn carriages filed through the city at mid morning, loaded with plain black coffins. A mass grave had been prepared in the Old City cemetery, and Queenstown reeked of death.

Anna heard the reports, of course. The great liner had gone down, hit by a German torpedo. The survivors' testimonies had spread like wildfire. German submarine. A heinous thing. She tried to ignore it, ignore the death count repeated at her shoulder. This did not concern her. Not at all. But she was edgy. She felt like a thousand eyes were watching her with suspicion. As she hurried to her job at the customs office now, she was stopped suddenly.

"Good morning, Anna."

It was one of those sailors she had met months earlier. One of those who didn't seem to notice her cold indifference to his attentions.

"I'm on my way to work," she said brusquely.

"Work? Most offices are closed today. Or hadn't you noticed?"

"Goodbye." She attempted to brush past him.

He chuckled. Who would laugh on a day such as this?

"Auf Weidersehen, Anna."

She didn't turn, though she felt his eyes on her back. She hurried through the crowd. And then another hand and voice restrained her.

"Anna! Haven't seen you in awhile."

The imposter was annoyed. "Hello, Jen. I'm on my way to work."

"Really? Bailey's let me have the day off. I'm on my way home for the day." She leaned forward. "Want to come with me?"

"No, I said I have to go to work."

"Oh."

"Goodbye."

They really weren't friends anymore.

Jen looked around. "Isn't it awful? What the Germans have done? All those bodies..."

Both girls shuddered, but Anna lifted her chin. "It is part of war, Jen."

She was gone into the crowd then, leaving young Jen Falconer staring.

"What has happened to my...hand?"

These were the first words the 'Lusitania girl' spoke to Maggie Falconer. Without opening her eyes, Kate must have felt her presence at the bedside.

"Aye, it is broken, lass. I've set it. It will hurt for a time, but it will heal."

Maggie did not like the listless tone from one so young. The voice was dull and had a hopeless quality. And clearly American as her son had said. Yet she herself was excited. The girl was coherent enough to speak. It was a beginning—an answer to her prayers. Padraic had told her what had happened during his vigil by the bedside. Maggie was not surprised.

"It was like she...was coming up from the sea, you know, gasping and...and surprised she was still alive. Afraid, she is."

Maggie had brought in the tray with food.

"Can you take a little nourishment, lass? You need it sorely."

The eyes opened slowly. Kate nodded cautiously and took the spoon. Then she began to tremble and cry, slow tears.

"I'm Maggie Falconer, as my son said," the older woman said soothingly. "You're in Ireland. We are taking care of you."

Enough information to answer some questions and start clearing away the confusion but not too much at once to bring back the horror.

"Can you tell me your name, lass? Your family, you know, will be so glad."

Kate turned her head and began to sob.

Constable Speight had never been so busy or felt so important in his term as peace officer of Kinsale. The *Lusitania* had sunk off the shores of his little village and suddenly his work included much more than dealing with complaints of a meandering cow in the neighbor's potato patch or some youngster pulling pranks or some local serenading too loudly at the pub on the corner.

The preliminary inquest would be held at the old market house of Kinsale, and the trial between the admiralty and Cunard lines would begin within the week at Queenstown. Suddenly the Irish fishing village captured the eyes and ears of the world as testimony from survivors came forth. The hotel overflowed with officials and newspaper people, as did the pubs. Kinsale was crowded with unfamiliar faces and loud automobiles. Everything had changed from that beautiful spring afternoon. With all the pressing duties, some detail continually nagged the constable's mind. Something about a passenger... The Falconers! He'd sent a survivor home with them four days ago.

"Mornin', Pad."

"Mornin' Jim, step in."

The tall constable ducked into the doorway of the Falconer kitchen. "Not out yet?"

Padraic made a sour face. "Who can sail with the crowd on the docks or newspaper types runnin' up here every hour to talk to me about the rescue? Aye, it's a circus. I'd just as soon it move on to Queenstown."

The constable chuckled. "Well, the pubs are doing a booming business, so we must take the good with the bad, Padraic, the good with the bad."

The bedroom door off the kitchen opened and Maggie Falconer emerged. "Aye, and I thought I heard your voice, Jim. Tea?"

"No thank you. It's a busy man I am these days."

"Too busy for tea then?"

"Well it is business that brought me here. Forgot altogether the *Lusitania* girl we sent home with you a few days ago. I could be getting myself into serious trouble from such a neglect. The Cunard officers want all the names, everyone accounted for, you know. Johnny Hogan is beginning the inquest this afternoon. So I need to speak with your girl, or have you moved her to Queenstown?"

Padraic watched his mother carefully. He knew the protectiveness she'd assumed with their "guest."

"'Tis the truth she is here with us. But you can't be speaking with her."

The constable gave Padraic a quick glance and a raised eyebrow. "Well, now, Maggie, we need to know who she is. Her family must think she's dead."

"Aye and that's the truth. But the girl can't be questioned like you have in mind. She's terrified and suffering and not even Admiral Coke himself could get past me to her."

Padraic inspected his boots carefully. The truth was the girl in there had no idea what a formidable defender she had for herself.

"Well what does Doc say is the trouble with her?" the constable asked. He saw her bristle; he saw his mistake.

"What is wrong with the girl, Maggie?" he corrected.

"Her hand is broken and she's badly bruised." Maggie looked down at her own hands. "But her mind is bruised in a way, too. There is a proper term for it, but I'm not one much for proper terms. She's lived through a terrible experience and been terribly shocked. She can't think clearly right now, lest she remember all the things she saw. So her mind pushes her back into semiconsciousness when the pain becomes too great."

"How long will she—"

Maggie stood up, her tone brisk again.

"I don't know. You'll just have to tell Cunarder we have a young girl survivor with us. Paddy and I both think she's American. I'll send you word immediately when I know more. Good day, Jim."

"He who dwells in the shelter of the most high, will abide in the shadow of the Almighty..."

The words were spoken in that lilting, almost musical tongue. Ireland. The Irish brogue, yes, that was it. Kate kept her eyes closed. She didn't want the musical voice to stop. The words were soothing and calming her. But...slowly, she raised her hand to touch. Immediately a hand gripped hers, and now she did not pull away or flinch. And the words did not stop.

"I will say to the Lord, 'my refuge and my fortress, my God in whom I trust.'"

"Don't leave me, please, until I go back to sleep. And if I wake, will you still be here with me?"

Maggie smiled. "Yes, little one."

Still Kate did not open her eyes. "You have a, a lovely voice. In a way it reminds me of my grandmother. In a way..."

Grandmother Sara. The face of the one she loved came to her mind and she was crying again.

"What is your name child?"

A sigh. "Katherine..." Kate tightened her grip on the hand. "Do you think I could call...do you have children? What do they call you?"

"Ma mostly...or Mum."

"Ma...I never called anyone mother or ma before. Is it all right with you?"

"Aye, Katherine, call me Ma," Maggie replied tenderly.

"Good, good...I'd like that. I'm so tired."

"Just rest."

"But if I sleep, I...I see them, Ma. I see the babies. I hear the ones trapped in the elevators screaming. There were 39 babies!"

Maggie smoothed her wet forehead. "I know, lass, I know. God is loving them now."

The eyes opened. "God? I don't...I don't think I can believe there is a God! I can't! Not now!"

"There, there, Katie girl. Listen, little one. You do not have to believe right now. I will believe for you. Hold on to my hand, aye tightly, and I will hold on to His."

Chapter 14

Chicago

♦ ♦ ♦ ♦ ♦

*T*he truth was, Ben Alcott felt more fatigued than amorous. But it wouldn't be polite, certainly not suave, to let Ellie Meyer know, so he tried to keep his mind alert, his kisses firm and directed—and not openly yawn in her face. He felt if he dared close his eyes longer than a blink, he'd be snoring in Ellie's ear. It wasn't that Ellie wasn't an understanding girl—she knew Ben put long hours in at the airfield, but he'd promised her this drive out on the lakeshore road for several weeks.

So they sat in the front seat of Ellie's coupe, looking on the unruffled surface of Lake Michigan. Clouds scudded across the sky and obscured the moon. Ellie snuggled close to Ben, sighing with contentment. She was talking, and Ben was only half listening to what she was saying, something about one of her friend's problem with a boyfriend. His mind was on an engine he'd left unfinished at the airfield. His life was planes and their assorted ills now. They were never far from his thoughts once he'd come to Nehi and begun fulfilling his dream. Girls like Ellie were definitely pleasant distractions—but only that.

"So, what do you think about the idea, Ben? Think you can go?"

"Huh?"

She laughed and poked him in the ribs.

"Ouch!"

"You weren't listening to me, Ben Alcott!"

"Sure I was!"

"You've been mumbling the last few minutes," she accused with growing anger. "You weren't listening!"

"I was. You were talking about Judith and her problem with Roy. Right?"

She crossed her arms. "That was 30 minutes ago."

"Really?"

"Really."

He shrugged. "Huh…well, what were you talking about?"

Her voice was cold. "I was talking about you going on a fishing trip with my father. You weren't listening."

Ben could think of no creative way to quell this sudden storm. He tightened his arm around her, kissing her with wide-awake passion. It worked.

Minutes later, headlights swung onto the end of the darkened lane where Ben and Ellie, and a dozen others were parked. The car stopped.

Marty Meyer sat on the top of his seat, peering into the night. "Hey ya, Ben! Ben, where are ya?"

Ben burst out laughing. Ellie was furious and slid down in the seat. "I can't believe what a tactless, embarrassing little brother I have!"

Ben stood up. "Over here, Marty! Third car to the left!"

"Ben Alcott!" Ellie fumed.

Meyer brought his car up beside his sister's. "Couldn't pick you out from all these couples. Hi, Ben! Hi ya, sis!"

"She ain't speakin' to you, Marty."

"Huh? Why not?"

"She says you're tactless and embarrassing."

"You both are!" Ellie hissed. "Marty, would you like it if I did this to you when you were with Julie?"

Her brother shrugged. "Sure, if it was important."

"And this is? Coming out here yelling like a maniac?"

Marty hopped out of his car and leaned on the running board. "Sorry you're in a cross mood, sis. Seen a paper in the last few days, Ben?"

"Nope, not in a week or so."

"That's what I figured."

"Marty Meyer, you came out here to talk current events? You interrupted us and—"

"Interrupted what, sis?" he asked with a sly wink at Ben. But his tone turned serious. "Maybe this isn't just any current event. When you went to Peppercreek a month or so ago, you told me your cousin, uh—"

"Kate."

"Yeah, her. She was sailing to England on..."

"On the *Lusitania,* why?"

Marty clicked on a flashlight and unfolded a newspaper in Ben's lap. "The *Lusitania* was torpedoed two days ago."

"Torpedoed?"

"By a German sub off the coast of Ireland. Never made it to Liverpool."

Ben saw Kate's excited, animated face in his mind, eager for her European adventure.

"How bad is it?" Ben asked, not wanting to wait to read the details in the paper.

"She sunk in less than 30 minutes according to witnesses. Early estimate...1000 lost."

Ellie took Ben's hand. It was cold.

"A thousand?" he whispered. His fatigue was gone—and any chance for romance.

The international reaction to the sinking of the *Lusitania* was immediate and clamorous, like the climactic breaking of a violent thunderstorm that was idling but very real on the horizon. Within hours the stunning details traced their way through the western world—the magnificent *Lusitania* was gone with an appalling loss of life. Newspaper headlines were grim in their brevity.

'*Lusitania* torpedoed and sunk...'

'World shocked by Germany's biggest crime...'

'Lusitania's death toll enormous, sunk without warning...'

'Huns' most cowardly act...'

Now the anti-German sentiment that waned over the winter months flared again with passionate intensity. Riots broke out in European cities against German citizens and their businesses. It ranged from the serious to the ridiculous—Germans dragged into the streets and beaten, their shops looted or boycotted, to renaming dachshunds 'liberty pups' and sauerkraut 'liberty slaw'. Some universities discontinued German studies, and libraries banned books with German titles and authors. Propagandists for the war effort found a wealth of opportunity in the tragedy—recruiting posters flourished in the British Isles.

The death toll rose to 1,198, with 128 of the dead, Americans. Would this bring the United States into the war at last? London and Paris privately hoped so; in Berlin, the kaiser was nervous and volatile. President Wilson had been firm in his notes to Germany, with phrases about 'strict accountability' if American lives were lost from German submarine attack. Ambassador Page in London had wired the president and cabinet in succinct terms.

'The United States must declare war or forfeit European respect.'

Yet the White House remained strangely silent. The country waited tense and expectant. Surely Wilson would soon give the marching orders. Men's clubs took bets to the hour that Wilson would declare war on Germany. But they were wrong. They had not counted on the tenacity of Woodrow Wilson, his commitment to neutrality, his aversion to war, and his peaceful upbringing as the son of a Presbyterian minister. He would carefully consider the proper course in the face of this German outrage. This was not yet the hour.

the Adirondack Mountains, New York State

A mild rain had fallen a few hours earlier, and now in late afternoon, the sky was cloudless, clear and pale between the frame of towering pines. It would be a clear night as the sun and moon orbited to their customary places—a million stars would be scattered and shining.

A thin muslin curtain fluttered lazily in the breeze redolent with wet pine in one of the open windows of Lilly O'Hara's summer cabin.

"Andy?"

"Hmmm?"

She smiled against his chest. "You sound content."

His eyes were closed. "Content is an inadequate word to describe how I feel right now."

"Andy, you know what...I was when you met me in New Orleans years ago."

"A lovely young woman."

She smiled again. "I was one of Max Hawk's girls."

His hand fingered her red curls. "Lilly..."

"Thank goodness I don't have to hide that from you, or try to explain it." She rolled over to lean on his chest, to look into his face as she spoke. "When I was with a man...I gave what he...paid for. But I didn't give myself, not all of me. What I did was wrong, of course, but...but I always felt that if I married I would give my husband something those men hadn't taken from me. And I thought with the man I married, it would be like I was pure again."

"Lilly, I love you so much. How can I show you? The rest of our lives I'll be thanking the Lord He gave me such a treasure."

Peppercreek

Sara Alcott knew her son and daughter-in-law were watching her with anxious eyes. It was a week of stunning news, they reasoned, hard on the composure of a 75-year-old woman. First, she learned her son had remarried after years of widower-hood—and to a famous Broadway actress at that! Then the shocking loss of her beloved granddaughter in a tragedy at sea, the innocent victim of a war on the other side of the globe.

They calmly told her the news of Kate—and expected her collapse in hysterics. But she did neither—for Sara Alcott did not believe it.

New York State

He walked slowly up the path from the stream that ran below Lilly's cabin. The sun was warm on his face and he smiled to himself. He couldn't remember when he'd felt so peaceful and contented inside. It was still rather amazing to realize that a little over two weeks ago he was in New Orleans, feeling his age, feeling lonely, working over ship designs with a devotion that had carried him through a span of comfortless years. Everything seemed gray back then, he mused to himself; now everything was in color, living, vivid color.

He had slipped away from their bed while Lilly slept, to walk to the stream and pray in the early morning. No words were adequate for how grateful he felt to the Lord for bringing Lilly O'Hara back into his life. And not only back into his life as a dear, old friend, but as his cherished wife. He imagined the shocked faces of his family and friends. And he thought of the words he must compose to Virginia Hollins.

He started up the steps to the cabin.

"I hope that's my husband," came a musical voice from around the back of the cabin.

Lilly stood over a large washtub that had collected rainwater. She stood in the sunshine wearing one of Andy's shirts and towel-drying her hair. Andy stopped. Her wet hair was red burnt living gold. Was there no end to her loveliness?

"It is your...husband," he said as his eyes went over her quickly.

"I borrowed your shirt." She fingered the fabric, her voice almost shy. "It makes me feel like...I belong to you, to wear your shirt. I hope you don't mind," she faltered under his gaze.

He came forward to take her in his arms. Amazed was the word, at the sudden color in his life—the red of Lilly's hair.

"I don't mind at all. Take everything..."

Nehi

"There is such a thing as a man being too proud to fight. There is such a thing as a nation being so right it does not have to convince others by force that it is right..."

Marty Meyer was reading the text of President Wilson's speech, his first public reference to the *Lusitania* sinking.

"So there you have it," Marty continued with unveiled disgust. "Woody sounds pretty noble, but it ain't much comfort to those with family at the bottom—" He stopped and shook his head. "I'm sorry, Ben. I keep forgetting."

Ben leaned over the airplane cockpit. "It's okay, Marty."

"Any word?"

"Went into town last night and called home. "My folks..." He shook his head. "She isn't on the survivor list in the papers."

The clanking of tools in the silence.

"Sorry, Ben. She sounded like a great girl."

Ben straightened up and brushed the hair back from his sweaty forehead. He tossed the rag aside. "Yeah, she...was. You would have liked her. You know, it was only a month ago and I was home and saw her. I can't quite figure, just like that, she's gone. She was so excited about going to Europe. Was going to write all about it. She liked writing like, you know, I like flying."

Marty was thoughtful a moment. "I have to go now, but I'll be back tomorrow. You takin' her up?" he asked pointing to the plane.

Ben grinned and thumped the side. "If Jimmy lets me."

The rich man's son lingered in the yawning sunlit doorway of the hangar. "You know, Ellie is getting to like you...a lot, Ben."

Ben was surprised at Marty's sudden serious tone.

"Yeah? Well, she's a sweet girl. I like her, too."

"Ain't exactly my affair, but what do you think about the butcher business?"

Ben understood the implication. "You're the heir, Marty," he teased.

"Ain't for me. Not yet, anyway. I have too much livin' to do before I sit in an office all day." He shrugged then grinned.

"Consider yourself warned. See ya!"

It was quiet in the hangar now, but Ben did not immediately return to his work. With Jimmy in town after a part, there was no need to hurry. And with so much on his mind, it was difficult to concentrate. He lounged in the shade of the hangar, looking out at the trembling heat waves over the airstrip. Farther on the corn was waist high. Perfectly still and quiet, remote. Ben could imagine he was alone in the entire world.

He thought of his red-headed cousin with her fun loving, mischievous ways. Gone. Too young...with so much life in front of her. It saddened him deeply—he was genuinely fond of Kate.

Wilson's continued neutrality. Like most, Ben was surprised. He tried to sort through his feelings over the conflict, German aggression, American involvement. He thought of blue-eyed Ellie Meyer. Could he sit behind a desk and count pounds of meat all day? But a rich man's son-in-law could own a lot of things—things a mechanic at 12 dollars a week could only dream about. His own airplane, or a house on Lake Shore Drive. He was not so backward from his rural raising that he did not know the proposition that was coming. If he was honest with himself, it was a temptation...to take a wife he did not really love.

I'll know the right one, David, when I look in her eyes, something will tell me she's the one.

That something had not spoken. He imagined his grandmother's disapproving face in his mind.

Is this the girl you want to spend eternity with, Ben?

He brushed the question aside. Back to the plane, gleaming muted silver in the hangar. There was something safer than figuring out the designs for a wife! He smiled—yep, much safer. Tomorrow he'd go up again. Tomorrow he'd fly!

It was a quilt of greens, russet and wheat, a slash of pale blue, bisecting roads of brown, scattered squares of silver from tin roofs, and the faded red of silos and barns. Ben was exhilarated. With Jimmy in the seat behind, Ben was up for another flying lesson. The older pilot didn't want to inflate Ben's confidence by saying anything, but the boy had obvious skill. He'd taken to the controls, easing, lifting, lowering the machine in all its cantankerous moods with a natural grace. And Jimmy could hardly conceal his amusement at Ben's obvious glee at flying.

A perfect day for flying, Ben wanted to stay up for hours, perhaps even swoop south to Peppercreek to wiggle the wings at his family! That would shock them!

But Jimmy tapped him on the shoulder. Time to start back to the field. Ben slowly looped and began the five-minute return approach. From this height he saw the road winding to Nehi perfectly—and the dust stream from a car. Curious, he lowered and could see the car and driver clearly. It was Marty. And his Bearcat he always bragged over.

"You can go faster on the ground than in one of those crates up there!" Marty had teased.

Ben had snorted and doubted Marty's intelligence.

Now he knew he'd get a royal chewing out from Jimmy for this, but he couldn't resist. He swooped parallel to the car only yards away. Marty saw him coming and waved enthusiastically. The race was on.

Ben pushed the stick foward all he dared, skimming ten feet over the cornfields, a swift gray shadow above the yellow-brown stalks. He could see Marty pushing the car to its limit. The hangar came into view quickly—Ben had won. He looped back up with a shout, then leveled for a landing. He climbed out, trying to conceal his triumph with a sheepish, repentant look. Jimmy crawled out gingerly. He lifted his goggles and stared hard at the young mechanic as his cheek worked up and down with a mammoth wad of tobacco.

"You could have killed us," he snapped.

Ben kicked at the dirt. "Yes, sir."

"Worse, you could have cracked up *my* plane."

"Yes, sir."

"You have a lot to learn. You're not a flyer yet."

"Yes, sir."

"Your take off was sloppy."

Ben nodded in agreement.

"Don't let it happen again." And he loped toward the hangar as Marty approached. "Beat ya, Marty," he said as he hurried past Marty's car.

"I came out to tell you my news," Marty said without preamble.

Ben eyed Marty with caution as he peeled off his overalls. He could never predict what new scheme the rich boy would come up with.

"Yeah? You gettin' married or taking your place behind the desk?"

Marty laughed. "Neither. I've joined the French foreign legion. I got the okay today. I leave end of the week."

Ben stood surprised in his shorts and undershirt. Another advantage to the airfield's remoteness. "You've joined the legion?"

"Yep, sail from New York in ten days, join up in Paris. I can't be sitting around waiting for Woody to make up his mind about this."

"I think he has made up his mind," Ben interjected.

"Well, he can keep his notes. I'm gonna join. The papers say Allies are having a hard time and the Krauts just can't win. I'm a German American. I'm going to add my two cents to this, maybe help push 'em back over their own lines and folks can go back to living decently, plowing their fields instead of burying their dead in them, and raising their families. You know the papers say the French countryside is being torn up. There's a cathedral in northern France that the Germans blew up for target practice, a beautiful old church—we saw it two summers ago. Think of it. This began as a gripe between the Serbs and Austria. Anyway, this *Lusitania* business is the last straw for me, all those innocent people." He shook his head. "I know I'm just one, but I can give what I can to make it stop."

Brave words, but they both knew the price for them could be high.

"What do your folks say?"

"Well, Dad's pretty riled up about the *Lusitania*. He's all for me going because he's convinced I'll come back. Mom's pretty teary."

Ben thought of what he'd read in the papers, the battle fronts, the deprivation and destruction. He knew the stories like Marty knew them. Now he personally knew someone who was joining the surge of men facing the fire.

"You sure about this, Marty?" he asked gently.

"Sure I'm sure. I'll go off and have my adventure. I'll come home and find a nice little gal and settle down to sell sausages!" He slapped Ben on the back. "I'm going, and I'll come back."

New York City

They would forever think of her in a paternal way, both St. John and Valentino, even though now she had a husband. They could not change overnight, or feel differently, less protective of her, because she now had the last name of Alcott. So George St. John was thumping the newspaper and Valentino was wringing his beefy hands.

"Oh, what a sadness! A great tragedy, St. John!"

St. John wasn't certain what the agitated Italian was referring to: the sinking of the *Lusitania,* or having to call a man on his wedding trip to tell him his child might be dead.

"They may already know," Valentino wailed. "Poor Miss O'Hara!"

The manager shook his head vigorously. "They won't know about it, I tell you! Lilly's cabin is remote and she firmly told me not to contact her for at least five days. She is so rarely firm, but she was adamant on that point. Told me she didn't want to hear a whisper from the outside world."

"But what shall we do?" Valentino despaired. "Her husband, his daughter! Surely they must know."

They both looked back to the newspaper where the first list of victims was published, along with the list of survivors. Alfred Vanderbilt, millionaire, had perished with so many others. But the list of victims was not complete.

"Alcott is not on...the list," Valentino pointed out.

"Nor is she on the survivor list," St. John growled. His finger traced the names on the list. Under the list, the newspaper noted that many victims were unidentifiable, and others were not yet claimed.

The two men looked to each other in sorrow. Katherine Alcott was not on the survivor list, so must be a part of one of the others. How could they break into a wedding trip with such news? Slowly, St. John reached for the telephone.

in the mountains

It almost frightened Lilly to feel such happiness. And to feel such pleasure in Andy physically. She wanted to touch him all through the day and night, as if to assure herself he was real and would not vanish as suddenly from her life as he had appeared. He was there to talk to, to tell all the secrets of her heart to, to eat and sleep with and to sit in silence with. And to pray with. Andy had opened his heart entirely to her about his daughter.

"I've got to change things with Kate. I've wasted so much time. Nothing else matters, but that I'm right with my daughter."

Five days, she had told St. John. Five days with no demands from her career or touch from the outside world. Five days alone with Andy in her cabin retreat in the mountains. No radio, no newspaper. The closest human contact was the general store two miles down the mountain from the cabin steps. Only the melodies of the forest, and only his rich laughter and voice. Hours to talk and walk and plan their future together.

She lay beside him in the darkness smiling before she fell asleep each night. They were sharing an experience supposedly reserved for couples half their age. She was a woman of 42, as eager and excited as a girl of 18 with her first boyfriend!

It was midnight now, and they had walked to the stream, to sit on the grassy bank in the shadows. The moon reminded Lilly of a huge yellow lantern in the sky. She sat in front of Andy, leaning against him, his arms around her.

"Is this a dream I'm going to wake up from?" she murmured.

"If you wake up from it, I'll still be here," he promised.

The young delivery boy from the grocery store had no idea he was the bearer of bad news. He only knew he was delivering a message from some imperative sounding voice in New York City to the actress lady's summer cabin in the hills. He didn't know he was about to bring darkness and pain into Lilly O'Hara's perfect world as he puffed up the trail that morning. He was about to bring five perfect days to a shattering end.

They heard his whistle from the end of the winding path. Lilly was trimming Andy's hair, and now their laughter stopped, their smiles faded. Someone had found their retreat.

"Hello!" Andy called with false cheerfulness from the porch.

"Mornin'!" the voice returned.

Lilly hurried into the cabin to make herself presentable. It wouldn't be wise to be seen in one of Andy's shirts—this 'uniform' of her honeymoon. Such a bit of gossip would be bandied across the county before dinnertime.

The young man appeared at the cabin steps. "Mornin'." He looked up at the slender man with the towel over his shoulders. "Come from the general store," he said jerking a thumb over his shoulder. He leaned against the step a moment to catch his breath.

"Need some water?" Andy asked. "That's quite a jog you've made to find us."

The boy grinned and shrugged. "Used to it."

"Uh, can I help you?" Andy prodded.

"Sure, if this is where Miss Lilly O'Hara is."

Andy nodded. "This is my wife's cabin."

Lilly appeared beside Andy then. "Good morning." Her voice was friendly to the intruder.

He nodded. "Brought you a message, Miss O'Hara." He pointed to his curly cap of hair. "Didn't need to write it down."

"Actually, I'm Mrs. Alcott now. But thank you for..." Lilly felt an apprehension that her voice did not reveal.

"Got a call for you from New York, from a Mr. George St. John. He said you're to call him at his home phone immediately. Was urgent. We're open till six this evenin' if you want to use the store phone, Ma'am."

Andy and Lilly exchanged a guarded look.

Lilly smiled weakly. They both knew somehow that this urgent message had nothing to do with a Broadway role.

Outside the night sounds were in full melody—crickets, frogs, the wind in the pines. Every other night, Lilly and Andy had listened to them as a background to their own words of love. Tonight these sounds only intensified the silence.

Andy placed another log in the fireplace then sat down again beside Lilly. Every other night the fire provided the perfect setting for him to take her in his arms. Tonight it was a screen to fix horrible imaginations on. She wanted to ask him if she could make him something to eat. He had eaten nothing since breakfast—the last meal before the boy from the store whistled into their little kingdom. Yet she knew he'd say no he wasn't hungry. He sat leaning forward slightly, silent, dry-eyed, and absorbed in the yellow-orange flames.

Remote. Lilly couldn't touch him. Not with her hands or her words. In these first few hours of shock, he withdrew into a private world of grief. Lilly O'Hara could only watch.

New York City

Black wreaths still hung on the gold embossed doors of the Cunard liner offices. This was a long and tiring week for the staff. So many phone calls. So many frantic family members pleading for a word on survivors. Government men asking questions. And, of course, the barrage of reporters.

Mr. Booth had spoken with dozens of hollow-eyed, gray-faced men like the one standing stiff in front of him. And immediately he recognized the famous woman with the red hair who stood beside him. She looked tired and sad, as well. Another time, under different circumstances, he would have told her he had caught her performance two years ago. She was wonderful. But now, no this was not the time. Not with the man at her side looking fragile with stress.

"Dorothy and Clark Benton?"

The official consulted his list. His frown deepened.

"I am sorry, Mr. Alcott, they did not survive. I deeply regret I can tell you no more. Your daughter's name does not appear on...on the survivor's list."

"I see," Andy said calmly.

The Cunard man, though he was practiced in it, hated to be so cold and blunt. He couldn't take away every shred of hope for the grieving man.

"The inquest in Queenstown is still underway concerning the sinking. New information comes in daily to these offices. There are still...victims that have not been identified. And..." He hated this part of the report worst of all. "And some...passengers are still missing."

Andy looked past the man to the ocean map on the wall. Then he looked to the open window where he could hear the sounds of the busy street.

"Then you're saying my daughter, Katherine, is dead."

Booth saw the woman slip her hand over the man's, clutching it.

"I...I can only tell you what I know from Queenstown, Mr. Alcott. I can not tell you to rule out all hope. There are passengers still recovering in the hospital who we have not clearly identified."

"But you know their nationality?"

"Two British women is all I know at this point, sir."

"My daughter is American..." His voice sounded dead.

It was one of those days Booth did not like his job in the vast Cunard office.

"Andy?"

Lilly stood framed in the bedroom doorway of her apartment. She wore a lovely white nightgown, but she could have worn rags from the way Andy looked past her. She had gone to bed to stare up at the ceiling while Andy sat in the darkness of the living room. He could be back in New Orleans for the gulf that lay between them. But it was a different loneliness for Lilly O'Hara than it was a month ago. Now she'd been held and loved, so now she felt the void. Those five days in the mountains were like a dream. She was choking with sadness to see Andy so destroyed with grief. Her apartment with him was quieter now than it was when she had lived alone. At least then she could sing out loud. Now, she didn't feel like singing.

He slept only when exhaustion overcame him. He ate little, hardly spoke or touched her or looked into her eyes. She turned away and cried when she heard the flatness in his voice as he called his family.

"No...no, she still isn't on a list...yes, I...know..."

"Clark...I'm so sorry..."

She stepped into the room now. "Andy, I'm afraid."

He looked up and she winced to see his vacant eyes.

"I'm afraid, Andy. You've...left me. You've gone someplace...I can't go with you. Please don't do this to me, please."

His voice was cracked. "I don't know...what to do."

"Talk to me...let me hold you, or, or comfort you somehow," she pleaded.

She stood in front of him, but still he looked through her, not seeing her.

"Andy, please talk to me. Don't close me out of your world."

"What can I say? Shall I tell you how I'm hating myself for so much...I gave in to her when I shouldn't have. It was wrong for her to go..."

He sunk to his knees, sobbing. "I've lost my daughter. There's no second chance. No turning back the years to start over...to stay at home and know her, and love her...too late..."

Lilly stroked his head as she would a child and cried with him. Now she knew what had happened to the tender man beside her when Amy had died. It was happening now. She was losing him.

Chicago

Dancing was one of Ben's favorite things—a girl in your arms or spinning around you, accompanied by some lively music. It made his list somewhere just under flying, kissing, and one of his mother's meals. And Ellie Meyer was a great dancer. So Ben was having a good time on the dance floor of the Lake Michigan country club, doing the fox trot. For the evening he could forget thoughts of war, Kate's death, Marty's sudden decision. He was wholly prepared to enjoy the night without sobering or weighty words or thoughts. Ellie Meyer seemed to be enjoying the evening, too, but then she led him to the terrace, where other couples had drifted, and he wondered if she might not have slightly different ambitions for the night. They stood with the inky blue sheen of the lake and the lights of Chicago in the background.

"Pretty nice shindig," Ben said with a smile. "Pretty gal, too."

They kissed in the shadows, lingering awhile.

"Ben?"

"Hmm?"

"Daddy and I were talking..."

"You've been warned, Ben," Marty had said.

"We were talking about you."

Ben had known this conversation was coming.

"Dad thinks you're bright and hard working. He likes you."

Ben liked the older Meyer, too. There was no posturing or snobbishness from one of the wealthiest men in the state. He didn't seem to notice Ben's obscure, rural upbringing. The whole family was likable and would make great in-laws...

"He knows I like you," she continued.

Ben tightened his arms around the young woman's waist. "Yeah? How much?" *Keep it light,* Ben told himself. *Another kiss.*

"I...I think the question is, how much do you like me, Ben?"

She had been raised by a successful businessman. She, unlike Marty, had adopted some of his tone and manners. She could bargain, be direct, be diplomatic.

"Ellie, you're the best girl I know."

She looked him directly in the eye. "Enough to become engaged to?"

He was sure he had paled just a shade underneath his healthy tan. "I'm a poor farm boy, Ellie, and now, a greasy mechanic."

"And I'm an heiress to something of a fortune. We both know where we're from, and where we want to go, so..."

"I..." He smiled lamely and shrugged. Here was the chance of a lifetime. How could it be a hardship?

"There's room in Dad's business for Marty and you, Ben."

Everything he could want. Suddenly he thought of his own parents, his grandmother and grandfather, his Aunt Meg and Uncle Barrett. They all loved each other deeply.

"I think my grandmother must be prayin' for me about now," he said shakily.

"What?"

He was surprised at his own deep tone. "Do you love me?" he asked gently.

She was surprised and obviously a little embarrassed by the question.

"I...don't know. I hadn't...I mean, I do like you very much."

He had taken out dozens of girls and never meant to hurt any of them. "I think we're supposed to love each other. I'm afraid if we don't, we could end up...making each other unhappy."

Everything had gone wrong. Jimmy, usually affable and unhurried, was in a sour mood. When their backs were turned, the Nehi cat had slinked up on the table and eaten their breakfast. The windmill that supplied water to the field had broken in the night. And the wind itself was strong and choppy. Hardly cherished flying conditions. Yet Jimmy was determined to make a test flight.

"Wind's pretty strong out there." Ben pointed to the wind sock that was taunt and perpendicular to the field. "And there's clouds over there banked up in the east."

They had reversed roles. Ben the impetuous, always ready to fly, had taken the cautious tone.

Jimmy polished his goggles with the elbow of his oily coveralls. "We have a show tomorrow and I want to try out that new cylinder."

"We could wait to take her up this afternoon. It'd give me more time to work over that oil leak."

"Stop frettin', Ben. I'm going up."

He did go up, and he came down—but not at all like either man had planned. By evening, Ben Alcott was out of a job.

Peppercreek

The family sat down for mid-day dinner. Ben was home in the middle of the week, and his mother had laid the table extravagantly. Sara said grace.

Her son Matthew looked up from his plate.

"Uh, Ma, you...remember what we told you about Kate? What, uh, happened to her?"

Sara surprised them with her irreverent-sounding laugh. "Of course I remember what you told me. Oh, Matthew, you don't think I'm losing my mind, do you?" She shook her head at her son.

"Ma..."

"You told me Andy married an actress named Lilly O'Hara and Katherine went down with the *Lusitania*."

All at the table winced at the bluntness.

"Uh, yes, Ma, that's right. Never mind."

She did hate to be patronized. "Matthew, what is the problem?"

"You prayed just now for, for Kate, Ma, that's all. Never mind, really."

"And why shouldn't I pray for all my children and grandchildren? Why shouldn't I pray for Kate?"

Millie Alcott was rarely diplomatic. "Grandma Sara, Kate is gone."

It was Sara's turn to cast them a regal and pitying smile. "I am praying for Katherine because I don't believe it."

"What?"

She calmly and daintily dabbed the corner of her cheek. Sometimes her family was so amusing.

"Oh, I believe you believe it's the truth, but I don't believe it's the truth."

"What?" her son gasped again.

She appealed to Ben with her eyes.

He smiled. "You're saying you don't think Kate died."

"Exactly, Ben. You have to have a body for a death. There is no body!"

Only Ben did not look shocked.

"Ma..." Matthew laid his fork down patiently. "I don't think this conversation is...is appropriate for the dinner table."

She smiled and shrugged. "You brought it up, son."

He looked exasperated with her. "Ma, this isn't a good way for you to think, that Kate is alive. It will only hurt more. She's gone, Ma."

"Her name is not on the survivors' list, nor the injured. That only leaves those missing. Missing people show up all the time. There was Harry Daniels. His family thought he was killed during the war between the States. They sent his mess kit and personal effects home and everything. Two years after the war, he shows up! And have you forgotten about your own brother Andy? Your father and I received a telegram that he was lost at *sea* and several weeks later he came home!" Her voice was triumphant.

"Ma," Matthew said tiredly, "this isn't like that."

"And why not!"

"There are some...bodies the papers say can't be identified."

Millie Alcott groaned aloud.

Sara felt every eye on her. She clutched her hands together under the table. Her voice was still as firm, though, her blue eyes still flashing. "I understand. You have your facts, that's fine. I'll hold my faith."

"Do you really believe Kate is alive, Grandma, or, or do you just really *want* to believe it?" he asked gently.

Sara smiled and tousled his hair from where he sat below her. Depend on Ben to ask her the hard questions. It reminded her exactly of the kind of question Kate herself would ask—direct, and perhaps not so gentle. Kate.

They sat together on the front steps, David had gone off for the evening with his girl, Bess, and Ben's parents had gone to bed, not wanting to deal any further with Sara's...peculiarities. Both were glad for the time alone, the bond of understanding very real between them. Sara was eager to talk over what had brought Ben home unexpectedly in the middle of the week, looking tired and troubled. But first, she must deal with his question.

"I doubt I can give you an answer that will satisfy you, any more than I could give one to your parents. I do want to believe Katherine isn't gone. Something in my...spirit tells me to keep praying for her. When your father told me, I didn't feel sadness or grief, I felt the urgency to pray. Something..." She closed her eyes and smiled. "Something tells me to have faith and hope. And I'm trusting the same voice will tell me...if it's time to stop praying for Katherine."

Ben gazed out across the purple-shadowed lawn. He wondered if his grandmother held him in prayer with such intensity. Feeling depressed and uncertain, he hoped so.

"Now tell me, Ben, tell me what happened."

As broad-minded and empathetic as she was, Ben knew his grandmother hadn't much affection for his profession. So he must condense and edit his remarks. No need to provoke a lecture, 'I told you how dangerous those machines are!' Later, in the privacy of their shared bedroom, Ben would tell David everything.

It all happened so fast. Ben still felt the shock of it, like hearing about Kate and the *Lusitania*. Jimmy on a routine flight with Ben looking on apprehensively. Dangerous and sudden thunderstorms, even tornadoes at times, were as much a part of an Illinois springtime as flowers pushing up in the garden or apple blossoms in the orchard. But the weather was not the culprit this time. Suddenly smoke wisped, then poured from the cockpit and the plane spun crazily. In these early days of aviation, such difficulties were part of the thrill. Ben wasn't thrilled this time and watched helplessly as Jimmy brought the machine in for a landing. It was, as Jimmy later described, 'The worst landing of my life. I hope you weren't watchin' too close, Ben. It was a crack-up, all right.'

But Ben's watching had saved the pilot's life. He'd run forward and pulled the unconscious man from the smoldering plane. Seconds later, it burst into flames.

In the hospital Jimmy was grateful. "I think I should be thankin' you for savin' my life."

Ben wagged a finger at him. "I'd rather you be saying you'll listen to me next time about oil leaks and things. I'm the mechanic, remember?"

And now a mechanic without a job.

"Jimmy has a few cracked ribs and some minor burns. The plane is a total loss. Nehi's out of business for at least six months while Jimmy picks up another plane. That's it."

A few cracked ribs and minor burns... What if Ben had gone up too? Sara chewed her lip. This flying business was so dangerous, and Ben obviously loved it. It was hard for her to restrain from saying the predictable, 'If men were meant to fly...'

"David is getting serious about Bess. What about you and this girl in Chicago? The hamburger heiress."

Ben laughed and shook his head. Ellie. When had his life suddenly become so complicated? Marty was leaving. His job, his passion were gone. His savings was meager. And Ellie.

"She asked me to marry her."

Sara Alcott nearly gasped out loud. Oh, the forwardness of these modern girls!

"I would have been a rich man, Grandma Sara, that was plain. I could have bought Nehi and a dozen planes!"

"Benjamin!"

"Well, it's true."

"To marry for money!"

He swiveled around to face her. "I had to turn her down. I...I didn't love her exactly. I...It wasn't right, you know, kind of like the feeling you have about Kate."

She smiled and patted his broad shoulders. They did understand each other.

It was after two in the morning and the Alcott brothers were still awake and talking. David's narrative of his evening with Bess was brief—he had found the girl who would "capture his heart." Ben in turn told him all about Jimmy's accident, Ellie Meyer's proposal, and his own frustrations. They talked of the latest war news. He tried to tell his brother what flying was really like.

"You can't imagine what it's like up there! So blue and, and clean, seeing everything for miles...you're like a bird up there!"

David yawned. "Except birds don't leak oil and crack up."

Ben ignored the jest. "It's the greatest thing, Dave."

David rolled over to face him. "Better than the best kiss?"

"Ooh, that's a tough one...but yeah, I think it's better."

They both laughed.

"So with Nehi shut down and no to selling sausages, what now?"

"What now? Well, Pa would take me working with him...I went to an airfield in Chicago and they don't have any place for me. I'm back to where I was six months ago."

David sat up and turned on the bedstand light. "I have news, Ben."

"You and Bess are gonna get hitched!"

"That's part of it."

"Congratulations, little brother. That's great. When?"

"Uh, not for...awhile. Here." He handed him a newspaper—an article was circled in red. Ben read quickly, feeling the intensity of David's look upon him. A group of college men in California were forming a group to go to France as ambulance drivers and medics. Ben looked up startled.

"I've joined them," David said. " I'm going over as an ambulance driver and assistant medic."

"But...but..."

"You're the first one I've told, besides Bess, of course. With the news of Kate earlier in the week, then you coming home suddenly and Ma and Pa...well, I'll tell them in the morning."

"But what about you and Bess? You said you were engaged."

"We are. She understands and agrees with me about the war. It'll be great medical experience for me, instead of just puttering around with my books."

"You were going to go to school in the fall."

"I will when I get back."

First Marty, now his own brother! He glanced down at the paper again. Young men, his own age, were also joining as aviators. Ben lifted his eyes and found David smiling. He didn't sleep much that night.

New York

He could see just a faint glimmer of water from Lilly's apartment window. He had loved ships and the ocean since he was a boy, but now it had claimed his youngest daughter. Andy was alone in the apartment—alone with his anger and fears and the pain that felt like a wave of darkness poised to overwhelm him. He stared at the skyline without really seeing it—all he could see was the *Lusitania* gliding down the Hudson and Kate waving from the rail. And young Clark Benton beside her and Dorothy trying to look dignified in spite of her worries.

Years ago he had struggled with the pain of loving another man's wife. Struggled until there was peace. Then he'd lost the woman he loved. He'd withdrawn from life then, slipping into some kind of emotionless void.

He would never forget those hours alone in Lilly's apartment that morning. He cried and prayed as he never had in his life. He could not ever quite explain to Lilly what happened, but suddenly the blackness was gone. Suddenly he knew that no matter what he lost, he was not really alone. He was still loved, still had hope. The pain of losing Kate would always be sharp, but now he had the strength to bear it.

Lilly. Lilly! He had hurt her, frightened her. He grabbed up his cap and dashed from the apartment.

She had hated leaving him alone when she went to rehearsal. And then the call came in to the theater during her solo in the third act.

"Lilly! An Alfred Booth from the Cunard lines is on the phone! Should I give him the shake?"

Lilly flew to the phone. Then, to the amazement of cast and crew, she was suddenly laughing and crying. She dashed to her dressing room, collected her hat and purse and waved at an astonished St. John on her way out the door.

"I'll be back!"

Miss O'Hara had never left a rehearsal! St. John stood gaping. What had marriage done to his star?

Her cab slowed to a crawl two blocks from her apartment. A water main had broken and dozens of children had appeared to dance in the cataract. A New York traffic jam was in full progress. She jumped from the cab with a toss of coins and started running. She knew she would attract attention, maybe even make the papers the next day, but she didn't care. She could have telephoned him. No, this wasn't the kind of news you telephoned if you could help it. So she ran, her hat gone in the crowd, her hair flying and tears streaming down her face.

They met at the steps to her apartment.

"Lilly!"

"Andy!"

He grabbed her and swung her up in his arms. "Lilly, are you all right?" he breathed into her hair.

"Andy..."

"Lil, I'm sorry."

"What? What did you call me?"

"Lil."

She laughed again. "Andy."

"I was coming to find you. I couldn't wait till you came back."

"Why?"

"I had to tell you how much I love you. I love you, Lil!"

She closed her eyes. "You're back," she whispered.

"I won't ever leave you again."

He kissed her as passionately as any young man could. And cheering rose from the opposite sidewalk.

"Andy, wait, I..." Her laughter bubbled over as he kissed her. "I have...to tell you. The Cunard office called at the theater. They've heard from Queenstown, or Kinsale rather."

"Kinsale?"

"Kinsale is the Irish town closest to where the *Lusitania* sunk, where they landed the first survivors." She gripped his arms and leaned back to watch his face. Never was a moment on stage more satisfying. "Andy, they have a girl recovering in Kinsale. She's about 19, slightly built."

He closed his eyes.

"She has red hair! She's suffering from trauma and injuries, so for several days they didn't know anything about her. But she has spoken— she's American."

"But...how did Cunard know to call you?" Andy asked hoarsely.

Lilly's tears spilled over as she drew him closer. "She spoke yesterday. She told them her name is Katherine."

They celebrated that night. Andy brought Lilly a huge bouquet of roses—and a new men's shirt that he held out to her with a smile.

The call came to Peppercreek, and only then did Sara Alcott cry. Kate was alive!

Peppercreek

The orchard was silvered and silent in the early morning dew. Ben stood at his bedroom window. He had looked down on this view for as long as he could remember. It gave him a steady, somehow reassuring feeling. It had always been there. And he wanted to come back to it and find it unchanged.

"Ready, Ben?" a quiet voice asked behind him.

The Alcott brothers had an early train to catch. They were going to France.

While David and Marty Meyer had arrived at their decision after careful consideration, Ben made his decision quickly. His job had ended so suddenly, and now just as suddenly, his plans and future seemed so firm and clear. He would go to France, to join in this war that so far was only statistics and battle reports with French names in the newspapers. He would add his muscle to this fight against aggression. He would hopefully fly.

"I *have* to go to watch over you two youngsters," he explained to David, grinning.

"And maybe learn...the language from a few young mademoiselles?" his brother returned.

So he left for war as his grandfather Ethan had done 54 years earlier. He left his family—their tears and prayers a benediction. And he left knowing that, unlike the orchard, he would come back changed.

Part III

Winter
1916–17

*Your breath first kindled the dead coals
    of war...
And brought in matter that should feed
    this fire,
And now it's too huge to be blown out,
with the same weak wind that
    enkindled it.*

—*KING JOHN*, ACT V
SHAKESPEARE

Chapter 15

The Reichstag
Berlin

◆◆◆◆◆◆

K aiser Wilhelm II was a fussy, petulant man—a puppet of his scheming subordinates at times, decisively independent and autocratic at others. "Unsteady" was the polite epitaph often whispered about him in diplomatic circles around Europe—there were others far less polite. Deeply militaristic in his haughty manner, he was a man of stormy moods, and morose silences. In the late summer of 1915, Kaiser Wilhelm was still brooding and cross over the international outrage concerning the sinking of the *Lusitania*. He did not like the German people cast as savages, though privately he was pleased at the painful strike at Britain's sea lanes. He was testy about the latest note that had arrived from Washington D.C. 'Strict accountability' was not a term he liked to be threatened with. Still, he could not ignore the American leader's posturing.

Within his own war cabinet the debate grew heated and querulous as he leaned back and stroked the dagger-like points of his mustache.

"We must press for the advantage! This is not the time for retreat! No!" The table was pounded to emphasize the point. "Our submarine fleet must continue their relentless attack without one moment of decline. They are having an effect on the British and it would be insanity to restrict them. Absolute insanity! We are superior on the seas!"

The opponent took his cue when a breath was finally drawn. "Insanity you say, Herr Hollweg? Yes, we agree! Insanity when Herr Wilson is so angry with this *Lusitania* business."

"He is angry for his British bedfellows!" the man spat angrily.

"One hundred and twenty eight Americans went down with the *Lusitania!*"

"They were warned," Hollweg replied with deadly calm.

"Even so, it is pure foolishness to ignore Wilson's anger and thereby encourage American participation! They will not be so patient again if our submarine captains unwisely target Americans. There will be no more notes from Washington. They will come blundering into our affairs in Europe if they are further provoked! We do not need Americans alongside French and British killing our good German boys. That would be the great insanity, Herr Hollweg, and would greatly imperil our advantage in this war!"

Hollweg uttered a curse. His voice was scornful. "You are afraid of the puny Americans? They have nothing! They are not ready for war! Our citizens are imperiled by this Allied blockade which will slowly starve them if our mighty navy does not destroy it! You would have us weak and subordinating to the whinings of this anemic-looking American president? No! The German people are not afraid and will not bow to him!"

"I did not say we are to put our submarine fleet in dry dock, Herr Hollweg, or bow to Wilson. I said—"

"Enough!" The kaiser straightened his tall, stout frame from the chair and stood looming over them. He was glaring and impressive in his wrath, and there was immediate silence in the room. "I have heard enough of this squabbling. You sound like kitchen maids! Our navy is the mightiest in the world and I do not bend or subordinate to a whiny American or anyone else! He can send a note each day and threaten what he likes, but I alone will decide this matter!"

He fingered the medals on his expansive chest and began pacing the room. "This Allied blockade can still be destroyed and shall be destroyed. But I will act prudently. German submarine captains will be notified immediately that they must choose their targets with greater care. They will not attack neutrals or passenger ships."

Hollweg moved in his chair to protest but thought better.

"I do not intend to have the United States enter where they have no business. We will appease them for a time. And I will dictate that. I will dictate who plays in this affair and when! Do you gentlemen understand?"

The heads nodded obediently, suffering silently in their relative fury or triumph.

He spoke with conviction. But like the dry leaves that skittered in every direction across the empty courtyard of the chancellery, that conviction could change with some passing whim. He was the kaiser of Germany, and he would hold back those interfering men from across the ocean. He smiled benignly at his war ministers before he left the room. His final words were ringing.

"I will not have Americans on the continent. They will not come!"

But he was too late.

the Atlantic

The Atlantic was kinder to his cousin who crossed in May. When Ben Alcott crossed this 'big pond', he found the sea inhospitable and churlish.

"I thought the ocean was supposed to be blue," he gagged.

This body of water was a yellowish green—like his own face. Years later he would remember little of his first ocean voyage beyond his unsteady navigation from the rail to his bunk. Other passengers of the steamer *Esplange* fared no better, with two exceptions. David and Marty were able to cross without lunging to the rail every time they came above decks. They could do more than groan in their bunks. But Ben, who was always strong and confident, rarely sick, always physically able, now could not eat and only stood with help. And he was far too weak to defend himself against their merciless teasing.

"Try this beef tea, Ben," David offered kindly.

"I...can't. Don't talk...about...beef."

"It's just broth. Come on. You have to eat some time."

"Don't talk about food, David. I mean it. I'll never eat again."

"Yeah, and you'll never flirt with another girl."

Ben leaned back in his bunk, moaning. He had no idea *he* could get so sick. "When will this tug stop lurching? Those waves must be a mile high!"

"It has been calm since lunch."

"No, I can feel it. We're pitching and rolling. And don't talk about lunch."

David smiled.

"How am I going to get home when the war is over?" Ben asked listlessly.

"What do you mean?"

"I can't do this again. I'll never step on a boat again in my life."

David shrugged. "Guess you could borrow a plane and be the first man to fly across the Atlantic."

Ben closed his eyes and imagined one of Jimmy's planes skimming over the green...all that green, churning water... Ben leaned for the basin his younger brother held for him.

David helped him clean up and then offered the tea again.

"No, I can't."

"Aw, come on. Now I see why Ma always said you were the biggest baby when it came to takin' medicine. You have to try to keep something down. If you don't, you'll be weak when we land and Marty and I will have to carry you off."

"Land..." Ben moaned again.

"Yeah, land. And we've heard lots of French gals are waiting at the landing, waving little tricolors, glad to see the American boys. How will it look if we have to carry this bag of bones off?"

Ben reached for the cup.

Ben was finally able to leave his cabin on the last full day at sea. Marty and David were still sleeping when he left. He knew how disappointed they would be to miss his erratic steps and pale face. But he was determined to make one final stand against this impersonal but powerful foe. He had to prove he could look at the ocean and walk, and not be overcome with sickness.

Though the ship rocked gently, Ben groped along the companionway and up the stairs. He had never felt weaker. The crossing did not seem like a mere six days—he felt like he'd been on the tub for weeks.

The crisp breeze hit him forcefully, but it was a welcome feeling. He looked out to the expanse of gray with almost no discernible line between water and sky. And no sight of land. He gritted his teeth as he felt a wave of dizziness sweep over him. He was slightly angry with himself. This was no way to begin an adventure.

"It's just like Peppercreek, ol' boy, only...wider. Yeah, a little wider...and deeper." He closed his eyes and inhaled deeply, grateful no one was in sight. He made himself think of something unrelated to this voyage and felt himself relax. That was it, ignore the motion.

The train trip East from Illinois. Uneventful and lazy, flirting with unattached females, playing cards, watching the changing, passing landscape. New York. Bright lights, buildings that pushed up into the heavens. People in a rush and lots of them, trains and subways. Uncle Andy and his new wife. Yeah, it was easy to see why the man had married. He was obviously dazzled by the red-headed woman at his side.

"Never remember seeing Uncle Andy so happy before," David commented privately.

"With a gal like that, who wouldn't be happy?" Ben returned.

"Which goes to prove gals are out there that have all *the* qualities they need to have and are still pretty and lots of fun."

"My sentiments exactly, little brother," Ben said with a straight face. "You got one, Uncle Andy got the other. So..."

But Ben was impressed with more than Lilly O'Hara's striking good looks. She was...he searched for the word. She was comfortable to be around. Laughing and smiling. Yes, just what Uncle Andy needed.

Andy had taken the three young men for an early breakfast before they sailed.

"And what do you hear from Kate, Uncle Andy?" Ben asked.

The table grew still. Andy carefully folded his napkin, the joy leaving his eyes. "You know, of course, she is still in Ireland. I hear from her...indirectly. The woman who is caring for her writes...some. Kate is still recovering, healing. I hope she'll be well enough to come home soon."

Andy and Lilly had shown them a few New York sights while they were there. The country boys were impressed but unpersuaded.

"Give me Chicago," Marty said under his breath.

"Their accents!" Ben agreed. "Did you see the price on the menus?"

"Haven't seen one girl even close to as pretty as Bess," David added.

Then it was time to sail, and they stood at the rail, waving down at Uncle Andy who suddenly looked pale and old. He was thinking of Kate, Ben realized. But there was Lilly holding his arm and smiling. He watched the edge of the world they knew grow fainter. The statue stood regal in a pale shaft of sunset. Only when all sight of land was gone, did he suddenly feel sick.

Ben thought of his cousin Kate again as the steward passed him. The sun rose lazily out of the edge of the water. The steward began to unclamp the metal covers over the portholes. One more night of running through the inky black water, muffled and darkened. Marty and David had told him the *Esplange* had entered Germany's declared forbidden zone. Shells were loaded in the deck guns. No deck lights at night. Lifeboats were inspected and prepared. The *Lusitania* was not prepared. The shock had come suddenly. Now he felt something of the fear Kate must have felt. Standing there, Ben grew sweaty and trembling.

"Get a hold of yourself, fella. You're going into a war zone, remember..."

Tomorrow they would land at Bordeaux, then go on to join the ambulance corps in Paris.

"Land tomorrow," he breathed, his face still ashen. "The happiest day of my life..."

Paris

After such an unpromising and unglamorous beginning, Ben Alcott finally arrived in France. He was not the first American to join the Allied cause, of course. Volunteers with assorted motives had filled the ranks of the French foreign legion since before the war had begun. But Ben, Marty, and David would be part of the first ambulance corps serving France composed entirely of Americans.

The French government had puzzled over the problem for many months until a bloody loss of young Frenchmen and a shortage of ambulance drivers stimulated their decision. There were propaganda possibilities of American drivers. These young men could be glamourized by the media. And this could swing sentiment in the United States toward fighting alongside France. This same attitude would prevail as eager young men came across the big pond to fly for France.

Ben regained his cheerful confidence and optimistic good humor once they were on land. He could even laugh with Marty and David over his pathetic experience on the *Esplange*. Marty shook his head and chided his friend.

"You're no seaman for sure, Ben. So how can you fly? It's not exactly calm and steady up there."

Ben looked up into the blue autumn sky of Paris. "I'll fly," he said simply.

Paris was different from New York, as New York was different from their prairie home. Paris was broad, tree-lined streets and the mild-mannered Seine River in its heart. It was a city of dramatic architecture and unpretentious sidewalk cafes. Few motor vehicles drove down Paris streets, but bicycles were everywhere. Taxis and fruit trucks were pressed into sevice as ambulances and troop transports when Belgium was invaded. A city of fashion—and fatherless children selling pencils and apples on the street corners.

The men climbed the three levels of the Eiffel Tower to the platform 905 feet above the city. A chill wind moaned through the iron girders though the day was sunny. It gave them a spectacular view for miles, well worth the breath-stealing climb.

"Got anything like this in Chicago, Marty?" Ben asked.

Marty ignored the taunt. "Still take the city by the lake any day."

"Think we could find a decent ham sandwich here?" Ben wondered aloud.

"Wish Bess were here..." David added absently.

Ten days of waiting in Paris for Marty and David. Ten days of discovering how friendly the French people were and how Ben's stumbling, awkward attempts at the language did not seem to matter. Somehow they always understood him and were quite obliging. Ten days of Paris nightlife and finding out that young French mademoiselles thought Americans were celebrities.

"And we haven't even done anything yet!" Ben reported happily. "We're heroes!"

David and Marty were eager to get to the business they had come for. No more loafing or sightseeing. The rush was on for their physicals and uniform fittings. They wore the blue of France. The little holiday, the ten-day interlude in Paris was over. Somewhere beyond those outlying hills was a war.

Bonjour, Grandmere!

Bonjour is French for hello. See, I may come home with quite an education. We left Paris two days ago for our sector. We ate in restaurants along the way, rather than set up our own messes. We had to drink nasty tasting wine because the water was unsafe. Davy and I greatly lauded the fresh water of Peppercreek! Little brother is persevering in his study of the French language, while Marty and I sit back and laugh. And all the

Frenchmen Davy tries to communicate with! In every little village the kids flock to see us as if we were war heroes already. They shake our hands and shout, 'Vive la France et les Allies, Vive l'Amerique!'

Most of the kids are barefoot and skinny. We were given a uniform and stern lectures on what we must do and not do. Then we were given our little cars. This will be 'tools' for our work, and away from our base, our home too. It will take a lot of working over to make these things respectable, but Marty and Davy and I will end up with the finest little buses in the fleet. Our unit is called the 'First Unit of Friends of France'. There are 20 of us American boys, and a doctor who is our commander and interpreter. He told us the French ambulance drivers are soldiers who were disabled in the war already, or did not pass the physical tests to begin with. Everyone else is away fighting on the front lines. The French people are friendly and continually ask in their broken English, 'When will the States join this war?' It is never, 'Will they?' Tomorrow will put us in our sector, about five miles from the lines. We have seen little evidence of war, beyond kids without enough to eat, and villages that are mostly older people, women and kids. We hear the big guns in the distance and see flashes in the night sky. Davy can't wait to get on duty and get some experience, but seeing men in pain, well, I wonder how brave I'll be. 'They' say there is talk of an all American flying squadron in the works, but the French government is puttering along about it. There are times, Grandma, I lay on my stretcher and think how different things are, and how far away I am from things that are familiar. And I think about you praying for us...Ben

They left Paris under lead-colored skies—without fanfare or touching farewells. The man in charge of their unit, Dr. Gros, was a Frenchman who was clearly suspicious of these brash young Americans who were always laughing and pulling pranks. He groaned aloud at their French phrases. "Barbaric..." he would mutter. And why did they have to wave their caps so wildly at every female they happened to pass? How was he ever to form these irresponsible schoolboys into a respectable unit that would honor France?

But he saw them transform before his eyes as they left the capital city. Suddenly, with no spoken words exchanged, they sensed their impending duty. The jokes and games remained, but their faces conveyed more. They knew.

They spiraled through the countryside by train. Ben watched with the same eagerness as David and Marty. He wanted to see everything—villages planted on hills, the sun gleaming off terra cotta roofs, houses of white stone with church spires rising solemn and steadfast among them. Old men nodding at the passing train, children on sleepy donkeys, women on bicycles. They passed barren fields and vineyards, and the roads they paralleled were occupied with multicolored military transports of every shape and size.

Finally the train ground to a stop, and Dr. Gros called to them sternly to gather their gear.

"Ambulance Americaine! Halt!"

A trip across the American midwest, a voyage across the ocean, then through the interior of France, and finally Ben, Marty and David had arrived at their destination.

Dr. Gros paced in the huge concrete barrack. He had talked for over an hour, and he was tired. He knew the young men lounging around him were tired, also. But he must be certain these boys understood—their lives might depend on how well they understood. There were, after all, rules to observe. Peals of thunder seemed to punctuate his words. He was glad of the dramatic effect—it sounded like artillery explosions only meters over their shoulders.

He had shown them the ambulances and the Americans had promptly nicknamed them 'chasers.' Fords painted gray with a spare on the roof and room for four injured in the covered truck bed. The driver sat in an exposed cab rather like the wagon seat of the American west. A canvas hood could be pulled up in a sudden rain squall or merciless sun. Very simple.

"You will work two days at 12-hour shifts, then be off for three days. Your duty is to pick up the injured and take them to the field hospital. You will transport more severe cases to the train station for Paris. Under extreme battle conditions, you will be called for duty regardless of your hours served, and all leaves will be suspended." His eyes were piercing and hawk-like. "Do not attempt to leave this post without permission. The French field service will not tolerate such insubordination."

Some young American in the back of the room was mimicking the long-suffering doctor, to the amusement of those around him. But Dr. Gros struck Ben as a kind man in a paternal sort of way, a man who had not really wanted the role given him, but was willing to make the best of it. So, despite his fatigue, Ben listened attentively. He found himself wanting to make this unit the best on the western front.

He thought about the ambulance the doctor had shown them earlier in the evening and imagined just where he would keep his maps and canteen, his helmet and gas mask. He would make his chaser sharp. American Ambulance Field Service No. 422.

"You are representing your country, gentlemen, yes, I remind you of that. Remember the rules I have spoken of and you will return to your country." He stood silent a moment so that his words would have full emphasis. "This is a real war with real bullets and shells and men wanting to kill you because you are on the opposite line. Consult me with your questions." He drew himself up to his full 5'4" height.

"Do well, you young Americans, and France will be forever grateful!"

He looked younger than his 23 years. His face was dusty and sunburned. His cap with the Red Cross insignia was pushed back on his head, and his dark hair was sweat-plastered to his head. It was an unseasonably warm fall in northern France, perhaps a gift before the bitter winter that was tardy in coming. They called this Indian summer back home. Back home...Ben shook his head. Home seemed like a million miles away. Grandma Sara, the Peppercreek orchard, his old Model T, Chicago, Ellie Meyer, Nehi Field and the unflappable Jimmy... A rut in the road meeting his right front tire jarred him from his thoughts. This was a road in France badly pitted by traffic and errant shells from ambitious German artillerymen.

He was on his way back to the field hospital with two couches (bed cases) loaded in his carriage. This was no time to daydream—injured men suffered with each pothole he failed to negotiate. He checked his gauges. Oil and petrol all in order. Ben Alcott was proud of his well-polished and humming chaser. Seven more miles to the hospital, and then his duty was over for three days. He would work on his car and David or Marty's if they needed it. Then, cleaned up and shaved, he'd head to the nearest village. An open cafe with a giggling mademoiselle across the table...a perfect ending to a long day. He smiled at the thought.

The road dipped slightly and ran adjacent to the railroad that brought them from Paris. Lately the Germans had found it a favorite target. Their biplanes would appear suddenly from the north, usually in a formation of four or five, swoop down like angry bees and lay their bombs quickly and capriciously. French planes would swarm up in eager response and artificial clouds of white would dot the sky. Ben watched these sparring matches with rapt attention. He could hear the drone of an airplane motor before anyone else.

"Hear come the Huns out of the sun, boys!"

If the planes flew low enough he could distinguish between French, British and German with a swift, casual glance. And unless he was en route with their wounded, he would stop what he was doing to watch the aerial contest. It fascinated him.

"That's what you want to do, Ben?" David asked quietly one afternoon as they climbed a nearby hill to watch. A German and French plane spiraled in the distance.

"Yeah, they look like they're having fun, don't they?"

David said nothing and Ben turned to his brother. "I'm just kidding. I know it's serious business up there."

"Still you want to join up."

"Sure. It's like you want to be a doctor. I want to fly."

The planes streaked out of sight in opposite directions. Their duel had come to no conclusion, and they would continue another day.

"You know it isn't all gallantry up there, Ben. I know we've heard from the British pilots—they wave at each other sometimes and such. But it can't stay so friendly. It seems to me a simple equation. Kill or be killed."

The older brother had no reply. Kill or be killed. That was war, but perhaps Davy should not be quite so blunt about it. This just might be one of those subjects you didn't really talk about. A universal understanding, unspoken but accepted. Ben had not yet been tested—he simply drove his little chaser around safe behind the lines. It was more than daring, exhilarating acrobatics a thousand feet above the earth. The brothers looked each other in the eye, then turned away.

Suddenly three French soldiers appeared in a rickety car in front of him, waving frantically, gesturing over their shoulders. Ben brought his ambulance to a reluctant stop.

"Bonjour, fellas. Okay, okay, slow down. What? You're gonna have to speak slower, a lot slower. I'm American, see?"

This was the closest contact Ben had had with Allied soldiers beyond the injured he carried in the back of his truck. The stretcher bearers of the field always loaded his van, and the orderlies at the hospital unloaded it. He was nothing more than a driver and had limited contact with the soldiers. He saw them briefly—nameless men, gaunt and unshaven, fearful and pain-filled eyes, filthy, bleeding through crude bandages. These three soldiers were anxious for him to understand something unseen beyond the line of trees.

"Look, I've got some of your buddies in the back here, and they're probably not too pleased with this little chat we're trying to have so—"

"Danger, American! Danger!" they shouted in unison.

"Yeah? Where? The lines are back there, way over that way, like seven miles or so."

One Frenchmen extended his arms.

"A plane?"

Then he heard it, over the hum of his own engine and theirs. The rumble, the shriek, the drone. The Frenchmen dove for the road culvert.

"Oh, boy, oh boy. Here they come!" Ben jumped from the seat to the dirt beside his truck just as the first plane skimmed over the trees. Surely these were just ambitious scouting-the-line pilots. No French planes had barked up to the chase. Then Ben heard the high-pitched whine of a bomb descending. The railroad 20 yards away was the target.

The air was suddenly smoky and Ben heard the zing of shrapnel. His injured screamed out in fear.

"Hold on, fellas!" Ben yelled hoarsely. "It's gonna be okay."

He clamped his eyes shut. His ambulance and the Frenchmen's truck were easy targets on the dusty road. "Easy pickin's," Marty would say.

The war was suddenly inches away from Ben Alcott.

He rolled under his truck and lay there trembling, trying to make himself invisible, or at least smaller. Then with lightning flash quickness it was gone, and the countryside was peaceful once more. Ben drew a deep breath then rolled out.

"Hey, Frenchies! You guys okay?" He trotted over to the ditch. The three lay sprawled as in innocent, exhausted sleep. Ben staggered. No. No... He backed up. He looked up and down the road, but no one was in sight. It had all happened in less than five minutes.

He felt weak as he turned back to his ambulance. He leaned against it, breathing heavily. His fingers felt the side. Number 422 was no longer the tidy polished pride of the unit; it was pitted by deadly shrapnel. No jabbering French, no moans or movement came from inside the chaser. His stomach knotted as he slowly opened the door.

Two patients. But only one raised his head and lifted his hand feebly. He looked at the man who lay so still with vacant, staring eyes, then pointed to his heart and shook his head.

Dr. Gros filled the coffee cup, but it remained untouched. The young American stared morosely at his hands. He looked haggard, his clothes dirty and blood-stained.

"Things like today, they happen, Monsieur Alcott. I told you this when you began."

"Yeah, yeah." Ben leaned back in his chair and closed his eyes.

"Do you want to quit, monsieur?" the little Frenchman persisted.

Ben opened his eyes. His voice was testy. "No, I don't want to quit."

"Fine. Go get some sleep."

But as exhausted as he was, Ben knew he would not drop off to sleep easily. The sound of the sizzling bullets, the cries from the men inside the ambulance...

"They saved my life," Ben said bluntly.

The doctor stroked his goatee. "God saved your life, monsieur."

Ben looked up. "And took theirs? That seems like a cheap deal."

"Indeed it would be if you wasted your life, or proved ungrateful. I have lived 65 years, monsieur, and conclude His ways are so often mysterious to mortal man. Still, I can trust they are best."

Ben shook his head. "You sound like my grandmother."

"She would be a wise woman, yes."

"Yeah..." Ben stood up wearily. "And I'd bet my last franc, Doc, that she was prayin' for me today."

Peppercreek, 1868

"...We all felt confident with General Grant in command. We heard the papers were calling him 'Unconditional Surrender' Grant. U.S. Grant. Now we were camped at Shiloh, Tennessee. I remember thinking how beautiful and peaceful the countryside was. A summer fair should be around the bend in the road, with men and women and little kids laughing together. But it was smoke and the scream of bullets. There were far more Confederates than the optimistic U.S. Grant had suspected. Men were falling everywhere around me. I was stumbling over boys in blue. My rifle was out and I was sweating and firing into the screams, not even thinking if I was actually killing some Johnny Rebs beyond the haze. Death...it was all around me, then strangely, eerily quiet. A fine woods for squirrel hunting I thought, but this was a day of battle, no pleasure in it. Silent, lifeless men—husbands, fathers, sons and brothers—gone. No more plowing or milking the cows or watching the baby's first step, or seeing the sunset. Death—a huge, yawning gulf. And that day in Shiloh, Tennessee, when the sun was warm and the air fragrant with spring for a time, I stood in the middle of that gulf, and thought I walked away alone..."

Chapter 16

Kinsale

◆ ◆ ◆ ◆ ◆

*S*he sat at the long wooden table peeling potatoes; carefully and slowly, she gave the task her entire concentration. With her mind focused on the work in her hands, how could she think of anything else? It was better this way. The girl looked older than her actual years because of her new thin figure. The skin, once praised for its creamy fairness, was even paler now. The eyes were dull and staring, and the mouth typically in a teasing pout, was turned down. Her shoulders sagged from an invisible burden. She bore the posture of early aging and the marks of inner pain.

"Like a ghost," Rory described with a shake of his head.

"An orphan," Denny agreed.

"Vacant," Pierce pronounced with typical brevity.

"She's so sad, so, so hopeless!" Jen added. "What can we do?"

What indeed? Maggie Falconer wondered. Yes, the body was healing, but it soon became obvious that healing must work in more than the flesh for health.

Padraic said little as he watched the girl—how long did it take for a person to slowly die inside?

Now the door to the Falconer cottage opened and two men entered, but the girl did not bother to turn.

"Afternoon, Kate!" Denny called cheerfully as he tossed off his cap.

"Hello, Denny. Hello, Padraic. Your ma had to go to the Shaws to check on their new baby. Here, I've laid out your food."

She crossed the kitchen and handed them each a plate.

"I brought you two letters, Kate," Padraic said.

"Thank you." But she made no move to take them. "I'm a little tired. I think I'll go rest awhile."

The brothers exchanged a quick look.

"Uh, Kate, you know it's crisp and nice out, the wind is down. Why don't you take Ma's sweater there and sit out on the bench? You can read your letters while we eat."

She looked at the table and sighed. "If you like."

While her back was turned, Denny gave Padraic a quick nod. She seemed to respond to him the best, even if it was often like a pet's listless obedience. This American girl had come into their lives so suddenly, yet now seemed a part of them. They returned from work each day with one unspoken challenge in their minds—to get her to respond, to want to live again, to smile. She'd been with them four months now, and never once had she smiled.

She answered their eager questions about the States. She worked beside Maggie in the cottage, quietly completing each task given her. But rarely did she step out of doors and then only from the back door. From the back of the Falconer home, she could not see the ocean.

It was crisp as Padraic had said, a fresh and blue sunny sky. The two took their places on a bench against the stone wall of the house. From this view they faced the rolling pasture—it was still green but quickly fading in the fast approach of autumn. This was the view that Kate preferred. Here the abbreviated hills were dotted with sheep and bisected by low gray stone walls.

Padraic ate, and Kate was silent. He was no longer nervous around her, even after they discovered she was older than they first thought. Eighteen, a young woman. He turned slightly on the bench to look at her. She sat with her eyes closed, the strength of the sun full in her face. Beyond the dark circles under her eyes and the pallor of her skin, her fragile beauty was apparent. The hair had deepened to a shining copper and hung softly in curls around her shoulders.

"Katie? How's your hand today? Did the peeling hurt it much?"

She didn't move or open her eyes. Her voice was weary. "Why do you call me Katie?"

He scratched his head. "Aye, it is Kate. I'm sorry, I don't know why...you just seem like Katie to me."

"I've never been called it before. Always Kate or Katherine. Mostly Katherine when I was in trouble." Her voice dropped. "Which was often."

She seldom referred to her life in the past or anything personal. The fisherman was uncertain what to say.

"Call me Katie if you want; it really doesn't matter."

Nothing matters to you, he finished in his thoughts.

She lifted up her right hand. After four months the break was mended, but it still ached at times. It was scarred and bruised.

"It's ugly now," she said flatly. "Women are supposed to have lovely hands."

Padraic shifted on the bench. This could get complicated—maybe even more so than his relationship with Anna.

"I don't think your hand is ugly."

"Well, I do." She closed her eyes again and leaned back. "Your ma says still it works, so I'm to be thankful for that."

But he heard only bitterness in her voice.

"Your letters," he prompted to draw her out.

'The more she talks, aye, the quicker she'll heal,' Maggie told her family. 'Isn't healthy for a body to have seen what Kate did and close up like a living tomb.'

"Who are they from?" she asked without interest.

"Well, let's see...Andy Alcott and Clark Benton in New Orleans. Did I pronounce that right?"

"New Orleans," she whispered. "Yes...Clark's father."

"Clark was the young man you were traveling with?"

"Yes," she replied stiffly. "I don't care to read either right now. You can if you like."

He smiled. "They aren't to me."

She made no reply. He looked out across the land—perhaps it was time to take the *Bluebell* out or find something that needed mending or clean the barn or... He could only imagine how her family must feel at her apathy, separated from her by an ocean like they were. Slowly he opened the letters. Aye, her father sounded like a nice man. He read the second missive.

"Well," he began carefully, "if I read this right, this Mr. Benton is asking about you and hoping you're better and—"

"And he wants to know about his wife...and son, all the last details of the *Lusitania*."

"Well, he's wantin' to know, I suppose as any father would—" Padraic continued gently.

The red curls shook. "No." Her voice was hoarse. "I can't do it."

"Aye, it would be hard sure...but maybe...healin' in a way too."

She jumped up and faced him, her eyes blazing with a light Padraic had not before seen.

"What would you have me write, Mr. Falconer? About the babies in the nursery? The bodies in the water? Screams from a woman trying to give birth?" The tears streamed down her face, and her voice was shrill. "Shall I write him that? Tell him his wife was terrified up to the last moment? That Clark...loved me, and I..."

Padraic held up his hands. "No, Katie lass, no. I meant—"

But, sobbing, she ran past him into the cottage and slammed the door.

Maggie found her oldest still seated on the bench when the sun had dipped in a rose-colored curtsy just beyond the farthest hill. His arms were crossed, his eyes were staring. They didn't speak for several minutes.

"Denny told me," she said finally.

"Aye," he nodded slowly. "I made her cry."

She patted his arm. "No, Paddy, you made her angry, you made her shout. That's good."

He shook his head. "I don't know, Ma, I don't think so. I can't figure it all out. I'm going back to work; 'tis easier, and that's the truth."

• • •

Kate stood at the upper bedroom window and watched Padraic disappear down the curving road. His stride was long and purposeful. He knows where he's going and what he wants, she thought, like I did once.

"Now I know nothing," she whispered. "Absolutely nothing." A crooked smile then. "And I even talk to myself...like an old woman with half her mind."

She looked at the fields, dusky and mellowing, the few trees, gray and barren. Winter comes quickly to the Irish coast, they told her. She still had difficulty believing she was in Ireland when it was once only a passing landmark from the deck of a ship, certainly not her immediate destination. Yet she had spent the summer here, not sightseeing or even working really, simply existing with this family called Falconer.

The Falconers. Raised by an absent father and never close to her only sibling, Kate found this quite a contrast, beyond the strange brogue and customs and foods. This family talked and joked and worked together. They were interested in each other, encouraging one another with a nod or look. No sullen silences or stormy scenes.

She would not forget that first evening when Maggie Falconer led her from the bedroom to the table to eat with the family. In another time and place she would have eagerly welcomed the four sets of masculine eyes upon her. But now with her frailty and weakness, she was sure she was about to faint in front of them. She wanted to hold up her arms and shield herself from their open curiosity.

Denny. Only a little younger than Kate, a fisherman beside his oldest two brothers. Tall and lanky, fair-skinned with thin straight brown hair, almost always smiling and teasing. His brothers stood when she entered the kitchen, but he had forgotten. The others all looked solemn in the one swift glance she allowed herself. But then he had come up to her eagerly.

"Kate, I'm Denny. You sit here by me. I'll make sure you get something. It's hard work with gluttons like the older Falconer boys."

Then Rory smiled, too. He could have passed for Denny's twin, except for the glasses.

"'lo Kate, I'm Rory."

Pierce Falconer looked nothing like Denny or Rory. He was heavy set, balding, with a mild face. He rarely smiled and Kate soon decided he must be the scholar of the family—he had a deep crease between his brows and he spoke infrequently. He gave her only a nod.

She sat down at the table and felt the impulse to cry suddenly. She clutched the wooden bench. Maggie was serving the food, and Kate could hardly follow the chatter.

"And there's our lass, Jen," Denny was saying. "She's at the girl's college in Queenstown. She'll be glad to welcome you."

The conversation flowed around her. She felt like a tiny object caught in a spinning whirlpool—the smells, the taste of food, the words. Was this a dream? Snippets of fishing talk, someone's new baby, Rory's day at the village school, and, of course, like a shadow over everything, the latest events of the war in Europe.

She took a drink from the cup in front of her.

"Sugar for your tea?" Maggie asked.

"No thank you. It's fine."

"Bet you've not had mutton and potato cakes in America, Kate?" Denny asked with chummy friendliness.

"No, no, I haven't."

But she hadn't taken a bite. Then a large hand removed her plate and quickly returned it in a moment. Suddenly it was silent at the table. All but one had forgotten her injured hand. The food on her plate was now neatly cut up.

"You're right handed," the voice said simply.

She looked up and nodded. Across the table sat the fourth Falconer son. Padraic or, as Maggie had explained, Patrick in the American tongue. He smiled briefly and returned to his food.

Tallest of the brothers, he was broad-shouldered and deeply tanned with wavy rust-colored hair and skin obviously weathered by the moods of the north Atlantic. Kate thought his brown eyes looked kind, though she could not explain why. His voice was Irish-flavored like his mother's, almost musical at times. She realized suddenly that Padraic was the one who had carried her from the lifeboat. Padraic had sat by her bed when the nightmare and pain held her prisoner. Padraic wiped her brow and calmed her. She looked back to her plate then up at Maggie. The woman was smiling.

Kate had felt love from the Irishwoman from the first moment she became aware of her. And it was almost as if Maggie Falconer were willing strength and hope back into this body of Kate's that felt brittle enough to break with a mild Irish breeze.

She had relayed disjointed pieces of the sinking to Maggie, enough to make her understand who she was and where she was from. Kate cried, and then so did Maggie. And it was Maggie who wrote the first letters to her father while she dictated.

"No, I don't want him to come over, not now, not yet."

"But why, lass? He hurts for you. He must see you're all right."

"I just, I can't explain it to you, and I'm not angry with him. I'm nothing, nothing right now. I want to get well, then I'll go back."

So Andy had not sailed for Ireland because of the fervent tone of his daughter's letter.

Kate could not imagine waking up from one horror to the next without this woman at her side. Even now after nearly four months, there were nights she woke sweating and terrified at the vision of water rising around her and the plaintive screams ringing in her ears. Alone in Jen's bedroom, she did not tell Maggie of these nightmares.

But now she'd offended Maggie's child. Padraic stalked off because Kate had yelled at him. She didn't mean to; she hardly thought she had the power in her to do such a thing. He was only kind to her and...he made her think of Clark.

"It's always the same," she whispered again. "Hurting them..."

She sunk to the edge of the bed in the room she shared with Jen Falconer when she was home. They'd given her privacy, and hadn't pushed and prodded. Her eyes fell on the stack of letters laying on the small oak bedside table. Three from her father, two from Melanie, two from her grandmother, one from Mr. Benton. She picked up the lilac-colored letter from Lilly Alcott. Her father had certainly gone beyond her original plan to simply reintroduce him to his friend from the past. He sounded happy, boyishly happy aside from his anxiety for his younger daughter. Lilly wrote her letter as if the two women had known each other for years.

"My father married an American actress after I sailed," Kate told Maggie one night as the woman changed the bandage on her hand.

"Aye, then blessings to them."

Kate shrugged. "Yes, they're happy. Everything is so different so suddenly..."

She was once happy and in control, with a future. She should be back at college now receiving congratulations on her summer's reporting from abroad. She should be clipping along the campus in a roadster with a boy smiling beside her, boasting that the famous Lilly O'Hara was *her* stepmother.

But she had sailed on the *Lusitania*.

Kate Alcott couldn't see beyond now in the cottage on the Emerald Isle. She felt stripped, naked and weak. And haunted by a hundred memories. Mr. Benton's letter...tell me about my dear wife and son...

The tears came slowly this time and without the anger. She had told Maggie Falconer she couldn't believe there was a God and, even with the Irishwoman's presence, Kate Alcott had never felt so terribly alone.

The streets of Queenstown were oily black with the rain that began at sunset. Long gray sheets of slanting rain varnished the cobbled streets and created muddy rivers in the gutters. The population of the harbor city was neatly divided behind the walls—those in their homes by the fire and those in the pubs. Conversation flowed principally with the same duo division—political unrest in Dublin and the battles between German and Russian armies in distant reaches of the globe. So it was a night to be indoors with the rain and raw wind scuttling up from the channel.

But a man stood in the chill shadows of a doorway, his hat pulled low, the collar of his black coat turned up. He didn't seem to notice the cold or his wet feet. His eyes were fixed on the second-story window of the building across the street; it gleamed orange-yellow through the thin curtains. He would wait all night in this shabby weather if he had to. But he smiled to himself—this vigil wouldn't last much longer. He'd kept appointments like this many times.

Presently the door of the apartment opened and Anna Ruebens and a man emerged. Huddled under an umbrella, they hurried as much as they dared down the sidewalk. Out of sight. They would go to the 'Northern Star', their favorite pub. They'd be gone over an hour. It would give him plenty of time.

At the door the man worked with practiced skill. Such a lock was a child's thing for him. He was glad the woman had left the light burning. He removed his boots quickly then strolled about the apartment—nice, classy things. He had never been here before; Anna had never invited him. He wondered how she could afford such pretties on her salary at Bailey's. He opened each drawer with cold, contemptuous glances. He looked in closets and under the bed. In part he was uncertain what he was looking for. Yet he knew it existed. Finally, he scoured her writing desk. In one look he knew the bottom drawer was fitted with a false bottom. He pried it up carefully with his knife. It contained precise stacks of letters, and instinctively he knew he had found what he was looking for— envelopes with a London return address, but the letters inside were written in German. He selected a letter and read it in full. From his travels, he could piece together the German phrases. He had no fear of the young woman returning. He knew her nocturnal patterns as well as his own. And if she did surprise him—he reached under his coat to feel for the knife.

Anna,
   Your most recent letter was greatly appreciated...Of course, you know of the sinking of the British liner *Lusitania* in the channel. I returned to Germany to receive the commendations of my superiors. But the politics of war are strange indeed; the kaiser is alarmed with the outrage. How can they be outraged when they were fully warned? Yet further evidence the British are foolish and arrogant in their confidence. The German navy is the mightiest in the world! For all your 'help', Anna, again my thanks. You are, even in your exile, a true citizen of Germany.
                                                              Cousin Walther
It would be prudent to destroy this letter.

The man's smile was thin. Anna had not been prudent at all—this letter was better than he had hoped for. He slipped it into his pocket and
returned the drawer without any sign of violation. Then he slipped
soundlessly back into the wet dark night.

A fire was laid in the Falconer kitchen though it was early afternoon.
Kate folded the family's laundry while Pierce drowsed in the big rocker
by the hearth. Maggie was doing some mending, and all was tranquil in
the room, when the Irishwoman spoke abruptly.

"'Tis time to be going for particulars."

"Going for particulars," Kate had learned quickly, was Maggie's
term for shopping. Pierce was immediately awake and rubbing his
eyes.

"One basket or two, Ma?" he asked with a terrific yawn.

"Two."

He stretched to stand, but Maggie shook her head.

"Keep your seat, Pierce. Kate can carry the other."

Pierce's eyes widened at his ma's peremptory tone, and Kate lifted
her eyes to the older woman. She hadn't ventured out so far, had never
been to Kinsale. Now there was clearly a challenge in Maggie Falconer's
gray eyes.

"I…" Kate began feebly.

"There's no denying you're in need of clothes, Kate. With the cold just
down the lane, you need new things and Jen's won't work for you any
longer. If we can't find what you fancy in Kinsale, we'll just have Pierce
take us up to Queenstown." Her tone was brisk. "Take in a tea shop if we
like."

Kate did not want to go, need or not. She was well satisfied with Jen's
dresses that hung limply on her. She felt a rising panic. This home was
her safe haven, her retreat. No prying eyes or awkward questions.

"Look, it's the lass from the *Lusitania!* The one still at the Falconers'.
Pale little thing, ain't she?"

"I've heard she may be…well, you know, teched in the head…"

"Mornin', Miss. Could you tell us…"

Maggie waited. A few short months ago Kate would have laughed
scornfully at being bossed this way. With a toss of the red curls and a
scathing word or two, she would have reduced her father to subjection.
But Kate Alcott knew the Irish midwife would be conquered by no one,
least of all this slip of a girl.

Kate sighed. This would be only the beginning if she gave in, that was
plain. All sorts of entreaties would follow.

"Run down to Sheffies will you, Kate, for that bag of meal?"

"Let's take a walk down to the beach, Kate…"

She met Maggie's eyes and could not ignore the kindness that lurked behind the line of determination.

"I'll get my sweater," she said calmly.

While her step was brisk, Maggie's tone had moderated. She chattered easily about the houses and neighbors they passed, the weather, the quality of shopping expected in the fishing village. She seemed to be apologizing in this way for her earlier firmness. But Kate said little—her teeth clenched in fresh determination, she looked neither right nor left at the scenery or village.

But even with this narrow and limited vision, it was foolish to think she could ignore things around her. She couldn't help but see the cobbled square and the pubs with their brass and wooden name plates, the public buildings crowded together, gray and weathered with their mullioned windows, the whitewashed Celtic crosses leaning lazily in the old churchyard, the farm carts with their loads of hay. And she saw only two cars on the entire trip. She felt she had stepped into the pages of a past century with New Orleans and New York sophistication a lifetime away.

Maggie made her purchases with swift efficiency and did not encourage prolonged conversation with neighbors or tradespeople. Kate was grateful. She felt their curious stares on her back, heard their whispers although she could not understand the words through the thick brogue.

At the dressmaker's shop the Irishwoman behind the counter eyed Kate's thin figure with blunt skepticism.

"You need some flesh on ya, lass." She shook her head. "We can look to the kiddies' clothes for something or cut down one of these dresses for young ladies."

Kate reddened and turned aside.

"Wool is the thing we want, Claire. Which color do you like, Kate?"

Kate wanted to dismiss the shopping visit with a shrug. "I'd like a dress in each of these colors, and I do not care for your kiddie fashions," she said to the merchant in an even voice.

The Irishwoman's eyebrows went up, and Kate knew the American girl's comment would be circulated to the farthest farm before they reached their own threshold.

On their return home, the road curved between the low stone walls where a man who was leading his sheep to pasture was blocking their way. Maggie stopped to lean against the wall. The farmer lifted his cloth cap to them in a cheerful greeting.

"Good mornin' to ya, Maggie Falconer!"

"And to you, Tate. How's Ell? Over that chill?"

"Aye. Needed me to warm her," he replied with a laugh and broad wink. "Some things can't be healed from a little brown bottle, Maggie."

She nodded, chuckling with him. "Truth you're speakin', Tate. Not comfort much from the big brown bottle either."

His weathered face reddened and he bowed. His eyes then went boldly over Kate who stood stiffly at Maggie's side. "So this is your guest, Maggie."

"This is Katherine Alcott from the United States."

Another courtly bow. "Well, a Yankee lass with a good Irish name! It's a real pleasure to meet you, Miss. And how are you findin' our fair isle?"

He was treating her like a tourist and not the notorious survivor of the *Lusitania*.

"Fine, thank you."

"Seen such beauty, have you?"

"No."

If he noticed her reserve, he did not reveal it.

"'Tis truth there's no place like our isle, and this west coast is to be above everywhere else. You'll find yourself caught in her charm." He leaned forward on his stick, his eyes sparkling.

"A lass with eyes like you have, and that red hair, well, you have your own charms that an Irish lad won't be blind to!"

Kate did not smile, but she felt herself relax. This was just a friendly, good-natured old man, seeing past her gauntness.

"Now there's Maggie's sons, all good lads sure. Couldn't do better. Have you sighted one?"

Maggie rolled her eyes.

"All the Falconer men seem to be very...kind, Mr. Tate. But I have no plans for them."

Moments later, they were back in the Falconer home, and as they pulled off their sweaters and sorted through their purchases, Maggie stopped to look closely at Kate.

"Was it all right then?" she asked almost timidly.

Kate thought of the wild Irish beauty, the picturesque town of Kinsale, Tate with his acceptance.

She nodded. "It was a nice walk, Maggie, thank you."

the channel

Padraic counted 14 vessels working along the coast south of Kinsale harbor to a few miles from Queenstown. He recorded each ship's name, nationality and tonnage in the little blue book Sir Coke had given him. The morning air was crisp but sunny and clear—a grand day for fishing. The *Wanderer of Peel* with Pierce at the wheel was among the local fishing fleet. But Padraic in the *Bluebell* was not working for the catch of mackerel today.

He was tacking farther out into the channel, away from the coast, in his patrol responsibilities. Only Denny worked with him, training his field glasses over the aft side while Padraic watched from the port bow. Their patrol work these eight months was uneventful beyond the dramatic *Lusitania* rescue. Twice they had seen submerged submarines and given the alarm, only to watch the sleek vessels dive with a spout of foam.

"Like a sea monster, they are!" Denny had said once in excited awe. "Under us and us not knowin'!"

Padraic had smiled. "Aye, and it keeps us on our toes, lad."

It was close to mid afternoon now when Denny came up to Padraic. "My stomach thinks my throat's been cut, Paddy, sure. I'm going down to fix us something."

But Padraic hardly heard him. "There's a steamer, two miles or so, there, do you see?"

Denny raised his glasses. "Aye, she's called...the *Sussex*," he said as he read the silver lettering on her side.

"British though she's flyin' no flag." Padraic stood closer to the rail.

"Maybe 1000 tons," Denny agreed.

"Let's hang back here on her stern awhile. Follow her till the Queenstown lads get her in sight."

"Think there may be trouble?" Denny asked eagerly.

His register from the admiralty let Padraic know what ships to expect, and what cargo they carried. He knew this vessel brought food stuffs for British troops.

"Aye, she may be a prize worth takin'," he replied thoughtfully. "The Germans wouldn't mind sending her to the floor."

So Denny ignored his stomach and returned to his vigil. This was a time to stay alert. The sun was shaded now with the sudden appearance of high, scattered clouds, and the sea had become choppy and lead-colored. Padraic turned his collar up and scanned the water. There was only half a mile between his ship and the *Sussex* when he saw it. He knew instantly what it was, and he gripped his glasses tightly.

He remembered a Cyclops eye from some old tale of mythology he had heard in childhood. A gray periscope rose from the waves now, solitary and coldly threatening. He watched with fascination as it slowly rotated. The *Bluebell* lay within its crosshairs. He lowered his glasses slowly, then turned and trained them on the opposite horizon. He knew whatever came would come quickly.

Willing himself not to hurry, he stepped from the rail along the port side and up the few steps to the small wheelhouse. "Den!"

"Aye?"

"Take my place. One's out there."

"One? You mean a sub?"

"Aye, between us and the steamer. Calm down, lad. Don't run. Just watch."

He turned to the radio the admiralty had installed in his boat. He would send the word to the British ship. He looked up for one final calculation. Denny shouted, and Padraic saw the burst of white foam, then streak. Of course, the submarine had not bothered with a local fishing smack. The torpedo, with arrow-like precision, sped toward the *Sussex*.

In less than an hour it was over and the *Bluebell's* decks were crowded with survivors once again.

"I'm sorry I got angry with you a few days ago, about my letters."

Kate had followed Padraic into the small Falconer barn. He looked up from the cow he was milking, surprised.

"Think nothing of it," he said easily.

But instead of retreating, Kate sat down on a bale of hay. The cat came to stretch luxuriously in her lap while she stroked it. They were silent several minutes. Padraic looked tired, almost gray as he worked in the warm, quiet barn. His shoulders sagged. She had not seen him look this way before.

"Is there something wrong?" she asked impulsively.

It was the first time in months she felt anything beyond her own pain.

He slowly lowered the pail, but he did not look at her. His hands hung limp.

"I'm thinkin' the *Bluebell*...is always too late. My patrol work does no good at all."

Of course, she should have known. Padraic and Denny had come in late the night before telling of the horrors of another sinking from a German U boat. She had heard only snatches of their words. She did not want to know the facts, the details. But, of course, a man like Padraic Falconer would take this latest tragedy to heart and feel the impotence of his efforts to stop it.

"Did anyone...were there any that you could not rescue?" she made herself ask.

He raised his eyes. His face was pale in the lantern light.

"Fifteen did not make it," he said slowly.

He looked away, resuming his work. She inspected her surroundings closer, forcing herself not to think of the men who went down in the cold dark water. Here she was 19 years old, her journalism career suddenly stalled, sitting in a drafty old tiny barn in Ireland with a man she hardly knew! She watched his large hands as they worked—tanned, rough and gentle.

"The war in Europe seems so far away, yet...it...keeps reaching out farther than...we think it can," she said finally.

Padraic nodded.

"I was so eager to...write about the war...to make my little observations. I thought it would be so easy, and everyone would tell me what a wonderful job I'd done..." Her voice was scornful. "The mighty journalist!"

She shook her head as tears came suddenly to her eyes. She had cried so little in her lifetime—now it was all she could do to keep from sobbing all the time.

"Well, I've seen the war, and I don't care to write a thing about it."

Padraic finished the milking. "You were going to Europe as a journalist, Katie?"

"For my college newspaper," she replied with steely calmness. "I won an award and the prize was a trip to Europe on the *Lusitania*."

He remained sitting, now fascinated. One so young and vulnerable had sailed alone then survived a nightmare. He thought again of her father.

The Falconer barn was more of a shed made of stones with a thatched roof than it was a barn. Nothing compared to the ones at Peppercreek. Yet even for its primitiveness, Kate could relax here. Padraic listened to her with kindness in his eyes, just like his mother. No challenges or threats or condemnation. She was impressed with his rustic, gentle strength. He looked a part of this place in his dark brown trousers and rough blue shirt. No teasing, no flirting, no deception.

"I didn't win the prize honestly. I wanted to win it very badly, enough to...I cheated. The old professor who held the power was...pliable in my hands."

She waited while the Irish fisherman considered her words.

He gave her a quick glance before studying the straw-littered floor.

Her chin went up. Surely he would say something accusing.

"I've shocked you," she said with the old stiffness.

He scratched his head. "Aye, a little. But I'm thinking 'tis a hard thing for anyone to admit...when they've done wrong."

"You know the story of Jonah, from the Bible."

He nodded.

"It's one of those stories I remember from my childhood. Not that I listened very well...much to my grandmother and father's despair. But I remember that one. And I think, late at night, was it my...sin of cheating that made the...made what happened?"

His deep brown eyes were riveted on her face. "You cannot think like that, lass. The *Lusitania* was full of sinners, not you alone. He's a big and loving God, and He's hearin' your repentance."

"I never said I was repenting," she replied archly. "I..." She shrugged. "I don't know...everything is confused to me."

He spoke up quickly. "So it was writing that took you to Europe. This writing must be a joy for you as fishing is for me."

"I thought it was."

He seemed to choose his words. "I'm thinkin' the college folk could see you had skill. It's a good thing when we realize the talent He has given us."

"You talk of Him like you are on the most intimate terms."

He smiled. "I'd like to think so."

"Like my grandmother, she's like that. But I don't know Him like she does," she said with a trace of defiance.

She stood abruptly. She had talked enough. The rawness was still there. It could not be healed in one evening.

Padraic stood also. "You know, Katie, I said earlier that the *Bluebell* is always late. Aye, it is truth, I wish there could be all survivors each time... But for you, I am grateful."

She felt strength and protection emanating from him. He was tall and broad-shouldered, and on her college campus, he would draw immediate attention and interest. Where once she could have felt attraction, now she only felt deadness. He was kind, like Clark was kind...

"Thank you, Padraic. Goodnight."

Later Padraic lay staring into the darkness of his bedroom. He was not thinking of Anna or German subs or even fishing. He was thinking of the young girl in the bedroom down the hall. Her words had startled him. She had come into their lives as a shell of her former self. Now she admitted lying and manipulating to take the voyage on the *Lusitania.* Now he could better understand her.

"Everything is confused to me," she had said. "I don't know Him..."

Padraic was satisfied as he drifted off to sleep. They had made a beginning in the Falconer barn.

Outside the wind moaned in a hollow voice. Winter had come to the Irish coast. The fire cast its warmth into the huge stone-flagged kitchen. It was a domestic scene, one that Kate could not ignore, either in observation or influence. This family had taken her in openly and generously, never questioning when she might leave. Maggie had stoutly refused the money Andy sent for his daughter's care.

"We can have you here, lass, with no hardship. 'Tis a blessing for us."

"Well, my father won't miss the money," Kate had countered.

Maggie ignored the tone and patted her arm. "We don't need it, lass, sure."

Kate sat quietly watching the Falconer family until Denny persuaded her to play a game of 8.

"I'll teach you in short order, Kate," he assured her.

Maggie was sewing, Rory poring over school papers, Pierce mending a pair of boots. Padraic was calmly staring into the fire. Kate found her mind wanting to create phrases for what she saw—the dull gleam of fire upon the floor and smoke-stained beams, the thick hands of Maggie as she sewed, Rory with a puzzled look and lock of hair in his eyes, the creamy yellow plates and cups upon the china dresser, Padraic in profile. She vaguely wondered what he was thinking. Were his thoughts on that girl in Queenstown she'd heard veiled reference to? But she wrote nothing down and instead took Denny's invitation to play a game.

Denny privately felt that once Kate understood the game, she would like it. It might even prompt a smile. But she played with intense concentration—and never smiled.

"'Tis a fact you're a quick learner, Kate. Paddy, you should take a try with her, she's good."

Padraic shook his head and smiled. "Too tired tonight, Den."

Denny stood and stretched. "A cup of chocolate, Kate?"

Kate arranged the cards. "Aye."

Instantly the room was still and everyone looked at her. Kate felt the color rising in her cheeks.

"What?"

Denny grinned broadly. "You spoke the Irish, Kate!"

It took a moment for her to understand. She had said aye when she meant to say yes. Seeing their childishly pleased faces, Kate Alcott smiled timidly. Denny had his reward, and Maggie went to bed with a prayer of thanksgiving.

In the kitchen dimness, though his face was turned from her, Kate saw Padraic's smile. And she knew it was because of her.

Queenstown

The man was past the shock and heat of anger. Now he quietly, and menacingly seethed inside. There was little room in his hardened heart for actual grief. Grief was a useless, debilitating thing, better left to women and children. He was a man of action. In many ways, he was like the woman he stalked.

His younger brother had not survived the sinking of the *Sussex* by the Germans. He could not strike the whole German navy in retaliation, but he wasn't without recourse. Just a little longer, and he would take action.

Chapter 17

Autumn, 1915
France

◆ ◆ ◆ ◆ ◆ ◆

*T*he European war had passed its first anniversary and was heading into its second autumn. Thousands of men from France, Britain, Germany, Austria, Hungary, and Russia had fallen, and the horrifying tally of death was rising with no sign of abatement. Lines of battle had moved by feet and not miles. Generals clung to their prescriptions for warfare, politicians to their resolve of nothing less than total victory.

Northern France became the largest sector of the western front, and it was here the fiercest fighting occurred between the Allies and Central powers—the terrain was soaked in blood. The pastoral landscape was scarred with a network of trenches, and miles of twisted barbed wire and shell holes. Villages were reduced to rubble, forests were shredded. When the guns were finally silent, these acres of battlefield became acres of memorials—hundreds of white crosses in neat, clean rows.

The French town of Amiens lay in the fertile province of Picardy. This large region of grain and sugar beet farms stretched across gently rolling plains between Paris to the south and the industrial town of Lille to the north. Valleys, forests of beech and oak, apple orchards, winding rivers—a landscape of beauty in the pathway of violence.

Molly Fleming loved the town of Amiens from the first day she passed through it to her aunt's home. Now after nearly a year, she was a part of this city of old men, children, and women, this populace trying to survive in the midst of food and fuel shortages and ration books, and on the threshold of fighting less than 50 miles away. Her command of the French language, and knowledge of customs and culture eased her transition somewhat from urban London life to French village life. Now she stood alongside the women of Amiens in the heat and cold for their allotted loaves of fresh bread. It was in these lines, where she might stand for hours, that Molly felt the lifebeat of Amiens, indeed of all French people who felt the effects of their country at war. Here she heard the local gossip, the weather predictions, the status of field crops, and about the recent savage actions of the Germans. Here she stood and watched the young mother, who the day before had lamented the price of coffee and trumpeted the news of her youngest's new tooth, stand rigid, pale and dry-eyed to receive her ration. All in line knew this woman had become a widow overnight.

Yet this was her life, and somehow Molly Fleming was happy in it. She felt a usefulness and purpose she had not felt in her secretarial position in London. Her days were full and busy with writing letters to her father and Martin, helping her aunt, and caring for the children who came as temporary boarders.

In these months she had begun to understand Madeline Chaumont— the woman held emotion and affection in strict reign. But Molly saw past the reserve and aloofness, past the often imperious tone. Madame Chaumont had lived a well-ordered, independent, quiet life in her home that was as polished and correct as the mistress herself. Then France fell for the lure of war, and everything seemed to change overnight in her proper world. Now she was no longer just the dignified spinster who lived in the lovely house at the end of rue de lilac. Now she took in dirty, frightened, hungry, noisy children called refugees. Townsfolk still saw her in her austere black silk. Perfectly coiffed, with her elevated chin and confident step, she bartered milk and eggs for children's shoes. Madeline Chaumont's unexpected service and generosity had shocked the townsfolk; she hardly appeared to have much warmth in her, much less tolerance for sticky-fingered children. At the market they wagged their heads in wonder as she passed by silently with only the briefest nod in greeting.

"Imagine! Lady Chaumont with her nose so high! The tykes must be terrified of her!"

"Well, cold and snobby or not, I admire her. She didn't have to take these children—"

"She just wants us to think highly of her, and I for one—"

"Oh, Louisa, what a thing to say!"

The grocer ended the discussion with a toothless grin preceding his eulogy. "Cold or not, she's a fine lady and I take my cap off to her. Shows the war changes more than just borders, changes hearts, too."

The woman in the bright red kerchief sniffed in offense. She would have the last word. "Well, it's the kaiser that needs a change of heart. Madeline has the young Englishwoman with her now. Bet the tykes are glad she's there."

"Her name is Molly and you know it, Louisa."

"She's a pretty thing…"

"Too bad our lads aren't home…"

Madeline Chaumont did not think herself at all noble. She merely took her New Testament literally. 'What you have done to the least of these, you have done to me…'

Molly Fleming was proud of her mother's sister, and pleased that the woman was willing to so generously give of her service.

Molly soon discovered that, while Madeline Chaumont was able to sacrifice, she was terribly irritated by the presence of war in her homeland. A German gain, however small, could send the controlled woman into a sudden, heated tirade. And a disaster for the French army pushed the older woman into moroseness and depression. Molly learned to carefully edit what she heard in the market lines. She would never forget the first time they went to church together in Amiens. They had paused at an outlying intersection as a column of ambulances passed en route to a field hospital. Rumbling past, they had raised a cloud of choking dust. Aunt Madeline, with typical decorum, raised her lace handkerchief to cover her nose. Then, a moment later, the street was so silent, Molly heard the birds singing in the trees.

"Aunt Madeline?"

The woman's face was still fixed on the retreating ambulances, and her voice was mournful. "Fathers and sons of France just passed, Molly. In the Revolution, so many years ago, a terrible, terrible thing took so many French lives. The guillotine has come back to France."

Molly followed her aunt's gaze. The papers told them more than Frenchmen were dying. "The war is a guillotine in Europe, Aunt Madeline."

The woman nodded. "Yes, and how much longer..."

David Alcott listened with half attention to Marty Meyer's words. As Marty drove and talked, David had enjoyed the French countryside. Here close to Amiens the land was not yet savaged and scarred. Here the poppies bloomed, the sky was blue and unstreaked with the smoke of exploding shells and the polar trees still stood straight and proud. David Alcott looked for beauty where he could find it, feasted on it—to counter the ugliness he'd seen in his months of service with the French ambulance corps. In this year of 1915, the real horrors were as yet unseen to him.

"Off in another world, Davy?" Marty asked with typical cheerfulness.

David shrugged and yawned. "Have you noticed the roads in this region?"

"I guess. They're pretty decent. Why?"

"One of the soldiers I picked up yesterday spoke passable English. He was a talkative chap. I think he was trying to keep his mind off the pain. Anyway, he told me most of the roads in this area were made a couple of centuries ago. They made them straight for the men marching off to battle. Planted all these polar trees so the way would be shady. The old conquerors used these roads."

"You like to pick up facts like that, don't you?"

"Yeah, I like to know about the people and the place I'm working in. Not like some folks who miss the beauty of a day like this because they're sleepin' it off." He grinned and jerked his thumb over his shoulder. Ben was asleep on a stretcher, his cap pulled over his eyes.

Marty shook his head. "Another long night in Paris. Your big brother is a real Don Juan. Think he'll ever settle down?"

"Maybe...if he doesn't wear himself out looking."

"I heard that," Ben mumbled.

"See? Now there's another picture of beauty I'd like to keep in my mind."

Two women stood waiting on the side of the road for them to pass.

Ben raised up lazily on an elbow. "Beauty? Brunette or red head?"

David laughed. "He's hopeless."

"That old gal looks pretty hot in that black silk. She must be in mourning. But yeah, that young one might be a beauty. Forgetting Bess already?" Marty teased.

David shook his head. "Nope, not a chance. I've seen that young woman before—I remember her dark hair. Last time, she was herding geese across the road. She was wearing a yellow dress. Like today in the blue skirt, and the old woman in her black, and the yellow fields in the background, the poppies. It's a French picture I don't want to forget."

He waved his cap at the young woman on the side of the road.

While Molly enjoyed the challenge of running a household with limited resources, and the opportunity to get to know her aloof aunt better, caring for the children was the real source of her contentment and happiness. She had always loved children and found it satisfying to work with them in a choir. But this was far different from leading a group of children through scales or an amateur Christmas program. The children who passed through rue de lilac, no. 10 were the war's youngest victims, as confused by the reasons for this sudden conflict as perhaps the generals or posturing politicians. They had left their home and everything familiar by the design of their concerned parents or because suddenly they had become orphans.

They came cheerful and curious or frightened and haunted by what they had already seen and heard. They all came hungry and tired but needing more than food and a bed. Madame Chaumont provided for their bodies as best she could, but her affection and attention were awkward. Years later, a few dozen French men and women who survived what was titled the 'Great War', remembered the tall, imposing woman, forever dressed in black silk. She had helped them survive that traumatic time in their young lives, and they remembered her with respect. They thought also of the young Englishwoman who had been at Madame Chaumont's side—Mademoiselle Molly—recalled her with affection, even love.

She was the one who held them close to her sweet-smelling shoulder when they were afraid and could not stop crying. She listened to them and told them bedtime stories. She laughed at their shy jokes and played games with them in the garden. She told them they were brave and that some day they would be the pride of a country no longer under the boot of war. She taught many of them bits of English. They came to Mademoiselle Molly with their cuts or bruises or stomachaches. She was young and pretty and helped fill the vacuum in their lives.

Molly's heart had gone out to these children from the first day Aunt Madeline explained the situation and introduced the "boarders."

"These children are smuggled out of occupied France by parents who do not want them to suffer for the duration, or they are orphans. There is a network all across Picardy, and my house is but one stop for them."

"Like a train station," Molly offered.

"Well, yes..." Madeline Chaumont thought train terminals loud, crude, congested places, and flinched at Molly's creative illustration.

"Some stay only a night before Pierre comes to take them to the next stop. Sometimes arrangements are slow farther south, so one night becomes several, or even a few weeks."

"And their ages?"

"All ages. One month ago, I had four teenage girls. Very trying. Last week, a six-week-old baby. Very difficult."

"A six-week-old baby! What happened to the parents?"

"I know very little from Louie who brought her, except she was from Arras and I had heard reports of a terrible battle there with heavy loss of civilians. So..." She spread her hands outward.

"How sad," Molly murmured. "Do you get...attached to them, I mean..."

Madeline Chaumont smoothed her skirt, avoiding the young woman's direct gaze. "I want them to, I want the best for them, to have a home somewhere, to be safe. But attached? No...no, it is better not to, Molly."

Molly was not certain she could be unemotional and clinical about this "work." "And the goverment?" she asked slowly.

"You mean what does Clemenceau and his cabinet do? Well, running the war, or generals, seem to occupy a great deal of their attentions. And trying to provide railway and such for the people of France. Refugees, well, they are a small matter when there are so many other matters. The government hopes the church will do its part, as it should."

Molly leaned forward. "They do give you extra ration cards for the children."

Her aunt perused Molly's face carefully. She had warned her that first day this was no romantic adventure.

"You have stated the problem exactly, cheri. No extra ration cards. We make do with one and the generosity of the merchants in Amiens and whatever else."

"But, that, that is outrageous! The children are hungry and, and..."

"That is war," Aunt Madeline returned simply.

And that was what Molly Fleming came to understand.

January 1916

Molly was dozing in the deep floral armchair drawn close to the sitting room fire. After the walk into the city over frozen roads, standing in line for rations, then bartering for fuel, she was tired. Outside the night was moonless and cold. Her aunt sat opposite her niece, her hands clutching a letter. Her brown eyes were fixed on the rows of pictures on the mantel—old and fading photographs in frames that needed polishing. A photograph of her parents as newlyweds, one of herself at 12 with Molly's mother, Adeline, on her lap, smiling and happy. Another photo of herself at 20 looking confident and proper even then, the wedding picture of Molly's parents. The final photograph was of herself at 16, with her younger sister and a friend canoeing on Lake Geneva. So long ago, when times were not as complicated...

Her eyes traveled to the young woman across from her, and her face softened. It was hard for her to express her feelings, so in these unguarded, private moments, her face revealed what her voice never could. She was glad her English niece had appeared suddenly on her doorstep. She was grateful for Molly's energy for now there were four hands and four feet to do the work of running the expanded household. Molly had taken over the shopping entirely. The burden of children and privations of war had become lighter with Molly's arrival. In her atrophied heart, it gave Madeline Chaumont a stirring of hope.

She looked at the girl's long, glossy hair, the oval face, the long dark lashes. It was like looking at her younger sister so many years ago. Her eyes returned to the portraits of youth on the mantel, and her mouth pulled downward in a grimace. It was true the war had more than a marginal effect on life in France, and in winter it was felt even harder. Other countries engaged in the struggle were suffering, too, she admitted to herself stubbornly. Food shortages from the Allied blockade in Berlin to Munich, bread riots in unstable Moscow, medical supply shortages in Vienna. She looked to the blackened square of window. Dark and cold. This small fire, that Molly had paid dearly for, gave little warmth—in their beds the children huddled under small mountains of blankets. But the men of France were freezing in miles of icy trenches. The men in

Kaiser's army were surely cold, too, but she did not want to think of them.

She shook her head, her mouth drawn in a grim line. Molly stirred and opened her eyes. "Did you say something, Aunt Madeline?"

The older woman shook her head. "No, cheri, I am just sitting here thinking and reading this letter."

"From a friend?"

"Oui, an old, dear friend, an Austrian girl. We grew up together, though I am much older. Her father, like your grandfather, was a doctor. They met in medical school and remained friends for many years. We would meet for summer holidays in Switzerland. They were happy times..." Her voice drifted off, and Molly tried to imagine what her austere-looking aunt was like at 15. Were there romances?

"We have kept in touch over the years, and this dreadful, dreadful problem has not kept us from that contact. Elise is in Vienna. She has been diagnosed with tuberculosis. Her husband died several years ago, and her oldest child, Kurt, is in the Austrian army. She has not heard from him in many months. She has a daughter, Anna, who is six or seven. I am worried for Elise."

"How do you get letters from Vienna?"

The woman's smile revealed she was proud of her little cunning. "We have a mutual friend at Lake Geneva. She sends the letter to him, he sends it on to me. Very simple. I thought of it. But now I must think of how to help Elise."

Molly smiled. This was her aunt. Almost an enigma, in ways. So vehement against the war, so thoroughly French in her patriotism, provoked by the inconveniences of war—yet reaching out to help whenever she could.

Carrying a candle, Molly softly entered the dining room. Six narrow beds lined the south wall. Another "adjustment to the terrible problem," Aunt Madeline had murmured sourly, then reluctantly agreed to Molly's plan.

"We'll close off the upstairs rooms since we can't possibly heat them and there's no use in trying," Molly had said. "The dining room is large enough for all the children we get, one or one dozen. And it's next to the kitchen, it gets some of that heat. So we have a dormitory for our children!"

Madeline had nodded soberly, silently thankful again for her niece. So the furniture was draped and pushed to the far end of the room, and the dormitory was made. Madeline abandoned her own room for the sitting room, but Molly would not give up her third-floor room.

"It's, it's ice up here, cheri!"

"Helps me to get up in the morning. Really, I don't mind at all."

"I will wake to find you frozen one morning!" Aunt Madeline continued in a horrified tone.

Molly laughed and squeezed her arm. "Only the water in my wash bowl is frozen. I'll be fine."

The woman gave her a clipped nod. "Perhaps in the spring we all can return to our own rooms...and sanity."

So each night while the weather remained frigid, Molly inspected each of the children to see that they were well covered. Seven 'boarders'—four boys, three girls. Molly stood watching their sleeping faces now as she did each night, so relaxed and at peace—when their futures loomed uncertainly and the war grasped at their innocence.

"Bonsoir, Molly," a sleepy voice spoke into the darkness.

She bent down. "Alexander, you should be asleep."

He rubbed his eyes. "Is it still 1916, mademoiselle, still the new year?"

"Yes, Alexander. It will be 1916 for many, many days."

"Will I get to see my papa and mama in this new year?"

"I hope so. Now, off to sleep and sweet dreams."

His thin arms reached to encircle her neck.

"You are good, mademoiselle. I will dream of you."

In her room, Molly quickly undressed with swift fingers, gasping with the coldness. She slid into bed, warmed by the bricks she'd placed there earlier. Warmed by bricks. She smiled wryly into the darkness. She was 24 with no man to love or warm her. Martin.

His last letter, like all his letters since she'd come to France, was brief. She decided Martin did not like corresponding or Martin was busy or... Even his Christmas greetings were, well...he could easily substitute his little sister's name for hers and the letter's tone would be the same. Molly looked for amorous letters, telling her he thought of her and missed her and... But it was not that way. For Christmas, he sent her expensive calfskin gloves. Gloves.

Her first Christmas in France had come and gone. Joyeux Noel. The huge box from her father had arrived one week late and somewhat battered from the trip and censor's probe, but intact. Tea and sugar, scarves and socks for the children, tops and picture books, chocolates for Molly and her aunt, and a popular novel.

Aunt Madeline had managed a thin smile. "Very thoughtful of Thomas, yes."

A long letter enclosed in the box brought him closer and eased the pain of this first Christmas they had ever spent apart. The last line of his letter warmed her more than anything Martin had penned. 'I love you, Molly, and I miss you terribly. But I am very proud of you.'

She burrowed deeper for warmth and thought of Alexander's words.

'I will dream of you.'

1916. A new year, an uncertain future.

"Are you dreaming of me, Martin?" she whispered.

The poppies were blooming in the fields of France again. Trees that had shed their leaves six months earlier saluted the season now in lush green. Crops were being planted and pushing up timid advances. The frozen earth had thawed, the winds were milder and the sky, bluer. The sun had lost its ineffectual shine. It was springtime in France. Budding trees trumpeted an ominous herald to the world, to the generals huddled over maps in their bunkered headquarters, to prime ministers and kings in their comfortable offices—it was time to get the war machine moving again.

Nineteen fifteen had been a stalemate year on all fronts, a ceaseless harvest of men, with peace and the prize no closer. It could not continue this way in the new year. The casualty lists with their staggering climb was reported daily in the press. Citizens demanded, politicians demanded, generals fumed and then demanded more troops, then sat down to design new plans. All sides called it the big push. Even the lowly privates in the trenches knew it was coming. In 1916 the war would take a sharp and decisive turn.

With such confidence and impetus, great military drives were staged on all fronts. The Germans would attack at the French town of Verdun and along the meandering Somme River. Austria-Hungary would fight the Italians in the east, and the Russians would battle the Poles. And the greatest naval battle of the entire war between the Allies and Central powers would unfold in the North Sea in early spring, called the Battle of Jutland. The war was not confined to the earth. In the skies above all fronts daring men in their country's colors battled their largely insignificant, but dramatic duels. The long, cold winter of hibernation was over. The quiet theaters were suddenly in full-scale production of a very ambitious play.

David Alcott had seen many pretty French girls since he had landed on the continent. They were generally friendly and equally impressed with the gregarious Americans who had come over to aid their country. He couldn't help but see them—Ben was constantly pointing them out or trying to strike up a conversation with them. With Bess so often in his mind, however, they made little lasting impression on him. So when he looked up from his French translation book, he was not surprised to see another lovely mademoiselle. He noticed her because she made an impression against the almost colorless background of a market bookstall—dark hair pulled back in a white ribbon, blue skirt and butter yellow blouse. She held a basket of tulips and daffodils. Everyone around her was chatting and preoccupied, so he chose to speak to her. She would surely be sympathetic to his bumbling French.

"Bonjour, mademoiselle," he began cheerfully.

She looked up surprised. Green eyes, yes, she was lovely.

"It's you! I mean, I've passed you on the road outside the city a couple of times. I remember you because—" He stopped. He was rambling in English and she was regarding him silently and cautiously.

Here was a young man in a blue French uniform. The insignia of the ambulance corps was on his pushed-back cap. Amiens was drained of its young men and was now bustling with military personnel. Molly was glad her aunt had not accompanied her. There was no predicting when she might take a rage against the current French general and his tactics.

"Bonjour, monsieur," she replied with the slightest inclination of her head.

"Comment allez vous? (How are you?)" he asked.

"Merci."

"Good, good." He consulted his book quickly. "Je suis Americain. (I am American.)"

"Oui."

"Oui, that's yes. Okay, now. Mademoiselle, I...uh, am trying to buy, could you help me, no...Okay, Je voudrais pommes. (I'd like to buy potatoes.)"

He looked proud.

"Pommes?"

"Oui."

Molly stepped over to a vegetable stall and picked up a potato.

"Pommes."

"Potato? Oh, no, something is wrong. My book says...hmm...non, pommes," he said with a shrug and a smile.

"Oui." Molly smiled in return.

"I know this part has to be right. Je voudrais...colettes!"

"Colettes? You mean, chops?" she asked.

"Colettes is chops?" he asked in alarm, too flustered to notice her very correct English.

"Yes, like veal chops."

"This is, my book..." He peered closer. "It almost looks like my book has been messed with...no...okay, how about...Je voudrais cervelle. That's it!"

Molly burst out laughing, and those around her looked up and smiled and nodded. Another funny, flirting American.

"Non cervelle?" he asked weakly.

It took some moments for Molly to recover.

"Cervelle is...is...the French word for...brains, monsieur!"

"Brains. Right. Wait. Parlez vous anglais? (Do you speak English?) I mean, you speak English!"

"Oui, or yes, monsieur. I am British or Je suis British."

David sagged against the table. "And I am very embarrassed. The only thing that saves me is Ben or Marty isn't here to witness this, this... Good grief, brains!"

"French can be difficult at times."

"Yeah, so I'm finding out. There's Ben, though. He doesn't carry around a guidebook. All he cares about is knowing the word for yes, no and you're very pretty. You should see how he gets by. And me? I better throw this thing away."

"Oh no, monsieur. Keep trying. Some people have a talent for language translation."

"Yeah...well, Ben has something all right. I was trying to buy stamps."

"Un timbre."

"Un timbre. Okay." He looked her full in the face then. She smiled and he began to laugh. "My name's David Alcott. I'm from the States."

She pointed to his cap. "You are in the ambulance corps."

"Oui. Yes, ma'am. For almost a year now."

She liked his easy, friendly smile. He stuck out his hand.

"I am Molly Fleming, Monsieur Alcott."

"I do not know that your father would approve of this, Molly."

Molly stopped brushing her hair and turned to face her aunt. "Approve of?"

"This, this rendezvous with an ambulance driver!"

Molly was in a teasing mood and tried to control her smile. "He was with the *Allied* corps...I think."

"Now, Molly."

"Aunt Madeline, really. It is not anything to be concerned about."

"He's an American!"

"Yes?"

"I have *heard* things about American men. Not the most flattering items."

Molly wondered where her aunt had received this American bias. The green grocer? The postal clerk?

"He was very polite. Simply a nice young man."

"But his motives, Molly, his motives!"

Molly could hardly keep from laughing. Aunt Madeline was taking her chaperon responsibilites too seriously.

"I think his motives are plain. He wants a guide to see Amiens, to see the Cathedral. Someone who speaks French. He has a little trouble with that."

"He could pay a young boy or old man to show him Amiens for a franc!" The aunt sniffed.

"Yes, I suppose so. But he did ask me, and I think it really is perfectly harmless, nothing to worry over."

"If he was French I would worry far less. I am your guardian in France. You are…a pretty girl and likely to catch many eyes. You admitted there are military men all over the city." She rolled her eyes. "I hear their dreadful rumbling trucks all night. The good people of France may be killed from a lack of sleep…"

"I could take Jonathan with me, if you like," Molly said.

Nine-year-old Jonathan was their only current "boarder."

Her aunt considered this suggestion.

"Or, if you really don't want me to go, I will stay."

"No, you have worked hard, and this should be a pleasure time for you. I cannot grudge you that."

Molly carefully tied her scarf. "Only a few hours, Aunt Madeline. I'll be back in time to make dinner. Monsieur Alcott will be gone."

Madeline Chaumont was skeptical. It was not likely the brash American would forget one lovely young woman quite so easily. Proof that Molly was naive and innocent and needed her protection.

"Very well. Au revoir, Molly!"

She stood at the iron gate of no. 10, watching Molly's light, quick step. Molly waved from the corner.

The older woman shook her head. "If only he wasn't American."

"Sure you won't come with me?"

Ben was sweating over the chassis of his ambulance. Of all in the "fleet," Ben Alcott's was undeniably the most fine-tuned. When he was not on duty, or carousing, he was working over his "chaser."

"I'm not much on touring cathedrals, Davy, sorry."

"Don't you want to see France?" David asked incredulously.

"I am seeing France. Hand me that crank, will you? Hope they get my new tires to me pretty soon."

"But the Amiens cathedral is the largest church in France, Ben! It's an architectural wonder! How can you not want to see it?"

"I have seen it. Drove by it the first day we passed through."

"He is seeing France, David, but not like you," Marty interrupted lazily. "He's seeing France one mademoiselle at a time!"

Ben laughed and David shook his head in disgust. "I think you're both blockheads."

Ben grinned broadly. "So you kind of like this English gal, huh? Bye-bye, Bess. What was her name?"

David ignored the tease. "Her name is Molly. She's just a nice gal. She's going to help me with my French."

"Uh huh…" Ben winked at Marty.

"You know, big brother, it wouldn't hurt you to look for nice girls for a change instead of those Paris cabaret types."

"Ouch," Marty murmured loudly. "I think we're about to have a little sortie between the Alcott brothers."

David smiled. "See you louts later."

Ben followed him out of the little garage. "You aren't mad at me are you, Davy? 'Cause I can clean up real quick and go with you if you want."

David gave him an affectionate punch. "Nope, you stay here and clean your dirty engine. I'll go get the culture."

Amiens was somnolent in the hazy spring sunshine—one could hear the sound of barking dogs and children laughing, good-natured bartering in the marketplace, the distant rumble of a truck. Old men nodded on sunny benches, the shopkeeper in his gray apron swept his sidewalk space, folks on bicycles pedaled over the cobbled streets, old women in dark scarves gossiped at the corners. David was flushed and damp from his ride when he met Molly Fleming at the prearranged corner.

"Grand day," he said cheerfully. "Thank you for meeting me, Miss Fleming."

"I was glad to come," Molly returned slowly. He was so friendly, so, so...American!

"I tried to get Ben to come with me." He shrugged.

"He is the one you work with?"

David nodded. "We work together, yes. But Ben is also my incorrigible older brother. We came over together and have managed to stay together so far."

"Did you say incorrigible?"

"Yeah, thoroughly. Here's a most recent example. You know how I was all messed up the other day in my French translation."

"Oh, yes, I remember."

David shook his head at the memory. "Yeah, cervelle, brains."

They both laughed. Molly had never felt so at ease with anyone so quickly. Never with a man her own age. This must be the American way. What could Aunt Madeline be so worried about?

"Well, Ben the joker decided it would be great fun to carefully erase some French words and write in some others."

"How awful!"

"It could have been worse. So there I thought I was asking you for stamps and I was asking for potatoes and—"

"Brains!" They laughed together again.

"That was cruel of your brother."

David nodded. "Incorrigible."

They wandered leisurely through the great Cathedral Notre Dame. Not as grand or famous as its cousin in the middle of Paris, this church in Amiens claimed its prominence from its size, its soaring asymmetrical facade, and Gothic rose-colored windows. Every building nearby was dwarfed. Their steps echoed hollowly on the cool, gray stone floor. Worshipers' benches had been removed in the primary nave, further adding to its cavernous appearance. David Alcott was impressed.

"I've never seen anything like this. I'm from a little prairie town in the Midwest. We worship in a one-room church."

"You are from?"

"A place called Peppercreek, Illinois. Land of Lincoln."

"Lincoln?"

"Our sixteenth president. He was an Illinois man."

"Yes, I have heard of him. He was the president during your civil war. The Gettysburg Address?"

"That's right. He was one of the great ones, like George Washington. My grandfather worked for President Lincoln," David added proudly.

When the tour was over, David suggested they get something cool to drink at a sidewalk cafe. He told Molly about his work and Ben and Marty.

"Ben wants to go into aviation as soon as possible. Marty and I are talking about transferring to the stretcher bearers corps."

"That is on the front?"

"Yes, the French government won't let us go into the trenches, but there seems to be a real shortage of stretcher-carriers. It doesn't take much to drive an ambulance back and forth—worst danger is the occasional pothole in the road."

"Isn't the work of a stretcher-bearer dangerous?"

"Maybe a little, but someone has to do it."

He shrugged and looked into the sunny street. It was more than a little dangerous, and everyone from general to mess cook knew it. These were the unglorified heroes of the war, brave men regardless of their allegiance. They knew dangers greater than even the front line men. It was their duty to enter the dreaded 'no man's land' at night. This landscape of shell-torn earth and blood-filled craters between the warring sides was aptly named. To cross it in the white heat of battle meant almost certain death. No man wanted to fall there injured. A stretcher-bearer could get lost on a cloudy night among the grisly geography. He could easily stumble into the trenches of the enemy. Any noise, a slip or stumble of the foot, the groan of the injured, could bring an instant barrage of fire. An eerie silence hung over "no man's land," a silence that magnified every sound or movement. One final danger existed for the team—if they were able to retrieve the wounded, and return to their own lines, they could face the fire from a nervous sentry.

"That would be brave of you," Molly said sincerely.

He smiled. "We hear rumors that a lot of troops are on their way up here, a real battle. Even General Haig toured the lines north of here. So, Marty and I figure, unfortunately there may be an even greater need for carriers. Please tell me about yourself, Miss Fleming, what an Englishwoman is doing in France."

So she told him about her aunt and the children they were trying to help.

"You call me brave, but I think you and your aunt are. Certainly very noble to work with such difficulties. We eat like pigs at the canteen. But now, when I think of what you're scraping by on…"

She smiled. "It is not so difficult, monsieur. God has been good to us. He provides for the little ones."

He leaned forward eagerly. "Do you know Him, Miss Fleming?"

"Yes, I think I do."

He nodded thoughtfully. "I'd like to meet your aunt sometime. She sounds like a grand lady."

"Well, she might be rather…cold to you, I'm afraid. She has a deep love for everything French and a suspicion of Americans."

He laughed. "Oh, I get it. She thinks we're the boisterous, obnoxious Americans."

Molly was embarrassed. "You know how…older people are. She suspects you are a rogue, flirting and all that. She did not approve of my meeting you this afternoon."

"The rogue is my brother. Besides, I have a girl back home, so your aunt doesn't need to worry."

Molly looked away. She didn't even tempt him to flirt, and her vanity was stung a little.

He saw her confused look. "Oh. You see, I can mess things up even in my own language. I didn't mean that you aren't, I mean, if I didn't have a girl…" He reddened. "You knew what I meant, Miss Fleming?"

"Yes, of course. You see, I have a ring. I'm engaged to a man in Scotland." She stood. "I better be getting back."

"Before your aunt has the gendarmes out looking for the American ambulance driver. Could we do this again sometime, while I'm stationed around here?"

She gave him her hand. "Yes, I would like that."

Aunt Madeline was diplomatic enough to ask few questions about her niece's afternoon. And Molly offered little comment beyond that it was a pleasant time. She went to bed thinking of the American ambulance driver—and wondering if she would ever see him again.

David Alcott informed his brother and friend that they had missed a pleasant afternoon in Amiens.

"Pleasant?" Ben asked, still in a teasing mood. "Does that mean your tour guide is pretty or the cathedral wasn't too boring?"

"Both."

He thought of her as he stretched out on his narrow cot. It was always Bess who filled his mind as he drifted off to sleep. But this night it was the Englishwoman with the dark hair. Could *she* be the one?...

Chapter 18

Kinsale

♦ ♦ ♦ ♦ ♦

*A*s thin as she was, it seemed it would not take much of a wind to blow her away. She felt her own frailty against the harsh wind and knew with an odd, detached sensation that it had the power to defeat her. Once she would have laughed at such an idea, once she would have shaken her fist defiantly at the storm. But that seemed like ages ago...

She had left the house when everyone had gone. She couldn't stay indoors another moment without screaming. She walked through the pasture, with no purpose, the wind tearing at her dress and hair. The sky held no definition or color, and as she walked, she imagined blending into the gray flatness, forgotten, no pain or memories or guilt. Painless to keep walking into the nothingness...

"Kate!"

She felt shock—that she was not alone. She turned slowly and stiffly to find Padraic coming toward her.

He came up to her, a huge coat in his hands. He jerked it around her roughly. His eyes were blazing, his face red with anger.

"Have you lost your senses then?" he shouted in the wind. "What are you thinkin' of to be out like this in only that thin jacket? All the boys are out lookin' for you, Ma's about wringin' her hands. Why'd you do this? Care nothin' for our feelin's?"

He towered above her, reminding her of a granite fortress. She closed her eyes and lowered her face into the coat as if he had struck her.

He knew then. "This isn't right, Katie lass, you know it isn't."

Even in the wind she heard the tender appeal in his voice.

"Won't you live again, Kate?"

She raised her red-rimmed eyes. "I don't know how anymore, Padraic."

"Let us help you, but you must pitch in with us."

He pulled the coat closer around her, and his voice returned to the familiar one she knew. "You've got to get out of this wind and soon. Can you walk?"

"I can walk."

The elation he'd felt at finding her waned a bit with disappointment. He had wanted to carry her. He shook his head.

"Is she all right, Ma?" he asked when Maggie tucked Kate into the warm bed later with the stone bottle at her feet.

"I think so. No fever or chills. She may be stronger than I thought. Sure and it is well you found her when you did, in such a storm as this. Much longer she..." Maggie shook her head.

"I think that was in her mind, to stay out there until..."

Maggie slumped into the chair. "Aye, as I thought. How did you find her?"

"I ran up on the south hill. I knew I could see miles from there. It was her hair I saw."

Maggie nodded and ran a weary hand through her own curls. "I'm stumped plain, son, and that's the truth. I've nursed her, taken care of her wounds. I've talked with her and I've listened. I've waited. I've made her get up and get out. I've prayed over her. I've prayed for her. Still...Still there's so little real life in her, no want to live. She has so little to do with her father. Aye, it is a mystery to me, one I can't seem to solve."

"You love her," Padraic said quietly.

"That's the truth. God has given me a love for this strange lass from America as if she had come from your da and me."

Padraic stared at his hands. "I don't know exactly the answers, Ma, except we can't give up...like she was wantin' to do this afternoon. Sure, and I'm stumped too. I fish and think why'd this lass come into our lives those months ago, and still here? And I think of Anna Ruebens and I get no clear answers. But I'll keep tryin', as you and Da have taught your sons."

Maggie smiled. "Aye, and I should be takin' my own dose, sure."

Peppercreek

Lilly could tell Andy was asleep from the even cadence of his breathing. She smiled. In seven months of marriage, she knew the little things of this man she deeply loved. She reached out and laid her hand on his chest, over his heart, praying that the pain she knew rested in the figurative heart of the man would lift. She knew for the Christmas season especially, he hurt for his youngest daughter. Stunning shock, grief, followed by the joy that she'd survived—now the coldness of her apathy and rejection from across the ocean. His frustration had boiled over into anger.

"Christmas in two days, and she's still in Ireland!"

"Because she wants to be," Lilly returned patiently.

"So do I give her everything she wants?"

"Of course not, but I don't think you can rush this...this healing time with Kate, as much as we miss her."

He paced the room. "You see, this is another example of her, her headstrong, manipulative ways! If I hadn't given in...to her...she wouldn't...this wouldn't have happened. This Irishwoman, Maggie Falconer, implies Kate's healed in her body, but emotionally..."

Lilly took his cold hands in hers.

"Andy, Andy this thing has happened. Kate is safe, but it will take time and our prayers. Even this can turn out for good in Kate's life. I feel confident of that."

"I don't see how," he persisted stubbornly.

"Andy, my father beat me. It was a horrible time in my life. But it drove me to New Orleans, and eventually to you and who you told me about. Careful steps in my life, some pleasant, some unpleasant. Kate has her own life with all the steps laid out—"

"But she isn't seeking Him," Andy argued.

"Neither was I when I came to St. Charles Park. But He was seeking me. This tragedy, this pain Kate is going through can work for her good."

"I hope so," he had murmured.

Queenstown

Anna Ruebens was annoyed to find Padraic Falconer at her door. He looked foolish standing there smiling and obviously pleased with himself. The landlady came up the stairs behind him and gave them both a cold, appraising look before she entered her own apartment. But Padraic was unruffled.

"Evenin', Anna."

She gave him a curt nod. She was finished with the Falconer family. Their attentions were too suffocating, too scrutinizing. And she did not really need them any longer. It was time she made this tall, boyishly simple, fish-smelling man understand.

"How are you?"

"Fine."

"I dropped by to—"

"You could have rung up, Padraic."

He felt as if a liberal splash of the north Atlantic had hit him squarely in the face.

"Well, I, uh, truth is I didn't think of it." He shrugged and glanced around, embarrassed to still be standing in the doorway.

"If this is a bad time for me to call, or you've company already, I can come back later."

"I am alone. Come in."

He felt awkward in the chair, gangling and provincial with Anna's unfriendly eyes dissecting him. Aye, something was wrong here, that was the truth. He took a deep breath; better to plunge in. He didn't have Rory's or Denny's practiced finesse.

"I was in Queenstown, and I dropped in to see, to ask if you'd like to come to the Kinsale New Year's dance with...me next week. It can be a nice evening. Jen will be home too, and you could stay over."

"You're not escorting that American girl in your home?" she asked archly.

Padraic did not know if he was more surprised at her tone or her words. "Take Katie? Why no, she hardly ventures out. Anna, is something...wrong? You seem, well, a little put out."

"I don't care to be surprised or interrupted this way, Padraic. Calling first is the gentleman's way."

While public opinion held the Falconer boys were good and honest, easygoing lads, they were not without a vein of temper in their decent Irish souls. Padraic could feel the color creep up the back of his neck. "What is this, this offense about? How have I behaved ungentlemanly to you? I've wanted only friendship—"

Anna's voice rose. "Ha! Men want more than friendship with a woman! Though you've been slow enough to the point."

He willed himself to stay calm, to steady his own voice. "I cannot explain your rudeness. Perhaps other men you accompany to the pubs of Queenstown each night are of that sort, but I am not. I was raised—"

"Spying on me!" she hissed. "And how you go on about your raising. Your fine ma with her religious snobbery!"

A tirade against himself was one thing, but slanderous words about his ma? He stood up.

"I don't know what's come over you, Anna. I won't bother you again."

"See that you don't!" she shouted as he left the apartment.

From her window, the landlady watched Padraic's broad, retreating back. She saw his clenched fists and scowl as he stepped into the street. And she nodded in a grimly prophetic way.

Padraic could not remember when he'd been so angry. And the ride from Queenstown to Kinsale did nothing to calm him. The few he passed who called a friendly greeting were shocked when the eldest Falconer ignored them entirely. He looked almost savage with his red face and snapping brown eyes.

He came into the Falconer kitchen like the hot blast from a furnace. Only Kate, Jen and Rory were at the table. The slamming door and his face stopped their words instantly.

"Say, Paddy, is something—" Rory began as he rose from the bench.

"Never mind!" Padraic snapped sharply.

The three exchanged looks with wide eyes. They listened to him muttering and slamming around in his bedroom.

"We have some stew here, Padraic," Jen said in false cheerfulness.

"I am not hungry," the big fisherman growled. "I'm taking the boat out *by myself* and I don't care to be bothered!"

Kate had heard only a reference to this temper from Maggie. "He's like the ocean he loves, Paddy is. Smooth and calm and generous most every day. But there are storms, then, like his da, he can be fierce."

Kate, despite her show of nonchalance, was intrigued. What had provoked the mild-mannered Falconer into one of his "storms?" He had given her no glance or greeting. With another slammed door, he was gone.

the channel

When the sea was rough, the waters would churn in waves of green foam—valleys between the peaks, with cold, drenching spray, almost humanlike with a vicious will to pitch out anything that floated on its expanse. The sea in its truculent mood was a fitting companion to Padraic Falconer, a mirror of his own disposition.

He had bid none of the fishing company loafing around the docks a pleasant good afternoon. The fisher folk knew each other like one large extended family, and none among them could miss the look on his face. Aye, there was a storm in Falconer's eyes, and one did not trespass on his humor or patience at such times. They watched in silence as the *Bluebell* eased out to the channel, then launched into a variety of speculations. Was it a domestic tiff with Maggie or one of his brothers? That did not seem likely. The odd American girl still living with them? That possibility was debated at considerable length. What about the Queenstown girl? What was her name? Padraic seemed to fancy her for all his nonchalance and evasiveness. Aye, a disagreement with her could have set Falconer on a sour course. Another puff of the pipe, another wag of the head. And wasn't it the truth, women folk were so often at the root of trouble?

Padraic left Kinsale harbor and his gossiping cronies without a backward glance. He felt the flame of his fury as intensely now as he had sitting in Anna's apartment. He grimaced freshly at the memory. In 30 minutes he was out of sight of land, the inhospitable sea creating a vastness of solitude for him. He slipped down to the deck and leaned against the ropes. Let a German sub slip right under him, or better, let one surface. He would ram it with the *Bluebell!* He laughed aloud at his own absurdity. Hadn't a woman tumbled up his reasoning like the sea around him churned? He remembered how foolish he must have looked as he had greeted the young woman and then her haughty, flashing eyes. He could hear her imperious tone over the waves. He recalled each humiliating, agonizing moment.

How could the young woman be so, so...unreasonable? Aye, more than unreasonable. He shook his head. It made no sense, and that was the truth. They had had pleasant conversations together over the months since Jen had first brought her home. He could still redden at the memory of their first meeting in the Falconer kitchen when he had kissed the top of her head. Even then her face was impassive, revealing nothing. Cordial enough, interested in his work. No discussions of her past or her family. No girlish laughing or teasing or flirting. What had Jen Falconer seen in this girl to draw her friendship? Indeed, what had he seen? What was the word Ma used for Anna? Guarded.

He admitted he was attracted to her despite that guard, that cool reserve. He looked forward to her company, to knowing her better. Then this sudden, unexplainable hostility. There on the *Bluebell's* decks, Padraic came confidently to some clear conclusions. There was no reason for her anger. And she had never really cared for him, Jen's big brother, the fisherman. She had tolerated him. The anger began to slowly fade as the shade of night was drawn. Now he felt the pang of disappointment and hurt.

He thought of Kate Alcott as he absently gazed at the sea. Yet another lass without the steady, amiable ways he knew from his own ma and sister and Kinsale girls. From the first when he had held her near lifeless body, he had felt a strong sense of protection toward her. As her body healed, he had looked for some return to the smiling, happy, optimistic girl who must have stood on the sunny decks of the grand *Lusitania*. But that girl was gone. The one in the Falconer home had haunted, pain-filled eyes. She spoke bitterly of her past, of deception and manipulation, and made vague references to a loveless childhood.

He had prayed for her diligently. That she remained in their home seemed a testament to Padraic, that their work with her was not finished. Yet for all his efforts, nothing seemed to work with Kate. Only days earlier, she had slipped away to try to end her suffering. What if he had not seen that flash of red from the frozen hillside? No, nothing seemed to work. Not with Miss Ruebens, and not with Kate Alcott. He sighed deeply, feeling old, and tired, and lonely. He didn't understand women, or how to please them. He'd do better as the bachelor fisherman he had always been.

Only when night fell in silvery darkness, did Padraic come out of his reverie. He stood up and sauntered to the wheelhouse. Even in the night blackness, he knew his location immediately. He watched the lights of a steamer some four miles to port side. The sighting altered his own course of thoughts. He had seen Sir Coke before he had gone to see Anna.

"Falconer, I want you to be aware that we are confident German spies exist in Queenstown, and along the coast."

"Spies, sir?" he echoed blankly.

There were still times when the war and all its peripheral activities amazed him, jolted him out of his security and routine life.

"They are as interested in ship movements through St. George's channel as we are interested in the submarine presence. They would like to know the precautions and measures we are taking to thwart their successes. Another little game of chess, if you will. So to the point, Falconer. Guard your information carefully. We need not give the Germans any further advantage."

German submarines. Now, spies. Where was this fast-changing world leading him?

Peppercreek

Dear Grandma,

By the time you get this letter it will be December 25th, so Merry Christmas! We received the package yesterday and have eaten everything already, right down to the last crumb! Many thanks for the socks, newspapers and all the other treats. We thought with such a mild fall, winter might bow out entirely, and we'd just move into spring. But it has come with a vengeance. (I borrowed that word from Davy. Yep, still borrowing after all these years. Glad I have such a generous little brother.) Anyway, it is very cold here and we have snow from time to time. Nothing like the blankets we get in Peppercreek, though. Marty was complaining about the cold, but I pointed out to him it seems to have reduced our little civilian population a bit. I think you call them lice back home. The war is mostly in hibernation. But we are busy transporting men who are sick and dying from different illnesses, like flu, that move through the ranks. Several of our unit are very ill. We work, work on our cars, play cards (no betting of course), loaf and practice French. Davy keeps me in line, you will be relieved to know. Spring will come, a thaw and "the blood will start flowing again." That line is from David. Some of the boys in our outfit are planning our Christmas feast. So don't worry, we will have a fine time. David says he will read from Luke for us. But it won't be the same, and I know we will miss all of you. Yesterday we got a surprise package from Uncle Andy's new wife, Lilly. She sent us a record of herself singing

Christmas songs and some other good stuff to eat. Marty has gone into Paris to buy a phonograph. He is the man with the big bucks. I was there myself a few days ago and had an American woman actually come up to me and ask me to light her cigarette! I was shocked to say the least. But I guess we country boys have to get used to these modern times. All Davy could comment was to ask me if I had flirted with her...

The old woman carefully folded the letter. She had reread it, along with the three others she had received from her grandsons now in Europe. She had also read again the two short notes from her granddaughter in Ireland. The world outside was undulating folds of whiteness and a slate-smooth sky of gray, but Sara Alcott was warm by her bedroom fire. The cold, the letters, and the fact that tomorrow was Christmas 1915 made her long for her three grandchildren so far away. Before Ben and David left for France, she had listened to war news from the lips of others, almost casually. Now she read each newspaper article with great deliberation. Now Ben and David were a part of that force of men called the Allies, and they were experiencing the hardships of winter along the western front. The newspapers called it a frozen wasteland. Sara could turn promptly to the page in Ethan's war diary which described the battlefields of 1862 in the same graphic words. The weapons had changed, she sighed, but so little else. Barefoot, skinny children without their fathers, Ben had written...

This letter was one of the first—before he saw things the papers could not describe. Now he saw the troops, the shell holes and mutilated villages and landscapes. Now he carried men both living and dead in his rickety little "chaser." Now he saw the real war behind the propaganda poster, just as his grandfather had. Sara knew her grandsons would come home changed men, as their grandfather had. Better men, she would smile. They would come home...

But sometimes, even Sara Alcott's faith and confidence trembled in the face of facts, if she thought too long on Ben's determination to fly in one of those dangerous flying machines. It horrified her to learn from the newspaper that there were now huge guns, like cannons, whose sole purpose was to shoot at those planes that defied the lines of battle on the ground. Perhaps Ben would be satisfied with his work with the ambulance corps and give up this frightening notion. And too, it was no small concern this wine-drinking because the water was unsafe...

And Katherine. Sara pulled her shawl closer around her shoulders as she stared into the flames. Kate still in Ireland. Kate with her languid-sounding letters. The only spirit she'd really shown was her insistence that her father not come to Ireland. How that insistence had hurt her son Andy. It was like Kate had managed to slap him from across the ocean.

Sara would be concerned for Andy—if it weren't for Andy's bride. Sara smiled when she thought of her new daughter-in-law. Lilly. A perfect name for the lovely, smiling woman who captured her son's heart and was helping him through this valley of pain. Lilly was restoring something of the man that was lost years before. But it would take time.

Take time for her granddaughter as well.

"Oh, Katherine," she whispered, "don't give up, little one…"

Kinsale

"Do you like boys, Kate? Did you have any beaus back in the States?" Jen Falconer asked in the bedroom they shared when she was home. She was brushing out her long brown hair, and Kate sat on the bed watching her. It was healthy, shining hair, a glory to Jen Falconer. Kate reached up and touched her own locks. Dull and dry. She was always the attractive, vibrant one in her circle of friends.

Jen Falconer never gave much thought to what she should say or not say to the girl who was staying in her home. She just spoke from her own natural honesty and curiosity. She was an easygoing girl who could sympathize but not understand the shadows of pain in Kate Alcott.

"So do you like boys?" she repeated with a smile.

Kate smoothed her dress. A funny question to stumble over, to have to think about. "Well," she began slowly, "I, I did…"

"You did? What made it did and not do?" Jen asked innocently.

Kate could not get angry with Jen; it would not be fair to the easygoing girl. "I've had…boyfriends," she said simply.

"Anyone special?" Jen pressed.

She remembered Clark. 'You know I love you. I love you, Kate Alcott…Someday you'll feel about some man the way I feel about you.'

Clark's words came easily, as if he stood just beyond her shoulder and whispered in her ear. She felt her throat tighten. Would she ever think of him without this guilt and pain? She couldn't tell Jen; she couldn't expose the tender wound.

She shook her head. "There is no one…special, like you mean, Jen."

Jen turned back to her mirror and arranged her hair, chattering over her own romantic prospects.

"Of course, the Kinsale boys are nice, but they seem so, so…what's the word?"

The tools of the craft she loved were always close at her command.

"Provincial? Rustic?" Kate supplied.

"Provincial! Exactly! After the young men I've met in Queenstown, they do seem rustic." She sighed. "But I'll go with Sean to the dance anyway. He's handsome and fun. Of course, I'm not sure Ma approves of him. He can be on the wild side. Who cares though? It isn't like I'm going to marry him! Well, at least I don't think I am..."

Kate smiled faintly. She suddenly had the feeling she was hearing herself, only now in the Irish-tinted tongue.

"Kate, you can't imagine what it's like having four brothers to, to scrutinize every young man who comes within a mile of your door!"

"You'd like their approval, though," Kate said with sudden insight.

Jen turned and smiled. "Aye, they are good brothers, sure. They wouldn't steer me wrong. Kate, will you go to the New Year's dance? It's only a week away and we need to be thinking of what you could wear."

Kate shook her head vehemently. "No, Jen, really, I couldn't."

"It's held on the top floor of the town hall. A band from Dublin this year! Eats and dancing, everyone goes. It's a grand time. The boys are fun coming home, singing carols." Her face glowed.

Kate was only half listening. Last year she had gone to one of New Orleans' New Year's fetes. She had worn a satin dress that cost her father over two hundred dollars. There was dancing until two A.M., a thrilling ride in Eddie's Bearcat, and then later in his arms in front of 2121 Old Manor... She shook her head again.

"No, I don't think I—"

"Why not? You can't stay in this house forever!"

Kate reddened, but this new Kate did not flare with indignation or a hot retort.

"No...no, I can't stay here forever. I've got to go home sometime," she said softly.

"I know lots of boys who would love to take you—"

"A novelty. The American lass who looks like a skeleton!" Kate said flatly.

Jen ignored the bitterness. "Rory and Denny have dates. Pierce never goes. That leaves Paddy. Or I can ask a boy I know."

"Padraic seems hardly in the mood for parties," Kate reminded.

Jen frowned and nodded. It was true. Since Padraic had returned from his solo voyage on the *Bluebell* days before, he was present to his family only in his physical body. His eyes and silence revealed he was far away in his thoughts. He answered when spoken to but volunteered little else. Kate recognized the look in his eyes.

The night he'd come in from the *Bluebell,* he had found her alone. She had watched him nervously as he removed his hat, coat and wet boots. He looked tense and worn as he lifted the lid on the pot over the fire.

"It is all gone. I've watched your ma make porridge a few times. I could try to make you something," she offered impulsively.

"Really?" he asked quietly.

"Well, not as good as Jen or your ma could make. I didn't, I mean I haven't...cooked much, you see. One of those weaknesses of being a rich man's daughter." Her voice was easy, and suddenly she smiled.

Padraic's big, rough hand rested briefly on her shoulder, a brotherly, affectionate gesture. "You smiled, Katie. Aye, you give me a little hope..."

Then he had shuffled silently to his bedroom.

"It's Anna Ruebens," Jen said abruptly. "That has to be what's got Paddy angry and scowling."

"Who is she exactly?"

Jen lifted her chin. "I thought she was my friend. But she made it clear she doesn't want to be friends anymore."

"Why?"

"Who knows? She is a strange lass, very moody. But I, well, we all thought Padraic was kind of taken with her. He was in Queenstown last week. I just bet he saw her and she was rude!"

Kate recalled his words. 'You give me a little hope'.

What had he meant?

Jen brightened with her ability to shrug off gloom. "So will you go to the dance, Kate? Please do. Will you have Padraic or another?"

'You must pitch in, Kate, you must,' he had said. 'Live again...'

"I'll think about it, Jen—no promises though."

Like so many other Irish cottages, the kitchen was indisputably the heart of the Falconer home, unpretentious and serviceable, yet an inviting and welcoming room. Kate Alcott thought briefly of her home in the fashionable and wealthy enclave of New Orleans. She tried to identify a room that embraced comfort and family tradition like the Falconer kitchen. But she could think of none. Even her bedroom, expensively decorated, and stamped with her personal tastes, was hardly a room to stir her affection and sentiment. There was no heart in the Alcott home at 2121 Old Manor, she realized in an unemotional and detached way. She knew her home would seem almost alien to her when she saw it again...

In long, quiet, undistracted hours, Kate revolved that question in her mind. When would she leave this Irish home, this island, and return to her country and her past? Would she effortlessly slip back into that life like she would one of her many satin dresses that hung in her bedroom closet? But confronting the question of when with her old directness made her recoil. She was not ready to leave this place. Not yet. It went beyond the horror of sailing in a ship across the vast, and now menacing, Atlantic. It went beyond leaving Maggie's love and acceptance, and her daughter and sons' friendship. Something else held her captive on this Emerald Isle, something undefinable and indistinct. But as Jen had bluntly stated—she could not remain here forever.

Now the Falconers were in the fervor of Christmas preparations. Holly was draped lavishly across the broad oak mantel and curled in the deep window sills. The brass was polished and red candles stood like sentinels around the room. They had a goose for roasting and plum pudding on the shelf. Maggie's best china and linens were brought out.

Then it was Christmas eve and everyone was freshly dressed as they gathered around the table in the dusk of late afternoon. Kate saw a mixture of solemnness and gaiety in their feelings for this holiday, excitement and reverence in their faces.

Denny had given frequent reports on the weather with childlike triumph. "Aye, there is snow now, coming down like feathers, it is!"

"It won't last," Pierce had prophesied soberly.

But Denny had winked and smiled at Kate. She smiled in return, unable to resist his enthusiasm and affection.

They walked to the old stone church after their meal. Kate sat between Jen and Rory, subdued in the quietness of the little sanctuary. It looked as if all of Kinsale had crowded into the church. Huge candles flickered against the gray walls and Kate felt as if she had stepped into a beautiful, holy place. The vicar stood and began reading the ageless and familiar story. But to Kate Alcott it seemed new, as if every time in the past were a hollow-sounding echo.

'...And the angel said to them, Do not be afraid; for behold, I bring you great news of a great joy which shall be for all people...'

From the corner of her eye, Kate saw Padraic wiping away tears. She bowed her head, uncertain of all she was feeling.

Their steps crunched on the thin veneer of snow as they began their trek back home. A spectator in this new drama, Kate was silent as Maggie linked their arms together. The brothers sang carols with Gaelic too broad for Kate's tongue. Greetings were called out cheerfully to those they passed on the road.

Maggie explained the single lighted candle in the windows of the homes. "'Tis a custom of Christmastime. Like an invitation to stop in before the hearth fire for a warm drink and a Christmas blessing."

They entered the kitchen, the boys laughing and teasing. Maggie bustled about serving the mulled cider and pastries. Jen was like a sprite as she passed out gifts from the small stack. They had given her gifts—a lace collar and hair ribbons, a book on Irish poets. Pierce presented her with a gift—heavy work boots. Everyone was quiet, waiting for her reaction. Heavy work boots.

"A practical gift, Pierce," she said with a serious face to rival his own.

"Aye." He nodded.

"Is this a way of telling me I need to be working harder, mucking out the barn perhaps?"

He looked confused. "Well, Jen has a pair, and I thought...aye, to be one of us, you need what we have."

"Thank you, Pierce," Kate said.

Later Kate stepped outside before she went off to bed. There was no wind, no lilting snowfall, only crisp coldness over the bare hills.

Padraic joined her. "Are you missing home?"

Her arms were crossed as she studied the night sky. "Missing home? No...not exactly. Just thinking...and trying not to think." Last year there was a Christmas dinner at 2121 Old Manor. The Bentons had joined them. Only a year ago... She shook her head. "This has been a lovely night. I've...enjoyed it."

"I have a gift for you," he said simply.

She turned. "You didn't have to do that, Padraic."

He stood tall beside her, and she let herself ask the question—was he handsome?

"Jen will scold me if she finds out I didn't wrap this in pretty paper, but I didn't have time."

"That's all right."

He hesitated. Why should he risk her rejection or scorn or...or any other unpredictable, female response? Only that in Queenstown he had thought instantly of her as he passed a fine stationer's shop.

He held out a book to her and watched her face as she opened it. Its pages were smooth sheets of ivory. She lifted her eyes to him.

"You see, I...remembered you said once that you lost your journal on the *Lusitania,* and I knew you loved to write. I...I thought this would help you to begin again."

"Begin again," she whispered as she ran her hand over the unmarred pages.

"It was the best one they had. Is it all right, Katie lass?"

He had thought to bring her pleasure, to help her with his gift.

"It was very sweet of you...to think of me this way, Padraic." She held out her hand to him with a trembling smile.

"This...this is an American way?" he asked, taking the slender hand in his.

"Well, sort of. I..." She stretched to give his cheek a quick kiss. "Merry Christmas, Padraic."

Queenstown

He felt as if the anchor from the *Bluebell* was suddenly wrapped around his feet. Going to face Anna Ruebens in her apartment again made him feel he was submitting to a beating. Aye, a beating with fists was preferable to an angry tirade he might receive from her unpredictable tongue. Yet Padraic was convinced this was what he must do. He had carried anger, resentment and hurt on his shoulders ever since he had seen her. His heart was cold and unforgiving—and he could not go on this way. Wasn't it forgiveness that so often came up when he talked with his fishing friends? He could not be a hypocrite. He and Anna must talk. It would surely be the last time.

He meant to leave Kinsale early in the day to reach Queenstown before sunset, but cutting peats for the fire delayed him. Now, as he glanced up at her window, Padraic's resolve was steady, though the chill, night shadows were falling. She answered his knock promptly and he gave her no time for greeting.

"I need a quick word with you, Anna, then I'll be gone. Please allow me that."

She hesitated just a moment, then swung the door wide. He stood in the middle of the room, nervously crushing his cap in his hands. Anna stood also.

"I came to say, that is, I came to tell you, that I was sorry about the words we exchanged. I shouldn't have made some of the remarks I did. It was ungentlemanly of me, like you said. I've valued our friendship and I want to ask your forgiveness."

The woman paled and her arms went limp at her sides. "You want my forgiveness?"

"Aye."

"But why?"

"May I sit down?"

She nodded.

"I've been very troubled since we talked last. Truth is, I haven't been able to put it out of my mind, or shake off the anger I felt at you. I finally saw my own uncharitable heart and so in the face of what I believe I had to come back to you."

"What you believe?"

He drew a deep breath. "You know about my faith, I've talked of it before. I try to live it, more than I talk it, sure. Christ forgave me and He wants me to be forgivin' like Him. I'm not to hold on to anger."

He waited for her to speak, but her eyes were downcast. This was hardly the defiant, unreasonable lass who had lashed out at him a week earlier.

"Is there something wrong, Anna? Is there anything I can help you with?"

"No, Padraic."

His eyes traveled the room, seeing two suitcases. "Are you taking a trip?"

"Yes, I leave for the United States in the morning."

"Oh." He nodded. Her voice, while not biting, offered no invitation for further confidence.

"Well, I wish you well then, in America," he said easily.

"Thank you, Padraic." She stood and Padraic knew it was time to leave. He stood also, facing her. He knew he should say goodbye and not press his proverbial luck. But he couldn't leave just yet.

"Anna, do you have any questions about Christ?"

He was sure his question would put her off, but he must risk it. She smiled then, a very tired and sad smile.

"You are a good man, Padraic Falconer, and I'll remember that. I have to finish packing now. Goodbye."

The man entered her apartment silently and unobserved. He saw the suitcases and he knew he was almost too late. Anna, appearing in her bedroom doorway, was shocked and frightened, then angry.

"What are you doing here? How dare you break into my apartment like a, a common thief!"

The man's smile was icy. "My brother was on the *Sussex*."

"Get out instantly, or I'll scream."

But he moved with the speed and agility of a cat. His hand clamped over her mouth as he twisted her arm behind her back.

"You call me a common thief? Is that so different from a common German spy...Marta Marie?"

Kinsale

Padraic did not know if he had accomplished much in his brief time with Anna. He only knew his own soul had profited from asking her forgiveness. He felt he could breathe, smile, enjoy life again. And he prayed as he returned from Queenstown that she would find real happiness in America.

Tonight he shaved and dressed with special care. Denny and Rory juggled beside him for a place at the dresser mirror—parting hair, straightening ties, polishing shoes and lots of laughter and teasing.

Padraic did not know how he had allowed Jen to talk him into this. Except that he would try to swim St. George's channel if she asked him to. And she must have used the same persuasive skill on the reluctant Kate. Of course, he went every year to the New Year's jig—it was tradition. Usually he took some local lass who did not want to appear at the affair unescorted. Sometimes it was arranged by his ma and some other zealous mother. But this night was different. Tonight he was taking Kate Alcott, the American girl.

He waited for her in the kitchen, flatly ignoring Maggie's amused glances.

"I am not nervous, if that's what you're thinkin', Ma," he said in pretended irritation.

She shrugged in innocence. "I have no complaint with you poking up the fire when it was fine or looking in the silver platter at your reflection." She winked and they both broke into laughter. She came to stand before him.

"Now I'm remindin' you she may be like a skittish colt out in public. You mustn't mind *her* being nervous."

He bowed. "I will keep your words in mind. I just want the lass to have a good time. She seems a bit better these days lately, don't ya think, Ma?"

"Aye, 'tis true. I think—"

But someone was clearing her throat loudly from the bottom of the stairs. They turned to see Jen and Kate.

She was still too thin and too pale. But somehow Jen had transformed the American girl. Padraic tried not to stare. She wore a softly draped dress of royal blue wool. A matching ribbon was threaded through her hair that was brushed to shining. She was looking past him, not smiling, and Padraic knew she was acutely embarrassed. He looked away. "Well..." was all he could mumble.

Maggie went forward with a pleased face. "You both look lovely, and that's the truth."

Kate took her hands. Maggie pulled her close and whispered into her hair. "Don't be afraid, lass. Everything will be fine. You'll have a good time."

Kate was introduced to yet another passion of Irish culture as she and Padraic stepped into the upstairs room of Kinsale town hall. Lively violin music greeted them. She looked up at Padraic for explanation.

"Jigging," he said simply.

Everyone was smiling, laughing and dancing. The young and old of the village were celebrating together the soon arrival of 1916. She was greeted at Padraic's side without speculation or question, and Kate knew these generous people, while not fully understanding her presence, had accepted her.

A Falconer neighbor bowed to her. "Lookin' pretty tonight, Miss Katherine."

"Thank you."

They sat and watched the dancers, and Padraic talked with friends. Denny finally persuaded her onto the floor to dance steps she could follow. Returned to Padraic she was flushed pink, her eyes sparkling. "It would take me a long time to get your dances down," she said with a laugh.

He smiled. It was good to hear her laugh. "You did fine, sure."

"You're not much for dancing, Padraic?" she queried.

He rubbed his chin. "Well see, it's these big feet. They're fine on the deck of the *Bluebell* or in the muddy potato field, but they can crush feet of lasses."

"Oh, you're being silly."

A man came up to them then. He was grizzled and bent with age. His face was sweaty and red, his eyes watery.

"Let me have a spin with the American lass, Paddy?"

"If she likes." Padraic nodded.

"Well, I...thank you, sir, but really it is too fast for me."

He tipped his cap and shuffled off. Kate fanned the air in front of her. "He...was rather strong."

"It's called stout."

"Yes, he was very stout. I *would* worry about my feet with him."

Padraic's laugh was booming. "No lass, stout. It's what he had a few pints of at the pub before he came, I'm sure."

"Oh...stout."

Later, as they returned home from the dance, Padraic was back to his old self, ever solicitous.

"You warm enough? Tired?" he asked without looking at her on the carriage seat beside him.

"No, I'm fine."

Padraic hesitated. "Did you...well, I..."

She turned and smiled. "Yes, I did have a good time, Padraic."

He exhaled loudly and she smiled again. The carriage jogged along in silence several minutes.

"You went to dances on New Year's in America?" he asked.

"Hmm? Oh, yes. There were always parties and dances to go to."

"Like this?"

"No, not quite like this."

He studied the horses. Of course not like this. This was an American girl from a rich family. How poor such a thing like this must seem to her. He frowned. He thought of how clumsy he had felt on the dance floor with her moving lithely in his arms.

"We aren't fancy here in Kinsale, not like you're used to."

She was surprised by his defensive tone. Her voice came slowly. "No, you aren't fancy, and I'm not used to this," she replied squarely. Another awkward silence.

"A lovely night."

"Yes, it is...Padraic, I'm sorry about leaving the dance...like we did, before it was over."

"I don't mind."

She clenched her hands together. They had reached the Falconer property, and Padraic guided the carriage into the barn. He helped her down, but she did not move away. For some reason, she must explain.

"It was the Strauss, Padraic."

"The Strauss?"

"The band was going to play Strauss waltzes." Her voice started to tremble and Padraic stepped closer. "I never want to hear Strauss again, Padraic, never..." Her tears boiled over.

Instinctively he pulled her into his arms. "It's all right, Katie lass, it's all right."

"They, they were playing Strauss...that last night...on the *Lusitania*."

"I understand, don't talk."

He stroked her head. Several minutes passed. She did not want to move away. But when her tears passed, she stiffened and stepped back.

"I'm sorry. I don't mean to dissolve into tears all the time. That isn't the way a date is supposed to end."

He loosened the harnesses. "Ah, well. Then how is it to end? I've been on so few myself."

She smiled. "In each other's arms of course, kissing and—" She stopped, stricken and embarrassed.

He smiled then, looking her in the eye, but she shook her head. Her words were hurried. "I wasn't thinking. I mean, I was being silly..."

He studied the leather with renewed interest. "Of course."

But she gripped his arm with sudden intensity. "You understand, Padraic? It can't be like that. It could never be like that...between us. I don't feel anything. I'm not like that girl at last year's Christmas dance in New Orleans."

"Sure and you aren't the same lass," he returned softly.

"Well anyway, thank you for a nice evening."

"And I thank you as well."

Her hand dropped from his arm, but their look did not end.

They stepped into the warm Falconer kitchen and were surprised to find Constable Speight warming his hands in front of the fire. He turned slowly. Maggie sat at the long table.

Padraic looked quickly at his ma. Her face seemed ashen gray. She gave him a nod, then looked to Kate.

"A nice time, lass?"

"Yes, Maggie, thank you."

"New Year's greetin's to you, Jim. What brings you out so late?"

A strange, foreboding silence followed while the lawman pulled at his whiskers. Padraic helped Kate from her coat. They were all waiting.

"Somethin's wrong," Padraic said clearly.

The constable nodded soberly. "You need to come with me, Paddy. Miss Anna Ruebens was found murdered in her apartment yesterday. I need to question you."

Chapter 19

Vienna

♦ ♦ ♦ ♦ ♦

*I*t seemed to the residents of Vienna that not only was the city being drained of its youth, but nearly every public building and many private homes had been requisitioned for military purposes, especially hospitals. It was a city of injured and dying and medical supplies that had almost dwindled to nothing. Their men went away healthy and determined, and if they came back at all, they were frail and spent. Vienna, the city of music, had fallen under a shadow.

In a long, crowded ward of one of the public hospitals, a middle-aged woman lay very ill. It did not trouble her much that so little could be done for her, but the ache in her heart for her dead husband was very real. Still, as she lay there staring past the circle of light cast from the shaded bedside lamp, she thought of her children. They would be left orphans. It would not be so critical with 19-year-old Kurt who was forced to play a man's role in this terrible war. But there was 6-year-old Emma, the joy of her last year with her husband, waiting patiently for her at their neighbor's apartment. How could she tell Emma she did not think she would be coming home this time? And if Kurt did not come home from the war... She closed her eyes. Please, not Kurt. But she must think, must prepare. It was all she could do in her ebbing strength.

The doctor had tried to be tactful and kind. "I know this is painful to discuss, Fraulein. I am sorry."

"It is all right, doctor."

"You have no...family?"

"No. My husband and I were only children. All relatives have died."

"Your church?"

The woman picked weakly at her bedcovers. "They will take Emma to an orphanage. But with the war, they are so over-crowded. You hear stories..."

The doctor nodded soberly. "Friends?"

"No one who could take another mouth to feed." She began to cry softly.

"Please, Fraulein, please. Do not worry yourself. We will think of someone. Someone for Emma."

If Kurt did come home from the war, would he be able to care for his little sister? Certainly he loved her. And his time in the army would have matured him. But Kurt was always so impressionable, so drawn to new, unconventional ideas. He seemed so interested in politics and all the turmoils it brought. His mother really didn't like this interest of his; it pulled him into circles of friends she thought questionable. Like Hitler. He had filled young Kurt's head with his ideas. She wished now she had forbidden their friendship. Sometimes she feared the older man had an almost hypnotic effect on her son. She began to cry. Leaving this world of pain...no, she did not really mind. Oh, but how she would miss Kurt and Emma.

British General Douglas Haig completed his tour of the western front as the frozen wasteland was beginning to thaw. He had studied countless maps. He had spoken with Allied pilots who had ventured over the German lines. He had argued with the French high command. This stalemate in northern France must be broken this summer of 1916. Call up the new recruits waiting in the camps across the channel. With enough men, and his "secret weapon," he would smash the German lines.

"A domino effect!" he exulted to his staff. "Our punch and the western front will crumble from Ypres to Verdun! Now is the time!" He pointed to the map, his finger tracing the Somme River. "We will headquarter here."

An aide strained over the general's shoulder to see the map. A French town called Amiens.

General Erich von Falkenhayn was very impatient with the war's exile into winter. He was also weary of Kaiser Wilhelm's constant harping for action. So springtime had come and it was time to put his new strategies into motion. He was proud of his plans, even if his staff was skeptical. He had the vision that they lacked. The German line along the Somme River was impressive, indeed "impregnable," he had boasted to the kaiser. Even the Allies with their darting planes and cameras did not know how strong his trench system was.

The chalk hills overlooking the Allied trenches were like fortified catacombs. No mere haphazard tunnels in the earth, these dugouts were timbered and rebutted with concrete. Electricity provided further comfort. An entire camplife with laundries and rooms with bunks. For the front-line soldier it was a comfortable life and he did not want to be disturbed from it. Huge guns were mounted in concrete pillboxes to discourage any foolish attack over "no man's land."

Falkenhayn received reports of increasing Allied movements along the Somme, before he could implement his own designs. No matter, he smiled. He perused the map again, pointing to the river.

"They will try along here." He smiled again. "A pity for them..."

Amiens

Molly Fleming felt a twinge of guilt, but she was just a bit relieved Aunt Madeline's headache was too severe for her to accompany her niece shopping.

"I will take Phillipe and Rachel with me," Molly said easily. "They can help with the baskets."

"If you find enough to put in the baskets," Aunt Madeline returned pessimistically.

"So that leaves you with Bertha, Mary, Louise and Raynald. All the girls will take long naps, but Raynald will wake them if he wakes up crying with another earache. I've put the medicine—"

Aunt Madeline shooed her out of the courtyard. "I can manage, go along now."

When Molly paused to latch the gate, she found her aunt still watching her from the steps. She gave her a nod and rare smile.

Phillipe noticed immediately. "Madame is smiling. Why is she smiling, Mademoiselle Molly?"

"She is glad your noisiness is gone from her grand house," 9-year-old Rachel retorted impishly.

Molly smiled. "No, no, I think her smile was her way of thanking me."

"Why can't she just say the words?" Phillipe asked.

"Well, because some words are difficult for some people to say, even when they feel them."

"I haven't trouble saying any words," Phillipe said as he skipped ahead of them. "I know lots of words. Marc told me words to call the Germans, you know, since they are our enemy."

Molly shook her head. "No, Phillipe. Calling them enemy is bad enough. We must hope soon they will just be our German neighbors again."

Molly found the city as congested with Allies as she expected. They had heard their trucks from the end of the street. Phillipe had discovered the attic window and unboarded it. From its height they could easily see the outlying countryside, the glistening river only a few miles north, and the road where columns of trucks were raising the dust to Chateau-Thierry. The rumble of trucks day and night had not gone unnoticed by Madeline Chaumont, of course. Molly had expected her to fuss, but instead, she was fearful.

"Molly, all these trucks and so many planes overhead each day. They must be planning a big battle near Amiens."

Molly chewed her lip. "You may be right, Aunt Madeline."

"Then we must face the reality of Amiens invaded."

"Surely they would give us warning."

But her aunt spoke with the conviction of a veteran. "There is nothing sure in war. We must prepare for you and the children to leave if it becomes so apparent—"

"The children and I? Aunt Madeline, you would come too, of course."

The chin had risen in disdain at the suggestion. "I will not leave my home."

"Now, really, Father sent me over here to—"

"There is no point in discussing this. I will not leave."

"But, what if...what if the Germans came and saw this fine house and decided to take it for their headquarters?"

Molly hated to be so cruel, but she had to make her aunt see the seriousness of her stubbornness.

Madeline had paled, but her voice was firm. "We shall see, Molly, we shall see."

Already the city library and municipal hall were converted into hospitals. The Allied staff had taken residence in the stone building across from the cathedral.

"So many soldiers, Mademoiselle Molly, look! They are everywhere!"

They were everywhere, loading trucks, passing through on convoy, in the cafes, and marketplace.

"We will do our shopping quickly, children. Stay with me."

Three dozen eggs traded for two pounds of lentils. Again Molly was grateful for Aunt Madeline's highly prized and prolific hens which provided her with a source of barter. No potatoes today, but plenty of onions.

"Butter? It is very high. Oh, it is you, mademoiselle, for you!"

After an hour of shopping, Molly had only half the items on her list, and proposals from four different soldiers.

"They are like bees around a flower," Phillipe pointed out, shaking his head.

After an hour she was tired and her feet hurt from chasing Phillipe who wanted to speak to each and every soldier.

"Bonjour, mademoiselle!"

Another flirting soldier?

"Cervelle today, Miss Fleming?"

She knew the easy going voice before she turned, laughing.

"Monsieur Alcott!"

"Oui." He nodded. "I was hoping I'd run into you."

She colored at the pleasure in his voice and approval on his face, glad she had put on a fresh dress before she came to market.

Phillipe studied the man with wide eyes. "An American, Mademoiselle Molly?"

"Oui, Phillipe."

"A boarder, Miss Fleming?" David asked.

"Yes, this is Phillipe and Rachel. They are staying with Aunt Madeline and me for a time. And as you can see, they are helping me with shopping today."

David eyed the nearly empty baskets. "This is all your shopping? Beans, onions, two loaves of bread, and six apples."

"There is a pound of butter, too," Molly pointed out. "We'll try again tomorrow."

"Are there more boarders at your aunt's?"

"Yes, four others."

He dug his hands into his pockets, thinking hard. "Kids eat a lot more than you have in that basket there..."

Molly waited. "Well, we had better be going."

"I'm on duty now. We're fixing up a hospital one block over. Can we get together tonight? I'm off duty then. We could just eat dinner, you know, and talk."

Aunt Madeline's face rose instantly in her mind. David guessed her thoughts. "Your aunt? She won't like it?"

"Well, I...there are the children to take care of."

"We can take care of ourselves, mademoiselle. Go with this American."

Molly was startled. "Phillipe, you have never let on you know so much English!"

He tapped his head. "Mama taught me to be wise, mademoiselle. I do not have to tell everything I know."

Molly laughed. "Yes, but it makes me wonder what I've said in front of you!" She turned back to David who stood waiting and smiling. "I will meet you here at six, monsieur."

"Great!"

On the return home, Molly cautioned Phillipe. "I'll tell Aunt Madeline about the American, all right? She gets...a little upset over Americans."

Phillipe shrugged. "Madame should not object even if he is a Yankee—"

"A what?"

"A Yankee—that is another word for American. Did you not know?"

Molly laughed. "Oh, Phillipe. You do know lots of words."

"Oui. He is a Yankee, but he is fighting for France. Madame should see he is—oay."

Molly concealed her laughter. "That's okay, Phillipe."

"Okay. Oui."

Just like back home they were fighting over the one small mirror in their tent.

"How long does it take you to shave, Ben? Come on, hurry up."

"Careful there, little brother. There, I'm finished."

He sat on the edge of his cot polishing his shoes. David claimed the mirror.

"You're humming," Ben pointed out.

"Huh?"

"You're humming."

"So?"

"So, you're pretty excited about going out to dinner with this English girl."

"I told you her name is Molly."

"Whatever. You are looking forward to this."

"Sure, why wouldn't I?"

"She isn't Bess, that's why."

David turned around and shook the razor at his brother. "Look, I've told you, you're thinking the wrong thing."

"Am I?"

David laughed. "Good grief! Now *you're* worrying over me about a gal!"

"I know, I know. I feel kind of fatherly all the sudden." He grinned. "Would Bess approve of you taking this English girl out to dinner?"

"Sure. She would understand perfectly."

"Uh huh…" Ben shook his head. "Whatever you say."

"I'd like you to come with me and meet her."

"Why are you so all fired for me to meet her?"

"She's nice."

"Uh huh…well, there's a gal with red hair who likes to dance who's waiting for me. She doesn't know a word of English."

"Bring her along. We'll make it a foursome."

"Another time, Davy, another time."

But David Alcott wondered if there would be another time.

Of course, this was bound to happen. That is what comes of having your peaceful little town overrun with soldiers. Aunt Madeline shook her head mournfully. With Molly going into Amiens for shopping and so many military men about, yes, it was bound to happen. She was a pretty girl—the men would have to be blind not to notice. She scowled again. Soldiers. Who could depend on them in, in…romance? They'd be here for a short time, then off to another assignment, and another pretty girl. Madeline Chaumont considered her options carefully. She could simply assert her authority and forbid her niece from going to dinner with the suspect American. No, that would not be respectful of Molly. She could claim that feeding and putting the six young boarders to bed was too much—her head still throbbed terribly. No, she musn't be dishonest. There was only one other possibility.

"There now. You will eat, then Madame has agreed to read to you."

Molly wagged her finger at them, though she was smiling. "No fussing about bedtime or going for a picnic to the river tomorrow may be in jeopardy."

"We will be angels, mademoiselle. Perfect angels. Go on to your American."

Molly blushed.

"He is not *my* American, Phillipe. You know that."

"He is not your sweetheart?" six-year-old Bertha asked.

"No. He is merely a friend. That is all."

The children looked away, and cut each other glances that seemed to ask 'Is it possible to look so pretty for a man who is only your friend?' Hmm...Molly was flustered. "Goodnight, children. Be good."

"Angels," Phillipe corrected.

"We will settle for good, young man," Aunt Madeline said dourly as she followed Molly to the door. "You look very...attractive tonight in your blue dress."

"Thank you. It is one of my favorites, though it is old and out of fashion now."

"The American will not care."

Molly smiled. "Monsieur Alcott."

"It will be dark when you return. I do not like you on the streets with all those—"

"I will ask the monsieur to bring me home. How is that?"

Aunt Madeline's lip pursed. Clearly Molly was eager to go to this American. Youth!

She laid her tactic. "What shall I say if Martin calls?"

"Martin?"

"The young man in Scotland. Is his name not Martin?"

"Well yes, but why would he call even if he could get through?"

"To say bonjour to his *fiance* perhaps?"

"But he has never called!"

"But he could. Would you mind if I told him you were out to dinner with a young man?"

Finally, Molly understood. Dear Aunt Madeline...

"I wouldn't want you to lie, of course. You would have to tell him I am out to dinner with a young man." She leaned forward in a conspiratorial whisper. "But try not to tell him the young man is American."

She gave her aunt a quick kiss and was gone.

Molly was having an enjoyable evening. The cafe's colored lights danced on the cobbled street, good-natured banter rose from the surrounding tables, and the thin strains of a violin drifted on the night breeze from another cafe. She enjoyed the meal unhurried and uninterrupted. David Alcott made her laugh and forget the war and the shortages and Aunt Madeline's worries. She liked the smell of his aftershave when he stood near her to pull out her chair. He seemed to genuinely enjoy her company.

"It was kind of you to invite me out this evening, Monsieur Alcott."

"I was happy to, but you know back in the States, we aren't so formal. You'd call me David and I would call you Molly. Could we try the American way?"

"Certainly David...though..."

"Yes?"

"Well, if I called you David in front of my aunt..." She smiled. "Well, her fears would be confirmed. You see, speaking so familiarly to you would be an indication that we are, that you are..."

David smiled. "I think I understand. My brother thinks the same thing."

"He thinks?"

"That I'm forgetting Bess. He doesn't know a man and woman can be friends without being more than friends. Ben doesn't know that."

Molly toyed with her silverware. This David Alcott was not handsome in a stirring way, but rather in a kind way. But he had such qualities that she realized looks meant nothing.

"My father would say..."

"Your father would say?"

"He would say a man and woman must be friends first *if* they are going to ever be anything more...than friends."

"Your father is exactly right."

She did not want him to misunderstand her. "But I understand what you are saying about your brother."

"Ben's a good egg, he just—"

"An egg?"

David laughed. "A good fellow. I asked him to come along with us this evening, but he had other...plans."

Molly dipped into her food. Already she was familiar with this older brother. "A date?"

David frowned and nodded.

"You don't approve?" Molly inquired gently.

"I don't know. Ben always goes after the showy kind. He could use better judgment. He'd sock me if he heard me say that."

"I see..." He's what the girls back in Whitehall would call a rake, Molly decided. And socking his brother? Did that mean punch or something to do with socks?

"He's a nice fellow, the best!" David amended quickly when he saw Molly's frown. "Ben is the greatest. He's just a little crazy when it comes to girls."

"Oh."

David spoke quickly. "He's loyal and generous and hardworking and, and honest and...he just goes for a girl's looks and..."

"And that concerns you?"

"I love my big, incorrigible brother. I just don't want him to get snagged up by the wrong gal. We don't have to talk about him all night, though. He's conceited enough," David laughed.

Molly brightened. "You have joined the stretcher corps."

"Yep. Marty and I both. Since we're familiar with this sector, they're going to leave us here. I'm happy about that."

So you can keep an eye on this brother with the roving eye, Molly said to herself.

"Have you started yet?"

"We just finished our training. We had to learn how to give aid if we got stuck out in the field for awhile. We went out a few nights ago, over near Cantigny. They put us with fellows that go out all the time, Frenchmen. You could tell they were nervous about being out with us green boys, afraid we'd make noise and the Huns would go to shooting." He looked at his hands. "It was scary, yet..."

"Yet you didn't feel alone. You were where you were supposed to be."

"Exactly! Have you felt that way?"

She nodded. "When I came here to France. I didn't know about the children. I only knew I was to help my aunt, but I didn't know how I would help her. I didn't know how she would receive me. Then that first night in my room, I was still a little scared, but I knew I was not alone. And I knew this was where I needed to be."

"Yeah, that's how I felt. It was so quiet out there in 'no man's land.' Quiet and misty. We didn't pick anyone up since there hadn't been any fighting. They were getting us used to it."

"Did the Germans hear you?"

"Nope, we were too scared to make a peep."

"You are very brave, David. You and Marty. I will tell Aunt Madeline. She will be proud."

"Say, Davy boy!"

A young American in civilian clothes came up to their table. His arm was draped loosely around a smiling young Frenchwoman. Was this...the rake?

"Hi ya, Pete," David greeted easily.

"This your girl, Davy? Didn't know ya had a girl." His voice was slurred.

"This is Miss Fleming. Molly, this is Pete Adams, one of the ambulance corps. This is his night off," David added significantly.

The American bowed to Molly. "Wanna come dancin' with us? They got a band over at—"

"No thanks, Pete, not tonight."

Pete leaned toward Molly and winked. "Wanna go dancin', Davy's girl? They got a great band—"

Oh, if Aunt Madeline saw this...!

"Thank you, but no."

"Okay, okay, adios!"

"This is France, Pete, it's au revoir."

The French girl at Pete's side giggled. Their laughter trailed behind them as they strolled down the street.

"You did hear me say that he wasn't on duty, didn't you?" David leaned over the table. "The corps isn't all like that."

"At first, I thought he might be the big brother," Molly admitted with a smile.

"Nope, Ben scores points there. He can't stomach alcohol, literally. Makes him sick as a dog."

It had grown late and the cafe was closing. "I've had a nice evening, David, thank you."

"I borrowed my old chaser tonight. Let me give you a lift."

"Aunt Madeline would be grateful."

They climbed in. "She and I agree then. The dark streets are no place for a pretty girl."

Molly heard nothing but "pretty girl."

Rue de lilac, no. 10 was quiet and dark.

"Aunt Madeline must have succeeded in getting the children to bed," Molly said pointing to the house.

"I'll meet her next time. Show her I don't have horns."

Next time...Molly smiled in the moonlight as he helped her down.

"Wait, Molly. I have a passenger back here." He opened the back of the ambulance and pulled out two boxes. "It was the best I could do on such short notice. But now that I know what to look for—"

"David!"

The boxes were full of fruit, potatoes, and bread.

"There's two pounds of bacon there at the bottom. Here, I'll set them on the steps."

"David, where did you get this?"

He was beaming like a proud schoolboy. "Oh, just happened on a few things, you know, just around."

She stood with her hands on her hips, waiting.

"Consider it a gift from the unit."

"But it's too much!"

"Are you kidding? We'll never miss it. I'm sorry to tell you, Molly, knowing how the civilians suffer, but they're feeding us like hogs."

They stood on the shadowed steps.

"This was very sweet of you."

"Will it win me points with Aunt Mad?" he teased.

"Definitely. She'll probably give my hand in marriage." Molly was instantly embarrassed at her impulsive jest.

"I wouldn't mind that," David returned easily.

A darkened porch. Suddenly Molly Fleming felt lonely. This should be Martin pulling her into his arms, or she should be the Bess from Lincoln land.

She sought to change the subject. "David, why are the troops pouring into this area? Do you know anything? Aunt Madeline is worried."

"You're right, they are pouring in here. Thousands, in fact, are filling the trenches. They haven't told us anything specific yet, but all leaves are suspended. We all think something big is coming. So I don't know when I'll be able to get off and see you again."

She must break this spell of intimacy. Her hand went to the door. "You know where Lilac Street is and...I'll be happy to see you anytime. Au revoir, David."

She stood in the hallway while he drove away, so many thoughts chasing through her mind. Something big was coming...it could mean a sudden threat to Amiens and trying to get stubborn Aunt Madeline to leave. But it would also mean David Alcott would be stealing out into the misty 'no man's land' for those who had fallen in the day—out there where the Germans listened with their fingers on the trigger. He would be in great danger.

She carried the baskets into the kitchen. Even the skeptical Aunt Madeline would be impressed with this Yankee. Her hand rested on the bread. He was a kind man to think of her and the boarders. He was kind to be watching out for his brother. Kind, respectful... She sighed with the loneliness she had felt on the steps. She must not make more of this friendship than what it would have to be. Friendship. He had made that clear. He was as honest as his clean shaven, boyish face. There was Bess, waiting for him. He was the kind who would be true.

She started up the stairs to her room. 'He wants a friend. I will be his friend. He will be my first American friend. I will write Dad about him.'

He yawned and pulled off his boots and threw them across the floor. Marty was deeply asleep with a book across his chest. Ben's cot was empty. David frowned. Ben wouldn't know a good girl if he ran into one.

That long ago conversation in Peppercreek. What had he said?

"I'll know her, Davy. Somehow I'll look into her eyes, and I'll know she's the one."

David was skeptical. He thought of Molly Fleming as she had looked during the evening across the candle-lit table from him—the gold gleaming on her dark hair, her embarrassment, her look of gratitude for the food. Yep, she was one of the good ones. She had all the qualities. Plus that charming English accent.

He leaned back, still smiling into the darkness as he thought of her. This was a priceless girl! He would have to write Bess a letter very soon...

July, 1916

"Over the top!"

Battalion commanders all along the line gave the order. Thousands of Britons and Frenchmen poured out of the trenches like some human reenactment of the seven plagues of Egypt. For days, artillery had rained explosions into the German defenses. Allied planes soared above to drop their deadly charges. Now, the basic element of fighting returned to the battle. Men against men. Across the wasteland with bayonets ready, rushing into the smoke, wave after wave. The new recruits ran forward eagerly in their vague fear and youthful optimism. They had disdained the worries and cynicism of the "old sweats." It was only a matter of their determination. They would push the Huns out of France in this one brave assault.

Men talked in low voices, in huddled groups, if they had energy to talk at all. Many sagged against whatever support they found, vacant-eyed, exhausted, filthy, starving. Man collapsed face down in the dirt, weakly hoping they had staggered back to the "right side." Still, they might be exposed to the enemy. But what did it matter? They were too weary and had seen too many horrors. They were past caring.

Ben Alcott looked as grim and spent as any soldier who had traveled into the wasteland. A week's growth of beard and circled eyes cast a hardened look to his face. He forgot the last meal he'd eaten sitting down. Most often it was a plate of beans shoved into his hands as he waited for his ambulance to be loaded. It did not take long to load his chaser. And there was no way he could keep his little vehicle spotless and well serviced anymore. The floor of the truck was stained in blood. He was either driving or catching a few hours of sleep.

It wasn't just the sights he'd seen, or the fatigue. A fear for David churned in his stomach, haunted him each time sunset came and he knew his brother was slipping into the target land of the Germans. David and Marty were both out there night after night claiming the victims of the day's bloody harvest. Ben was in danger, too, from the long-reaching shells, but still he was behind the lines, driving his chaser away from the violence. He saw his brother only in snatches of time—looking like a mirror of himself, only thinner. Ben knew the Germans were furiously mowing men down like a scythe in a field of ripe grain. His little brother was out there—one false step or stumble and the stretcher bearer would fall beside the one he had tried to rescue. Ben was terrified for David. And there was nothing he could do.

Dr. Gros came up to Ben.

"I have an assignment this morning, Monsieur Alcott. You take six others and go four miles to Arras. There you will find a field."

"Yeah?"

The doctor looked old and pale in the morning light.

"You all right, doc?"

"Yes, yes...I saw your brother there this morning."

"Is Davy all right?" Ben asked quickly.

"Oui. He and Marty worked most of the night."

"Doc, how long is Haig or Joffre or whoever is in charge gonna keep throwing men into this battle? Are we gaining any ground?"

"The general does not consult me, Monsieur Alcott. He expects me to...clean up his mistakes."

When he stepped from the ambulance, he was assaulted by the smell. Planes skimmed overhead, big guns blasted past the horizon, troops moved lethargically along the dirt road. David had seen him coming. He came up to him, pointing to four large trucks.

"That's your assignment, Ben. Load them and take them to the cemetery they're making east of Amiens."

Ben walked a few steps past his brother. He could not pull his eyes from the scene. Row after row of men, all still. They stretched across the entire field. David came to stand beside him. They took in the sight in silence for several minutes.

"Marty and I stopped counting at...a thousand."

Ben was arrested by the hoarse croaking of David's voice. He turned to look closely at his brother. "Did you...do this all night?"

David nodded. "Somebody had to sort the living from the dead."

"How long have you been up?" Ben asked.

He shrugged. "I don't know. Yesterday morning, I think."

"You get in my chaser right now and go straight back to camp." His voice was sharp as he leaned toward David threateningly. "I don't care what the doc says, you're off duty. Now go on..."

"You have to have help loading them," David replied tiredly. Ben knew his brother was nearly in tears.

"I brought help with me. Now go on, Davy boy, no arguments."

David gave him a crooked smile. "You gonna thrash me like you did when we were kids?"

"If I have to, yeah."

David laid his hand briefly on Ben's shoulder, then walked to the ambulance.

Ben turned back to the field. A field, Dr. Gros had said.

"A field of death," Ben muttered.

Sixty thousand British soldiers had fallen in one day.

There were few visitors to no. 10 rue de lilac, so Aunt Madeline was surprised when the front doorbell rang in the middle of the afternoon. Pierre had brought boarders the day before and was therefore not expected for another several weeks. And the tradesmen always came to the back door if they were so bold. Perhaps it was one of the children playing a prank. Molly had taken them to the field past the garden, to watch the haying. She quickly checked her appearance in the heavy gold leaf mirror.

A young man in civilian clothes stood on the front steps. Instinctively she knew who he was. Yet they eyed each other for several moments in silence.

"Madame Chaumont?"

The American! She knew it! She stiffened—then remembered the boxes.

"Oui."

"Parlez vous anglais, madame? (Do you speak English, madame?)"

A perfectly atrocious accent!

"Oui."

He gave her a faint smile then. "I'm David Alcott, a friend of Miss Fleming's."

She waited very still in her regal bearing.

"Is she home?"

"No, she is not."

"Oh."

He seemed to lose energy then. He turned slightly and leaned on the iron railing by the steps. His voice sounded hollow. "I was hoping...she'd be home."

Madeline Chaumont's eyes went swiftly and critically over the young man. He was obviously tired and under some distress. Would he collapse on her front steps?

"You may wait for my niece if you like...monsieur."

He raised his head slowly. "Can I?"

He was hurting. She could see that. She swallowed hard. "Oui, please step in."

She led him to the sitting room, but he hesitated just inside the door. "I...Miss Fleming said you have a garden. Would you mind if I sit there and wait for her, Ma'am?"

It seemed vaguely improper...but she consented with another stiff nod. They stepped into the garden. Quiet, cool, shaded, fragrant.

He exhaled loudly. "Yes, this is what I wanted." He went to the bench and sat down.

Alarmed, the mistress of the house turned away. She hurried through the large kitchen then past the outbuildings and down the grassy slope.

Molly looked up from the blanket where she sat with the children. An apparition in black was flying down the sunny hill! Aunt Madeline! She had never imagined the older woman could move so quickly.

"Aunt Madeline! What's wrong?"

On another occasion, Molly would have struggled to hide her laughter. The gray hair had escaped from its dignified and restraining coil, the cheeks were red, the blouse loose, the skirt covered in nettles.

"There is...you have...Oh my..." The aunt clutched at Molly's arm.

"Are you all right? Here sit—"

"No, no,...I'm...fine. You have a visitor, Molly."

"A visitor?"

"The American. Monsieur Alcott. He is waiting for you in the garden. He does not look well. I will bring the children. You go ahead."

Molly slipped on her shoes, but her aunt stopped her. "Should you go to your room first and change, tidy up?"

Aunt Madeline could not dismiss tradition and decorum entirely. Molly smiled and hurried up the hill. David had come after nearly a month since their dinner out. David ill?

He sat on the bench, his arms hanging limp, his head lowered. Molly stopped at the trellis. He had heard her step and slowly looked up. Molly was shocked. He looked terrible—thin and white with sunken eyes. This was not the easy-going David she had met in the marketplace. He looked like a small boy, lonely and afraid.

"Hello, Molly."

She stepped foward cautiously. Even his voice was different.

"Bonjour, David."

They were openly staring. She had not bothered to go to her room first as her prudent aunt had suggested. So her hair was windblown, her cheeks colored by the sun.

"Are you all right?" she asked softly.

He nodded slowly.

"Can I get you something? We have tea."

"No thank you. I don't want anything but to sit here awhile."

She was never nervous around him before, but now she was. He was too withdrawn, too intense with his looks.

"I tried to sleep. But I can't...sleep. I thought by coming here and seeing the garden you told me about...do you mind if I rest here?"

"No, not at all."

Certainly, he had been through some terrible experience—something that had not touched his body, but something inside.

They heard the sound of running feet and childish laughter. A young girl ran into the garden, but stopped abruptly when she saw the mademoiselle and the man who looked ill. Four other children appeared behind her, equally curious and wide-eyed. Aunt Madeline's voice was sharp.

"Children! Come out of there at once!"

David raised his hand. "Miss Fleming, let them stay awhile please. Let them play in the garden."

"You don't want quietness?" she asked.

He shook his head. "No, I've seen enough quietness. I want...life."

Molly appealed to her aunt with a look. The older woman nodded, her heart softening for the weary young man. She had forgotten for a moment he was American.

The children fashioned boats and sailed them in the fishpond. They played tag and made things from sticks and leaves. They brought their creations to Molly's lap and ventured bold looks at the man who would then smile at them and ask them their names. He seemed to have strength to do little more. Finally Aunt Madeline came and took them to dinner.

"Tell me what you've been doing, Molly," David asked quietly.

She told him of the children and news from her father in London.

"And what is the name of the man in Scotland?"

"Martin."

"Do you hear from him often?" David asked pointedly.

"No...he is very busy." She looked away, embarrassed.

Aunt Madeline came to the garden again. "Will you join us for dinner, monsieur?"

Molly looked to her lap and smiled. A small French-American victory.

"Thank you very much, Madame Chaumont, but I'm not really hungry and I do need to be leaving soon."

But he lingered another hour. Molly sat across from him. They talked very little. Mostly David sat with his eyes closed, though she knew he was not sleeping.

"I guess I can go back now and try to sleep."

Her heart ached for him. His eyes filled with tears. "I needed to see some beauty and peace, Molly. I needed to see you and the children, to hear your voice."

She nodded. "Is your brother all right, David?"

"Yeah, he's okay. Just tired like all of us."

They were friends. They looked at each other a long moment. Surely, he was thinking of Bess, needing to hold her, to be comforted. She could do nothing...

They had heard the battle of the Somme for over two weeks now. Day after day of explosions thudded through the earth, night after night of flashes and distant thunder. They had climbed to the attic like witnesses spellbound to watch from their premium seats.

Molly held her aunt when the old woman broke down and cried. "They are killing my country! Think of what the land must look like just past our view, Molly."

And, of course, the children needed comforting in the nightly barrage. The mayor of Amiens had told the townspeople the Allied line north of the city was holding firm. The commanders had promised him no less than four hours notice if the city had to be evacuated. But Aunt Madeline had drawn little comfort from that.

"When will this end? Oh, cheri, that you are here with me!"

It was the encouragement Molly had needed from her reticent aunt.

"David, is...it almost over?"

He sighed deeply. "I think so. I don't know how...much more they can pour into it."

He stood stiffly.

"I'm praying for you," Molly said shyly. "I know you face such dangers each night."

He took her hand. "Thank you. I will think about that." He held her hand, looking at it as if he had not seen a woman's hand before. She knew he was enjoying the smoothness of her skin.

At the front door, he paused. "Thank you again."

She smiled and nodded. The tears she had held back spilled over.

"Don't cry. It's all going to work out."

"I wish you did not have to go back to those..."

He nodded and took one final look into her deep brown eyes.

"You're the right one, Molly," he whispered and was gone.

The battle of the Somme was over. As the dead and wounded were carried away and the guns grew temporarily silent, it had become another statistic, another contest to be recorded in the history books. In England, some villages had lost entire neighborhoods of young men. It was a bloody fight, and both sides were left with broken pieces, and no laurels.

The pre-battle barrage of artillery from the Allies had had little effect on the German entrenchments. So line after line of French and British had faced the murderous defenses. It was the slaughter of a generation: 600,000 British, 500,000 Germans, and the lines had not moved in either direction more than a few feet. A general's nightmare, the battle of the Somme toppled Falkenhayn from his place of power, and replaced him with another stoic militarist named Hindenburg. In Britain prime minister Asquinth was replaced by Lloyd-George in the public outrage. The French city of Amiens had sat in the balcony of the battle of the Somme—throughout the summer the fighting raged just outside their city gates. In the spring the city had been flooded with wave after wave of optimistic boys. But in the fall, the tide brought back a depleted and ravaged army. With its shortages already painfully felt, the influx of wounded heightened the critical situation. The citizens of Amiens looked at each other in the marketplace with anxiety. The prophesy was that 1916 would bring a very hard winter indeed.

David Alcott gradually recovered from the nightmare he had witnessed. His letters home put the case simply.

> ...I would love to come home. I'd love to say I don't care
> anymore or this isn't my fight, or even the American fight. The
> British and Germans are simply butchering each other. But I
> cannot leave until I have given my best. I keep on going for
> those men who fell this summer, and for Aunt Madeline and the
> children who are living in a world that is stealing their
> childhood, and for Molly who is trying so hard with so little.
> I can endure a little hardship. Ben and Marty feel the same as
> I do...

The battle of the Somme had strengthened the three young Americans' resolve. Ben was more determined than ever that his place was in the sky.

"You guys can slug it out in the mud," he said jerking his thumb skyward. "I'm going up there."

Dr. Gros brought the news when the ambulance unit and stretcher bearers had sat down to dinner in the mess hall. He was sad to lose another Alcott. Ben was one of the best drivers, certainly the best mechanic. He cleared his throat significantly.

"I have received a call from Paris. We are losing another of our unit. But I trust he will go on to continued service in the cause of France. Monsieur Alcott, we salute you."

He handed Ben the slip of paper. Ben's smile was wide as he looked up from it. He was accepted into flight school. He was going to fly for France!

Chapter 20

Ireland

◆ ◆ ◆ ◆ ◆

*S*pring in Ireland. As a city girl, she had never fully known the complexion of the budding season. Maybe it was there in front of her, she decided, but she had never had the eyes to see it before. You couldn't ignore spring in Ireland even if you wanted to—which Kate Alcott did not want to do. It was a comparison she shied away from, but like the land thawing in rebirth after the months, of cold, she was waking up. There were moments, though, that the waking up was painful—and she wondered if it might not always be this way.

When the winter still held the earth in its tenacious clutch she'd awakened one night, screaming, in Jen's bedroom. Jen wasn't home, and Maggie had flown into the room in her flannel nightgown to calm her.

"Maggie, what would I do...without you?" she sobbed.

Since she had come to their home, the Irishwoman could see the American lass had gentled.

"Sure, and you'll do fine without me, but I'm here now. There, there..."

Kate laid back on the pillow. She could almost imagine the horrors just past Maggie's soft shoulder in the darkened bedroom corner.

"Another bad dream, lass?"

Kate nodded. She did not want to voice it as talking might bring it back in strength. Her voice was hoarse.

"Why, Maggie, why? Why did I have to go through the sinking? My life was fine before. It haunts me. It changes everything. The other survivors have gotten on with their lives, but I can't seem to. Like you said, the boys have the smell of fish in them, I can't get the...*Lusitania* out of me."

"Have you thought, lass, it isn't the sinking entirely? It is like the sinking simply made you look at a dozen things in your life you've not wanted to really think about before."

"Like?" Kate responded cautiously.

"Like your relationship with your da. It isn't right. Of the young men you've known. You know better those things that you say are haunting you. Perhaps you're to look at them now and understand."

Kate looked away. Maggie was right—but it was so hard.

Maggie smoothed Kate's forehead and smiled.

"The sinking, 'tis a part of who you are now, Katie, though you did not choose it. It has the power to add to you or take away, and only you can choose that."

In Ireland, with the coming of spring, Kate Alcott was finally finding life again.

She understood exactly what Maggie meant—it was a torture to be indoors during the spring. It was color and freshness outside. Maggie Falconer was busy with her midwife duties, and Jen had gone to Dublin, so Kate was left with the household responsibilities many days. She had gotten over the brothers' good-natured, but relentless teasing over her cooking and her well-intentioned attempts at mending. She had to laugh when she thought of her friends back in the States—'Kate Alcott, domesticated!'

She hurried through her chores so she could take her journal and a picnic and go walking. She could tramp for miles through the green fields or meandering dirt roads.

"I might just walk to Dublin!" she declared one morning.

"You wouldn't get far," Denny countered.

"And why not?" she returned with mock indignation.

"The lads on the way to market would be stopping, wantin' to give the pretty American lass a lift, sure. No, you wouldn't get far."

Kate smiled. It was nice to be called pretty—even if she didn't quite feel pretty.

It should have been a near perfect time in the Falconer family. Jen had a secretarial job in Dublin, the fishing had been respectable, Denny's romance with a local girl was blossoming. But it was not perfect. Even in the best of moments, a shadow hung over the household. Padraic sat in the Queenstown jail charged with murder.

Kate sat on the sunny slope, one of her favorite spots under a lone beech tree. She could see all of the Falconer property from here. She was writing—feeling the old thrill of inspiration and energy flowing out of her was very satisfying. She had begun to put some of the things Maggie had referred to on paper. It was a small beginning. She paused, looking down at the smooth, creamy sheets. Padraic had given her this journal. She missed him. She had a unique relationship with each Falconer man— with Padraic gone, there was a void. He had helped her, encouraged her, done so much for her, like Maggie had. What could she do for him?

The cart rolled up to the cottage, and she watched Denny help Maggie down from it. Kate gathered up her things and hurried down the hill.

"What happened?"

The Irish midwife was disgusted even in her pain.

"Oh, and the foolish one I feel. Twisted my ankle, shooing the rooster out of Flanigan's kitchen, when I had the new babe just asleep. He comes in throwin' his chest out and yellin' to wake the dead. Makes me mad that Jake Flanigan can't keep his creatures penned up, sure!"

Denny shook his head as he helped his ma to a chair in the kitchen. "You should have left well enough alone, Ma. You know the rooster rules the roost," he said with a serious face.

She wagged her finger at him. "And the hen rules the rooster. Now quit your foolishness and help Kate draw the water for my foot."

They sat the bucket before her. Gingerly she lowered the swollen foot. "Goodness! Do you think I'm a mackerel to boil?"

"Ma, you're a terrible patient."

Maggie frowned. "Today I was going to Queenstown. Now..." She threw up her ample arms in impotent frustration.

Maggie Falconer had been confident, optimistic, even stoic in the face of this trouble that had come upon her family. She broached no hint of gossip or speculation with even her well-intentioned friends.

"I'll not wag my tongue over this ridiculous charge!"

Pierce was conciliatory. "Ma, Paddy is in trouble. There's that witness. The magistrate isn't convinced like you, that the charges are ridiculous. That's why he's holding Pad."

"He will be convinced they're ridiculous, and sure! He's holding Padraic because he has no one else! Do you suspect your own brother, Pierce Falconer?"

Pierce lowered his head. "Of course not, Ma, only we shouldn't be...be blind to how serious things are with Paddy." He retreated to the corner with his pipe. It really was more prudent to be a man of few words.

But for Maggie's assurances, they all knew this problem was taking its toll on her. You could see it in the new lines around her eyes. Eyes that sought out the lane from Queenstown, as though expecting her oldest son to stride down it at any time soon. And, of course, the day Kate had slipped past her bedroom but not before she saw the mother quietly weeping, her son's shirt in her lap. Instinctively, she knew this time it was better not to intrude on the proud woman.

"I'll go to Queenstown," Kate spoke up. She had not seen Padraic in the weeks since they had moved him from Kinsale.

"And I'll take her and see him, too!" Denny chimed in. "We'll go just as soon as we get his basket ready."

Maggie looked skeptical. They were children really. This was a terrible prison. No place for... She shook her head.

"No, no, I doubt they will let either of you in because of your age."

"I'll make them!" Kate said stoutly.

Maggie chuckled at the passion in the American girl. "All right, you try. Paddy will be glad to see you."

Queenstown

It reminded Kate of something from a French novel—the Bastille or a fortress in *The Count of Monte Cristo.* Apparently, Queenstown fathers of long ago had wanted a building that inspired fear and respect from its citizenry. This prison was built with deliberate design.

"How ugly! I don't suppose they build cheerful-looking prisons, huh, Denny?" Kate said softly.

The building on the port city outskirts inspired her to whisper. Denny shook his head. "Poor Pad...I see now why Ma's not said much about it. All these years, I've never seen this place."

It looked like it was carved from the huge gray rocks that challenged the Atlantic along the coastline. Hopeless, fearful, foreboding.

"A few window boxes with geraniums would help," Kate joked.

She slipped her hand in Denny's. But when she stepped forward, Denny restrained her.

"Wait, lass."

"What's wrong?"

He tugged off his cap. "I've no feeling to go into a place like this without prayin' first." He closed his eyes in boyish, innocent appeal. "Uh, Lord, we come askin' You'd guide and protect Kate and me as we go into this place. Truth is, Lord, it frightens me a bit. But we're needing to see Paddy. Open the doors for us, please...and help our brother to come out. Amen."

Kate would not admit it easily, but she was glad the youngest Falconer had prayed.

They were shown into the head jailer's small, bleak office. They glanced at each other nervously.

"You're his brother?" the man asked without preface or greeting.

"Aye, I'm Denny Falconer."

"We don't allow youngsters to see prisoners."

"I'm 20, sir."

"Where's your ma?"

"She's ill," Kate spoke up quickly. "She couldn't come. We came in her place to see Padraic."

"You're not family. You've no right to see him."

"She's like family," Denny said eagerly. "She's like a sister to us."

"You're an American," he continued in an unfriendly tone.

Kate Alcott was having a difficult time not lashing out at this pompous little man. But she felt Denny's hand on her shoulder.

"Sir, we're askin' to see our brother, nothing more."

His eyes boldy swept over Kate. He nodded at her.

"You can wait in here while he goes in."

Kate felt Denny stiffen. "No thank you, sir, the lass goes with me."

The man leaned forward, his eyes beady as he jabbed a stubby finger at Denny. "You keep a civil tongue in your head, lad, or it may be quite a time before you see that brother of yours."

Kate turned to Denny with innocence. "You know, I just thought of this, Denny. We could go see the American consul. I'm sure since I'm an American citizen, they'd be happy to help me."

The jailer snapped to his feet. "They'd have no business here!"

Denny and Kate stared at him calmly.

"You can see him for 20 minutes and no longer. Next time it's your ma or no one."

"I thought all Irishmen were friendly," Kate whispered fiercely as they were shown down the hall.

"Where did you get that consul idea?" Denny whispered back.

She smiled, shrugged and batted her eyelashes.

Her smiled faded when they were shown into the small visiting room where Padraic Falconer waited. Yes, Kate agreed with Maggie Falconer— this was ridiculous. A good man like this being held in this archaic-looking dungeon. Indignation rose in her.

He turned from a small barred window when he heard them enter. He looked swiftly at Denny, then his eyes lingered on her—almost in a caress. He looked the same—tall, strong, only a little tired. It would take much to pull down a mighty one like this Irish fisherman.

"Hello, Paddy," Denny said easily.

Padraic nodded. "Lad." They shook hands, then Padraic pulled his brother into a rough embrace. "You're still lookin' the same, though Ma tells me Janie has a pretty determined hook in ya'."

Denny blushed and shook his head. Padraic turned to Kate waiting beside Denny. "And 'tis a...pleasure to see you, Kate. You're looking well."

"Well?" That was all? Kate felt disappointed with the brief words.

"Thank you, Padraic. How are you?"

He indicated the benches for them to sit. "Fine. First tell me how it is that Ma didn't come."

They explained and it made Padraic smile.

"And Pierce and Rory?"

"They are fine, sure. 'Tis truth we're all missing you," Denny said.

Padraic glanced at his hands and nodded. He seemed not able to speak for a moment. Then he began a barrage of eager questions—like one starved, Kate thought. She suddenly felt guilty for enjoying the beauty of the spring, and here Padraic sat in this dismal place.

"The fishing? Are they running? In the channel or further out? How's the weather been? Seems I heard a squall the other night. Did Pierce get the rudder mended? Aye, use those nets I've put in the locker on the *Wanderer.*

The big man leaned forward as Denny answered each question. Kate realized this was the real torture for the Irish fisherman—to be separated from the sea he loved. She did not know until that moment how much she had really missed this man who had become her friend, and how she longed to help him.

"And have you been writing, Kate?" he asked abruptly.

"She totes that book you gave her around everyplace!" Denny volunteered. "Calls it her Emerald Portrait."

"Emerald Portrait. I like that," Padraic said with a smile.

Kate felt embarrassed. "I've been writing a little."

He nodded. "I'm glad to hear that."

"Tell us how it is with you, Pad. Ma didn't say much from her last visit."

Padraic sighed. "There isn't much to tell. I...don't like to talk about it much because it centers on me and my part. And the important thing gets pushed aside—that a young woman...was murdered." It seemed hard for him to say the words.

Denny nodded and laid a hand on his older brother's shoulder. "I understand what you are saying, but if you are silent, well, you may...stay in this place. And we can't be forgetting the murderer is still out there. He must be brought to justice!"

Padraic stood up. "Justice, aye..."

Denny looked to Kate. This apathy in Padraic was not good.

"So the lads are pitchin' in on the *Bluebell,* Ma told me."

"Aye, Jeffery took her out with us, then brought in the entire catch. A nice sum."

The local fishing fleet of Kinsale had rallied around the Falconer family. Padraic's innocence was unquestioned. Even if some had shades of doubt, he was like family, guilty or not, and you stood beside each other, especially in a squall.

Kate stood up, her eyes flashing, her hands on her hips. "Now listen, you two, you're going on and on about fishing, but we only have ten more minutes! Do you have a lawyer yet?"

Padraic was leaning against the stone wall, almost casually, a slow smile spreading over his face. "The court says they will appoint a lawyer when they find one. They've taken my statement, and that's about it."

"So you sit in here for weeks and weeks while they take their time to find a man for your case? What about a private lawyer?"

"Ma looked into that a few weeks ago. Their fees are too high."

She took a deep, calming breath. "Padraic, you've got to help yourself. As Denny said, the real murderer is still at large. We must do something!"

"Beyond praying, I don't know what to do. I've told the truth."

"But...but..."

Earlier she had appreciated prayer. Now she resented it.

"There's a lawyer named Huntly. Dan Flanigan says he's a good one and perhaps we can pay on the fee," Denny declared stoutly.

"No, Denny. He'll charge you just for stepping through his door, sure. I won't have the family going into debt over this...this trouble."

"You act like you want to stay here!" Kate flashed hotly. "Like a martyr! Don't you know what this is doing to your ma?"

Her face went scarlet. She had said too much. This was her only visit with Padraic for how long, and she had ruined it.

Padraic came to stand in front of her and tilted her chin up.

"I'm sorry," she said simply, not meeting his eyes. "I just want to help."

"I know that, sure...I'm glad about your writing, Kate. Maybe some time, if you feel you could, I'd like to read your work. It'd be a pleasure for me."

Why did he keep going on about her writing? Didn't he realize how serious this trouble really was?

The jailer rapped sharply on the door. "Time's up!"

"Here's the basket Ma sent, Paddy. They've already been through it."

"Thanks. Give Ma a kiss for me, and tell her I'm fine. And give my deep thanks to all the lads pitchin' in for us."

They shook hands. Kate felt she was strangely alone with Padraic—just the two of them.

"'Tis truth you look more than well today, Kate. You—"

"Time!"

"Goodbye."

"I'm not allowing myself to think of Padraic's anger when he finds out about this," Maggie Falconer said grimly.

Kate shook her head. "Nonsense. There's no reason I can't help."

"He's proud," Maggie countered.

"Too proud, then, if he won't let me help. What if I'd been proud when I was...in the water? You've all done so much for me and I've lived with you without paying rent. Even this is small payment for all you've done."

"Still he won't like it."

"The Irish have no corner on stubbornness," Kate replied with a toss of her unruly red curls. "I can be just as determined as Padraic Falconer."

The Irishwoman smiled but said nothing.

Perhaps it was a little intimidating for all of them to crowd into the Queenstown lawyer's office. Maggie's three tall sons stood behind their mother, all with their arms crossed. Maggie alone looked formidable with her aggressive posture draped in her Sunday best. Even the American girl was unsmiling.

He wiped his brow and adjusted his glasses. Clearly this Falconer family expected great things from him.

"As I've explained, Mrs. Falconer, this is a straightforward case against your son Padraic. He is charged with the murder of Anna Ruebens. She was found stabbed to death in her apartment by the landlady, Mrs. Cornelia Mellis. Mrs. Mellis testified it was your son who, earlier in the evening, entered the deceased woman's apartment. She saw him leave less than one hour later. Only his fingerprints, besides the victim's, were found in the apartment. So—"

"So because a man visits a woman and she's found dead later, he is the murderer?" Maggie sputtered, after she had reasoned in her own simple way.

"The police have learned that your son visited Miss Ruebens the week before and they were overheard arguing by Mrs. Mellis."

Maggie Falconer's fears temporarily took away her charity. "A busy woman," she muttered.

"You call this case straightfoward, Mr. Huntly, but I see many holes," Kate said.

The lawyer nodded. "The strength of the case against Padraic Falconer lies in Mrs. Mellis's witness."

"And motive?" Kate continued.

The lawyer shifted uneasily under the five pair of eyes. "Padraic Falconer was known to have an...interest in the deceased—"

"Please don't call her deceased," Maggie interrupted tiredly. "Her name was Anna."

"As I was saying, Miss Ruebens was know to frequent the waterfront. We may presume their earlier argument was a lover's quarrel."

Maggie blanched. The poor girl had struck her as a troubled one from the very first. She shook her head.

"That is indeed a presumption, Mr. Huntly, until we have Padraic's side to this. I've been angry myself, and had a few...lover's quarrels, as you say, but it has never driven me to murder. If you knew Padraic Falconer even slightly you would know he did not commit this terrible crime. Now."

The Falconers were openly gaping. They had never heard the American lass so confident and assertive before. She spoke with authority.

"Here is the strategy, Mr. Huntly. Enough of Padraic sitting in a jail cell with no counsel. You must go to the prison and take a detailed statement from Mr. Falconer. I want you to then hire a private investigator you trust to look into the background of Anna Ruebens and the reputation of Padraic Falconer. When the trial comes, you will be ready. Oh, and you must tell Mr. Falconer you are the court appointed lawyer."

"But—" the barrister began.

"Money should not concern you, Mr. Huntly. You will work your hardest and do your very best. I will place bank drafts into your account regularly. Now, have we covered everything?"

Maggie Falconer cleared her throat and Kate looked to her. The older woman leaned over and whispered. Kate hesitated only a moment, then gave the lawyer a stunning smile.

"Will you *please,* Mr. Huntly?"

Then the lawyer and all the Falconers were smiling.

It was a scene of domestic peace that most anyone could appreciate—a cat napping on the hearth, an older woman working a huge lump of bread dough in a wooden bowl and a young woman bent over a stack of papers at a long table.

Maggie greatly enjoyed making bread. It relaxed her. But she didn't have much time for it these days. Her trips to Queenstown to see Padraic, tending the kitchen garden and mending her sons' rugged work clothes took most of her time. And, of course, the knock at the door at all times of the day or in the still of the night with a breathless, 'It's time Maggie! Come quick!'

The Irish midwife smiled to herself. With so many lads and lasses being born these last few months, surely county Cork's population had doubled. Because of so much to do, she almost wished this begatting would slow up a bit. She glanced at Kate so absorbed in her writing. Maggie watched the pen scratch the paper in quick rushes. The lass must have a lot on her mind, a lot she needed to be saying through this passion with her pen.

Maggie loved Kate Alcott as a daughter. She rejoiced that the girl was alive again, completely alive. The older woman knew it was only a matter of time before she would come to them and say it was finally time for her to go home. Then Maggie would know the healing was almost finished. Her love for the girl had deepened when she saw how much Kate wanted to help her son in prison.

Maggie gave the dough a powerful thump with her strong, thick arms. Padraic should be home, fishing and laughing with them in the evenings.

Her son...sitting in that damp, smelly prison cell when the real murderer walked the streets. Maggie shuddered. What if Paddy became ill before his case came to trial? She could not allow herself to think such things—the fear and worry would swallow her up. Yet, Mr. Huntly and the investigator had found nothing new in the case that differed from the Queenstown constable's view.

"I think the key may be in her background," Kate insisted to the lawyer. "Please keep pressing there."

"But why do you think so, Miss Alcott? She held a respectable job."

"For the very reason that she was so closemouthed about her past, her family. It makes you wonder."

So Maggie hoped and prayed the team Kate had hired would find something soon, and Padraic could come home. She looked up again when she heard Kate sigh. The girl had laid down her pen and was looking out the window. A look of sorrow shaded her face. She was a hundred miles away or out in the channel again. Sorting through all the pain. 'Lord, help the lass...'

The sunlight reflected off the girl's hair, and Maggie saw her now as a lovely young woman. No longer too thin or anemic. She would make some man a fine wife. It was easier to think about something silly like this, a harmless daydream. The pragmatic Maggie Falconer did not engage in such very often. But now she did. Four unmarried sons and a lovely unmarried girl in their home. All affectionate and kind toward Kate, like a sister. She had even heard Rory refer to her once as their "American cousin." Could it ever become more for one of them? She had always held a bias that none but an Irish lass would do for a wife for her sons, but now...

Kate was finally finished. She felt completely spent, as if something living and vital were pulled from her through her fingers. She held back the tears while she wrote, though more than once she'd felt a choking panic and overwhelming sadness creep towards her.

Five letters in a neat stack. It was over. Everything was there in black and white. Unless she snatched the letters up and tossed them in the fire, they would not really be complete until they were in the hands of the ones they were addressed to. Five letters. Grandmother Sara, her father, a coed at Amherst who truly won the Clifford prize, Amherst, and Clark Benton Sr.

She stood up suddenly, clearing away her writing things. Nothing was ever so difficult in all of her life. She wanted the tools out of her sight. She might feel differently later, but now the writing was like a traitor. Now it brought her pain instead of pleasure.

"You're going up to see Padraic soon?" Kate asked in a brusque tone.

"As soon as the bread is done. Did you want to ride along?"

Kate shook her head vigorously. "I'm going for a walk, a...long walk."

"Are you all right, lass?"

Kate nodded. "Fine. If you'll just post these letters for me."

"I'd be happy to."

But Kate lingered, her eyes resting on the stack of letters. She looked up into Maggie's eyes.

"He asked me…if there was anything I could share with him of my writing, that he could read…perhaps these letters…"

Maggie waited.

Could she do it? Padraic was her friend. He would see her cheating and ugliness.

Her voice was low and sad. "Take these if you will, Maggie, and let Padraic read them if he wants…then post them."

Queenstown

There was no explaining the workings of the man's mind—the same mind that carefully put the pieces together of Anna Rueben's jaded past and treacherous present led him to stalk her, then kill her. Yet, the evil act had only satisfied his need to avenge his brother's death. He was an arrogant man, tolerated but generally disliked along the Queenstown waterfront, principally because of his continual boasting. By his estimation there was no more seasoned traveler than he, or expert of Irish politics or the war, no better fisherman, no finer ladies' man. So it was with growing frustration he watched the events unfold surrounding the German spy's murder. He felt no compassion or concern that an innocent man sat accused in the Queenstown prison. But he was more than a little disgusted. A lover's quarrel, a mild-mannered fisherman gone murderous with anger. He alone knew Marta Marie Schweiger alias Anna Ruebens was a German spy, that she had worked against the Allied cause. The knowledge was festering inside him, never mind the implications to his involvement. He could take care of himself. But how long could he keep what he knew to himself?

The men who worked beside him had figured out long ago the man was the sort you listened to with half attention, nodding at the appropriate times to appease him. He was a brash, bumptious windbag, full of stories. So as the trial of Padraic Falconer approached, the waterfront gossip naturally focused on it. And the man in his typical fashion was intimating he knew more about the case than most—insider stuff.

"Aye, but I'll admit, I've been mad at my lass enough to strangle her…like when I caught her makin' eyes at the butcher."

"But you're no murderer, Danny boy, and to my thinkin' neither is Pad Falconer."

"The constable is bumbling as usual," the man spouted, "picked up the first man he sees! Luck for you, Johnny, you weren't out and about that night!"

"The old lady seen Falconer and no one else."

"Doesn't mean there couldn't be anyone else. Did she have her eye cracked at the window the whole hour?" the man protested. "And I hear tell this Ruebens wasn't ever her real name!"

They looked up from their nets.

"Where did you hear that?"

"Around," he smirked. They rolled their eyes and returned to their labor. "Maybe she wasn't even British like she *claimed*. Maybe she was German!"

They shook their heads. 'Tis truth, he could spin big ones.

"It's my feelin' the constable is holdin' the wrong man entirely."

He enjoyed this. It thrilled him to hold power like this.

But they were off on the latest war news, ignoring him. All but one who lounged along the quay. He found what he'd overheard a little intriguing.

"What do you suppose happens if he gets caught in a shower?" Kate whispered to Denny as she watched the judge in the powdered wig take his place behind the tall, dark desk. Denny grinned and nodded.

Kate felt like she'd stepped into some strange lapse of time—a court-room drama from the 18th century. She could not wait to write about it—the austere-faced panel of judges in severe black robes and wigs, the somber high-ceilinged room with slender-paned windows. She half ex-pected the court reporter to be scribbling his notes with a quill pen. The chief magistrate rapped the gavel sharply. The trial of Padraic Falconer was in session.

The Falconer family occupied most of the front row of the crowded courtroom. People stood lined along the walls. This trial promised a splash of intrigue and sensation in their mundane lives—a local charged with murder. Despite her joke to Denny, Kate felt anything but light-hearted. She glanced at Maggie beside her, and her heart ached. The woman looked worn and old in the subdued light of the room. Her chin was up, but Kate saw the fear clouding her eyes. It was that way for all of them. Things did not look good for Padraic.

The defense's case was weak. No new evidence, nothing of signifi-cance to help Padraic. Unless you counted the score of Kinsale folk who had come to testify to the fisherman's fine character and that of the Falconer line for generations. But Kate was skeptical it would hold much weight with the dour-faced judges. She was disappointed to learn this Irish court did not do things the American way with a trial by jury. And compassion did not seem like a prominent quality in these men.

The chief magistrate began talking, but Kate could hardly follow him. Even after exposure to the heaviest of Irish brogue, there were times like now it was nearly unintelligible. But she did understand when he spoke, "Bring in the prisoner!" The courtroom hushed and stilled, a side door opened and the tall fisherman strode in.

Some in the crowd may have expected a gaunt, broken, embarrassed looking man to appear. But Padraic wore neatly-pressed clothes. His head was up, and in his eyes was the same look of kindness and good nature that he was known for. Now Kate knew why Maggie had insisted on one final visit to Queenstown. She would not have her son looking uncared for. If it weren't for his manacled hands he could have been striding into the Falconer home. Strength seemed to radiate from him, and when he saw his family, his face was illuminated. Kate felt her throat tighten. There must be some hope. She looked to Maggie, and the woman was beaming now. No matter the outcome, this son would not bring her shame.

It was clear the prosecution and magistrates expected this to be a swift trial.

"They expect it to be over this afternoon?" Kate whispered to Denny. She was shocked.

Denny nodded with anguished eyes.

Mrs. Mellis, the apartment landlady appeared proud of her center stage position. The room hung on her every word.

"...and their voices were raised, very angry, his mostly..."

"Did you hear the exact words, Mrs. Mellis?"

"Exact words? Why no! That would be eavesdroppin'! But I can tell you he was angry, sure...and he left an hour later. I seen him in the street from my parlor window." She leaned forward to almost hiss at the enthralled crowd. "And her apartment was still as a tomb, I tell ya, a tomb!"

"Thank you, Mrs. Mellis, you may step down."

Kate was disgusted. Denny was angrily drumming on his leg. Maggie was scarlet with suppressed rage. Only Padraic appeared unruffled. He gazed at the floor, head slightly bowed, face impassive. Kate had seen him look this way before the hearth fire at home.

"If I were an artist I would paint his portrait and call it 'Gentle Strength,'" she said to herself. But she was rudely drawn from her thoughts by the magistrate's imperious call.

"Miss Katherine Alcott, approach the witness stand!"

Maggie's hand tightened around hers. Mr. Huntly leaned over, his face beaded with sweat. "I'm sorry, Miss Alcott. I should have warned you. The judges can call witnesses."

Kate had never faced the *Lusitania* inquest or been put on such public display since the sinking. At the witness table, she calmed herself and sought Padraic's eyes. He nodded, and she saw he had confidence in her.

She looked to Maggie, and the woman smiled. She could not let them down.

"We called you, Miss Alcott, because you are living in the Falconer home, but are not a family member, and can therefore testify. Now, repeat this oath..."

They hurried through the first, routine questions.

"Now, Miss Alcott, would you agree that it was generally known in the Falconer family that the accused was...romantically interested in Anna Ruebens?"

"If it was spoken of, I didn't notice. I was dealing with...with other things at the time. I didn't notice much of anything. But it may have been referred to."

"You saw Padraic Falconer on the evening of this argument, correct?"

"Yes."

"The fishermen of Kinsale remembered that Mr. Falconer looked and acted very unfriendly, even angry that evening when he took his ship out. Would you describe him for us?"

Kate's heart sank. She couldn't make things worse—not when she so wanted to help him. It would look all wrong to these men who had already decided the verdict in their minds. Another appealing look to Padraic. If only she could tell him she was sorry. He nodded—and she knew he was willing her to tell the truth.

"Miss Alcott, you will answer the court."

"Mr. Falconer appeared a bit upset when he returned from Queenstown."

"A bit?"

"He was upset," she asserted firmly.

"Angry?"

"Perhaps angry, yes."

"And did he tell you why he was angry?"

"No."

"Did he ever talk about Anna Ruebens to you?"

"He never mentioned her."

"The night of the murder, you saw Mr. Falconer."

"Yes, we were all at home."

"Describe how he seemed that night."

"Perfectly normal."

"Relieved?"

"About what?"

"Did he tell you or his family he had been to Queenstown?"

"No."

At the noon recess, Mr. Huntly could hardly offer the family comfort.

"There must be something you can do," Pierce said slowly.

"I can bring character witnesses, and Padraic himself. But you must understand, Mrs. Mellis puts him in that apartment. He was the last to see Miss Ruebens alive. No one else was seen. His fingerprints, and of course, the motive."

"What about the investigator looking into the victim?"

"I haven't heard from him in three days...I'm sorry."

They were stunned. This was like a horrible, very realistic dream. "The court has another case on the docket for in the morning," Huntly continued mournfully.

They understood. The verdict would be handed down this afternoon. Murder...Padraic Falconer would hang.

Padraic did not want to do this. He had contended with Mr. Huntly over it. But the lawyer was firm—and blunt.

"You must, Mr. Falconer. If not for your own sake, then for your mother's and brothers'."

So with a heavy heart, Padraic mounted the witness stand in his own defense. From Constable Speight's announcement of the murder weeks earlier to this moment of public scrutiny in the courtroom, the fisherman had experienced an odd mixture of emotions—shock and grief, outrage and apathy. He had weighed the situation carefully—did he fight, protest, challenge or submit and trust the truth to prevail? He felt the testimony mounting against him. Many in the Queenstown courtroom knew Padraic Falconer. And many thought he had never looked so fine, almost noble as he stood before them. Tall and strong, yet patient and kind. He was a good man. Of course, he did not do this heinous thing— no matter what the magistrates thought. They were, after all, English. Padraic betrayed no sign of fear, or worry, or nervousness.

"What was your relationship with the deceased?"

"Miss Ruebens and I were friends. I met her through my little sister Jen."

"Only a friend, Mr. Falconer?"

"Only a friend, sir."

"You were seen with her walking about Kinsale on several occasions. You appeared at her place of employment and in an eating establishment. You were seen at her apartment on two separate evenings and you were alone with her overnight on your ship."

The crowd stirred, but Padraic did not flinch. "That is all truth, sir. And we were friends."

"Then, did you desire more than just friendship with Miss Ruebens, Mr. Falconer?"

"Aye, for a time I did. But...nothing came of it."

"You were aware Miss Ruebens saw other men? That she was seen in the company of sailors along the waterfront district?"

His voice dropped slightly. "I...knew."

"And that made you angry and jealous!"

"No, it did not make me angry and jealous. It made me...wonder."

"Wonder..." the voice sneered. "You were heard to argue with the deceased on a night, a week before she was found brutally murdered. What were you arguing about?"

Padraic did not like to think of that time, and he hated having it so callously exposed to the throng.

"We had words...because Anna, Miss Ruebens, seemed upset with me, and I didn't know why."

"You didn't know why?"

"No, I...I'm not...you see, beyond my ma and sister, I haven't...been around lasses that much. I suppose I don't understand them too well."

"Relate the argument as you remember it, Mr. Falconer."

So he did, and Kate pictured the scene in her mind. Padraic humble and confused, Anna Ruebens arrogant and cruel. She suffered for him as he sat there, so vulnerable before all who knew him. And the oddest impulse seized her. It had not come upon her even when she was at her lowest after the *Lusitania*. She closed her eyes. She must pray for Padraic. There was nothing else any of them could do. His voice dropped to a deep monotone, and she felt a peacefulness come over her.

"So you argued. Then what?"

"Then I left. I had no reason to ever see her again."

"Except you did see her again! And you were very angry when you left her."

"Aye, that is the truth. I was angry. Then after a week I went back."

"You went back!" The magistrate was triumphant.

Padraic looked directly at the panel of judges.

"I went back to apologize. I did not understand Anna, but I wanted no hard feelings between us. I told her I was sorry I upset her. She was leaving for America in the morning...and I wished her well. Then I left."

The magistrates leaned toward Padraic expectantly.

"I did not kill Anna Ruebens. I would not ever even strike a woman. I could not, sir." His voice wavered just a moment. "You'll decide my fate as you wish, that I cannot change." His voice grew louder. "But before my family and friends, the ones I love, I tell you I cared for her as a sister. I would not harm her no matter how angry I became."

In the front row, Maggie Falconer quietly wept, beaming with pride for her son.

The black-robed judges waved him away and huddled together, whispering furiously while the crowd hummed with speculation.

The gavel came down, sharp and ominous, as the judge stood. Still expectancy filled the big room while everyone waited to hear the verdict.

"This court finds Padraic Falconer guilty of murder!"

Chapter 21

France

♦♦ ♦♦ ♦♦

*T*he desire to fly, to soar above the earth was an ageless longing. Men of every civilization had looked up to the sky, admiring and envying birds. The flight of the American Wright brothers in 1903 brought that desire down from the clouds. For several years after the event, however, the world took little interest in the development. Its importance and potential had an evolution to pass through. Could the airplane ever be more than an expensive and very dangerous toy?

So it was when the war began in the summer of 1914 this new invention was hardly a consideration. French commander Joffre had voiced a feeling unanimous among his military contemporaries.

'The airplane is fine for sport, but to the army it is useless.'

Wars were always won or lost by masses of men on the ground. Winners took key cities and fortifications, specific landmarks and boundaries. The sky seemed unchartable and therefore did not figure prominently into the general's strategies. But as the war progressed, this prejudice began to dissolve. Each camp slowly began to recognize the dynamics of the airplane. World War I would one day end, with the airplane responsible for little actual territorial exchange, but it had brought the invention from obscurity and question to a usefulness in war and peace. Thirty years later, when Europe went to war again, the airplane had a legitimate and prominent place.

Until the middle of 1915, the airplane was used by each nation principally for observation. The early planes were little more than wooden skeletons held together by wire and covered in canvas varnished in a highly flammable liquid. Pilots sat in cockpits open to the elements. The seat was wicker and rested on the fuel tank. It was like straddling a bomb. The pilots knew the peril. If hit by enemy gunfire they knew their plane could ignite in seconds. Many would choose to leap to their death rather than burn up in the sky. They accepted this danger with philosophical calmness.

'Fire is our third passenger.'

Pilots were given a simple challenge in the early days of the war—find out what the other side was up to. This soon expanded when pilots came back with startlingly accurate and detailed reports. Now they could direct artillery fire though a wireless radio.

'You're short 100 meters! Same angle and direction.'

They could take a passenger along to photograph ammunition dumps and installations. They could dart in low and quick in advance of infantry to spot landscape problems and troop concentrations. While these flights involved a definite element of danger both from the plane itself and antiaircraft gunfire from the ground, the pilots of opposing countries were largely content to perform their assignments and return to base. Encountering planes of another country usually meant a few loops around each other in a sort of aerial sparring, followed by a friendly wave. But such chivalry was destined for exploit. Soon pilots were carrying pistols and shooting at each other. Machine guns were fixed on the nose of the planes. The relatively friendly flying days came to an end. The next move was pilots dropping crude bombs by hand over train lines and other targets. Duels and 'dogfights' became the premium drama in the skies. And for such a drama there must be equally dashing personalities. Scores of British, French, Germans, and Americans filled the colorful cast of characters.

The average age of the World War I pilot was 20, his life expectancy flying over the western front a grim 6-8 weeks. Of the 180 Americans who volunteered to fly for France before the United States entered the war, almost half died in combat or were captured. These aviators flew into battle above trenches and barbed wire, the lethal killing ground of 'no man's land', above mud and boredom and anonymity. They considered themselves a breed apart. They were not part of a mass but relied on their own instincts in attack and retreat. Their skill and courage, or lack of it, were on a vivid stage for all to see. The loser plunged to earth in flames, the victor glided off into the blue for another contest. They were not confined to uniforms but could dress in their own flamboyant style. They became the pampered heroes of the press. Casualties on the ground were measured in the thousands, but the death of an aviator brought national grieving. It was easier somehow to understand the death of one man.

By the summer of 1916, names like Albert Ball of Great Britain, George Guynemer of France, Eddie Rickenbacker of America were well known. Their glorified duels in the sky made the front page. Schoolchildren prayed for their heroes at bedtime and kept a tally of downed planes like they kept track of baseball batting averages. A duelist recorded his victories and became an ace at five downed enemy planes. Germany could boast the ace of aces, Manfred von Richthofen—the Red Baron with 80 Allied losses. Ben Alcott had joined this select fraternity of men, and like them, would quickly find out just where the thrilling adventure ended, and survival in the sky began.

Amiens

Travel across France and the English channel was too difficult and dangerous for Molly Fleming to attempt a visit to her father over the Christmas holidays. As much as she missed him this second Christmas apart, she felt she could not leave her aunt. The winter was as gruelingly hard as the French people had anticipated. Even with David's 'gifts' and money from her father, Molly was pressed to the limit of her bartering and improvising skills. The soup was getting thinner and thinner. The town simply had too many mouths to feed. Everyone struggled to feed their own hungry family. The tradesmen were not so generous with the pretty English mademoiselle and her "boarders." Molly went to bed many nights in her unheated room with the fear there would be nothing to put on the table before the children. What then? But the next day, somehow, there were always a few more potatoes in the basket, or an anonymous package at the step, or something from a kindly neighbor.

"Like the jar of oil that never goes empty because He provides!" Molly said happily, and Aunt Madeline was forced to smile at her niece's faith.

Aunt Madeline was tested in ways she would never have dreamed of that winter. She was forced to sell many fine, old pieces that had been in her family, and a part of no. 10, rue de lilac for years. The furniture brought only a fraction of their worth but provided another meal on the table. Many of the rooms were cold, and now bare. The lovely old home had given up its best for France. Molly expected a tirade or depression from her aunt. But again, the older woman surprised her.

"The armoire is left. We will use it for…firewood if we must."

"Oh, Aunt Madeline, I am so sorry."

"Don't weep. This is…this is very little. Your grandmother would say, 'Hold things very lightly, and people very tightly. Dear Mama…" Her head went up as if the kaiser himself stood before her. "The boys in the trenches, Molly, we must think of them."

She swept from the room in her spotless silk and Molly knew she had gone to her room to weep just a little.

"Your aunt is one in a million," David said. "A very brave woman."

He came as often as he could and he made the long winter endurable for Molly. Aunt Madeline had accepted him in her own cordial and reserved way. On fine, sunny days they would drive in a chaser out of the city to the smooth fields of snow. He made a sled for the children, and they spent long hours on the slope behind the house. He told her of his childhood on the other side of the globe.

"Ben let me tag along with him everywhere. He never complained. He'd stick up for me, share things with me. Nobody could have a better brother…"

"You miss him."

"Yeah." David sighed. "But I'm hoping come spring, he'll be posted at one of the airfields in this sector."

On Christmas eve he escorted Molly and her aunt to the services at Cathedral Notre Dame. Later she sat with David in the sitting room. He had brought cocoa sent from America.

"I'm going to Paris tomorrow to see Ben. Is there anything you want?"

"Hmm?...No, thank you."

"Molly, you're pretty quiet tonight."

"I suppose I'm just missing my father."

"Is that all?" he pressed.

She stared into the fire a moment, then reached into her skirt and withdrew a folded letter. She handed it to him wordlessly. David read it quickly, then looked up. Molly was crying. He did not think of the possible consequences, or what Aunt Madeline might think if she appeared suddenly. He hated to see her hurting. He came to sit beside her on the sofa and put his arm around her. She relaxed into his shoulder.

"I'm sorry, Molly."

"I feel so rejected...so...so ugly!"

Martin had written his typical brief letter. But it included more than just lines about his medical training. Martin had married a nurse.

David held her while she cried. How could anyone reject this lovely girl?

"Molly, don't feel ugly. Believe me, you're not ugly." How could he comfort her? "This Martin guy, he wasn't the one for you. I know it hurts now, but it really is better this way. I know you want the one He planned for you."

"But David, I get so...lonely sometimes. I want to be wanted."

She was soft in his arms. He could smell her hair. He closed his eyes. He knew. He felt the same way.

"Molly, we...we understand each other. But would you mind if we just sit here awhile like this? It's the best Christmas eve I could have in France."

He held her as the fire burned low—and she did not resent the American girl. Tonight he was holding *her*.

Paris

The tall, broad-shouldered man slipped quietly into the shadowy sanctuary. Already the parish minister had begun the service. The man stood against the closed doors, scolding himself for being late. The little church was full of Christmas worshipers and every seat seemed to be taken, except in the very front. He hesitated and considered backing out. It was an impulsive idea he should have ignored anyway. But his family had always gone to church on Christmas eve. It was a tradition that he vaguely wanted to keep. A man in the back row stood and indicated he could have his place. The young man was tempted, as folks were turning in their seats to stare at him. But he shook his head and smiled at the man. There was an entire row in the front. He would sit there.

He wore a leather jacket with the maroon sweater of the University of Chicago underneath and tight, tan-colored trousers that were tucked into tall boots. Any other time he wouldn't have given his clothes a second thought, but he had hurried from the field and there wasn't time to change. He felt obvious and showy in these surroundings; you didn't come into a place like this looking like a pampered pet—even if you were one. Those in the pews recognized him immediately. Not personally or individually, of course, but his confident step, his air of invincible manhood, and his clothes identified him. He was a flyer. He was one of those brave, young men, French, British, or possibly American, who was risking his life for their country. His exploits might have little to do with the duration or outcome of the war, but he could bring a needed spark of glamour to the monotonous news from the western front.

Life was never better for Ben Alcott. He flew nearly everyday as weather permitted, he enjoyed the camaraderie of the flyers and he loved the nightlife of Paris.

His six-week training at the base near Versailles, 11 miles southwest of Paris, was over. The large airfield was fine and level and surrounded by wheat fields. One of the finest Allied bases in France, it was a beehive of aviation activity. Ben soon distinguished himself among the other cadets. Ben Alcott could take off and land on a pocket handkerchief or "tight squeeze." The long summer days at Nehi with Jimmy's slow, but thorough training had now paid off. The discipline of this new life also profited the American. Life at the ambulance corps, while busy, was informal and casual on off hours. No longer. Now there was morning roll call. The days were for flying, and nighttime brought lectures in the mess hall. The cadets were allowed only an occasional romp to nearby Paris—which Ben took full advantage of. Five minutes in the capital had shown him just how popular aviators were. He had not flown above the lines, or into enemy territory, or even seen a German plane—still French children pressed him for autographs on the street.

Midway into training Ben was faced with a decision.

"We tell some men what branch of aviation they must enter, Monsieur Alcott," his teacher said. "But our better students, they have a choice. And so, you must decide."

The choices in aviation had expanded in the three years of the war as the evolution of plane service in wartime unfolded. Bombing pilots, called 'truck drivers' for the heavier, slower planes they flew, were lowest on the aviation scale. Infantry liaison planes swooped in to direct advancing troops through a wireless during heavy battle and were only slightly higher. Photo planes were in constant danger as they penetrated far into enemy lines. Ground artillery waited patiently for any plane, to send up "flaming onions." Still other pilots took the task of "balloon busting." Huge sausage-shaped observation balloons were sent up over enemy lines. Attached by cables, they were ringed by protecting guns. A plane must fly in low and fast. These pilots were considered the daredevils of the flying corps, and unlikely to survive the war. Only a handful volunteered.

Pursuit pilots were those who dueled in the skies. They were considered the cream of the crop, the darlings of the press. Their 'work' was perhaps least important, yet they were the ones with immortalized names. One in 19 who trained for this position would never reach the front. They would crash in training, often from show-off stunts. They were a select few.

Ben did not reach his decision quickly or impulsively. He took long walks through the adjacent wheat fields. Flying in any squadron would be flying. The pursuit division had the best and fastest planes, but speed was secondary to Ben—being in the sky was the important thing. As a pursuit pilot he would be pitted essentially against one man. Kill or be killed, David had said. That grim equation. Yes, that is what it would come to. An anonymous man in goggles, only meters away from him in the air, trying to destroy his plane and kill him.

Ben Alcott did not want to kill anyone, German or not. But he had known the reality when he made the decision to come to France and join the Allies. This was war, and he had chosen a side. He thought of David facing a German firing squad each night. David would never pick up a gun, yet his brother was in danger. Ben must face the danger, too, and if each did their individual part, they might put an end to the killing.

He had left the States without consulting anyone. He had made his own decision. But now, he knew he did not want to make this decision alone. He must ask...someone. Lines from Kate's last letter came to his mind.

..."I have made most of the choices in my life...and so many mistakes have come from them. Now, today, I don't want to make choices all alone. I never valued wisdom before. I do now. There is in this Falconer family a quiet strength and wisdom. It isn't flashy. Ben, I think it is the same 'thing' that Grandma Sara has. And now I'm ready to know more about it. Can't you imagine her smiling?..."

So the day came when Ben stood before his flight school commander.

"I want to go where I'd be most useful, sir," Ben told him. "Send me where you need me, balloon buster or photo pilot, whatever."

The man looked thoughtful a moment and tapped a paper in front of him. "This request came an hour ago. You have heard of Raoul Lufbrey, perhaps?"

"Sure. Everybody has. He's the leading American ace so far."

"He has written me requesting a flyer for his squadron. General Mitchell has agreed and leaves the decision to me. They want the best flyer from this school to join them. That is you, monsieur."

Pursuit pilot.

"You must understand, Monsieur Alcott, this request is not without cost, shall we say? This opening in the squadron was made by the...death of two of its aviators in the last month. It is far more than adoring mademoiselles and children wanting to touch you and give you flowers. Lufbrey himself has said the flowers he is given will probably be his funeral wreath...." He stopped to let the words sink in.

"At the moment the German's Flying Circus is very active in the sector."

Germany's Flying Circus. The Red Baron's squadron. Ben understood the warning. This German ace was already responsible for over 50 Allied losses.

"Three weeks of fighter training then...the opening is yours if you want it, monsieur."

"I'll take it."

Lafayette Escadrille—a group of rugged young men formed into an all-American squadron flying for the Allies. Already the squadron was notorious back in the States as it had become in France. Names like Frank Luke and Eddie Rickenbacker had become American heroes in a country still standing neutral. Young men seeking thrills and adventure at a high price. The identifying insignia painted on each Lafayette plane was an Indian chief in war paint and feather bonnet. Now he would join them. He would return north to the sector called Verdun.

The Christmas eve service was over and a light snow dusted the little French town outside of Paris. Ben knew where half a dozen Christmas parties were in progress, but he did not feel like parties tonight. He wanted quiet, like he had found in the candlelit sanctuary. This was his first Christmas away from his family. Not even Davy was here. If he couldn't have his family tonight, he didn't want anyone. He decided to walk the two miles back to the airfield. It would give him time to think without distraction.

Tomorrow he would spend the day with David and Marty. Christmas in Paris. Peppercreek, Illinois seemed a planet away. Grandma Sara...she would be praying for him. Would his decision to join Lafayette Escadrille please her? He could almost imagine her voice.

Now, Ben...You're a pursuit pilot? The kind the papers write about? Sure you get the glory, Ben, but what about the dangers? What about honor? What about having to kill?

Ben Alcott was a different man now than he was a year ago. He wasn't sure how or why, but he knew the beginning point. That dusty road near Amiens when the three Frenchmen had warned him, then died in the grassy culvert. Carrying their bleeding bodies had brought a change in him—something quietly undefinable. Then the summer battle of the Somme. Thousands dead. Men who wanted honor and glory, something of what he would get at Lafayette. But their future was gone in a moment. He felt the change when he thought of David and his family. They were important to him, more than he had realized before. He felt the change when the men whom he lived with expressed some view or idea that went against what he was taught as a boy. Outwardly he seemed the same, still fun loving and easygoing, still very interested in the mademoiselles. But he felt the difference even if he could not give it a name.

'What about honor? What about killing a man?' His grandmother's voice seemed to echo in his mind.

Soon he would find some answers.

Ethan's diary
1861
...It was hard for me to sleep. Pa's question chased itself through my mind all night. 'Will you point a rifle such as this at a man and pull the trigger, as you will be expected to do?' If I signed my name to the Union army, I would be saying yes. I would go through all the training of attack and retreat. Training. Then it would come to that moment in battle. A man born in the South would be my enemy. A middle-aged man, perhaps, with a wife and children at home, or a young man like me, unsure and nervous, eager, wanting to do the right thing, and be honorable in the process...

over the western front

Six of the seven pilots waddled out to their planes in their heavy flightsuits with their favorite good luck charm—a rabbit's foot, a mother's picture taped to the dash, the silk stocking of a girlfriend, a rosary, a helmet from a captured German soldier, an eagle's feather. The seventh and newest pilot to the squadron did not carry a talisman. He was not a superstitious sort. He just hoped his plane would cooperate and he could get a respectable take off among these veterans. The men settled into their open cockpits while the engines jerked and sputtered to life. A mechanic at each plane grabbed the propeller and gave it a strong downward pull. As the propeller began to spin, other ground crew held the tail and wings. These planes, like most that flew over

France, were not equipped with the luxury of brakes. The pilots nodded
and the crews released their hold. Mud spattered up from the field dot-
ting the windscreen and pilots. Then, in a neat single-file pattern, they
rose easily into the morning sunshine. Another mission for the Lafayette
Escadrille and the first mission for Ben Alcott. Training was over; they
had practiced hairpin turns, loops, rolls and the important corkscrew
dive. They had gone through emergency procedures and machine gun
practice. The long hours and the lectures had come to this flight.

The formation of seven broke through the clouds and climbed slowly
to ten thousand feet where they settled into a v shape. Ben's plane took
middle position—protection on both sides for the newcomer.

"Things have been quiet the last few days, Ben, so we may not see a
single Hun plane. But the archies are hot over this sector, so stay on
your toes and we'll help you along," Lufbrey warned the star pupil in the
briefing room.

Archie. Ben quickly searched his mind for the slang. He did not want
to have to ask. Anti-aircraft cannons—termed archies by the British.

This was the finest, sleekest plane Ben had ever been in or flown. He
wished he could give the affable Jimmy back at Nehi a spin in it. Yet, he
felt a momentary panic. There was so much to watch for—the instru-
ment panel with oil pressure and fuel gauge, the big guns on the ground,
enemy planes appearing suddenly, the plane in front and behind him.
Was he too close or too slow? He had watched baby ducks frantically
hurrying after their mother, lest they be lost or gobbled up. He grinned
to himself now—he knew how they felt. He was sweating in the heavy
flight suit though the air was cold. Finally, he began to relax and look at
the earth below him.

The countryside was sharply visible in the clear winter air. A river like
a silver serpent curved toward the west. A few scattered buildings and
lonely-looking roads, a patch of forest. Ben sighed. At nearly two miles
up, the world seemed peaceful—war must only be a rumor. He checked
his instruments and position; everything was going smoothly. He would
be surprised if they did not encounter German planes on such a fine flying day. The miles slid away quickly with the music of his humming
engine. Then Ben leaned foward suddenly. He lifted his goggles and
crouched behind the wind screen. Surely his eyes must be...deceiving
him.

The land below had changed suddenly, abruptly, harshly. He had
always seen the trenches and 'no man's land' from a peripheral and level
perspective before. This...he could not pull his eyes away. Later, he
would try to describe it to David.

"It was like...like a giant's hand had plowed, no, flattened everything
in its path. Completely barren, a few sticks, very few, that I later figured

out were charred trees still standing. But the holes...these huge shell holes in the ground, some filled with dirty water. It was like looking at...you know, the craters on the moon on a clear night. It was nothingness. I won't ever forget the sight of it...I've seen...dead Frenchmen, now I've seen their dead land."

Sudden white puffs toward the lead plane jolted Ben from the ground sight. The formation was descending. This was not time for daydreaming or inattention. The objective of this mission was simple—penetrate the enemy lines as far as possible to see what the latest German troop movements were. The French were planning an advance in the next 48 hours.

Lower now, Ben could see pencil-thin, dark lines across the scarred land. Barbed wire. Row after row, like the savage claw marks of some mammoth animal. The trenches. The German ground archies had spotted the incoming formation and now shells were bursting all around the planes. Ben followed the example of the plane directly in front of him and began banking his plane slightly left then right. He could see the pilot swiveling in his seat. German planes could pounce anytime, from any direction, above or below. Ben turned to check the position of the sun, a favorite hiding place of attack for the famous 'flying circus' pilots. But no planes appeared. The ground fire was vicious and Ben's plane rocked with the explosions. Suddenly the lead plane, Lufbrey's, nosed down. Ben understood his intention. Give the German ground guns a little "American howdy." All seven planes pitched forward now in a screaming dive. Ben saw the roads leading to the trenches more clearly, but it all became a confusing picture that rushed at him. Men in green uniforms and spiked helmets plunged and dove for cover as the Allied planes sprayed them. Horses reared in the smoke. Ben squeezed the trigger on his machine gun and then pulled up sharply. The planes reformed. Ben counted quickly. All seven. He felt himself drenched with sweat inside his flight suit. No rumor of war any longer. He had found it.

They continued on peacefully for five minutes longer. Soon the lead plane would wobble his wings as the signal to return. But instead Lufbrey's plane suddenly broke out of formation and twisted upward. His machine gun cut loose. Glancing over his shoulder, Ben tensed. A swarm of brightly painted planes were coming down fast, like zealous and angry bees. Blood-red machines with black Maltese crosses on their wings—the German flying circus against the Lafayette Escadrille.

The sky that was once calm, lightly tinged blue, and peaceful, was now crowded with twisting, diving, zooming planes. The airships of the Indian war chief were greatly outnumbered. Troops on both sides of the line took their eyes off each other for this thrilling interlude. They had grandstand seats. They could relax and cheer the fight.

Ben had never worked so hard, and as thorough as his training had been with long hours of talking with other pilots, nothing could really prepare him for this. The air, once thin, crisp and fresh, was heavy with the smell of burning oil. The sound was deafening with the high whine of engines and the deadly shriek of bullets. It was a schoolyard brawl with planes spinning wildly. Ben was convinced a head-on crash with another plane was imminent. He willed himself to calmness and clear thinking, to remembering the tactics. He heard a burst of gunfire at his back and knew a German had chosen him. Had he somehow sensed Ben's vulnerable newness? The new cadet had made a critical mistake—never let the enemy get on your tail. Great for offense, but suicidal in defense. He threw the joy stick forward roughly and plunged his machine into a spiraling dive, hoping his engine would withstand the strain.

Once level he eased up and looked around. His dive had broken up the free fall, and others in his squadron were banking sharply right and following him south. Their mission was complete. Ben gave one last glance to the German planes that circled above, almost taunting. He could imagine their boasting.

'Ah, today! Today we sent the famous Lafayettes whimpering for home!'

And today, Ben wasn't too proud to mind. This was enough.

When the airfield came into view 20 minutes later, Ben turned off his motor so he could glide in quietly. It was a tranquil, sunny winter day again. Once landed, he pulled himself from the cockpit. His suit was soiled in spewed oil, mud and sweat. His legs felt weak. Lufbrey came up to him immediately, his face revealing his concern. He was a kind man and did not tease Ben about his pallor.

"You okay?" he asked.

"Yeah."

Lufbrey lit a cigarette. "It was kind of tough, meeting up with the Baron's boys your first time out."

Ben attempted a casual shrug. "Was *he* up there?"

Lufbrey's grin was wide. "Didn't bother to look too closely. I was kind of busy myself."

They both laughed. He slapped Ben on the back.

"You did fine, Ben. That dive was a great signal to get us out of there."

He walked off, leaving Ben alone. He leaned against the plane and closed his eyes. He could hear the voices of the other pilots as they headed toward the hangar. He had expected his first encounter with the enemy to leave him exhilarated and eager for more. But it had shaken him. And he realized his success at the training school did not guarantee his success out of school. It took incredible nerve and skill in such a fight as he had just experienced. He had a lot to learn, and for the first time, Ben Alcott did not feel quite so confident. He could not forget the collage of images he had seen today—the terrified horses and scattering men, the sky full of twirling planes, the French countryside that had become a corpse.

After his time alone, he joined the men and he could be as animated and speculative as they. But today's baptism had left him drained. Now he understood the dangers. Now he understood how closely death stalked in the sky.

Vienna

It was a very long, very hard winter in the old Austrian capital. The hardest winter thus far in the war, people said mournfully. It was a sentiment shared by millions across the scarred face of the European continent. Man had been too long at war, the harvests were meager. The blockades created massive shortages. The economies of the belligerent countries were geared for war, so the civilians suffered under a third winter of privation. It was a suffering as old as the first wars.

To the healthy it was a desperate time, but to those ill and dying, there was little hope. The Austrian woman died quietly in her bed at the end of the long row of beds in the crowded city hospital. The new year of 1917 was only a few hours old. Her son Kurt had seen her the day before on a one day leave from the Austrian army. He had held his mother and cried.

"I must go back, Mama," he whispered hoarsely. "I wish I didn't have to...Mama, what will happen to Emma?"

"I have taken care of Emma. Do not worry, son."

Her doctor had carefully written down her dictated instructions. "To Lake Geneva, Fraulein?"

"Yes. There is a man there, an old family friend. He will send my Emma on to a good woman in France."

"France, Fraulein?" he asked in a shocked tone.

She nodded weakly and smiled. "In France, there is my oldest friend. War does not change true friendships, doctor. No, it cannot. Emma will be cared for. She will be loved. It will be all right."

He wagged his head skeptically. It seemed the patient was comforting the doctor.

Amiens

Molly hurried into the alcove of the Amiens post office just as the slanting sheets of rain poured down. The wind had whipped her hair around to blind her and her arms held a box. And so her last step was actually a jump—against the occupant emerging from the building who fell back with a "humph."

"Oh, pardon, pardon," Molly began although she could not see clearly the person in front of her. She was helpless. Then through the rain, she heard a chuckle. Someone was carefully parting her hair out of her face.

He was the most handsome man she had ever seen. He stood there smiling and with a slight look of surprise on his face. He was tall, dark haired, blue-eyed, and his face was well tanned. He wore a leather jacket and she could smell a masculine scent. No military insignia. She knew somehow he was not French. His eyes moved over her quickly, and she felt herself blushing.

"Well, this is a pretty situation," he said to himself.

American.

"Pardon, mademoiselle," he said smoothly. He still blocked the door and did not appear eager to let her pass. For her to move one inch backwards would be to get thoroughly drenched. So she remained where she was, almost pressed against him. It was embarrassing and awkward for Molly Fleming.

His eyes rested on her face.

"Pardon, monsieur," she said, lowering her eyes and indicating he must step aside.

"Parle vous anglais, mademoiselle?" he said agreeably.

"Non anglais, monsieur."

Why had she not told the truth to the bold stranger?

He shrugged. "It's okay. I can help you with your box." He began to take her parcel.

"No, monsieur, merci."

"Oh, come on. I don't mind. I can carry it for you. We could have a bite to eat somewhere when the rain lets up."

He thought she did not understood a word, and could simply be won by his magnetism. The brash, confident American! The sum of Aunt Madeline's horrors! Good-looking or not, Molly was not amused. She did not feel like swooning at this man's feet.

"Pardon, monsieur, sil vous plait. (If you please.)" She pushed against his chest with the box—and he laughed.

"You are very pretty, mademoiselle," he said in French. "I am an American."

He waited for her to understand. She should be impressed. It always worked with the friendly girls of Paris.

The arrogance! If her hands were not full she might have slapped him. But the door behind him opened and Molly pushed past. The door slammed.

He shook his head and shrugged. Turning up his collar, Ben stepped into the rain. "Kinda chilly in Amiens today."

"Molly, this just doesn't sound safe."

She smiled. "You wouldn't have Aunt Madeline go, would you?"

"Of course not. I'm surprised she's letting you go. Traveling through occupied territory, alone and unescorted."

David was pacing in front of her in the garden. His concern was touching.

"I have the proper passes and permissions, everything is in order," she assured him. "I will be fine."

"Passes or not, things you didn't plan for can happen. Trains stall or are taken over by troops and you get stranded. A single girl alone, a very pretty girl. The Germans..." He shook his head. "No, I really don't like this."

"You wouldn't have her waiting in some strange place after losing her mother, would you? She's only six years old. I must go for her."

"Yeah...I just wish..."

"You wish, David?"

"I wish I could go with you, all the way to Switzerland. It is such a long way."

Molly laughed. "Aunt Madeline would never approve. Traveling together, it would be improper."

He snorted. "Okay. Then I wish Ben could fly you there. Just plop you down on the lawn of the resort and pick up—what is her name?"

"Emma."

"Pick up Emma, and bring her back."

Molly's laugh deepened. "And you think Aunt Madeline would approve of your American aviator brother?"

"Once she meets him her fears would be put to rest. My grandmother is a classy lady like your aunt and she thinks Ben is tops."

"Family prejudice perhaps?" Molly asked with a dimpled smile.

He sat down to face her. "Ben is different lately."

"Different?"

"Yeah. I'm not sure why, but when I'm with him I can tell he's thinking like he hasn't before. You know what he told me the last time I saw him?"

She shook her head.

"He told me he'd gone out on a training exercise alone. He had to fly a triangle. That's a plotted course from a map. He saw this level hill overlooking a pasture and he decided to land. There was nothing in sight so he put it down. He climbed out and sat on the hill for about an hour. Said it was beautiful up there, made him think of our place back home. He said all of the sudden he felt like Grandma Sara was just behind him whispering a verse he'd learned in Sunday school. 'Be still and know that I am God.' He asked me, 'Why do you think I thought of that verse all of the sudden, Davy?' I told him, maybe it wasn't Grandma he heard..."

Molly carefully filed the story in her mind. "Still all the mademoiselles concern you?" she asked playfully.

"Well yeah, that hasn't changed. But it will. I just have to be patient."

"You sound confident."

"I am." He leaned forward. "You will be careful, won't you? You won't take any chances?"

"Absolutely none. And you will look after Aunt Madeline for me if you've time?"

"I'll make time. We'll both be waiting for you."

London

Thomas Fleming sat in his parlor, a stack of school papers on his knee. The fire was burning low in the grate, but he was too tired to replenish it. Tonight he missed Molly. He could picture her across from him—her dark hair shining in the lamp light, her smile, her dark eyes. He heard her teasing voice in his mind.

"Dad, are you grading papers or napping?"

"I'm meditating over them, my dear, merely meditating."

But she was not here this night of fog and chill. She was across the channel, far away where all the bombs were falling. And now she was going to Switzerland. Oh, she was capable and healthy for the trip, but... He fingered her latest letter on the table. Cheerful, newsy, funny stories of the children and Aunt Madeline's proper ways, the war. And this American, David Alcott, the stretcher bearer. He was in every letter these days. No more Martin. Fleming smiled at that. Good lad, but not the one for Molly. This American then? "He is the kindest, most honorable young man I have ever met, Dad," she had written.

He closed his eyes and prayed, and the tears he could hold back no longer spilled over.

Amiens

Molly could not get to sleep. She would begin her long trip tomorrow, and she should rest, but there was too much on her mind. Aunt Madeline had given her at least an hour of cautions to remember. She must be as decorous as possible, and avoid friendliness to any man, no matter how innocent. And then the old woman had hugged her and told her in plain words how thankful she was for her. Molly smiled in the darkness. Little Phillipe, now gone south, would have been proud of Madame's affectionate little speech. Then Molly thought of David and his concern.

David. There was no Martin. No David, beyond friendship.

"I never imagined staying out of love could be so hard," she whispered just as sleep came over her.

Lake Geneva, Switzerland

Molly hesitated in the dim hallway of the summer hotel. The little girl with the long brown braids was thin and sickly looking. The child stood rigid, as if paralyzed.

"Hello, Emma," Molly spoke slowly in French. "I am Molly. I've come to take care of you." She ventured a step forward and kneeled. "Would you like to show me the duck pond?"

It took two days before Molly felt she and her new charge were ready for the return. She dreaded the long, uncertain train trip back into the war-torn country. It was quiet here. The child had come from war, and back to it she must go. But once at rue de lilac Molly could begin the tender healing work the little girl so needed.

"We must leave now, Emma. Aunt Madeline is waiting and eager for you. We must go to France. Will you trust me?"

The little girl silently slipped her hand into Molly's.

Amiens

The English girl living in France with her spinster aunt was nervous— and hoping it didn't show. David had come unexpectedly to the Chaumont house early one morning as she prepared breakfast for the children. He rarely came empty-handed these days. This morning it was a box of oranges. Aunt Madeline, while grateful for the young man's generosity, was mildly alarmed at his frequent appearances. Would Molly's father approve of an American son-in-law? Aunt Madeline did not know. Perhaps she should write the Englishman and inform him that...that... Molly kept insisting they were only friends, that Monsieur Alcott was quite serious about a girl back in his own country. But Aunt Madeline in her limited romantic experience had never seen two young people who enjoyed each other's company more. Molly was bright-eyed and animated when David was coming. He was respectful and kind. Often Aunt Madeline heard their laughter from the garden. Could they remain friends only? That American girl was, after all, an ocean away, and Molly was very pretty.

David came into the kitchen. She could see he was excited about something. "Molly, I just need a second."

He pulled her gently into the hallway. But in the hallway, he forgot to let her hands loose, and she did not think to remind him.

"Molly, Ben is here at the base. He's agreed to go out this evening."

"Go out?"

"A foursome. You and I, he and some gal."

"Oh."

"Can you get away? We thought we would go to dinner then to a movie. They're showing an American movie at the base."

"Well...I don't know."

"We could have a nice time."

She was silent. She knew he had wanted this meeting between she and his brother for a long time. And in the face of all his kindness, how could she refuse?

He looked at her curiously. "Are you worried about meeting my brother, Molly?"

She avoided his eyes and shrugged.

"Look, Miss Fleming...do you like me?"

"Oh, David." She laughed.

"Okay, forgive the arrogance, but I know you do. So, if you like me, you'll really like Ben!"

She looked skeptical.

"What do you like about me?" he continued.

"Well, certainly you are ridiculous at times."

"Okay, besides that."

"You are kind, generous and honorable—there."

"You've described Ben perfectly!"

The 'rake' was honorable?

"Tonight?" he asked appealingly.

She sighed. "Tonight."

So Molly Fleming was as nervous as if this were her first date. She shouldn't be nervous, of course. This was only David's big brother. She would see him tonight to satisfy David, then he would go away to his flying career and...his mademoiselles.

David picked her up promptly at six.

"Slight change in plans. Movie first, dinner after. Something Pauline wanted. Is it okay?"

"Pauline is Ben's...date?"

"Oui," David answered with a frown that made Molly smile.

"The movie first is fine."

They drove along the bumpy road to Soissons. David cast her a side-long glance. "Molly, you're not nervous, are you? It's only Ben."

"Who is kind, honorable and generous even more than his little brother," she teased.

"Exactly!"

When they arrived, David's brother and a giggling redhead came up to the ambulance. David stood at Molly's side, beaming proudly.

"Bonjour, mademoiselle," Ben began, then stopped. His voice was amused. "It's you."

Tall, broad-shouldered, smiling, the most handsome man she had ever seen. The American. The rake.

"Bonjour, monsieur," Molly replied in her most conservative tone.

David pushed back his cap. "You've met?"

"Well, I don't know. The girl I bumped into didn't speak English."

He looked at her intently, teasingly. He knew. Molly's face was scarlet.

"Must have been another girl 'cause—"

Ben's date interrupted in a bored pout. "The movie is starting and I am not going in there late."

Birth of a Nation flickered on the screen in the makeshift theater. David leaned over. "Okay?"

"Yes, this is fine."

Molly was grateful for the darkened room. Ben and his girl sat behind them, and she could imagine his amused look at her back. 'So this is the girl that David's been raving about, the one who said she knew no English...Hmm...'

Molly should have found the situation amusing, but instead she felt guarded and cautious. This good-looking, confident American was the lady's man, David's brother. Even now she heard an occasional whisper and smothered giggle behind her. Part of her wished David would put his arm around her—and another part was terrified that he would. There was still dinner to come in a brightly lit cafe, and across the table she would have to face David's brother. Relax. Enjoy the evening.

After the movie, they walked down the street to the cafe. Ben and his date walked ahead of them. David looked at Molly and rolled his eyes every time Pauline giggled and leaned on his brother, which was often. Molly laughed. They understood each other's thoughts.

"Well, she is pretty," Molly offered generously.

David tilted his head in a speculative look and shrugged. Molly laughed again. David was funny with his almost paternal protection and exacting standards of suitable women for his brother.

The cafe was crowded with other servicemen, but Ben seemed to stand out, smiling and laughing. He drew the eyes of women easily and Molly also noticed that the flashy girl at his side provoked looks from the men. She suddenly felt plain—and angry at herself for her feelings. Why should she feel intimidated by David's brother? She willed herself to smile and relax—and concentrate on those qualities David had almost promised were present in Ben.

The waiter came to their table correct and bowing.

"Parle vous anglais, monsieur?" David asked.

He shook his head vehemently.

David passed the menu to Molly. "Okay, it's up to you to rescue us. Or else it's bread and water."

"Or pommes and cervelle?" she said to him, and they laughed together.

Molly then placed their orders perfectly.

"Being from England, Miss Fleming, how did you become so good at French?" Ben asked.

"We were taught it in school and my mother was French. I was raised with...two languages."

"See, that's the way, David. You have to be raised with it. Not try to pick it up at our age. You end up insulting people! When we first came over, David was always trying to strike up a conversation with folks. You should have seen some of the looks he got!"

The brothers laughed while Pauline smiled and stroked Ben's forearm.

"I think David has done extremely well," the English girl said firmly.

The table became awkwardly still, and Molly colored with embarrassment. Why had she said that? She could not look at David.

"So, how long have you two been...you know, an item?" Pauline asked Molly and David.

"Uh, Pauline, you remember I said Molly and David are friends, just friends," Ben spoke up easily.

The girl's smile dropped. "Oh." She took another bite. "I never had a boy for just a friend before."

She looked at Molly as if she were a novelty, and David laughed.

"So, we're all here in France from different countries," David said cheerfully. "Ben told me your father does what, Pauline?"

"Daddy's a secretary to a general in the Canadian army." She giggled. "I forget his name. Anyway, Mother didn't want to stay there alone, so we tagged along." She squeezed Ben's arm. "My folks are very happy with Ben."

Another awkward silence while Ben looked intently at his silverware.

"Paris is such a pretty town," she continued. "We've had such fun."

Fun. Molly met Ben's eyes for just a moment. He was embarrassed. David was embarrassed. Molly wished she had stayed home.

"What are you taking up now?" David asked.

Ben shook off his embarrassment easily. "A pretty little Spad. Smooth as silk. On your next day off, I'll get permission to take you up."

"I want to go!" Pauline pouted.

"Uh, it isn't allowed, Pauline. Sorry."

"You can at least let me sit on your lap then. Just to say I've been in a plane would be a thrill!"

"Well, see I'd rather you didn't come to the airfield. There aren't women there."

"Oh?" Her voice was teasing. "I've heard stories about women smuggled in—"

"Well..." Ben cast David a nervous glance and Molly nearly laughed out loud.

"The flyers would fight over me?" Pauline asked archly.

"Yeah..." Ben nodded. "They sure are taking a long time with our food."

"Are they what I've heard flyers call, 'dogfights,' monsieur?" Molly asked Ben directly.

David burst out laughing, and Pauline looked confused. Ben managed a nod and slight smile.

Molly was freshly horrified. Why had she made such a joke?

"Would you like to go up in a plane sometime, Molly?" David asked.

Molly smoothed her skirt. "I don't know. I suppose...I've never really thought of it before."

Ben leaned back, his smile expansive. "I'm sure you would enjoy flying, Miss Fleming. But it would depend on the pilot. You know, if you could trust him or not."

Molly had found during the evening she could meet Ben Alcott eye to eye. She did so now with a nod. "Perhaps you are right, monsieur."

The evening wore on with the conversation flowing principally between David and his brother. The two seemed to have real affection for each other. Molly, who felt a suspicion of Ben Alcott that her aunt would be proud of, was forced to admit it was not a one-way affection.

Ben leaned forward when the meal was over and the table cleared. His smile and jesting was suddenly gone. "Are the Germans still using the green stuff, Davy?"

Even Molly knew Ben referred to the deadly gas that had blinded or killed many on both sides of the western front.

"It was out one night last week," David replied casually. "They put it up every once in a while to try to catch us off guard."

Molly boldly watched Ben who was unhappy with this news.

"I don't like you going out in that, David." His voice surprised her with its gentleness. "Do you take your mask with you?"

"We all have them now. Keep 'em with us all the time."

Ben tapped the table nervously. "Does the doc make you go if it's out there?"

"He lets us wait until it thins and drifts. Sometimes we take the pigeons with us if things aren't too fierce."

"That's still too dangerous!" Ben replied hotly. "I've seen what it does...to men."

"I've seen too, Ben," David answered with a sudden weariness in his voice.

Molly knew David had seen many things as stretcher bearer—too many things.

"We can't leave the boys out there, even if the gas does come. Sometimes...they drop their masks in the fight. Sometimes..." He stopped.

"Now I think you two are being gloomy gusses," Pauline said. "Enough talk about things like that. We're supposed to be having fun. Right, Molly?"

Molly shifted in her chair. But the cafe owner's arrival saved her from replying. He presented the bill to David and spoke fluently to Molly. He pointed to Ben and smiled.

"What's he saying, Molly?" David asked.

Molly looked uncomfortable. "Well, he says times are hard and he must make a living, of course. We were all charged for our meals, except...Ben."

"What?" David exclaimed.

Ben looked sheepish and shrugged. "Sorry, Davy."

Pauline snuggled closer and looked proud.

"What gives?" Davy demanded mildly.

"He does not want payment from the flyer who wears the Indian head on his jacket," Molly further explained. "It is a point of honor with the merchants. He says it would be rude to accept money when the Americans are in the sky with danger. They volunteered for France."

David grinned. "Reminds me of when we were kids. You were faster than me, so you missed a few lickins that I got."

"That's the way it goes, little brother. I could try to pull a few strings for you in the aviators' corps."

Molly was indignant. Didn't David risk his life each night that he ventured out to rescue a fallen Frenchman in the nightmare land?

David left the table to pay the bill. Pauline was engaged in a conversation with someone at another table. Molly stared into her lap, but the strength of Ben's gaze forced her to look up.

He gave her a careful, appraising look, and a smile played at his mouth. For a fleeting moment, she wondered what he was thinking. When she had run into him in Amiens, he had said she was pretty. But

that was just a line, wasn't it? Did he really think she was pretty? Like
David thought.

"You don't agree with the waiter, Miss Fleming," he said calmly.

"He has every right to choose whom he favors."

"But it should not be...spoiled aviators."

She drew a deep breath before answering. "You worked in the ambulance corps yourself, so you are aware of the dangers your brother faces,
far better than I. The merchants of France cannot be generous to everyone."

"You're impressed with David's work."

"I'm impressed with his courage, his selflessness."

Ben colored. He thought of the sights he'd seen. "And you don't think
there's any danger or...courage needed for flying?" he asked cooly.

"I'm sure there is, monsieur. You would know best."

On the sidewalk they parted. Pauline could not wait for privacy. Her
arms were around Ben's neck.

"Uh, Ben, uh...Molly and I are going now. See you back at the base."

"Sure. Don't wait up for me, though." He winked at his brother and
cast a roguish look at Molly. "I'm glad we were able to meet, Miss
Fleming. Davy's talked a lot about you."

"Yes...thank you. Goodnight."

Moments later they sat quiet and still in the ambulance before no. 10.

"David, I'm sorry."

"What for?"

"For tonight. Things didn't go...I know you were hoping your brother
and I would, as you say, hit it off. I was rude to him. I don't know why."

"You were just nervous. It's okay. You'll be friends with Ben. We'll try
another time."

But Molly Fleming wasn't sure she wanted another time.

Chapter 22

*I*t was carried on the front pages of nearly every newspaper in Ireland, and when the full story came to light, tabloids in the United States published it as well. Incredible courtroom theater that kept folks talking for weeks and remembering for years. A local fisherman of no particular distinction accused of a brutal murder while maintaining his innocence. Then the commanding voice of the judge. Guilty. The defendant pale, his mother weeping on his brother's shoulder. The dramatic entrance of a man, hurrying forward, saying 'Wait!' The thunder of the gavel and the scowls from the bench.

Her name was Marta Marie Schweiger, a woman of 22 years, a native of Berlin. A woman with a background of deception and dishonor. She'd manipulated the men of the waterfront for one clear purpose—to attain information about British vessels in St. George's channel. A spy! A German spy! And most incredible, the woman's contact in passing information was the German submarine captain who had torpedoed the grand *Lusitania!* Murdered by her jilted lover who had pieced together her past and current crimes and was seeking revenge for the death of his brother who had died from a German submarine. Readers were spellbound for weeks.

The murderer had entered the stunned courtroom unshaven and disheveled, brazen and bold in the company of policemen. In his mind he was a hero. He had killed a German spy. No different than a man in the trenches firing at a Hun across a few meters.

Shocked, the judges could only stare. The family hugged each other and cried for joy. Yet the defendant sat apart, remote and oddly quiet. He did not look like a man whose neck had come close to the noose. They called her a spy. The conversations returned to his mind then—all the questions about his work, her time at the waterfront—and Sir Coke's warning, "We have reports of German spies…Be careful." Aye, he shook his head. He thought of the victim he had known as Anna, the girl with the troubled, painful past. She was all he could think of.

It looked and sounded as if all of County Cork had crowded into the Falconer home. Fiddles competed against each other and laughter rose from dozens of glad hearts. It had been this way since midday when most of the shops in Kinsale had closed and the fishing fleet had landed.

It was time to welcome Padraic Falconer back home. And it looked to Kate Alcott as if the celebrating would go on till sunrise.

She was exhausted, and one look to Maggie across the room with a tray full of cups confirmed the older woman was fatigued also, but as hostess, Kate knew she would stay up with the staunchest reveler. Finally, Kate went up to her room and stretched out across her bed. She woke some hours later to the fiddle still weaving its tunes. When she looked out the window, she saw that it would be dawn soon. She had never taken one of her walks at this time of the day. Downstairs the kitchen was still packed with people looking as lively as ever. She slipped her shawl from the peg and stepped into the night.

A full moon splashed gold on the emerald hills, and the fragrance of jasmine hung heavy in the night air.

"Going for a walk?" Padraic asked, stepping into the moonlight.

Kate laughed. "You are the guest of honor. What are you doing out here?"

"Ah, that's the thing, lass, with the Irish. Be it wake or christening or welcoming home one thought dead, with such it will go on for hours and hours. You can slip in and out without notice."

"True. I went up and slept awhile."

"Aye, see there, Ma's in on the parlor sofa, while two ladies are gabbin' hard across from her."

"Good, I'm glad," said Kate. "She's worn out."

"Aye, so are you taking...one of your jaunts?"

"I thought I would. It really is too lovely out, to stay indoors."

He fell into step beside her, and they walked in silence down the path.

"Ma told me about your paying Mr. Huntly with your da's money."

She smiled without looking at him or slowing her steps. "I wondered how long you'd be home before you brought that up."

"I'm not wanting to sound ungrateful, but I wish you hadn't done that. It was money your da sent for—"

"For me to do with as I pleased, which pleased me to do as I did." She stopped and faced him, hands on her hips. "Really, Padraic, you know nothing beyond fishing. If you walk with a girl on a night like this, you don't go along fussing at her! And that 'tis true."

He smiled. "Okay."

She laughed and they resumed walking. Soon the Falconer house was distant, and they could only hear thin strands of melody and laughter.

"I've not had a chance to tell you how much I enjoyed reading those letters you sent. I...I know it was a difficult thing to do."

Kate felt sensitive to being reminded of that painful exposure. "It was nothing. Hardly literary," she replied almost curtly.

Padraic was silent. The road dipped and forked. Kate stopped. She had always taken the left turn—it ribboned through the countryside.

The right wound past Kinsale then to the bluffs that faced the Atlantic. Even now, she heard the surf and immediately felt her heart begin to pound. In the time she had spent with the Falconers she had steadfastly refused to look at the ocean. Now she stopped.

"Kate?"

It was a calm, tranquil night. Why should she be afraid? And with a friend beside her.

"I…I want to see it now. Will you come with me?"

"Aye."

With each step they took the thunder grew deeper and stronger, the crash of waves louder. The path wound through tall grass, then to the bluff, past the lighthouse. She stopped. It was a huge panorama, so big and endless in the night that was now paling to an opal-like gray, a thin thread of scarlet on the horizon. Spellbound, Kate stepped closer. So beautiful yet, frightening. Out there… She was trembling and perspiring. This was Padraic's friendly sea, but it terrified her. She sank to her knees, crying.

The sun came up pouring scarlet and saffron and silver on the water. Gulls circled. Kate sat hugging her knees and watching the new day for what seemed like hours.

"Katie lass?"

She looked up, pale, her eyes rimmed in red, but she was smiling. She had forgotten Padraic completely. She held up her hand and he lifted her up.

"All right, lass?"

She looked to the ocean, then back to him. "All right."

Against the background of the ocean he loved… He could not release her hand, and never mind if anyone saw them. She tilted her head to look up at him.

"What are you thinking of, Mr. Falconer?" She knew exactly what he was thinking.

"I'd like to…kiss you, lass," he replied in his simple way.

"Aye, I'd like you to…" She smiled.

It was a kiss Kate Alcott enjoyed very much. It was good to feel wanted again.

She stepped back. "Now what are you thinking of, Padraic Falconer?"

"A line from a poem…came into my mind."

"Oh? An Irish poet of course." She smiled.

He laughed. "Sure and there are no others."

"And will you tell me this line of poetry I've inspired you to remember?"

He looked to the sea then back to her. He stroked her cheek. "From Mr. Yeats, 'I have spread my dreams beneath your feet…tread softly….'"

The Irishwoman was on her knees in the garden, the morning sun warm on the back of her neck as she worked over the soil and prayed.

Life had returned to its smooth, predictable routine, free of shadows. The *Bluebell* was back at sea with its captain at the helm. The mackerel were running, aye, life was good. Then she heard their laughter, like music in the clear morning air. She stood up and shaded her eyes as she looked down the road.

Denny, Jen, and Kate were bicycling from Kinsale. They were having a race. Denny was hollering and the girls were red-faced and laughing.

"No fair!" Jen was laughing as they pedaled up to the house. "Denny Falconer, you cheated!"

"Ah, poor losers always make that claim. And how was I cheatin'?"

"You saw I was going to win and you tried to run me off the road!"

"You blame me that you can't steer?"

"Ha!"

"Well, I would have beaten both of you if I didn't have this package to worry over," Kate panted as she came up last.

Jen and Denny entered the kitchen still arguing. Kate took the package from the basket and set it on top of the low stone wall. Maggie came to lean beside her.

"A package from your da?"

Kate smiled as she held the brown wrapped parcel. "No, it's from Peppercreek, Illinois, from my grandmother."

"Ah..." Maggie nodded. The grandmother seemed to be the one relative Kate had a healthy relationship with. She could see the girl was eager to go off alone and open it, and she hated to detain her.

"Lass, Meg Donnerel was over this morning with a plate of currant buns and a question."

Kate turned to her, still smiling. "Let me guess. Does it have anything to do with a certain young man with flaming red hair?"

"Aye, it does."

Kate was not blind to the young man's obvious interest each Sunday morning in church. Even the Falconer brothers' frowns had not discouraged him from a few hurried words when the services were over.

"She's testin' the waters for Johnny, so to speak, seein' if the interest might be mutual." Maggie laughed. "She thinks her son and the American girl are destined for each other with their hair color!"

Kate joined in her laughter. "She makes courtship sound very simple and unromantic. Hair color!"

"Aye. Sometimes folks go to lookin' for mates for their children. Sometimes it works, sometimes not."

"And so what did you tell the designing Mrs. Donnerel?"

"I told her plain that I did not know the inclinations of your heart."

"Oh, Maggie, that was a well-phrased answer!"

The Irishwoman shrugged.

"I...I really...I'm not interested in Johnny Donnerel."

"Well then...perhaps..." Maggie was suddenly embarrassed.

Kate was curious. "Yes?"

"Interested in...anyone else, lass? Do you think you ever want to marry, Kate?"

Kate looked down to the smooth, warm stones under her hands. How could she explain to this good Irishwoman that part of her, the loving part, seemed stunted? Marriage, even deep love for a man seemed unattainable. Something held her back, made her take from men, without ever really letting them get close to her. No, Maggie wouldn't understand. She thought the American girl was all healed from the tragedy she had passed through. Kate was a different young woman. But some things had not changed. She didn't know if they ever could.

"There isn't anyone...I, I don't know, Maggie, about marriage. It doesn't seem likely, or at least soon. I just imagine I'll have a career as a journalist."

She knew she sounded flat and cold. She felt awkward now in the kind woman's presence.

"I can't think what it would be like to have never known the love of a man, the right one, of course, such as I had with my Dennis. 'Tis a wonderful gift, something unique, different from the love I have for my children. But I can see that there are all kinds of good things in life to make us happy if we've lost, or haven't found the right man."

"You don't mind me not being interested in Johnny Donnerel, do you, Maggie?"

"Of course not, lass. Meg will simply have to keep looking for the lad. And knowing Meg she'll not give up till she finds the proper shade of red."

Kate hopped off the wall, relieved the Irishwoman did not seem offended. Maggie laid a plump hand on the young cheek.

"Back to my garden, and on to your package."

A leather bound book. Kate had walked to her favorite tree, sat down in its leafy shade, and opened the package. Her grandmother had sent her the journal her grandfather had written.

'There will come a time when you're ready for it...' she had said.

Now across the vast miles that separated them, Sara Alcott had decided it was time. No letter accompanied the book; it would speak alone to her without amendments or explanations. Kate was pleased with the confidence her grandmother had placed in her.

It was the story of a young man whose life had taken a long journey across a varied panorama of experience—walking across the Midwest as a young orphan boy, adoption and growing up in a loving family, serving in the Union army and later the 16th American president, a crippling attack, marriage, fatherhood.

Kate had always looked at her grandfather with detached but curious interest; now she saw him as a young man full of ambitions and pride and confidence—like her. A man shocked by the rawness of life, and near death, like her. His testing had come in the war between the States, a refining fire; hers was the tragedy of the *Lusitania*. He had emerged and found the One who was there from the beginning, the One her grandmother knew so intimately.

She sat on the sunny hill in Ireland in a sea of gently waving grass and read the journal completely. She reread some passages. But the last line, before her grandfather signed his name, revolved in her mind like a beacon—words she had surely heard before, yet not really heard at all...

'And you will know the Truth and the truth will set you free...'

"Free from what?" she said aloud.

Free from everything, the past and the hurt and the anger, the bitterness and the disappointment.

She felt small and fragile under the huge canopy of blue sky. Very small and needing freedom.

"I want to know the Truth, I want to know You..."

She had come into their lives on a day that had begun so routinely and without premonition. She had lived with them and been a part of them for over a year. From another country and culture, a stranger had become family. So it was not easy for Kate Alcott to speak after the evening meal one night. Every face at the long, plain table had become dear to her. It was hard to say goodbye.

"I have something to say," she began nervously.

Maggie Falconer's cup stopped in midair, as if she knew what was coming. Perhaps they all did.

Kate wore a plain cream-colored dress. She knew she was not the same gaunt figure she had once been. She looked at her hands, then to Maggie. "This isn't, really isn't easy for me to say." She drew a deep breath. "I left the United States for England. I was going to London to report on the war for my college paper. But you all know what happened, of course. You saved me and brought me back to life. You have loved me. So leaving isn't quite so easy as I once thought it would be. But I have decided to go home. I think I'm ready." She gave them all a brave smile in the shocked silence.

"You can sail?" Pierce asked gently.

"I think I can. You all have helped me so much. I think I can get on the boat and sail. My father wrote me he showed, or rather his wife Lilly showed some of my writing to a friend of hers that works for Colliers. That's a big magazine in the States. Anyway, I can have a job, just a bit job, if I want it. So...so I think I'll take it."

She had not expected this sober, sad response. They would hardly meet her eyes.

"You sure, Kate?" Denny whispered hoarsely. "I can't think what it will be like...with you gone."

Her throat tightened. "That's very sweet of you. I will miss all of you very much, too."

"We are so thankful you're well and strong, Kate, but sure and we will miss you so," Maggie added.

"'Tis truth," Pierce nodded soberly.

Kate smiled. Pierce and his brevity of words. She would miss his quiet, comforting friendship.

"With Jen gone, they'll be no one to tease," Rory said mournfully. "When are you going?"

"A ship leaves from Queenstown in two days."

She glanced up at Padraic who had not spoken. Finally, he looked away from the hearth and gave her the smile and nod she knew so well.

Kate had gone up to her room, Denny and Rory out for the evening, Pierce to bed. Maggie and Padraic sat at opposite ends of the long table. They heard the ticking of the clock and watched a gentle breeze flutter the curtains. Padraic lifted his eyes from his folded hands in front of him. Pain-filled eyes. Maggie winced. He shook his head.

"Goodnight, Ma."

She watched him as he crossed the room, suddenly stooped.

Alone in the kitchen, Maggie understood. She sighed. "There is a lass whose name is written on my son's heart. Aye, this was the one."

crossing the Atlantic

The young woman's posture and the look in her eyes did not promote conversations as she strolled the deck or dined in the salon of the *Charleston*. Yet some determined young men could not ignore the fragile beauty in the navy skirt, white blouse and navy hat. She appeared completely unescorted, and good looks and singleness were too persuasive a combination. So they tried a little friendly flirting—and were meagerly rewarded for their efforts. Kate Alcott wanted to be alone on the six-day crossing, to give her time to adjust to life away from the Emerald Isle and to what lay ahead once the shores of America came into her view. A part of her wanted to see if she could recapture something of her old life, however, and since holding men in her power was part of her past, she did not wholly discourage their attentions. But it was not the same— something was different now. That difference came to her as she leaned on the rail with a stranger one evening. The Falconer brothers appeared in her mind, as they always did. Honest, hardworking, respectful and affectionate—good men. These flashy men aboard the ship seemed...hollow in comparison. She sighed to herself. Maybe the old ways were gone—and maybe it was good that they were.

It was enough that she faced the challenge of the Atlantic and leaving rural, uncomplicated Ireland—and seeing her father again. The first 24 hours at sea were the hardest. Even though the seas were calm she felt the strangulation of panic. Water, deep, dark water. Endless water. Cold and sinister. Suddenly, she left the stranger standing at the rail and rushed to her private cabin where she sobbed and longed for the Falconer family. Another battle to face, this crossing, as she had known it would be from the first hour of her decision. But there was no Maggie or Padraic to comfort her.

She closed her eyes and pictured Maggie Falconer on that sunny day they had stood on the quay at Queenstown. The goodbyes, then going to Maggie's outstretched arms. They were both crying.

'I...love you, lass...tis true.'

Kate felt overwhelmed with her love. This woman, there was never anyone like her in Kate's life before. Accepting her as she was...

'Ma...' Kate cried.

She had sent her grandfather's journal on to Ben in France. Now she read from the other book her father had given her long ago. She touched it hesitantly, then opened the cover. "Amy Cash Alcott, 1898."

Her mother had treasured this book. With calmness stealing over her, the daughter began to read.

New York

When she had first sailed away with bright hopes and big dreams, bands were playing and streamers were flying in the May sunshine. Now she was returning, sailing into New York harbor with no fanfare or attention. Only two people who seemed small and frail from her position on the deck of the liner, were expecting her. They were clutching hands, as if for support, as if this moment was one of the biggest and most important in their lives. And it was. Katherine Alcott had come home.

She started down the gangplank grasping her leather bag, her stomach tumbling with nervousness. The couple moved forward hesitantly as she approached the dock. Lilly O'Hara stood back smiling broadly at her. Her father looked older and tired, and afraid. Not at all as she had expected. She knew in a moment he was tense with fear—fear she would reject him. Tears rose in her eyes.

They stood looking at each other like strangers—with so much to let go of, and so much to pick up. They must begin as they never had before. Face to face.

She smiled and he reached for her.

Part IV

Spring
1918

*He makes wars to cease to the end of the
earth,*
He breaks the bow and cuts the spear in two,
He burns the chariots with fire.
Cease striving and know that I am God,
I will be exalted among the nations...

—PSALM 46:9

Over there! Over there!
Have you heard, spread the word, Over there!
*for the YANKS ARE COMIN', the YANKS
ARE COMIN'!*
the YANKS ARE COMIN' OVER THERE!

—GEORGE M. COHAN, 1914

Chapter 23

The Reichstag
Berlin

◆◆◆◆◆◆

*A*s long as Germany kept its U boats under control, the American president was willing to be patient and give diplomacy its full reign. But the German high command knew they had a valuable weapon in the submarine, and keeping their navy on a leash only empowered the Allies even more. The gains along the western front were not impressive, so the kaiser, with an imperious wave of his hand, erased his earlier edict. Total, unrestricted submarine warfare.

"Without pity or limit!" the kaiser shouted as he jabbed at the map—the waters around the British Isles, France and Italy were again a war zone. "You will leave for Washington tonight, Herr Bernstorff. Tell the Americans. Tell them this!" He had worked himself into a sputtering rage. A vein along his neck throbbed purple. His ministers shifted in their chairs uneasily. Would the kaiser collapse in front of them?

He pounded the table. "Tell them they may sail one ship a week. It must arrive in Europe on a Sunday and leave the following Wednesday. It must fly a checkered flag and no cargo of war material will be on board, of course." He gave them an intimidating glare, then stalked from the room.

No one lifted their eyes from the table for a long minute. They dared not speak a word. But for once they were in agreement—the kaiser had gone too far. The Americans would not like this.

Washington D.C.
The White House

Woodrow Wilson was a man of peace. He hated war. As a man of 62 he could still conjure up the childhood memory of Union soldiers, worn and weary, marching past his front porch. He had been patient, tolerant, forgiving, diplomatic. He was staunch in his belief that the United States must remain neutral in the European conflict even when the *Lusitania* had plunged to the bottom of the Irish sea with innocents aboard. He'd spent long hours alone thinking over the troubling problems on the continent, and the implications to his own country. Now he sat back in the deep leather chair in the oval office while the debate swirled hotly around him. Leaning back, quiet and relaxed, he appeared a minor player.

"This...this is the last straw! Germany attempting an alliance with Mexico against us! Invade Arizona and New Mexico! Are they insane in the Reichstag?"

Another official's voice was grimly calm. "No, they're just ready for the U.S. to throw in with the Allies."

Still a third voice spoke up. "And this concession, this privilege to allow us one ship a week! It's preposterous! And flying a flag like a, a kitchen tablecloth! The nerve!"

Then someone noticed the president. Silence was telegraphed around the room while the leader stood up slowly and tiredly. He removed his carefully polished glasses. His voice was firm.

"Call a special session of the Congress tomorrow night, gentlemen."

The weather was wet and dreary—fitting for what the Presbyterian minister's son must do tonight. Wilson sat in the darkened limousine oblivious to the flag waving crowds along Pennsylvania Avenue, or the Marine sharpshooters on the capital rooftops. His bride squeezed his hand to comfort him, and he gave her a smile. This was the right thing to do, he was convinced of that. But this was the hardest thing he'd ever done in all his years.

Once inside the House chamber, he was shown to the rostrum. It was silent in the packed gallery. He adjusted his steel-rimmed spectacles. Again his voice was firm and unwavering.

'...We must fight... The world must be made safe for democracy...'

With a rebel yell from a Civil War veteran, the chamber exploded in thunderous applause and wild cheering.

Later Wilson returned to his darkened cabinet room in the White House. He felt old and tired and drained—not victorious or exultant. His popularity had soared with the declaration of war, but Wilson felt little joy. He spoke softly to his personal secretary who hovered anxiously nearby.

"My message was a message of death for our young men. How strange to applaud that." Then he bowed his head and cried.

Magnolia Bible College
Mississippi

It was a sultry afternoon, yet Viney Jefferson always found a reason to hold an informal party, no matter what the weather was like. It gave her real joy to send out the call for friends and family scattered across Washington county to gather. But today was not a birthday, or celebration of a new baby or graduation. Today the friends and family of Seth and Viney Jefferson had gathered on the broad green lawn behind 'Magnolia Bible College' to say goodbye and wish well the couple's oldest son. Gideon Jefferson had enlisted. He was going to war in Europe, answering the call of Uncle Sam. Viney Jefferson wanted the party, not for the social reasons this time, but so that those gathered could lay hands on and pray for her son. She could only face his parting knowing he was well prayed over.

She stopped in her serving a moment to look at him across the lawn. He stood there holding hands with his girlfriend and they were laughing. She treasured the picture of her tall, strong, healthy son. Gideon was always such a good son. She smiled and handed out another plate of food. But her mind remained on her child.

"Over there, Lord, in that strange land, please give him someone, please, Lord, someone special that knows you, someone for my Gideon..."

"Dear Grandma Sara,

Today is Sunday and I have a few hours to knock around on my own. The weather has been pretty nasty the last few days, rainy and windy during the day, foggy in the morning. That keeps us grounded and makes the time slog along. They're pretty stingy with leave lately. If I can't fly, I'd at least like to run over to see David and Marty. They are about an hour and a half from here. But I did get to fly this morning. I have to look over my shoulder to make certain no bunkmate reads that Ben Alcott got scared today, but since you've always held my secrets pretty close, I can tell you. We went up, three of us, for a routine check over the lines. All was quiet along the front, except for an occasional archie, which seemed to be put up pretty half-heartedly. We hear from prisoners that the German army is rather depressed and eager for this war to be over. The fellows we see are glad to be prisoners. They get better food. War is strange, isn't it? Anyway, after about an hour the lead plane signaled it was time to head home. I decided on a nice smooth loop to bank right. It put me right in a cloud that I hadn't really noticed. The thing seemed to go on forever, my compass was spinning wildly. No sound, or wind, nothingness. It was really eerie. If my engine decided to conk out I was in a real jam. It felt like I was in there for hours, when it finally began to thin. I broke through and it was blue. I saw the ground, but I didn't recognize a thing. None of my planes were in sight. No lines or roads or river landmarks. I was really sweating it. I had the uneasy feeling I'd gotten over Hunland. I've heard all the stories about pilots going down when their fuel runs out and they become a 'guest of the kaiser' for the rest of the war. Yet another worry was patroling Germans. I'd be easy pickings for a squadron. Then I spotted two Germans underneath me. They seemed to spot me at the same time. One lone wolf came up to look me over. This is it, I thought. No buddies to pull me out now. He circled me and we went round and round a few times. He squeezed off a few rounds and I did the same. Then he seemed satisfied I was harmless. I guess he figured I was a famous ace just toying with him, or someone not worth wasting lead over. Figuring I must have gone a little too far north, I swung my plane south. In a few minutes I caught up with the rest of the group. Funny, but the German actually helped the lost sheep home. Now, let me tell you about David and his English girl..."

He'd been flying for nearly six weeks now. While each day was different, Ben had settled into a routine, vigilant as he flew, but somewhat relaxed. His work was principally defensive—patrolling Allied lines, escorting photo planes and protecting observation balloons. He was well liked among his squadron mates—known for his skill at mechanics and his willingness to lend a hand in any situation. He had proven his skill in flying, his instincts. But his mates noticed he did not lust for the German kill, becoming an ace. His commanders held a private view among themselves concerning the Illinoisan. He was an excellent pilot and shot. He kept a clear head and avoided unnecessary risks. He wouldn't seek a fight, they decided, but he would be deadly when pushed to the wall.

Today Ben was flying rear position in a formation with two other planes. He hummed some long-ago tune to himself as he enjoyed the sky flamed in scarlet, and the mounds of fluffy clouds with golden undersides. No artificial lights from the ground war marred the beauty at this moment.

"Wish Davy could see this," he said to himself. "This would be a great picture for his French collection."

Then as he watched the sky and the planes in front of him, he began plotting. How could he convince his commander to allow him to fly to Amiens and give his little brother a ride?

They received the report then that a single German photo plane was approaching the lines. Their assignment was simple—'encourage' him back home before he snapped any important pictures. Typically a slower plane, it should be an assignment without problem. But then four red planes appeared unobtrusively at Ben's left—nearly an even match. The ground spotter had missed the accompanying four-plane escort.

Ben whistled. "Somebody wasn't lookin' too good."

The photo plane circled back at the sight of the three Lafayettes. But its attendants decided to stay. It was time for a tete-a-tete. It began as always, a spinning, diving free-for-all. But after a few moments, the planes paired off, with one German circling. Ben was again faced with the realization this was no Sunday afternoon outing. The bullets zinging around him revealed his opponent's earnestness. He tried to fire, to keep the Hun off his tail, and to keep some watch on the fate of his fellows. His German was diving at him and Ben turned the full strength of his guns on him. Then the plague of so many pilots happened—his machine gun jammed and silenced. The German knew it and came on with greater intensity. Bullets pinged along Ben's wing supports. He was in serious trouble—no firepower and the German smelling a victory for the ace column.

He dove forward in a corkscrew. To those on the ground it looked like the Allied pilot had lost control. But he brought the plane up sharply and leveled at 100 feet above the ground. The sound of an engine just over his shoulder informed him the German was not fooled by this ploy.

"Jerry Hun wants me in 'no man's land' and nothing less," Ben muttered to himself.

His only asset seemed to be that his Spad was flying perfectly. The long hours over his engine were well invested. He skimmed over the ground, one last hope to ditch his pursuer forming in his mind. It was as dangerous for him as it was for his opponent. He banked left, still low, and flying slower. He wanted the German hooked on his tail. The Allied lines loomed abruptly into view. He flew directly at them.

"Wake up boys and take a good look!" he shouted over the side.

Just as he hoped the ground fire barked to life. He only hoped they could distinguish between an Allied Spad and a German Albatross. They were directly over the lines now. Ben climbed a little higher in narrow loops. The German was on his tail like a burr.

"You're a poor shot, Jerry, or I'd be down long ago," Ben said grimly. He turned sharply to face the German, when the ground guns found their target. The German plane ignited instantly, spinning crazily to earth. Ben opened the throttle wide to join his squadron. He could not watch the red plane's plunge. Kill or be killed...

The sun was going down in a rosy glow when he found the two Lafayettes still dueling. Two Germans narrowed in on one Allied plane, and Ben zoomed in. He couldn't worry about his dead guns. Then the burst of flame flashed in the sky, and shrapnel flew everywhere. Smoke poured from the cockpit. Feeling overwhelmed with helplessness, Ben gripped his controls tightly in agony. The Lafayette was going down. If only he could fly closer and rescue the pilot somehow. It was over in seconds. The Allies were leaving, the Germans returning north. Both sides had drawn blood.

Ben wandered alone to the perimeter of the airfield. He was exhausted and had a growing headache. He had left the Lafayette mess hall. He wasn't hungry and the room had been painfully quiet. Yet the empty chair across from him had made a loud, eloquent statement. Everyone had sat hunched and picking indifferently at their food. No teasing or joking or boasting. He had been there for midday meal; he had slept across from Ben. Ben knew about his hometown, his girl back in the States, and the red hound he liked to take hunting. One German bullet had found him.

And some German mother or sister or sweetheart had lost the one she loved. Ben drew a deep breath. His risky tactic to shake the enemy from his tail had succeeded. He slid down against a beech tree and closed his eyes. He didn't feel much like the cocky American aviator who French merchants admired and young women swooned over. He felt alone and lonely. He couldn't imagine even his wise, steady little brother being able to comfort him. Kill or be killed... He shook his head. "I don't know..."

His own death would have been a fraction of an inch closer with misaimed ground fire or German machine-gun blast. He stood up shakily. He needed to go to sleep, escape—and tomorrow his old reliable confidence would surely return.

"So, are you serious about...Pauline, Ben?"

Ben took a final bite of his apple, then lobbed the core in a nearby corner. "Who?"

David fell back into his cot with a sigh. "I guess that answers that."

"Oh, Pauline!"

"Yeah, the one who is having fun in Paris," David continued dryly.

Ben shook his head. "She dumped me. Found an airman stationed in Paris. She explained it wasn't anything personal, just a matter of convenience." He laughed, betraying no wounded ego.

David coughed, then broke into a spasm of sneezing.

Ben eyed him critically. "So I guess this means no night out for you."

David blew his nose loudly and closed his eyes. "Sorry, Ben. I'll probably feel better tomorrow."

"Tonight is my last night of leave. Do you want me to hang around and play nursemaid?" he teased. "Ma would want me to."

David laughed weakly. "No she wouldn't. She'd be afraid you'd give me the wrong medicine. But you can do me a favor."

"Sure, what is it?"

"The British Red Cross has brought over a band to play for their boys. They're giving a little concert in the square in Soissons."

"Yeah?" Ben's tone was edged with suspicion.

"So, I told Molly I would take her."

Ben's arms were crossed defensively. He was silent.

"She's been real busy with the kids and all she does. She needs an outing. I'd like you to take her."

"No thanks," Ben replied bluntly.

"Why not? You told me you don't have any plans tonight."

"I suddenly have plans." Ben's voice was calm.

"Yeah, like?"

"Like…like going on back to base and washing my plane. I ran through a dirty cloud yesterday."

"Why don't you want to take her out?"

"Any other girl or request I wouldn't mind at all."

David leaned up on an elbow. "Molly too decent?"

Ben's smile froze. "I'll allow that you're probably feverish, otherwise we'd be down on the floor right now. I don't want to take her out for the simple reason she won't want to go."

"And why wouldn't she?" David demanded.

Ben was irritated. "Look, Davy boy, we haven't talked since that double date flop a few weeks ago. But two things were plain from it. Miss English isn't overly fond of me, and is very fond of *you*. I don't think she'll appreciate me showing up on her doorstep when she is waiting for you."

"What do you mean very fond of me?"

"Good grief, David! You're an, an infant when it comes to women! I don't see how you snatched up Bess."

"Yeah? Well, if I'm an infant, what does that make you?" David countered testily.

"Look, it's obvious to me. It was obvious to Pauline. The English—"

"Her name is Molly Fleming."

"Molly Fleming likes you, she likes you a lot. One little snap of your fingers and she'd be all over you!"

"Ben, you've got it all wrong," David returned tiredly.

"Yeah, yeah, you keep sayin' that. You've said that for months now. She knows about Bess and she has a guy back in Ireland and you have an understanding."

"The guy was in Scotland and he got married."

Ben slapped his leg in triumph. "There, you see! She's a nice girl, but she isn't the kind to throw herself at you without a little encouragement. You're a decent, healthy guy, and she's a young woman. Good grief!"

David shook his head.

"David, you can see it when she looks at you, and hear it in her voice."

'I'm impressed with his courage…' she had said. Ben could not forget that.

David lay back silent and thinking. Could it be true? Had Molly misunderstood their friendship?

Ben's voice was patient again. "So, I think—"

"Then that's even more reason for you to take her out. Get her mind off of me."

Ben laughed. "You!" He shook his head. "She's not my type. The English are too serious. I want to take out a girl who wants me. Look, it would be like me taking out Bess when she's pining away for you."

"You would prove a disappointment to her," David agreed soberly. "But still, I hate to think of Molly getting ready and me not showing."

Ben stood up and stretched. "You lie back and sneeze all you want. Big brother will go take care of this."

"What are you going to do?"

"With my natural charm and finesse, I simply go and explain you're sick and you'll see her another time. She'll be disappointed, but she'll get over it. She won't have to suffer with me, and I'll go on to the concert and find...someone who likes aviators."

When he was gone, David lay back and smiled.

Ben was pleased with this little assignment. He rang the bell at rue de lilac and waited calmly and confidently. Finally the heavy door swung open, and a young girl regarded him with gray, serious eyes.

He bowed slightly. "Bonjour, mademoiselle," he greeted her cheerfully.

But her face remained impassive. He stepped inside the cool hallway. "So..." He looked at the little girl more closely. David had said something about a little girl Molly had brought from Switzerland. This child looked fragile. She'd seen too much of war, Ben decided. Another time, and he would like to make her smile.

"Do you think you could find Miss Fleming for me?"

A discreet cough caused him to turn. Molly stood at the landing of the stairs. She wore a dress of icy blue, and her hair was drawn into a loose chignon. Ben involuntarily took one step forward—to assure himself this was the Englishwoman. She came down the stairs and stood before him. She was neither smiling nor frowning.

"Monsieur Alcott," she said politely.

Even her voice could not quite break the hold. Ben was openly staring.

"Monsieur Alcott?" she ventured again.

"Huh? Oh. Hi ya," he said slowly. And he began to stare again.

Molly looked to the young girl and smiled. But the little girl was staring at Ben. Finally, Molly met his gaze directly. He scratched his head, as if he wondered why he had come. The little girl sneezed.

"Bless you, Emma." Molly handed the girl a rag from her pocket.

"That's it!" Ben replied brightly. "So, here I am!"

"Yes...you are," Molly agreed.

"I...the fact is, Miss Fleming, Davy's sick."

A line creased her brow. "David's sick?"

He shrugged. "A cold, nothing really serious. But he's feeling kind of low, sneezing and coughing all over the place. Pretty messy. He hated to miss taking you, so he asked me to take you, to the...the..."

"Concert."

"Yeah, the concert."

"I..." she began slowly, toying with the little girl's braids.

A startled, slightly alarmed voice came from the end of the hallway. Aunt Madeline hurried forward as if one of the kaiser's footmen had entered no. 10. Her unfriendly eyes raked over Ben boldly.

"Aunt Madeline, this is Monsieur Ben Alcott, David's older brother."

Madeline Chaumont gripped her wrinkled hands together. Ben was relaxed and smiling now, his hands thrust loosely in his khaki pockets.

"Pleasure to meet you, Madame Chaumont," he said easily.

She gave him an almost imperceptible nod, and turned slightly to Molly, lifting her eyebrows in question.

"David is ill, so Monsieur Ben has offered to take me to the concert."

"Ready to go then?"

Aunt Madeline looked horrified—'These slangy Americans!'

"Yes," Molly replied with a deep breath as if she were plunging under water. She stooped to give Emma a kiss on the forehead. "I'll look in on you when I get home, I promise."

Aunt Madeline made an ungraceful clutch at her niece's hand. Her look was eloquent. 'Is he...safe?'

Molly smiled and squeezed her hand.

"I'll bring her back safe and sound, Aunt Madeline," Ben spoke up roguishly.

The Frenchwoman blanched.

Outside in the old Model T, Molly carefully smoothed her dress. Why in the world had she agreed to this? David would certainly have understood if she refused.

It was a ten-piece British band trying valiantly to bring some cheer and pleasure to its sons at war. They had assembled in the cobbled town square of Soissons and ran through their menu of songs several times. But the crowd of soldiers and medical staff seemed to enjoy it. The band had brought a touch of home from across the channel—to men who had forgotten their reason for fighting. Ben turned to Molly sitting decorously on the bench beside him. He did not recognize any of the tunes, but she was leaning forward and smiling.

"These are all British?" he asked.

She nodded without turning. "Yes, old favorites."

They spoke little throughout the concert. Molly was drawn into the world of a little English village and it made her miss her father. It was a world this American, almost a stranger, did not know of. But David would have understood. Already, she knew about his prairie home, the apple orchard and creek, the venerable grandmother who 'reigned' from her wheelchair.

When it was over, Ben insisted on dessert at a cafe. Molly agreed reluctantly. At least she would be able to tell David she gave her best effort.

"You are enjoying your flying?" she asked at the restaurant. He was a flyer—what else was there to talk about?

She was surprised by his suddenly pensive face. He traced the edge of the table with a slender brown finger.

"I'm enjoying the flying. I love it, and I like all the guys in the squadron. But...I—"

"Bonjour, Benjamin!" A French girl approached their table and gave him a quick kiss on the cheek.

"Uh, bonjour, Nicole."

The smiling girl pouted. "I am Ninette! Where have you been?" she attempted in shaky English.

"I've been pretty busy lately, you know. How do you say 'busy' in French, Miss Fleming?"

Wasn't this the one who had played the prank with David's translation book? It was a temptation she chose to resist. She told him the word.

The French girl understood. She cast Molly a quick, unfriendly look and left. Ben shifted uncomfortably in his chair and avoided Molly's smiling face.

Finally, "Ready to go, Miss Fleming?"

She nodded. Outside the cafe, Ben was accosted again.

"Ben! Ben Alcott!"

Molly smiled to herself as she watched the flyer cringe. He turned around slowly. Pauline. She came up to him with four other laughing young women. They surrounded the tall man.

Oh, he loves this, Molly thought.

"Hi ya, Pauline. You're in Soissons."

"Yes, and—" She noticed Molly waiting in the car and gave Ben a bold wink. "Took her from little brother, huh?"

"Uh, no, well, I better be going."

"We're off for a drive to some old ruins somewhere. We're going to picnic under the stars. Mary brought champagne! Want to come along?"

"Uh, thanks, but not tonight. See ya!" He hurried to the car.

They drove in silence, each staring rigidly ahead.

"You could have gone, monsieur, with your friends," Molly said softly. "I could have made my way home."

His head swiveled around. "No thanks, I didn't care to." Molly was startled by the coldness in his tone.

"I only meant, it would not have offended me, and—"

"You really think I would do that, huh?" he asked brusquely.

"I just want you to understand you could—without worrying over me."

"You expect me to be a complete hooligan and dump you. Right in character, huh?"

"I didn't think it would matter to you," she ventured stiffly.

It was the wrong thing to say.

Ben's voice was tight. "I don't dump my dates, Miss Fleming. Even if you think David is the only Alcott with a shred of—"

"I never thought...and I certainly thought...and I do think, you'd want to go with someone you prefer to be with instead of—"

"You, huh? And you wanted to be here with me tonight, too, Miss Fleming?"

She was silent.

"You wanted to be with him tonight and it turned out to be me, so you've, you've pouted all night!"

"I did not pout, Monsieur Alcott!"

"This is the most life I've seen in you tonight. Well, you certainly didn't—"

"Throw myself at you and giggle every time you opened your mouth?"

"No, Miss Fleming, you are not the kind of girl who throws herself at anyone. You're too careful."

"And you are conceited! I throw myself at whom I want to throw myself at when I'm ready to throw!"

The car lurched to an undignified stop in front of no. 10. Ben tapped the wheel in an angry staccato. "I'll show you to the door, Miss Fleming," he said in an icy tone.

"You needn't bother."

"No bother."

She hurried up the steps. Ben came up behind her and put his hand on her arm. She turned and waited. They looked at each other a long moment.

"I do not melt at your touch, monsieur."

He shrugged. "I know that." A shaft of moonlight fell across the steps. "I'm sorry, Miss Fleming."

She felt as if he had thrown water in her face.

"Monsieur Alcott...I—"

"It's okay. I didn't mean to make you angry or give you a bad evening, really."

She stared at his boots. "I am sorry, also."

"You won't tell Davy, will you? I'll have to let him thrash me if he finds out I upset you."

Molly could almost smile. The tall man sounded like a penitent schoolboy.

"You highly value your brother's feelings," she said softly. She could not see his face clearly.

"Yeah, I do. He's the best little brother in the world. And I value your feelings, Miss Fleming. Goodnight."

He was gone before she could reply.

He didn't have as much time as he wanted. It must be a rushed conversation for the First Friends of France ambulance corps was moving to a new sector that afternoon. So David Alcott hurried to Amiens to see Molly. He wanted to say goodbye, and with the uncertainty and the dangers of war, he didn't know when he would see the young Englishwoman again. But it was more than saying goodbye and that he would miss her.

She was just leaving for a picnic behind the house with the children when he appeared.

"Hello, Molly."

"David! You're just in time to join us on a picnic. We made doughnuts with that flour you brought and—"

But he shook his head. "I'm sorry. I can't stay."

"You can't stay?" He would be the perfect addition to the outing.

"No, we've been ordered to a sector just west of Verdun. We're off this afternoon."

"Verdun..."

"Yeah, I was hoping we'd be stationed here for the duration of the war, but..." He shrugged. "Gotta go where they need us."

"Of course," she agreed slowly.

They stood in the trellis-shaded garden path. The children had run on ahead of Molly, and they were alone. He looked tired, she decided.

"So I came to say goodbye. I don't know when we'll be sent back to this area."

Molly stared at the brick walk, then looked up and met his eyes.

"I'm sorry I won't be able to bring stuff for awhile," he continued.

"We will manage. You have done...so much for us already."

"It wasn't that much."

Why did she feel awkward and nervous with him? Suddenly this saying goodbye seemed...intimate.

"Molly, there is something else. I don't know exactly how to say it."

She watched him as he fumbled. The easygoing, uncomplicated American was actually nervous. She smiled. "David, you're nervous!"

"Yeah...look, Ben and I had this talk...about you."

"Oh?"

"He's convinced in his own stubborn way that...that you, well, to quote Ben, you really like me. You know, more than as friends."

David was obviously embarrassed, and Molly felt she had blushed to the roots of her hair.

"So, you see, I came because I didn't want there to be a misunder-standing between us. I'd never mean to hurt you."

She looked away from him.

"I'm sorry to be so blunt, but this is important since I'm going away for awhile. Was Ben right?"

Finally she faced him. "No, David. You don't have to worry. I've under-stood all along. There is Bess."

"Yeah..." Still he felt awkward.

"Your brother does not know everything about women. Apparently, he thinks friendship only is impossible," Molly replied with a little tart-ness in her tone.

"Oh, he's a good guy though. He messes up, but his heart—"

Molly interrupted impatiently. "David, why do you go on and on about this brother? Why are you trying to convince me how good he is?"

Now it was David's turn to search the ground. "Yes, I have tried to convince you, and I've made a mess of it. You see, I thought Ben needed help finding the right girl, and I...I could find her for him."

He looked so embarrassed and guilty. The truth flooded over Molly, and she stared at him. "You, you wanted me to like you, then, then, you step out of the way, and there's big brother!"

He hung his head and nodded. There was a long, flat, strained silence.

"Molly, I know this sounds—"

"Perfectly...designing and, and cruel!" she flared.

His voice was pleading. "Please let me explain. We met. I liked you for you. You're a wonderful girl. At first I didn't think of Ben. We were friends and I was glad. Then, I admit, I did think of Ben. All he seemed to go with were floozies. I knew you were one of the good ones, the prize kind, and that's what Ben needs, so I thought, well, I thought maybe you two could hit it off. Except every time I tried to promote Ben, I scared you off from him. Then he got suspicious of you for some silly reason and everything was going wrong. Then he tells me if I snapped my fingers, you'd be all over me."

Molly blushed again.

"And I began to see setting up romances is for the novels. I'm no good at it." He hung his head. "I'm sorry. I sure didn't mean to hurt you." He slowly reached for her hand. "There's one other thing to this. I...if there wasn't Bess, I'd have snatched you up in a second."

Molly's laugh was shaky. "Now you sound like Ben."

He sighed. "I gotta be going. You're not mad at me, are you? I couldn't stand leaving and having you angry."

She smiled. "I'm not angry."

He had called her a prize. She would hold on to that.

"Besides Bess and Ben, you're one of my very best friends."

Tears rose in her eyes. "Please don't say that. It sounds like you're saying goodbye...forever."

They enacted a scene that had been repeated hundreds of times with no respect to military allegiance in London or Vienna or Paris. A young man tenderly holding a young woman as she cried. They were saying goodbye.

Paris

They moved as a steady current down the Champs Elysees to the Arc de Triomphe. The sound of their polished boots could not be heard on the wide, tree-lined avenue. The citizens of the city, in desperate need of hope and a cause to celebrate, turned out en masse to welcome these newcomers. The young ones laughed and danced, and the old ones wept with joy. They lifted their children on their shoulders. They waved tiny French and American flags. They shouted, 'Vive la American!' The Yanks had come to Paris.

Row after row of General John J. Pershing's American Expeditionary Force passed, stepping proudly, grinning broadly in their drab olive uniforms. Confidence seemed to perfume the air that sunny morning on the Champs Elysees. Few watching could help but feel that these men, wave after wave of them landing on France's shore, were indeed the tide to sweep war from their ravaged land. These men would fight beside their own weary, depleted army. These men would push the Hun back over the Rhine. Then France could live and breathe again. Her fields could be planted and harvested. Brothers, sons and fathers who were spared the scythe of war would come home. The Americans had come to help them, yes, perhaps save them.

Ben, David, and Marty had received permission to go to Paris to see the Americans' arrival. They were part of the human crush that packed the capital city's main thoroughfare and watched the procession of doughboys with pride. The column reached its destination at the Picpus Cemetery where so many French heroes lay. One of the General's staff officers stood to speak in front of the tomb of the Marquis de Lafayette. He looked out over the crowd and the troops who waited at attention. In his nervousness and fragile French, 'Black Jack' Pershing had insisted

Stanton address the crowd first. Pershing's short speech would be forgotten. But with four words, the American officer captured the intensity
and drama of the moment.

"Lafayette! We are here!"

He had uttered a line that would be repeated in newspapers interna-
tionally and preserved in textbooks. The French people went wild with
cheering. Ben jabbed David in the side.

"Okay, you're the brain of the family. Who's this Lafayette? We didn't
cover much French history at Peppercreek Elementary, you know. Marie
and her rolling head is all I remember."

David laughed. "It isn't just French history, Ben. It's also American
history. A stirring line for the captain to use."

"So fill me in."

"Lafayette was a French nobleman who came to the colonies during
the Revolution to fight alongside the patriot cause. He was a real hero.
He and George Washington became chums."

"So Stanton is saying, you helped us, now we're here to help you."

David nodded. Ben scanned the cheering, holiday-like crowd. He
admired the sentiment and patriotism of the words, but he must be practical.

"Lafayette, we are here," he repeated thoughtfully. "Yep, I think it will
work."

"Work? What do you mean?"

Ben's smile was as wide as any of his fellow Americans passing in
review. "Impress the young mademoiselles, yep."

Chapter 24

*I*t was an epic year on the European and Asian continent. The United States had crossed the Atlantic in boatloads of doughboys. In Russia, Czar Nicholas I, the head of the ruling dynasty, was toppled from power. And the new landlords of the country were not ready to withdraw their hungry and exhausted troops from the slugfest along the eastern front. The year was falling into twilight as autumn approached. To Allied or Central powers, it seemed these three and a half years of hardship and bloodshed would stretch on endlessly. The politicians, the ruling heads of state, the generals and their masses of men, could not bring a conclusion.

"Will it come down to the last bullet one starving soldier has to fire?" Aunt Madeline wondered. Another winter...

It was well after dark, and a group of Lafayette pilots were clustered together smoking and drinking coffee in the open hangar. Ben was bent over an engine. The big guns booming on the western front seemed right over his shoulder or just past the wheat field. But it was several miles away. David and Marty would be busy tonight.

"There you go, Stanley," Ben said as he tossed down a tool. "She's all ready."

"Thanks, Ben."

He joined the pilots at the huge hangar entrance who were watching white flashes cross the darkness. They stood transfixed.

"The fireworks at Coney Island on the fourth are pretty tough to beat, but this about does it," a pilot from New York muttered.

"Huns are gettin' pretty close tonight."

"Okay, fellas enough loafin'," Lufbrey called as he joined the group. He came up to Ben. "Alan's sick, Doc won't let him up. I know you haven't had any sleep—"

Ben smiled. "I'll grab my gear."

He couldn't help but be excited. This was his first night flight as a pilot. He hurried to his locker and grabbed a canvas bag. Ben Alcott now had his own good-luck piece.

But to Ben, it had nothing to do with luck. If he was downed and survived, he wanted this pack with him. It might make things go a little easier. An extra pair of socks, a first aid kit, matches, a few cans of bully beef rations, the Bible his grandmother had insisted on, and a map of France.

"What's up?" he asked Lufbrey as they hurried to their planes.

"Jerries are pounding the boys between Amiens and Verdun pretty hard." He pointed to the bomber plane taking off. "We're to act as escort and take care of any trouble."

They sailed off into the darkness, an impressive convoy of eight. Ben was tense with eagerness and nerves. He'd already talked with other pilots about night flying. It was vastly different from flying during the day. Once off the strip, Ben knew why. Like the extravagance of brakes and enclosed cockpits, these planes were not equipped with landing lights. He must follow his squadron by sound and the smudge of gray they made against the black night. If their guns barked to life, he could pinpoint them even more. All familiar objects and landmarks faded effortlessly as he gained altitude. Definition of land was gone, no orienting horizon.

It reminded him of swimming at night. He wasn't quite sure where anything was, up or down.

In five minutes, he received a bearing. The brilliant white and blue flashes from the lines gave him some perception of how far beneath him the land was. The bomber plane seemed certain of its target and minutes later, unloaded its deadly cargo. The Lafayettes circled high above the explosions—with a wary eye for the zealous German squadron. But none appeared and the mission accomplished, the bomber plane and the four Lafayettes began their return to base.

Ben leaned back and sighed contentedly. It was an uncomplicated, successful, uninterrupted flight. He was grateful. It was too beautiful a night for fighting. It was as pleasant as a summer evening on the front porch at home, listening to the frogs at the creek and watching the fire-flies and stars come out.

A million twinkling stars. He imagined leaning over and grabbing one. He wished he could share this with David.

They approached the last mile of "no man's land." It was only five more minutes to the airfield when Ben's attention was pulled down to earth. A yellow-greenish mist was creeping like an arthritic fog, slow but deliberate. Ben checked his position to make certain of the sides. What was this? He descended a few hundred feet to get a closer look. Then he knew. The sight of it had brought the ground guns to a temporary silence. The Germans had released the deadly gas. It was a supremely cowardly and unfair way to fight. Amiens was somewhere to his left. David would be working hard on a night of bombardment like this. David was down there.

Ben's anger mounted. The beauty of the night had suddenly soured. He knew his impulsive anger might get him into trouble, but right now he didn't care. He banked his plane sharply and headed directly for the German lines. He descended as low as he dared and opened his machine guns wide, emptying his entire belt along the line.

"Got the message, fellas?" he shouted hoarsely.

Maybe it had helped David or some other man crouched in the cata-combs of earth or a crater in the vast lunar surface between Allied and German trenches. He hoped the Germans understood. At any rate, he returned to the airfield feeling better for it.

Later, as he drove down the pitted road, his eyes darted to the dark clouds massing on the horizon. He'd never make it back to the field before the storm hit. Then he saw her. Molly Fleming was walking briskly along the side of the road in front of him. He had not seen her since their fateful date weeks earlier. Many French girls wore their hair in braids, yet somehow he knew it was her.

He drove up beside her. Might as well give it a try. This wasn't the kind of weather one walked in, and on a lonely stretch of road.

"Hello, Miss Fleming! Can I give you a lift somewhere?"

She stopped and turned slowly. Ben drew in his breath sharply. The whiteness of her face was accented by her dark hood. Her eyes were circled.

"Miss Fleming," he repeated gently. Wordlessly, she opened the car door and climbed inside. He continued driving. He didn't turn to her. "Are you okay? Is your aunt all right?"

She pushed back her hood and nodded. "We're both fine, Monsieur Alcott, thank you."

Never was he so careful in every little word he spoke to a girl. This was Davy's friend. Davy had seen qualities that impressed him. He'd just have to trust Davy's judgment.

"Where can I drop you, Miss Fleming?"

"I am trying to get to Arras," she said simply.

"Arras! That's over four miles. You were going to walk?"

She did not speak or face him.

He calmed himself, and spoke casually. "Actually, I'm on the way there myself. I have to pick up some parts. It will be no trouble."

"Thank you."

He knew she didn't really want to talk, but he had to know what caused her to want to walk eight miles in such inclement weather. A pretty woman alone... He shook his head.

"Seen Davy lately?" he asked.

"No, not for six weeks since he was transferred."

"Me either. Longest we've been parted, you know. It's a shame he and Marty got moved right when we're posted within ten miles of Amiens." He shook his head again. "The generals of both sides seem to favor this area for chewing each other up and spitting each other out. I feel sorry for folks like your aunt who live around here."

"Why, monsieur?"

"In the sky you can see how badly they've torn it up. Most of us will move on when this is over, but the locals will be kind of shocked to see the looks of things."

Molly sighed, still not looking at him. "Will it ever end, Monsieur Alcott?" she asked softly.

He glanced at her. She sounded weary. "I think so, by the spring, or summer at the latest."

Finally they arrived in the city. "Well, here we are. Where to?"

She pulled a scrap of paper from her cape and consulted it. She directed him to the center of the French city where he stopped before a jeweler's shop. The small leaded windows cast an orange and scarlet glow into the gloom and wetness of the street. She was still. Was she actually reluctant to leave his presence?

"Thank you again, for the ride," she said.

"Like I said, I was coming this way. I'll pick you up in 30 minutes. Will that give you enough time?"

She shook her head, then stopped. "Yes, 30 minutes will be long enough."

Thirty minutes for Ben Alcott to pick up the airplane parts and figure out how to get Miss Fleming talking. What was the problem? Why was she so sad? Why should he care beyond giving her a gentlemanly lift? Return to Lilac Street in Amiens—and prove, perhaps, he was...trustworthy? For the first time, Ben felt he needed his little brother's advice.

He was waiting for her when she emerged from the shop. A look of gladness passed over her face. But she masked it again quickly.

"Anywhere else?" he asked as if taking her on errands was commonplace.

"No thank you. That was...all."

Again the flatness in her voice.

Between Arras and Amiens, the rain poured down in torrents. Ben leaned forward to see through the cracked windshield. A solid wall of gray blurred the road and countryside. He slowed the car to a crawl.

"I have to find a place to pull over." He drove the car off the road and stopped underneath a small grove of beech trees. It seemed as if they were sitting in a thundering cataract—an enclosed, private world.

"Look, I didn't plan this!" he said defensively.

She turned to him, a question in her eyes.

"You know, run out of gas or get stranded in a storm. I didn't plan for this to happen."

Molly smiled suddenly. "I...have thought you arrogant in the past, monsieur, but I know even you cannot control the weather."

He exhaled loudly and smiled, still holding her look. "You know, back in the States we aren't so formal. It would be Ben. Can we try that?"

She nodded and looked back to her lap. Fifteen minutes passed as the rain continued.

"Can you tell me why you were walking to a jeweler's shop in Arras on a day like this?"

She did not turn. She twisted the strings of the beaded bag in her hands with long, slender fingers. He glanced back to her face. Thinner. She was losing weight. There was not enough food, and Davy was not around to provide extras.

"Molly?"

She was crying.

"Please tell me what the problem is. Maybe I can help. I'm not completely worthless."

"I have not thought you were worthless...Ben. This..." She held up her purse and shook it. Nothing fell into her lap.

"Mu aunt sold most of her fine furniture last winter for food and fuel. I know it was only furniture, but...I felt so sorry for her. Her country invaded, all the shortages, the fears of the German army advancing so that she would have to flee her home, the house stripped. This season, it is hard again, of course. Coal and food. Now the doctor says Emma needs medicine and it is hard to get and therefore very expensive. So...so my aunt is selling her jewelry. These pieces were in her, my, family for years. She showed me each piece very slowly, told me the history, who had worn it. Some belonged to my mother. It was to go to me, she said..." Molly shook her head as the tears fell. "I don't care so much for the jewelry, I just want...I'm tired. I want the war to be over and everyone to go back to just...living."

It was a rare moment in Ben's life. He wanted to pull a girl into his arms with no passionate intent. He wanted to comfort this English girl. But he knew he could not do it. She would misunderstand. She wouldn't trust him. It was enough he had given her a ride to her errand.

But he received his reward when she slipped quickly from the car in front of her home. "Thank you, Ben. You are very kind."

He glanced at his watch, hoping no one was waiting for him or the parts from the airfield. He must hurry back down the shelled road—and presume upon the goodwill of the French merchant. Just now, Ben Alcott was happy to be an American aviator.

It was one of Molly Fleming's favorite times of the day—when she could sit with the children at bedtime. She would read and sing softly to them. She felt her own weariness like a heavy garment, but she didn't mind as she sat there beside their beds and watched their little bodies relax. Her ambition was to send them off to sleep with smiles on their faces—a defense against the nightmares, loneliness in the dark, and the reality of separation from family. Molly had refined her purpose over the now nearly three and a half years at rue de lilac, no. 10.

She wanted to grow closer to her aunt, of course, and to help her by physically serving the household demands. But beyond that she wanted to give the children who passed through her aunt's home for a few days or a month, a rest from the troubling world around them. She wanted to help them hold on to their childhood. War should not rob them of everything.

Young Emma from Austria had proven less of a challenge than Molly expected. At first, she had looked so haunted and remote. Even now, the look could return as she remembered the pain. But Molly was delighted and surprised to see the relationship that blossomed between her aunt and the child. Molly suspected that her dying mother had prepared her for the proper Frenchwoman, as far as was possible. Emma had come up to the old woman and taken her veined hand in her own. It had touched Madeline Chaumont immediately. Most children were intimidated by the tall, rigid-looking woman in immaculate but worn black silk. But Emma was not. It was clear she favored young Emma, but Molly saw a new softness in her aunt toward all the children.

Molly sat beside Emma's bed now. They were talking, yet Molly still clutched the hand of two-year-old Raphael who had fallen asleep in the next bed. Emma had many observations on the war she felt she must make the young Frenchwoman understand.

"So you see, Mademoiselle Molly, if Kurt hadn't listened to Adolf he wouldn't have gone off to war and he could have taken care of Mama and me, and she wouldn't have gotten ill."

"The government would probably have drafted your brother," Molly pointed out gently. "And who is this Adolf fellow? You've mentioned him several times."

"Only Kurt's best friend. They met at art school. Then Adolf went to join the German army, and Kurt with our Austrians'. But Adolf wrote him letters and they saw each other on leaves. He got him to join the army and listen to poli—polotigs."

Molly smiled. "Politics."

She nodded vigorously. "Politics! That's what Mama said. Kurt should not have listened to Adolf's politics!"

"Well, young men do that kind of thing and—"

The little girl sat up. "I hate him! I hate Adolf! What if Kurt dies like Mama died? It will be his fault!"

"Emma, there now, lay back. You'll wake the little one." Molly smoothed the little girl's hair. "You mustn't hate anyone."

"But Adolf—"

"Not even this Adolf. Hate is what makes wars, Emma, and we want wars to end. Now let me tell you this little story. It is from the Bible..."

· · ·

It became a game at no. 10—hurry to the front steps to see what was left during the night. The children knew it would not be every morning, but several times a week. It was a treat to be the first one to make the discovery—a basket of cabbages, a box of coal, a crate of eggs or apples.

"Mademoiselle, is this an angel who brings these things?" one of the children had asked excitedly.

Molly held an apple close and smiled. An angel swooping down in his airplane? "Sort of, Pierre."

Aunt Madeline was not so fanciful. "Monsieur David is gone. So who is bringing this?" she demanded suspiciously.

Molly smiled and shrugged. Aunt Madeline would have to solve the mystery on her own.

When Molly stepped into the hallway one cold afternoon, she stopped abruptly. An odd sound...from one of the children? No...it was...Aunt Madeline was laughing! Molly hurried to the sitting room where she found Aunt Madeline sitting in her floral chair and Ben Alcott across from her, a tea cup balanced precariously on his knee.

He stood up and his eyes rested on her face. He was smiling—and looking a little proud. "Miss Fleming." He bowed.

"Monsieur," she returned correctly.

Aunt Madeline stood up also. "Will you come back for tea sometime, Ben?"

"Sure." But he was watching Molly.

"Bonjour."

Ben! Her aunt had called him Ben! Molly was openly gaping. Aunt Madeline swept past Molly, her cheeks flushed. She whispered fiercely in her language, "His French is atrocious!" Then she smiled and left them alone.

Molly pulled off her scarf slowly. Aunt Madeline's behavior would have been no more shocking if Molly had found the woman serving tea to the kaiser. Ben looked pleased and confident, and Molly looked to the floor and smiled. Certainly, he thought he had won some victory...

"So, how are you, Miss Fleming?"

"Fine, thank you. And you?"

"Great."

"Have you heard from David lately?"

"Saw him last week. Doing fine."

They stood facing each other in the silence of the great house.

"You made my aunt laugh," Molly said finally. "I have never heard that."

Ben shrugged—a mannerism she now recognized.

"She's got this funny idea that I come here at night and leave food and stuff on her front porch, so she's quizzing me. I tried to say the names of the things in French, and I guess that made her laugh."

Molly nodded. Why had he come?

"I came by to see if you'd like to go out for a drive in the country. We do that at home a lot. Since I've flown all over here, I know where the best roads are and what isn't torn up too badly. There's this grove of trees by the Somme about ten miles from here...and I have this basket of stuff to munch on, and some chocolate my ma sent...I thought maybe..." Suddenly he appeared nervous.

"I am sorry, Ben, but Emma is not feeling well, and I should really stay and care for her."

Aunt Madeline appeared suddenly and noiselessly behind her. "I am perfectly capable to taking care of the child," she said with dignity.

"Oh, I know you are, but there's Raphael starting to sniffle, and—"

"I never thought caring for two children a burdensome thing, Molly. You've been up with Emma at night. You need a...rest from it. A drive in the country would do you good."

Molly's mouth fell open. Was this a conspiracy? She looked back to Ben. Aunt Madeline had never really encouraged her outings with David. Then she smiled wryly to herself. David had once told her his older brother was a charmer. Apparently this was true.

They stood beside the little girl's bed so Molly could say goodbye. Emma told Molly she thought she and the tall man beside her made a handsome couple. Molly blushed.

"What did she say?" Ben asked.

But Molly would not repeat it.

The little girl gave Ben a long, speculative look. Her English was halting. "Are you one of them?"

"One of them?" he repeated and looked to Molly for explanation.

"One of the ones trying to kill my brother Kurt," Emma explained.

Ben stood still and rigid while Molly smoothed the bed covers around the little girl.

"Monsieur Ben is trying to help end the war, Emma," she told the little girl.

Molly guessed that Ben's eagerness was sapped by Emma's question. His smile had a forced quality to it as they drove away from Lilac Street, and she decided that his confidence masked a very sensitive side.

He had spoken the truth about knowing the roads and geography around Amiens. He drove through countryside that Molly had never seen before, the land relatively unmarred by fighting, turning in its coat of autumn. He talked easily as they drove, or they were silent which gave Molly time to again wonder why he had called for her.

There were dozens of eager young French girls in the villages and city for him, girls who loved aviators and uncomplicated fun. Yet he took time from his nocturnal pilgrimages to leave gifts at the Chaumont home. On other nights of the week, he saw the Paulines and Ninettes, she concluded. He had come calling out of sympathy, obligation to David, pity?

He drove to the summit of a gently sloping hill where the sky flamed gold and scarlet and the Somme River glistened a deep silver.

"Pretty, huh?" Ben asked without looking at Molly.

"Yes...Ben, did David ask you to...take me on this outing?"

She regretted the question when she saw something in his face. Hurt?

"No," he replied slowly. "He wondered how you were doing and said he was eager for his next leave so he could come see you. This was my own idea."

He turned back to the view, and Molly scolded herself. She now knew why David had said his older brother was a forgiving sort.

"He can get pretty sore and upset, and you think he'll never forgive you, then you look up and he's smiling and sayin' 'let's go for a swim.'"

He was eager and excited again. "I took Davy up for a flight last week. It was his first time. It was great. He didn't want to come down, except when I did the loops." Ben laughed.

These Alcott brothers loved each other very much.

"It was kind of you to take David flying," she said simply.

He turned to her with a frown. "You know what the little girl said, about me...trying to kill her brother..."

"She is young and has seen many painful things," Molly soothed.

"I know, but in a way she's right. The German I led over the lines could have been Kurt or in the line when the gas went off... You told her I was trying to end the war, and I am. I'd like it to end tonight." He rubbed his chin thoughtfully. "But if I keep flying and dueling, then in a way, I keep it going."

"You like flying, and that is what you want to do. But shooting down men, that is what bothers you."

He nodded. "The other guys, they're a good lot. Most of them don't like the killing either. See, you take pride in your flying skill, but it's no game up there. The bullets are real...I'm sorry, I didn't mean to get so serious."

He was honorable.

"I don't mind," she replied softly.

They ate the food that Ben had brought, and he coaxed her to speak of her life in England. And for just awhile, Molly Fleming forgot that he was the rake—and that he had brought her here for brotherly kindness.

"This was a nice evening, Ben, but perhaps I should get back to care for Emma. She is always restless at night."

"Sure."

They drove through the darkness and he was humming. Was he thinking of a kiss on the steps? Was he thinking of another girl waiting patiently at a cafe in Amiens?

The house was dark. He followed her up the steps, and she turned to give him her hand.

"I think I left my cap in your sitting room," he said smiling.

So they went down the darkened hallway together. Molly was acutely aware of his tall masculine presence behind her.

"The kids are cryin'" he said.

She stopped and tilted her head. He was right. Wordlessly he followed her into the dormitory bedroom where Raphael and Emma were both whimpering. Then he was in the sitting room, the young boy in his arms. Molly sat across from him in the rocking chair with Emma. She had not asked him to stay, and he had not offered to help. Yet, it seemed perfectly natural to be sitting together in the shadowy room. Ben closed his eyes while Molly sang softly in French. Two hours, three hours passed and Molly woke with a jump. Emma was gone, and Ben was stretched on the sitting room sofa, Raphael sprawled across his chest in sleep. Unruly, dark hair curled slightly around his boyish and honest face that was turned to her in sleep.

She should not, no...she shouldn't. But she did. She reached out to touch Ben's hair—just to touch a man in one innocent, fleeting moment. He stirred and opened his eyes.

He stood up and carried the sleeping boy to his bed. Molly followed him. Emma was sleeping untroubled in her own bed. Ben had taken her there when she fell asleep. They went to the front door where they heard Aunt Madeline's prize rooster greeting the new day. They faced each other. She had told him once she would not melt at his touch. That was no longer true. She waited.

"Good morning, Miss Fleming."

And he was down the steps and in his car with a cheery wave.

the western front

Gideon Jefferson was certain he would never forget the sights and smells of a battlefield trench. His father Seth nearly begged for letters— detailed letters about everything his oldest son was seeing and doing. But Gideon could not adequately describe the tunnel of earth he was crouched in with his squadron, and he wasn't sure he wanted to try. He'd already described the size and ferocity of the trench rats in a letter home with such vividness that his father had written back it was better for his mama's sake if he did not mention rats.

He had been in the trench for six hours, and now daylight was coming. He knew what that meant. The Allied commanders were waiting. And the Germans were waiting too. Then word came just as he expected it would, whispered down the line. He hurriedly finished the prayer he'd been composing all night. Bayonets glistened in the first pale light. All the faces were collages of fear, eagerness, anxiety.

"Over the top, boys!" The 369th squadron surged forward.

It was like a non-ending, supernatural thunderstorm. Flashes of manmade light split the sky. Shells thudded and rocked the earth, sending up geysers of dirt and rock into the night. The Allies and Central powers seemed determined to go all night with this battle that had begun at sunrise. But how many days before, David Alcott had lost count. The big guns were off to his left, but he couldn't measure the distance in the unreal light. After months of work on the field, a stretcher bearer's nightmare had happened to him. He was caught in a shell hole in the wasteland, the battle exploding all around him.

"What time is it?" Marty whispered hoarsely, though there was no need for quiet.

David checked the luminous dial of his wristwatch. "Midnight." They had been here nearly four hours. It had begun like any other routine and dangerous trek into the land between the lines. Except that the fallen soldier was a black American. Two stretcher bearers close to David's position had made disparaging remarks.

"Let their own kind go out for 'em. I ain't risking myself for no—"

David was known as mild and even-tempered. But he had worked too long without sleep, had seen too many dying men. He grabbed the man's shirt front roughly.

"You don't deserve to be a carrier. You don't deserve to go out there. Don't you know his blood is as red as yours?" His voice dripped with disgust. "You ready, Marty?"

"Lead the way."

David slid down farther into the hole. The soldier lay at his feet. Silently he checked the man's pulse. "Still hangin' in there, Gideon?"

"Yes, sir. Just restin'."

"Sir is for men my pa's age. I'm David."

The black man nodded.

David pulled off the man's jacket to use for a pillow under his head and then wiped the sweat from his face. "Better?"

"Thank ya...David."

"I notice your coat. How come your division isn't wearing the doughboy green?"

Gideon smiled. "Kinda funny 'bout that. Seems with the States in the war all the sudden like, they ran out of uniforms. Some supply fella was diggin' around in…Washington and he finds all these clothes wrapped up in 1863 newspapers. We's wearin' us old Union army uniforms!"

David whistled. "You have an accent. I'm from Illinois. Where you from?"

"Mississippi. Place called Greenville…"

"Yeah? I think my family, or my uncle lived around that part for awhile. He had this big estate, then he moved to New Orleans."

"That so? What's your last name?"

"Alc—"

Marty slid down beside them. "You two are yakkin' enough to be heard in Berlin. Cut it out. I think we should try for it, David."

David listened as the battle raged and waned.

"Yeah, this could go on for hours and we're out of water and Gideon here needs to get in. We can't wait until light. So…"

"You do what you think is best, David…" Gideon spoke up. "It's all in the Lord's hands."

"You know Him?"

"Sure do."

"Let's go."

They were within 25 yards of the Allied lines when the German guns blazed red and deadly in the night. The carriers lunged forward in a desperate sprint, but they did not drop their "passenger." They slid the final feet into the trench where eager hands reached out, grabbing them.

"We made it!" Marty laughed.

Even in his pain, Gideon Jefferson smiled. But David Alcott was puzzled by the sudden warmth down his back. And the detached feeling. And the strange aloneness.

It was a day that had begun newly washed in the early morning and then came up from its baptism sparkling, crisp and clear. It was a perfect day for flying—a faint breeze almost scented in spring though it was early January, the sky a vivid, cloudless theater of blue. The young aviator of the American 94th squadron called the "Hat in the Ring," climbed down from his cockpit and came, laughing, across the tarmac. His goggles were pushed back in his sweaty hair, and a white silk scarf fluttered around his neck. He pulled off his leather gloves while he talked, but he fingered them a moment, almost affectionately before stuffing them into the deep pocket of his coat. He was eager to grab a bite to eat, then return to the sky. There were airmen and mechanics all over the base, but he stopped when he saw one man standing by an ambulance beside the barracks. It was Marty Meyer.

Ben took one look at Marty's ashen face and climbed into the ambulance. He didn't want to know the details, he didn't care. He sat in the rickety ambulance now as it rocked and swayed down the road to Amiens. He stared straight ahead as Marty drove. Only one question was important.

"Is he okay?"

Marty groaned. His knuckles were white on the steering wheel. "Ben, it isn't good. The doctors just don't know..."

"Hurry up," Ben snapped.

A few moments later, the doctor was too tired and too busy to be diplomatic.

"The bullet passed through his back. He's lost a lot of blood. There's nothing more we can do. Say...what you need to say."

Ben glared at him. He wanted to punch the little man, but he brushed past him into the ward.

David looked like he was taking a nap. He was a little pale underneath the growth of beard was all. Doctors could be alarmists... Ben pulled up a chair.

David's eyes opened. He gave Ben a long look.

"I've been waiting...for you." He cocked his head. "You look mad."

Ben fumbled with his hat and looked away. "I...am."

David smiled tiredly. "It's okay, Ben."

Ben reached out and awkwardly took his brother's hand. The tears slid down his tanned cheeks but he didn't care. He bowed his head. David sighed. "Your hands are cold...been up?"

Ben nodded.

"Ben, this...it's only going to be like a, a little separation, you know. Like...like when you went to camp that summer and I bawled for two days and Ma finally packed me off to you."

Ben leaned his head on the bed. "I promised Ma...I'd take care of you. We were supposed to go home together..."

David stroked his brother's head. "It's okay, Ben. You...did a good job."

'Say what you need to say...'

"Davy, I found her." It had happened when Ben wasn't looking. Molly Fleming, the English girl, was the one.

"I knew you would. You've always been so...conceited that only you could find the good ones..." Another smile.

"Davy, I love you..."

Amiens

The people of Amiens needed a reason for an impromptu celebration, and the pilots of the 'Hat in the Ring' squadron had given them one. Four ambitious German planes had escaped ground fire and French pursuit planes and penetrated far into Allied territory. Their target was the train terminal at Amiens. But six equally determined members of the American squadron had shot down two within sight of the city. Two more were chased back to German lines. If the Germans had succeeded in their attack, the casualties among the citizenry would have been high for it was a middle of the week market day. The French people were magnanimous and decided to award the brave Allied pilots with the Croix de Geurre, the country's highest award for gallantry. The town mayor stood in front of city hall and addressed the crowd, lauding the pilots' heroism in prolific terms. Then the Americans stood to receive their award and gave a little speech in their awkward French. The last pilot stood slowly and came to the front. Unlike the rest, he was not smiling. He held the medal in his palm and looked at it curiously. Then he looked up at the crowd which had grown still and expectant.

Molly Fleming stood on the perimeter of the crowd. She had not seen Ben Alcott in weeks—ever since David had died. Tears rose in her eyes as she watched him. He looked older and tired—and suffering.

Ben took a deep breath. "Thank you, I mean merci, to all of you. I can't speak French very well, so maybe...someone will tell you what I say." He shrugged and looked back to the medal. "I'm very glad my fellow pilots and I were able to...to take care of the Germans who came so close to your town...but this medal..." He shook his head. "My little brother deserves this medal. He was out nearly every night for months carrying in your wounded sons and husbands while the Germans tried to pick him off. I'll take this...tribute, but it's for him. Thanks."

Molly watched Ben as he tried to disappear into the crowd, but faces were smiling and hands were patting him—even handing him flowers. He hurried, almost to a run, down the side streets.

Molly followed him down the street and into a cathedral. She sat behind him on a bench near the door. His shoulders were hunched and she felt tortured. Finally, after an hour, he stood up. She waited—and he saw her.

They looked at each other a long moment.

"Hello, Ben."

"Hi, Molly. I haven't been around...I've been pretty busy. No, that isn't it. I just needed a little time, you know?"

She nodded, not trusting her voice.

"How's your aunt and the little girl?"

"She's fine. She took Emma to Paris yesterday, to see a heart specialist."

"Hmm..."

Molly twisted her purse. "Were you going back to your...base?"

He shrugged. "I don't have any plans."

"Well, would you like to come back to my aunt's for dinner?"

He gave her a wavering smile. "Sure, I'd like that."

She made him a simple supper of stew and fresh bread. They spoke little during the meal. Her pain for him threatened to overwhelm her. She must keep a clear head, she told herself in a respectable Aunt Madeline imitation. He stood looking out the sitting room window as Molly cleared the few dishes. A light snow was falling, frosting the barren garden in beautiful lacework. Molly sat on the sofa, gazing into the flames of the small fire, and trying not to show her nervousness. Then he came and stood beside her. She felt him hesitating. He sat down and pulled her gently into his arms. And he began to cry. He told her about David and how much he missed him, and how hard it was to write his family with the news. He told her about the black soldier named Gideon Jefferson who had come to him and told him David had given his life to save him. And the incredible story that this Gideon lived on the estate his Uncle Andy had given Gideon's father years ago. He held her—and Molly Fleming closed her eyes in happiness.

She knew he was exhausted, and soon he fell into a deep sleep in her arms. She stretched him out on the sofa, tenderly pulled off his boots and covered him with a blanket.

In the morning, he appeared in the doorway of the kitchen, his hair tousled, his shirt untucked, standing in his socks. Aunt Madeline would have been completely scandalized. Molly wore a yellow apron and had started cooking his breakfast.

"Hi ya," he said with a crooked grin.

"Good morning."

"I'm sorry about last night. I usually don't fall asleep on a date."

She joked to cover her nerves. "I'm that boring?"

His eyes seemed to bore into her, and his voice was serious. "Not hardly."

She untied her apron. "Actually, I can't stay to eat with you. The market is open in 20 minutes."

"I'll drive you."

"Oh, no, I don't mind walking. I need to…walk. It's a beautiful morning."

"Yeah." His eyes rested on her face.

"Besides, you haven't eaten," she said hurriedly.

He glanced at the table. "Okay."

She pulled on her coat and scarf and took up her basket. Then she opened the kitchen door and stepped into the snowy path.

"Goodbye, Ben." Her heart was pounding.

He nodded, watching her. He was frowning.

Molly stopped at the end of the path, her hand hesitating on the gate. She turned. Ben opened the door. She ran to him.

"Ben!"

"Molly!"

He pulled her into the room and slammed the door. Molly Fleming had finally found someone to "throw at." Her arms went around his neck and he held her tightly. They stood that way a long time.

"Molly...Molly...." He stroked her hair. "I don't want you to leave."

"I know. I don't want you to leave."

She felt his heart pounding, smelled his aftershave. She didn't want to let him go. It felt so right in his arms.

"Molly, " he said, holding her away from him, "I...Molly, you are the most beautiful girl I've ever seen."

"Do you mean that?"

"I wouldn't say it if I didn't." He took her hands. "I want to marry you."

She searched his face. "You told David you weren't the marrying kind." She laughed nervously.

"Why do I always get misquoted? Look, I said I won't marry until I find the right girl. You are not only the right girl, you are the only girl for me."

"Ben—"

"Don't argue with me, Miss Fleming. I held you in my arms last night."

She blushed.

"This morning, I wake up and find you cooking my breakfast looking like a million in that red apron."

She smiled. "It was yellow."

"Yellow. See, you affect my eyesight!"

"Ben, marriage is...is more than just feelings. Feelings might change."

"Uh huh. Do you think that I'm the kind that marries on a whim? Me? Hey, I think I forgot the most important part. I love you."

It was a long kiss. One time in London she had asked Martin what passion was. Now, she knew.

"I don't have leave again for another four weeks." He counted up the days then named a date. "That's a Friday. I'll be here by 11 o'clock. You have the priest or whatever here, or we'll go to city hall. Arrange everything. Except the ring, I'll take care of that. We can come back here and you fix dinner and I'll make the fire. Just like last night. Then we'll curl up on the sofa and then—" He stopped abruptly and Molly had to laugh at his embarrassment.

"You get the idea, right?"

"I think so," she whispered.

His smile dropped. "I forgot about Aunt Madeline. I have to ask her for your hand. She won't—"

Molly laid a finger across his lips. "I'll take care of my aunt, although she really was the first one you charmed in this household."

He laughed and pulled her into his arms again. "Will you trust me, Molly?"

She took hold of his shirt. "Please be careful, Ben, please."

"I will. And I'll come back."

over the western front

Ben had never been involved in a worse dogfight. Never had his plane responded so badly—guns jamming, oil spewing in his face, the beginning of a fabric tear after a desperate dive. And never had he felt death breathing so closely. Never had he worked harder to stay alive. For weeks after Davy had died, he wouldn't have cared if death came to him. But now there was sweet Molly waiting for him. Seven German planes, ten Allied. The sky was full of smoke and spinning planes—and death. The flying circus was feeling especially vengeful on this cloudy afternoon. The 'Red Baron' had perished by Allied hands days before.

Ben banked his plane and decided to climb up above the fray to see whom he might help. Ben sighted squadron leader Lufbrey's plane as it climbed then dived at an Albatross. His guns were firing short burst. He closed in on the tail of the plane; it was an almost certain kill. But the German plane broke away sharply, pouring lead into Lufbrey's gas tank. The cockpit exploded in flames.

Ben was horrified—and crying. Lufbrey had vowed he would not go down with his plane in flames. Ben watched as the pilot climbed over the edge and jumped. Ben hadn't time to think or react. Two angry Germans were on him. For the following 15 minutes he tried every maneuver he could think of to shake them. His fuel gauge was dropping; he had barely enough to reach base. Ben Alcott knew then in a cold sweat this was the flight of his life.

"I don't know...what to do, Lord," he gasped.

One trick he had never tried. Never needed to try—until now. He descended in erratic spirals, hoping the eager German pilots were new to this and would think his plane was in trouble. In the confusion of the descent, he watched the ground. Ben knew he was over enemy territory. It was a forested region, but Ben spied a small square of open field. It would be tight, but he squeezed the lever forward and headed for it. Glancing over his shoulder, he smiled grimly to see the Germans had followed him.

It was a perfect, if bumpy, landing. The American rolled to a stop, the two German planes rolling in behind him. Ben could only see a dim reflection in his windshield. He sat perfectly still, waiting until both German pilots had climbed out of their planes and were coming slowly forward. He raised his arms in surrender though he did not turn. "Come on, fellas, a little further, that's it...come on."

He could hear them talking. Ben's eyes measured off the ground in front of him. It would be the hardest take-off of his life—clear the trees, or become impaled in them. Then, when the Germans were 15 yards from his plane, he threw the lever forward, counting on the fact that like him, the advancing pilots carried no pistols. He scrunched into his seat as the propeller slowly began to revolve and the engine sluggishly turned over. The Germans stopped and looked at each other in astonishment.

"Come on, don't let me down now," Ben coaxed the engine.

His plane inched forward slowly as the Germans ran back to their planes. More speed, the trees coming closer, the bumps jolting the Spad mercilessly, the fuel gauge dipping lower. Even if he could get up and away, did he have enough fuel to make it to Allied lines? Up, up!

Ben cheered. He turned to see the German planes still struggling on the ground. He checked his direction, turned and headed over the forest. Allied lines should be no more than 10 minutes away. He'd ride in on fumes.

Then, one clean shot and the Spad was twisting down in plumes of smoke. Ben Alcott had not seen the ground artillery hidden in the trees placed for advancing Allied pilots.

Chapter 25

Amiens

♦♦ ♦♦ ♦♦

*F*our weeks was time enough for a man to get cold feet—very cold feet. Feet to rival the poor men who huddled in trenches across the new wastelands of France. Four weeks was time enough to consider all the implications of a hasty proposal—a questionable exchange of bachelor life and its luxuries for responsibility and fidelity. Molly hovered in a curious mixture of suspense and joy.

Back among his hard-drinking, carousing friends, Ben would see the stark truth. Marriage! And the temptations! But when Molly remembered the tender and loving look in his eyes, she could dismiss her fears easily. 'You are a beautiful woman, Molly. I love you.'

"Monsieur Ben has proposed marriage to me, Aunt Madeline...I accepted," Molly said carefully.

Her aunt sat still and straight. "I see."

"He loves me. I love him. I love him very much."

"Well, we will make the best of it," Aunt Madeline answered mournfully.

Molly laughed. "I thought you liked Ben."

"I want only your happiness, Molly."

The day drew closer, two weeks, three weeks. What if he did keep his word? What if he did show up on her doorstep with a smile, and a ring, and a claim on her? Aunt Madeline scoured the kitchen, polished the sitting room and aired Molly's bedroom. She brushed her black silk and ventured to the market to secure the items for a respectable wedding dinner.

Molly cleaned and pressed her best dress and accepted the crisp, new sheets that Aunt Madeline gave her. The spinster woman looked uncomfortable, and Molly was blushing. She arranged for the vicar.

"He will bring the ring, Molly?"

"He said he would."

Molly sat primly on her chair. Nine, 10, 11 o'clock. Her throat tightening, she went to the window. The promise of snow hung in the sky. She smiled. Ben would have the first of his hopes. Noon, one o'clock. She could not meet her aunt's eyes. The Frenchwoman put up the food with tears in her own eyes.

Ben had not come.

Aunt Madeline slipped from the house and hired a car to take her to the airfield where Ben was stationed. She would demand to speak to the brash, thoughtless American who had broken her niece's heart. He was probably laughing in a cafe with some girl on his lap!

But the airfield was abandoned. The 94th squadron had moved two weeks earlier.

Back at no. 10 rue de lilac, Molly stood at her bedroom window watching the snow fall.

'Trust me Molly,' he had said.

She did not cry. "I did," she whispered.

The Allies were pounding the western front from Ypres, France, near the channel coast, west to Nancy near the Swiss border. The British and French high command were sensing a breakthrough and victory this year of 1918. There were encouraging signs that even the irascible old kaiser himself could not ignore. Intelligence reports confirmed by German prisoners of war revealed declining morale in the German army. Reports of desertion, mutiny in the German navy and riots in cities across Germany filtered in to Allied sources.

But it was more than the enemy crumbling. The Allies now had numerical superiority in troops. The Yanks were fresh, energetic, and eager beside the weary French and British. By August, one and a half million Doughboys would enter the trenches. The summer of 1918 became decisive and conclusive in ultimate Allied victory. After July 18th, the Allied offensive did not stop until the armistice was signed four months later. Battles at Belleau Wood, Chateau Thiery, Amiens, Verdun, Ypres, and the Meuse Argonne region. Bloodshed on both sides...but the guns would soon be silent.

It seemed as if the sky had suddenly split with a solitary peal of thunder, rain beating down in a hard, drenching torrent. The three men crouched under the trees were grateful for the downpour. One of them gestured toward a road that curved into the valley in front of them. The Germans would come rumbling down that road, and the mud and rain would not slow them forever. Already the two German planes were circling overhead before they hurried back to their airfield as the storm worsened. One partisan shook his fist at them, then the three rushed forward.

Ben struggled to stay conscious as he hurled toward the earth. He knew he was wounded by shrapnel just as he knew his plane was hit by ground fire. And so he would make one last effort to bring the plane in without completely smashing up. The ground rushed up at him through the screen of acrid smoke filling the cockpit. Going down...into Hunland. He worked frantically. Trees and one small stretch of grass pitted with rocks.

The 'Hat in the Ring' Spad hit the ground just as the rain came. Ben slumped forward in pain and weakness. Pain in his legs, warm moisture along the side of his face. Molly...

Hands grabbed him roughly, but he had no strength to protest. A hurried, unintelligible language. German. 'Guest of the kaiser'... Ben groaned. Then they were lifting him, rain soaking him.

He knew they wouldn't understand, but he didn't care. He struggled for his pack. "My pack, please, my pack...I have to have it."

He did not recognize the French words. "Hurry! I see them! Come!"

They carried him free of the plane and stumbled back into the trees. The three were well hidden in the gray curtain of rain and the plane wreckage. But nothing, not even the rain, could bring Ben Alcott back to consciousness.

Ben had lost count of the days. His only real testament to the passage of time was the trees which, from his bed, he watched turn from green to scarlet and gold—and the sunlight that streamed in the one small window had a fading quality. He could not remember how long he had lain in this bed before he realized he was not in a German hospital or even a prison camp. The men had fed him and tended his wounds, but it was days before he clearly understood they were not German. They were French! He had cried with gladness. They had grinned and poked his chest, saying, 'Vive la Americaina! Vive la France!' He had been rescued by French partisans.

When the days of intense pain and confusion passed, he finally began to understand where he was and what had happened to him. Days before he had crashed into German-occupied northern France. Three Frenchmen who lived in the wooded region, fighting their German oppressors in their own way, had seen the Allied plane plunging to earth while they were out hunting. Ben was not the first Ally they had rescued. The three, a grandfather, his son, and grandson lived in a remote and secluded cabin that thus far had gone undiscovered by the Germans. The older man had some basic, if not crude medical skill. He had set Ben's broken leg, bound the three cracked ribs and bandaged the lacerated scalp. The man had done his best with the meager supplies he had.

So the days and nights became an endless parade for Ben as he recovered on the cot in the primitive cabin. Beyond a few French words he could hardly communicate with his benefactors. Often they left him alone during the day as they went hunting or scouting for Germans. Long hours for Ben Alcott to think...of Molly, and David, and his family, and himself. One night when he had been in the cabin nearly three weeks the young French boy was washing up the few dinner dishes as his father and grandfather sat by the open fireplace smoking their pipes.

Ben was counting the knotholes in the heavy beams over his bed. The young boy suddenly turned from his chores, talking and gesturing excitedly. Ben did not understand a word. The boy hurried to a darkened corner, where he pulled blankets and debris from a pile. He lifted a canvas pack triumphantly. Ben leaned forward eagerly. His pack!

He opened it quickly and spread the map on his legs. The three gathered around. Finally he knew where he had crashed. At least 20 miles from Allied lines. The grandfather stroked his beard and shook his head soberly. Ben understood. It was too far to attempt an escape. They went back to their pipes.

The next morning when Ben was alone and thinking he'd likely go mad from isolation, he remembered the journal. He dug frantically into his pack. It had arrived from England two days before his final flight. He held it almost reverently in his hands. This was a treasure. Kate had sent him their grandfather's journal. Home...

A letter from Kate had come with the journal.

'...I have now read this journal of Grandfather's several times. I'm so thankful Grandmother Sara sent it to me. It is one of our family treasures, Ben. I wanted to read this two years ago, but she knew I wasn't ready for it. And I see now, that I wouldn't have been. I would have read it to examine the writing style, and missed the meaning of the words entirely, that they could mean anything to me personally, that I could learn something from it. I had to go off to Europe, sail on the *Lusitania* and go through that horrible time, lose friends, make new friends, and on and on until I felt completely hollow inside. Grandfather losing his arm, his best friend, his girl and more, he felt hollow—he knew he needed something else in his life. Now I wonder if you might not be ready to read it. I can imagine your feeling uncertain being so close to danger as you fly over the fighting. And hurting from losing David. So read this, dear cousin Ben. I hope you find what I have in this book...'

Ethan's journal, 1865

'...Everything I've been through, all that I have lost and all that I have gained, it all comes to knowing the one who loves me as I am, who died for me...'

Ben had practiced walking all morning with the simple crutch the partisans had made for him. His ribs were tender, but healing—to breathe no longer brought a sharp pain. He could leave the cabin for short walks in the forest. But the Frenchmen had cautioned him—Germans were constantly moving near this area. He must be careful for their sakes, as well as his own.

It was a long, tedious day for him. He had never felt so confined before. His days had always been so full, and now he had hours to limp about and think. He felt powerless and frustrated. The partisans had little use for keeping track of time or dates. Ben's watch was crushed in the crash, and the Frenchmen kept no calendar. They watched the changing seasons as their almanac, grimly noting another winter was approaching with their country still occupied.

But Ben could not accept the passage of days so calmly. According to his calculations, it must be the end of October. What was happening in the war? Were the Allies still advancing? How was the squadron? And of course, Molly. She must certainly have returned to her first unimpressed opinion of him.

He had felt the frustration mounting that morning. As soon as he regained a bit more of his strength, after maybe another week, he would try to return to the Allied lines. No matter the risks, anything would be better than this. He stared into the flat gray sky above the trees. His wings had been clipped, he smiled wryly.

"Why?" He spoke out loud.

He fingered the journal on his knee. He had only a few pages left to read. He turned slowly back to the front page—and his eyes began to blur as he saw his grandfather Ethan's name and the signatures of his sons and...

'Matthew Alcott, Andy Alcott, Daniel Alcott.' And one grandson, 'David Jeremiah Alcott.'

"Davy..." he whispered, tears tracking through his beard. "What do I do now, Davy? I sure miss you..."

Now Ben understood. That last morning before he and his brother had left for France, Sara had taken each aside for a private conversation. Now he knew how David had spent part of his time with the old lady. She had shown him this family book, and because he knew the Lord, David had signed his name.

The war would end, and he would return to Peppercreek without David at his side. Ben flipped to the last pages of the journal, and read. He and his grandfather had faced so many similar struggles.

'...Everything had been allowed for a purpose, nothing was an accident. Nothing. He knew...'

Ben looked back to the sky.

'Be still and know that I am God...'

He closed his eyes. The crash, the journal, the time of isolation, the healing. Now he understood—like he had never understood before.

What had David said? 'This is just a separation Ben, like summer camp. We'll be together again.'

Kinsale, Ireland

The Kinsale folk were pleased—the Falconers were giving another wedding party. First Denny, then Rory, now Jen. Only two sons left in the midwife's household. Aye, it was good fortune at last for Maggie Falconer. A blessing she would agree—two new lovely daughters and one fine son. But truth was she missed the boys and her girls deeply. And she began to have that nagging dread the Falconer house would soon be still—no slammed door, or teasing, clattering dishes. Only she and the cat. Aye, it was not a pretty prospect.

'Now you can't be so selfish and ungenerous, Maggie,' she chided herself. 'Even Pierce and Padraic must have their own lives.'

The neighbors were less in awe over three Falconer weddings in one year than they were the sudden interest Pierce Falconer was showing a young local widow. That left Padraic, handsomest of all.

'He won't have a girl after being stung by that German girl,' they gossiped.

'The German girl? Oh, you've no eyes in your head, man. It wasn't the German girl that broke him. Have you forgotten the little slip of a lass, the redhead?'

'The Lusitania girl...'

'Aye, the American lass. Set him against all women, maybe...'

'Then Maggie may not be so lonesome, sure...'

So for once the gossip was true. Kate Alcott had sailed away with something of Padraic Falconer's. Time did not seem too generous to give it back. And Maggie Falconer knew it best. She had watched him, seen him appear so normal and easygoing—and then in the evenings, melancholy and lonely. Sitting before the fire with a hundred memories, she imagined, all with a redheaded girl he had rescued from his sea. He worked hard, harder than he ever had before—and she knew why. As a distraction, he would push himself and not feel the void.

In all the months Maggie had not spoken one word to him directly about his feelings for the American girl. Kate's letters arrived punctually each month, cheerful and informative. She's in New York, she's back in New Orleans, she's working, she's going to school.

"It sounds as if she and her father are doing much better," Maggie commented.

"Aye." Padraic nodded. "That's the important thing."

And she knew he waited for the letter that Kate would sign with a different last name.

Maggie, Denny, and Padraic went out to cut peats one afternoon, and when the wheelbarrow was full, Maggie glanced up at her oldest son. He was leaning against his shovel, his eyes on the far hill. Maggie looked that way, to the tree that Kate always sat under. Denny looked up and followed the stare. He understood.

"Why don't you go to her, Paddy?" Denny asked quietly.

Padraic looked at him startled. "What?"

"Why don't you go to the States and get her?"

"He's right," Maggie added. "'Tis truth you should have never let her go, but that's done. And you should never have let it go on this long."

Padraic looked shocked at their bluntness. And perception perhaps? They stared at him, and he shifted nervously.

"Now, look—" he began.

"Here come the excuses, Ma." Denny smiled.

Padraic threw up his hands in frustration.

"You say go to her like she was something I could go into a store and ask for!"

"Ah, it needs to be that simple for you." Maggie shook her head.

"Ma—"

"Truth is you've moped and looked like the inside of a broken heart since she left!"

"I haven't moped," he said contritely, looking to his feet.

She laid a gentle hand on his arm. How she loved her sons. "Son…"

"Don't you see, both of you? Have you forgotten she's been gone nearly a year? She's back in her old life, with friends and…and others."

"She's mentioned no man in her letters," Maggie pointed out firmly.

"That's truth, Paddy," Denny said. "Sounds like she works and travels with her father."

"She's wealthy. I'm a fisherman. I can't give her nice things like she's used to!"

Maggie snorted in disgust. "Foolishness has grabbed my normally steady son! Pure foolishness! Did she complain about not having the nice things while she lived with us over a year? Did you ever hear the lass complain? Tell me, did you?" she asked as she punched his chest. Maggie Falconer could be fierce when she needed to be.

"Well, no…"

"All right then, now…" Maggie forced him to meet her eyes. Her voice softened. "You say you can't give her the nice things she's used to. Can you give her your heart, son?"

He looked to the sea that was vivid blue and sparkling. He smiled back at his ma. "Aye, I can give her all of that."

France

It was a slow, peaceful, drizzling rain. The Compiegne forest of France had seen much remarkable history over the centuries, but perhaps none so significant and dramatic as this wet November morning. The German delegates entered the railway car stiffly and solemnly. Their faces were proud, yet weary. General Joffre represented the Allies. One flourish and stroke of the pen from a German and a Frenchman on the eleventh month at the eleventh hour and the armistice was signed. The long war was over.

Berlin

The doctors ordered the patients brought into the army hospital's main hall. In one brief announcement, they would inform these men of their country's defeat. A thin soldier with a drooping mustache, pale face and dark flaming eyes stood at the edge of the room. He was suffering from the effects of poison gas, and so leaning against a table for support. Even now when most of the others wore the drab hospital robes, he had insisted on wearing his corporal's uniform.

His mind had, for the moment, wandered away from the momentous news. He was thinking of so many friends who had died, or worse, deserted him over the years. Men who counted trivial things more important than the idea of a great and glorious Germany. Like Kurt. Kurt—so pliable and promising. Gone. Back to care for his little sister. So foolish!

Then his mind snapped back to the pastor's words. Germany was defeated! Humiliated, broken. Angrily he left the room and staggered back to his cot. He threw himself on the bed cursing. Corporal Adolf Hitler vowed revenge.

Amiens

It had begun on a fine summer day four years earlier in Sarajevo. A single shot had begun a cataclysmic series of shots. Now on a chill November day, the shooting had ended. Madeline Chaumont and her English niece stood in the cold attic garret that gave them a spectacular view of the road from Amiens. Mile after mile of trucks and men were leaving the trenches and going home. They looked at each other in some dismay. Of course they had known it would end some day, but now that it had, they were shocked by the suddenness. It was an ending—and a new beginning.

Molly was chopping vegetables later in the warm kitchen. Aunt Madeline was knitting socks for Emma who was reading the English primer that Molly had made for her. Occasionally the Frenchwoman looked up from her work and stole a glance at her niece. Invariably she would frown. Too pale, too thin, too quiet. Even the children noticed the subdued mademoiselle.

"Where has her smile gone, Aunt Madeline?" Emma would ask.

Aunt Madeline would shake her head. "Wherever her broken heart has gone…"

The sound of an airplane overhead seemed to fill the quiet room now. Molly paused and felt her aunt's penetrating look. They met eyes for a fleeting moment, then Molly went back to her work. He had told her he loved her in this room. He had held her and shown her what passion was. In the hallway, he had promised her he'd come back. Over four months ago… Molly hurried from the room. Her aunt followed her.

"Molly, moi cheri…"

The young woman was crying. "I'm sorry, Aunt Madeline."

"Do not be sorry."

Molly stood in the middle of the sitting room. She glanced at the couch where Ben had once slept. Even looking happy and content in his sleep. 'You are the one…' above all others.

Madeline Chaumont took her niece's hands. "I think it is time for you to go home, Molly."

Molly dried her tears. "Aunt Madeline, there's still so much to do, and Emma and—"

"Non, cheri. I am stronger than when you first came. You have strengthened me through so much that you gave of yourself. My country is done fighting. I can rebuild with them. But you must go back to your country, to your father. And you will begin too."

Begin with…what?

Aunt Madeline pulled her into her arms. "I love you."

Molly clung to her. The future was so bleak, but perhaps it was time to go home.

Tons of confetti poured down in the burroughs of New York. Men and women danced in the streets. Along the western front men tossed down their guns, lit barrels of oil for celebration bonfires, embraced each other and wept. American flags and French tricolors flew along the Champ Elysees in Paris. Church bells tolled in London. There were tears and joy and stunned disbelief. It was really over.

And in a forest cabin three Frenchmen came up the forest trail singing. Ben saw their faces. And then they hugged him and spoke in quick garbled phrases.

"What? Now wait. Slow down, guys."

Then—there was one word they had heard in the village and could put into English. Armistice!

London

He paced the platform of Victoria station with nervous energy. With the return of the troops, she might not be on this one. But Thomas Fleming was determined to meet each train. His step had a new energetic lift to it. His hands were clasped behind him, his head was slightly forward. He could not appear casual.

He looked very natty in his tweeds. Like the one he waited for, he was thinner. And the hair had gone white.

Then the passengers were disembarking. Laughter, tears, embracing. He saw her. "Molly!" He could no longer be the dignified professor.

"Dad!"

New York

Lilly O'Hara Alcott's apartment afforded a stunning view of the parade. Line after line of doughboys marched by in an avalanche of confetti. New York was hosting a huge welcome home party. Even with the window closed, Andy, Lilly and Kate heard the cheering crowd on the street below. Waving flags and streamers and bands playing. The Yanks were coming home. And for a moment Kate Alcott was reminded of when the *Lusitania* had sailed away on her final voyage.

Lilly came to stand beside her daughter-in-law. Together they watched in silence for several moments. Then Lilly took her hand.

"What are you thinking of, Kate?" she asked softly.

Kate did not want to throw gloom over the celebration. This was the armistice. "For awhile…I was thinking of…of Clark Jr." Lilly squeezed her hand. Kate drew a deep breath. "Then I was thinking of Ben being shot down and missing. And David gone…but right now I feel…I just feel…" She looked away from the window.

"Lonely?" Lilly prompted gently.

Kate's eyes filled. "I'm thinking of Ireland and, I don't know what exactly, but I feel I left something there."

Amiens

Madeline Chaumont felt especially tired. It was not from caring for Emma or the shortages or missing her niece. The Frenchwoman had had two visitors during the day—and now she felt drained, yet oddly exhilarated. It had begun just after the morning meal when she and Emma were doing the dishes. There was a ring at the front door.

A young man stood there—very pale, very thin, almost skeletal. His hair was cropped short, and he was showing the beginnings of a youthful mustache. His clothes were odd to her. They inspected each other suspiciously. His eyes and mouth...something was vaguely familiar about them. Then Emma came skipping up beside her. She stopped as if she'd run into a barrier. Her eyes were huge and her hand sought the Frenchwoman's.

He stooped over. "Hello, Emma. It's me, Kurt."

Madeline Chaumont stiffened. This was the...enemy. One of the kaiser's own.

It began as a formal conversation. Emma sat close to the Frenchwoman. Madeline Chaumont was grateful the young Austrian had such an excellent command of her language. They were frank with each other.

"Take her back to Austria? Vienna is in ruins!"

"But she is my responsibility, my sister, the only family I have."

"But you have no job, you're tired and weak."

He hung his head. It was true. He had nothing.

"And what about your involvement in politics? That Hitler fellow?"

"I am done with him. I just want to live peacefully with my little sister."

Madeline Chaumont sat very straight. She cringed at the thought of parting with Emma. Her eyes swept over the young man. He was lonely-looking. But...but he *was* the enemy. He fought against her countrymen.

'And if you do it unto one of the least, you do it unto me...'

"You must stay here and heal. We can work together. I...need your help."

The second visitor arrived as the three sat down to dinner. Again, Madeline Chaumont was shocked speechless. Was a member of the defeated German army in her home not enough? Now, now...an American! But when he left an hour later the old woman was in tears. He had given her a cheery wave as he climbed into the battered ambulance. But when she smiled at him, he bounded back up the steps and kissed her warmly on the cheek. Then he was gone. Madeline Chaumont stood staring—and clutching the leather bag full of her family jewels.

London

Molly entered the cottage humming. Her class was enthusiastic that day as usual, and obedient to her leading, which was not so usual. She was happy that she and her father were able to leave London and return to this English village. Thomas Fleming had been commissioned to write a book on Greek studies, which he was very happy about. Things were back to the old, predictable routine. After dinner, Molly anticipated a good book by the fire. She glanced into the parlor expecting to find her father.

"Hello? Dad?"

"In here!" he called from his small bedroom.

"Dad—" But she stopped abruptly right inside the door of his room. His suitcase lay open on his bed, half packed. She looked at him. He was smiling, and she saw here was a glint of something in his eye.

"What's going on? Why are you packing?"

He wagged a finger at her. "You see, I've kept after you not to depend on predictability."

"What are you talking about?"

He brushed past her with a low chuckle. "Ready for tea?" he called from the parlor.

She followed him. The tea things were laid. But he had already had his tea. On the table sat two cups and only crumbs were left on both plates. She met his eyes with an unspoken question. He watched her, obviously delighting in her confusion. She had to laugh. "Oh, Dad, really, you should have been a drama teacher." She laughed again as she shook her head. He was like a child with a surprise behind his back.

He held out her cup. "Tea, my dear?"

She rolled her eyes, took the cup and sat down. There was no hurrying him—let him have his fun. He took the chair across from her.

"I suppose we can dispense with how was my day, since you look like a cheshire cat," she said with a smile.

"If you like," he agreed with a nod.

"So will you tell me why you're packing?"

"I'm taking a little trip. You remember the Kents?"

"Yes, they're the friends that always ask you to winter with them in Italy. You mean—"

"Well, I won't spend the entire winter there. But I'm already imagining the warmth and sunshine. The Mediterranean…" He waved his arms to finish.

"But why now? What made you decide to go now? We both know the rail systems are a mess across Europe. Why not wait until spring?"

"Spring is lovely in England. But winter can be tiresome. I'd like the change."

"What about your book?"

"A manuscript fits nicely in a suitcase."

"But…this is so unexpected and…and…"

Molly didn't like this sudden change. But he was still smiling. He leaned forward. "Now you had your French adventure, didn't you? Are you begrudging me a little fun?"

"Well, now really...I..."

"Yes?"

"When were you thinking of leaving?" she asked in a small-sounding voice.

"Tomorrow."

She slumped back against the chair. The cottage would be so quiet. Don't depend on routine, don't depend on predictability. Hadn't she learned that yet? Didn't she learn anything in France? Hopes...

"Well, if this is what you want to do, then—"

He looked thoughtful. "Did you really love that young American flyer you met in France?" he asked gently.

Such an unexpected question! "Dad, I..."

"Can you tell me, Molly?"

She set her cup carefully on the table, avoiding his gaze.

"The young man your Aunt Madeline was suspicious of, then charmed. The one you had rows with, that thrilled you when you saw him. That—"

She held up her hand to stop him. "Dad—"

"Please tell me."

"Yes, I loved him. I would have married him."

There was a long silence.

"I had a visitor today."

She looked up from her lap.

He peered at her over his glasses, a smile spreading slowly across his face. "Can you guess?"

She shook her head.

"It was a pleasant and most enlightening visit. I enjoyed it greatly."

She watched him as he took a book from the mantel and he extended it to her. "He left this...for you."

Molly took the volume, her heart thudding. She ran her hand across the smooth, unmarked cover. She had never seen it before, yet somehow she knew where it came from. She opened the cover.

"The journal of Ethan Alcott."

She raised her eyes to her father, only then realizing she had begun to cry.

Her father took her hands. "Ben was here this morning, Molly. He knew you were at work and he wanted to talk to me. Sort of the advance reconnaissance team, you know." Her father smiled tenderly and blotted away her tears. "We talked for nearly two hours. He's a fine boy, just like your letters described him."

She hugged the book as she wept, unable to restrain the flood of pain.

"Now, let me tell you briefly what happened. He can fill in the details. He was shot down two days before he was to come to you. He was cared for by partisans but was in constant danger. And he had a leg injury to complicate matters. He didn't abandon you. He told me that when he woke up, all he could think of was that you would think he jilted you. He left this book for you to read. He marked the spot where he wanted you to start. He suggested you read it tonight."

"Where....where is he?" she whispered hoarsely.

"Why, in the village, of course! At the inn and keeping out of sight as any bridegroom must do. I remember when—"

"Dad!" She clutched at his hand.

His laugh was deep. "Here is the message I am to convey to you. First, you're to read the journal tonight. Secondly, I'm to have the vicar here by eleven sharp. He was firm on that point. He'll bring the ring. Let's see, what else?"

Molly was crying again.

"Then after the ceremony and appropriate toasts, you both will see me off on the four o'clock train for London."

"Dad—"

"Now be patient. I must get all these details right. He wants dinner after you return from the station. Must be stew and fresh bread. No divergence on that. You're a lovely cook, Molly, so we won't worry about it. He'll make the fire. Then you draw up the sofa here, and he'll hold you. He turned a bit red at this point but was resolute. Something about warming his feet on the fender. I'm sure you understand this message, Molly?"

"Yes." She smiled and tenderly touched the journal.

"Oh, one last point. He loves you, Molly, very much."

Her voice was a whisper. "Ben..."

The next day Thomas Fleming met his soon-to-be son-in-law at the cottage door at 15 minutes until 11 and showed him into the parlor. The vicar was waiting and smiling. Ben tripped over a stool and fumbled with his cap.

"She, uh, was she, I mean, she is?"

Fleming was pleased—the bridegroom was nervous.

"Oh, yes, she was, and is, Ben. Molly, dear?"

Ben turned to see Molly hesitating at the top of the landing. He went to the bottom of the steps and waited.

Her hair was gleaming in a loose chignon. Her dress, a soft cranberry. "Hello, Molly."

She gave him a nervous smile. He was more handsome than her dreams.

He reached for her hand. "Sorry I'm a little late. You know how tricky flying can be."

They stood at the little train station—a new bride and her beaming husband, a pleased-looking father-in-law.

"You are a beautiful bride, Molly," Fleming said as he held her close. "Isn't God good to us, my dear? The author of perfect gifts."

"Yes, He is."

"God bless you both."

Ben shook his hands warmly. "Thank you, sir, and God bless you. Thank you for your daughter." He gave Molly a quick look. "I guess I feel like your King George V!"

They rode back to the cottage in silence—not touching, not meeting eyes.

"Molly, I know I'm a sentimental fool, but will you do something for me?"

"What?"

"Let me go into the cottage first. You wait on the path about 30 seconds, okay?"

He dashed into the cottage and threw off his jacket and tie. He tossed off his shoes. Then he turned the doorknob. Molly turned on the path. She ran into his arms, laughing and crying.

He held her, and kissed her—and didn't want to ever stop.

"Ben!"

"Oh Molly! Molly…I'm sorry it took…what happened and I knew what you were thinking…"

"Ben…"

She made their dinner as clouds massed in the late afternoon sky. She wore a yellow apron. She burned the bread as Ben hovered around her in the small kitchen, pulling her into his arms, tasting her neck, her eyes. The stew needed salt. They ate in front of the fire, and it was Molly who sensed it first. She hurried to the window that faced the barren garden.

"Ben! It's snowing!"

He smiled with his mouth full. "Of course."

They sat with their arms about each other, looking into the flames, as Ben told her of his accident.

"You read the journal? The part I marked?"

"Every word."

"Reading those words, and thinking about you was the only thing that kept me from going crazy."

She extended her arm in front of her. A beautiful ring sparkled on her finger. Even now it hardly seemed real, though she could touch it. He had secured her aunt's jewels and placed the one Aunt Madeline had chosen on her finger. She thought of David now. So loving, and so wanting the best for his older brother.

"If you like me, Molly, you'll really like him. He's honorable and loyal and generous and..." She smiled. David had told her the truth.

Ben seemed to read her thoughts. "We have...Davy to thank for tonight, you know. I was able to tell him. I'm real glad of that."

He poked the embers in the fireplace—but did not add another log, she noted significantly.

"The evening was perfect, Molly, the whole day, in fact. Now we've eaten and curled up in front of the fire. We even got the snow."

"I remember the first time, you added, 'And then...'"

"I wondered if you'd remember that part." He smiled as he pulled her closer.

"I couldn't forget it, Ben..."

New Orleans

It was obvious to the New Orleans cab driver that his passenger was nervous. The man drummed on his knee, or adjusted his collar, or glanced at his watch. The cabbie took in the plain, rural-looking clothes. A foreigner. But he was not adept in discerning accents.

"From Scotland, maybe?" he finally asked.

The man laughed and shook his head. Imagine being mistaken for a Scotsman! Ma would laugh.

"It's Ireland, man," the passenger said easily. "How much farther now?"

"'Round the next corner."

Padraic Falconer studied the houses in this New Orleans neighborhood as they passed them. Fashionable, Jen would say. Like the northern part of Dublin, Denny would compare. Wealthy anyway, Padraic decided. He nervously twisted his cap. The cab slowed.

"I don't want you to stop entirely," Padraic explained quickly.

The cabbie cocked his eyebrows."You don't want me to stop?"

"No, just go by slow-like."

The cabbie nodded with obvious suspicion. "You said 2121 Old Manor?"

"Aye."

"That's it there."

Padraic took a long look. It was a two-story set back a little ways from the street, black grillwork, roses bushes and a privacy hedge—immaculate, and no sign of life on the grounds or behind the curtains. It was just as Kate had described. Aye, her father was a rich man.

The cab passed the house, then turned at the end of the street.

Padraic was confident—before. Now he wasn't so sure. Kate Alcott was wealthy. She was…social. She was probably surrounded by admirers even now. She had come back to her old life. Certainly, he had lost her…

"Look, Mac, are we drivin' or stoppin'?" the cabbie asked irritably.

"Back to my hotel, and thanks."

'If she's the one for you, then, she's the one,' Maggie Falconer had said. Her optimism and certainty was enough for Padraic to get his passage, say goodbye and sail for America. Maggie and his brothers had stood on the quay at Queenstown smiling and waving. Padraic had smiled, too. He would bring home his bride.

Now he was here. He'd made the long voyage. And all the doubts that had come to him on the trip over, resurfaced. But he couldn't sail home without at least seeing her…could he?

"I love her," he whispered to the quiet hotel room. "Aye, and shouldn't that be enough?"

He was greatly relieved that the cab driver who took him to 2121 Old Manor that evening wasn't the same one as before. But this time the house was different. Padraic leaned forward in alarm. Light streamed from nearly every window, and cars lined the street. He could hear music from the grand house. People hurried up the steps—wealthy-looking people.

"What is it? What's wrong here?" he asked.

"What d' ya' mean?" the cabbie asked gruffly.

"At this house. All the lights and…"

"It's a party."

"A party," Padraic replied dully. He felt his stomach sink.

"So, am I letting you off here or what?"

She was in there, so close, yet…

He couldn't go home and face his ma.

'You didn't even see her?'

'What happened, Paddy?'

'Aye, he got scared.'

'By a party?'

"Aye, I'll stop."

The butler gave him a cold, appraising look.

"Do you have an invitation…sir? This is a private party."

Padraic heard an orchestra and laughter from the room down the tiled hallway. "Truth is, I don't have an invitation. Still, I'd like to see Miss Katherine Alcott."

"Not without an invitation."

"But I'm a friend."

The butler began closing the door, but Padraic brushed past him with authority. "I understand about the invitation and you're just trying to do your job, man. But I'm here now, and I'll see Miss Alcott."

The butler stepped back. "I will get Mr. Alcott. He will send for the police."

Padraic shrugged. "Do what ya must."

The butler scurried away, indignation radiating from him.

Padraic stood rocking on his feet. He had sounded bold. He did not feel too bold now. He felt rustic and what was that word Kate had used with Jen? Provincial. He took a deep breath. He heard hurried steps, and then the butler returned, looking very triumphant. But it was not Mr. Alcott with him.

The redheaded woman came toward him eagerly. Kate's stepmother, the actress, Lilly. She was smiling. She didn't seem to notice his homespun clothes or heavy boots.

"Hello, Mrs. Alcott," Padraic said with a little bow.

Her smile widened, and she took his hands in hers. The long look she gave him made him feel she was glad to see him, like she'd even been waiting for him.

"You are Padraic."

He nodded. At least Kate had spoken of him. He drew his eyes away from her pleased face.

"I've come at a bad time." He glanced towards the party room. He looked to the sharp-eyed butler waiting at the woman's elbow. "With no invitation."

"A friend of Kate's needs no invitation."

He gave another uneasy look down the hall.

"This is Kate's birthday party, Padraic," Lilly explained.

Her birthday. The Irishman groaned.

Lilly took his arm. "She'll be happy to see you. Let me introduce you to Kate's father."

She led him down the hallway. He stood in the open doorway. It was just as he expected. Lights, music, people dancing, color and...wealth.

"Padraic, this is my husband, Andy Alcott."

He was not as Padraic expected. Tall, slender in a tuxedo, and kind-looking. Kate's father stared at him with open curiosity.

"Andy, this is Padraic Falconer, from Ireland," Lilly said with the beginning of laughter in her voice. "He's come to see Kate."

"Sir."

They shook hands and Andy Alcott smiled warmly.

"I'm glad to have this chance to thank you personally, Mr. Falconer. My daughter has spoken highly of your family. You did...so much for her."

Padraic nodded. "Thank you, sir, aye, and it was a blessing for us, sure."

Lilly stood beside her husband, her hand entwined in his. It seemed to Padraic that she was smiling like she knew a secret. Padraic drew confidence from her. He cleared his throat and faced Andy squarely.

"I've come a long way, sir."

Andy nodded slowly.

"The truth is, I love your daughter and I want to marry her."

Lilly nodded and Padraic turned.

The song ended. The dancers were breaking up. He saw her. This was the way she would have looked before the *Lusitania,* before she wore Jen's dresses—a long silver dress that reflected light, her hair shining and riotous, a young man at her side.

Then she saw him. She stopped—and her smile faded.

He moved toward her. He might as well get this over with. She wouldn't want to leave this, but he must tell her. They stood face to face now.

"Hello, Padraic," Kate said softly.

He nodded. "I've come for you, Katie lass."

The birthday guests had left and Andy and Lilly had discreetly left them alone. Tall candles still burned in the party room and the orchestra still played. But there were only two dancers now—one with heavy boots and clumsy steps, and one who closed her eyes in happiness that she had found something she thought was lost to her forever. She thought of the woman waiting for her son back in Ireland. She could not wait to see her again and tell her how much she loved her.

Then she went to the orchestra leader and made a request. Kate Alcott was dancing to Strauss once again.

Peppercreek

Sara Alcott didn't have to turn her head toward the open window to catch the scent of apple blossoms. Apples...that was Peppercreek. She smiled weakly to herself.

She knew that one of her three sons, Matthew, Daniel, or Andy was sitting beside her bed because that was the last thing she had seen, an anxious face. But now she was just too tired to open her eyes. Just too tired...Ethan, I'm coming...

Faintly she heard a door open, but still she did not move. It took too much effort, and breathing took all of her strength right now. Someone grabbed her hand, eagerly, almost roughly—not at all like the gentle ministrations she'd been receiving. Distantly she heard a voice, as if at the end of a tunnel. When she finally recognized it, she understood why her hand was grabbed.

"Grandma Sara! I'm here! I've come home! It's Ben!"

Ben. Though her face betrayed nothing, she smiled inside. Ben had come. But he sounded afraid. She wished she could tell him everything would be all right. He need not worry—where she was going there were no more tears or pain. Did he remember the things she told him from the book they had read from on her lap?

"I made it back from France, Grandma. The war is over…can you hear me? Can you understand?"

She wanted so to tell him she did understand. She was so tired, but to hear his voice…

"Grandma, I'm going to believe you can hear me. I have so much to tell you! I…I don't know where to begin exactly…"

His voice was shaky and Sara wanted to reach out and squeeze his hand, but not a muscle would respond.

"I'm married, Grandma, can you believe it! She's right here beside me. Her name is Molly. She's an English girl, and she's beautiful, and I know you'd love her. She's the girl you told me once I wouldn't ever turn loose of. Remember the talk we had? You asked me if I knew a girl I'd want to spend eternity with. I found her, Grandma, and eternity seems too short…"

Ben married. Well… Sara rejoiced.

Then another voice, shaky in the same way Ben's was, but slower, deeper. Was this Ben's English wife? Sara could not immediately recognize it. Oh, this was frustrating!

"I'm here too, Grandma…I've come home. It's Kate."

Kate! But not sounding at all like Kate. Sara strained to open her eyes. But they weighed tons.

"I brought you a book, Grandma, a journal I wrote while I was in Ireland. And I read the journal you sent me, Grandma, I read…" The voice cracked, and Kate was crying. "I…I read every word…please don't leave us, Grandma, please!"

Oh, Katherine, don't cry. I know you love me.

The old woman felt her face being stroked even as she had so often caressed her granddaughter's face the last time she'd seen her.

"I love you so much, Grandma, I do! You're the very best grandmother a girl could have. And I…I've learned the most important things, Grandma, you know, the ones you prayed I'd learn…"

Katherine, we won't be apart long, really. We'll be together.

Sara felt her hand lifted to the soft cheek of her granddaughter. She did not need to struggle to open her eyes now. Katherine had come home!

Ben's eager voice was beside her again. "Grandma, this journal that you sent Kate, the one Grandfather kept, well, you know that part where you sign your name? My name is there now, Grandma…That's what I wanted you to know."

Benjamin, what are you saying? You signed the book?

"My name is in the journal now, Grandma, right under Davy's. And Kate signed it too."

So they know…Ethan, they know!

"I don't think she can hear us," Ben cried. "We're too late."

Oh no, Ben, don't be silly. You're not late!

"Pray, Ben," a soft voice said above her. Meg? No, it's an English voice. Ben's wife, Molly Alcott. She knows, too! Sara had never smiled so widely in her life.

Ben was praying. Sara had never heard her grandson pray before beyond grace at meal time. Suddenly her hearing was perfect—better than it had ever been, clearer and magnified. To just lay here and listen to Ben's prayer. Never had she felt so peaceful. There was no pain, no heaviness.

"I love you, Lord! You had your hand on my grandfather when he didn't know You. You've had your hand on Kate and myself…Thank You. Tell…tell Grandma, please tell her how much we love her. We'll be there…"

The air she breathed now was lighter and fragrant. She took deep breaths of the freshest, coolest air she had ever breathed. Where had it come from? It was better than a spring morning scented with apple blossoms.

Ben was finishing his prayer. "Even so, come quickly, Lord Jesus!"

A tear slid down her cheek as she smiled. All those years, Ben was listening.

One last word for her children—*please, Lord, give me the strength. Just to tell them.*

Her voice was a weak whisper, but all in the room heard Sara Alcott's last word.

"Amen…"

They lie on a windswept hill now, these silent keepers of history. Yet, living still in the most important, most precious way—their passing of the faith, that living heirloom they called…the Alcott legacy.

Afterword

World War I is generally less studied than the big war that consumed Europe and nearly the entire planet some 30 years later. Then there would be flamboyant and dramatic figures like Churchill, Roosevelt, Stalin, and the one man who seems to represent all the horrors of that conflict: the German dictator, Adolf Hitler. We remember World War II generals like Patton and MacArthur and Eisenhower. But how many generals of World War I can be named? Still, this war of 1914–18 was a time that claimed the prime of a generation and extracted a terrible toll from the civilian populace and landscape. When it was over, the political geography of Europe was greatly altered and the seeds of the next great battle were sown. Still, with optimism, so many who had survived believed this war that had ended really was "the war to end all wars."

There really was a Lafayette Escadrille, composed of young Americans who had volunteered to fight and fly for France. Few of them survived the crudeness of those early planes and the dangers of war to tell their grandchildren the colorful stories. It would be left to others to remember their daring heroics.

The details of the *Lusitania,* the ship itself and her final voyage, are all accurate. The huge liner sank in 18 minutes within sight of the Irish coast. Walther Schweiger was the captain of the German U20 that torpedoed the Lucy to the bottom of the Atlantic. Like so many tragedies, this one was full of intrigue and near misses, almosts and what-ifs. To this day the question remains unanswered if there really were explosives unlisted on the cargo manifest, bound for the Allies, that caused the second explosion and sent the ship to its watery grave much, much quicker than it should have gone. That was why the German submarine captain was so surprised. Even the *Titanic* had listed in the water for two hours after her fateful meeting with an iceberg.

The *Lusitania* had left New York two hours later than scheduled because of tardy passengers and the loading of their cargo. If she had left on time, she would have been up the Mercy River and out of the submarine's deadly path. The German embassy did publish a warning to passengers in many American newspapers the day before the sailing. Only one passenger canceled because of it. And there was a regiment of black Americans who wore Civil War uniforms into the European conflict.

With the background of a war, Padraic and Kate, Molly and Ben told their story, (And yes, it was hard for me to "kill off" David.) Beyond their story, however, is Kate and her father. Theirs was really the most important relationship. Beyond pride and through forgiveness they found a way to be as the Designer of families intended.

To my wonderful husband, kids, and friends, for their encouragement and enthusiasm, and to those who wrote me with kind words about Book 1 and Book 2, again, thank you so much.

In Him who blesses abundantly,
MaryAnn Minatra